Silent Hawk

a novel by

Alfred Patrick

Pick your trails, always
ride point and never
lose sight of the
    Chuckwagon.
Enjoy the journey with
    Silent Hawk.
        Happy trails,
        Al Patrick

About the Author

Al was raised on a ranch in southwest Montana and attended a small country school.

During the summers he had few opportunities to be around children his own age. He used the hillsides, creek bottoms, and the wide-open countryside for his magical playground, stretching his imagination to the limits. This imagination would never leave him.

Al joined the United States Navy and left Montana when he was twenty. He married a California girl and remained in California after he served in the Navy. He worked, raising his family while attending college. He graduated from California State University-Hayward with a bachelors' degree in finance. His career to make ends meet was finance; his career to live was writing. He would write short stories for his young children and felt inspired seeing the happiness on their faces. While writing these stories, an increasing desire to write a novel began to build. He always had a keen interest in history, particularly the old west, and his passion for Montana never diminished. Building upon these interests and passions, he found his story called Silent Hawk.

Silent Hawk

Alfred Patrick

Although <u>Silent Hawk</u> is based at a historical locale that involve some historical events and characters, it is strictly a work of fiction, and the reader should not consider any portion of this novel as historical truth. All other names, characters, places and incidents are products of the author's imagination. Any resemblance to current events or locales or to living persons is entirely coincidental.

ISBN 978-0-6151-7218-7

Library of Congress Control Number: 2007908333

To contact the author or order 'Silent Hawk':
<u>Silent-hawk@comcast.net</u>
<u>allpatri@aol.com</u>

Published in the United State of America

Printed in the United States of America

I am dedicating this book to three special people who have given me direction and unselfish love in my life.

First, I dedicate this book to my wife, Bonnie, who taught me the meaning of love and the importance of sharing one's life.

The second person is my mother, Josie, who had love, understanding and kindness that filled her heart and soul every day of her life.

Thirdly, I want to dedicate this book to my father, Sam. He died when I was a young man and I had not yet learned how to express my love and admiration. This poem is written in his memory.

No man ever stood taller,
Yet he never rose above me.
His gentleness never surpassed
By any man I ever did see.
Not once a complaint I heard
About the life he had,
I guess I never knew
If he was ever sad.
He was very giving,
Often more than he should,
I wish I had known,
But back then, I never fully understood.
With the passing of time,
His greatness I came to know,
And sometimes I wish
I could tell him so.

-Alfred Patrick

-Acknowledgments-

Writing a novel requires many hours of solitude, but it is also an undertaking that requires the help, patience and understanding of many people and I would like to acknowledge some of them. I shall begin with my wife, Bonnie, my wonderful companion over the years, who has been by my side offering encouragement and an unwavering love; and to my three children: Shannon, Robert, and Paula, who patiently listened to my stories when they were small, giving me the desire to keep writing. I have to give particular thanks to Paula, who has served as my advisor and editor. I cannot forget my grandchildren: Haley, Hannah, Violet, and Quentin, who give me renewed youth each day of my life.

I must thank all those dear friends and family, who offered encouragement during the roller coaster times of writing and publishing <u>Silent Hawk</u>, and to Laurie, a special thanks for being a good editor in a time of need.

I also want to take a moment and remember my dear brother, Chuck, who recently left us here on earth.

I also need to thank the characters in my novel, which took over my mind and guided me through the story from beginning to end. They made me do it-so to speak. There obviously would not be <u>Silent Hawk</u> without them.

I must acknowledge one particular source I used for my novel that I found very helpful. It is <u>Golden Gulch</u> by Dick Pace. I would recommend it to any of the readers that enjoy the historical events of the Montana gold rush.

HISTORICAL BACKGROUND

Near the mid-nineteenth century, the cry of 'gold' rang out in the West echoing the call through the Eastern United States and around the world. It ignited a stampede into the Western frontier never before imagined. People of all cultures and backgrounds poured into the previously uninhabited lands like floodwaters through a narrow ravine. Some came to start a new future, others to hide their past; but all to seek their fortunes-whether by honest work or by unscrupulous means.

Until the rush, the rugged terrain of the West beyond the vast prairie was considered by most to be a land for Indians, trappers, and frontiersmen. It was a land to read about-fantasizing its enchantment, adventure and danger. It was a land to be left to a few hearty souls. Beyond the Great Plains stood the forbidden barriers of the Rocky Mountains rising defiantly to the sky; and to the south lay the vast barren desert thirsting for the blood of the unsuspecting soul. What sane person would venture into this treacherous country and for what possible sane reason?

But gold changed that philosophy. Now there was a reason, whether it was sane or not. Stories came east about men without a cent becoming rich overnight. Gold was everywhere for the taking. But seldom mentioned in these stories were the hardships and dangers facing those who dared venture, and never mentioned were

I

those forgotten ones who returned poor and broken in spirit, or those who never returned.

The gold rush started in California and quickly spread to Oregon and Washington. But as these camps filled or the claims played out, miners in search of new dreams often retracing their steps, pushed into the barren lands of Nevada and the mountains of Colorado to find more discoveries.

By the late 1850's, prospecting had pushed north past the Mormon settlement at the Great Salt Lake and into the regions of the Salmon and Snake Rivers in the Idaho territory where still more gold bonanzas flourished.

To the north of these new found strikes was the rugged Continental Divide winding its way like a deadly snake through the treacherous mountain ranges of the Northern Rocky Mountains. Some fifty years earlier, Lewis and Clark led their expedition through these same isolated mountains, but since, few white men had ventured into its unforgiving habitat. Many Indian Nations, finding their lands overrun by the onslaught of the white man from the East, found this land to be one of the few remaining sanctuaries as they desperately struggled for survival.

By 1860, the United States was in turmoil and civil war was inevitable. A few adventurous miners were beginning to push their way into this northern mountainous land that in years to come would become part of the Montana Territory, but prospecting had given little hope until the summer of 1862. Some men camped along the Beaverhead River discovered considerable color in what became known as Grasshopper Creek. Even in this isolated country, word spread quickly of the find and by the fall of 1862 three hundred hopeful miners resided in camp. The camp was named Bannack after a nearby Indian tribe. Winter temporarily slowed the rush, but in the spring, the area swelled to over a thousand residents.

As Bannack grew, the overflow of disappointed miners began spreading out in search of still new findings. In May of 1863, six men, headed by Bill Fairweather and Granville Stuart, having missed their connection with a larger search party headed for the Yellowstone

II

River wearily set up camp along Alder Gulch near the river called the Stinking Waters. They had earlier encountered irate Indians, and avoiding certain death had escaped and spent several days eluding them. The miners were tired and hungry, but like all good prospectors went to the stream to test for color. To their excited disbelief, they made a major find.

The next morning, excited, but sworn to secrecy, they began the seventy-five mile trek back to Bannack to register their claim and replenish their supplies; however their secret was short lived once they arrived. When they began their return journey to their findings, they soon realized a large following was traveling close behind them. Seeing no alternative, they admitted their discovery. A new bonanza had started and would soon become the biggest and most deadly strike ever. Alder Gulch, unknown and isolated, had suddenly been thrust into chaos.

PROLOGUE

Sarah Templeton's Diary

1863, June 1

It has been one month today since we left our home in St. Louis-a wretched month. I believe it has rained every day since we left. I am homesick for my family and friends. I am also homesick for a warm bath, a cast iron stove, and perhaps most of all, a soft down bed. If I were not so weary by day's end, I think I could not sleep a wink on the hard, damp ground.

We rise at four and have eaten breakfast before the first sign of light. By seven, we are moving across this endless prairie, and except for a short stop at noon, we travel until dusk. Then the supper must be prepared, clothes washed, horrid buffalo chips gathered for fire, and all the other endless tasks that are needed for the next day's journey.

Some of the younger folks often dance to a fiddle at night. Where do they find the energy after such a grueling day? I am so weary; I find difficulty holding this pen...yet we still have so far to go. I fear sometimes I will fall by the wayside for the picking of the buzzards.

1863, June 8

A few days ago we crossed the Platte River. We had to raft our wagon across its merciless waters. I have never encountered such terror. The *terrain is worsening. The rolling prairie now behind us seems so kind. They say the worst is yet to come. I pray the Lord is with us. How shall I ever endure? I try to be strong for Sam and the children...but I know I am not.*

1863, June 11

My heart aches tonight. A second child, Jennifer Platten, died last night. She had lived only eight precious years. Young Johnny Tinsley was the first, dying two days ago. I must never forget their names so that I can always remember them in my prayers. The terrible pain one feels leaving such little ones behind. I am blessed that thus far Hezekiah and Cynthia are well. I pray that it shall remain so. I am terribly frightened for their well-being.

1863, July 8

I fear that we shall never make it to Oregon. Today, a man arrived from a train ten miles ahead of us. Indians have been pestering them-driving off their livestock. He called them Sioux. His train will wait, allowing us to travel together for safety.

The terrain continues to worsen. They say in a few days we will enter the mountains at a place called the South Pass. In the distance, they look impassable.

The journey has been so difficult for Cynthia. She complains continually...for good reason I might add. I am afraid she is too much like me. Will we ever be able to adjust to the life out here? Hezekiah is like his father in appearance, action and thought. He seems so excited with each new day. He is growing tall and handsome like his father, but I fear what this terrible land holds in store for him. He is trying to become a man, but he is still a mere child, barely fifteen.

1863, July 22

We crossed the South Pass and have arrived at Fort Bridger. We plan to stay three days before proceeding...to rest the animals they say, but I know

I shall enjoy it the most. They say we are a week behind schedule. Mercy, how could one travel any faster over this treacherous land?

Thank the good Lord, we have seen no sign of Indians since crossing the pass...such relief. They frighten me so.

The mountains are a beautiful feast for the eyes, but the body finds them otherwise...hot by day, cold at night, and they make travel so difficult and terrifying.

There is word here at Fort Bridger that a big gold strike has been discovered north of here at a place called Alder Gulch. They say it is bigger than California. Sam and some other men are discussing whether to change plans and go there instead of Oregon. I fear it will be more desolate than Oregon. The one light of joy...it would shorten the remainder of our journey by more than half.

1863, July 25

We are going north to Alder Gulch, perhaps as many as ten families. I am pleased the Kyles are going. Mary Kyle is a kind, pleasant soul. She has been such a help to me. She handles all the misery of this journey so well. Besides, Hezekiah has become good friends with their son, Isaac. It would be such a disappointment for both of the boys if they had to part ways.

1863, August 12

The road, if such a name can be given to it, is wretched. We have crossed the pass that will lead us to this unknown land. I admit the land and mountains are breathtaking, but how can a mother do properly by her children in such a wilderness. I can only try.

1863, August 22

They tell us we will arrive at our new home tomorrow...joy for the end of the journey...fear for what we shall find. Lord, give me strength...I know I shall need it.

Silent Hawk

CHAPTER 1

Virginia City at Alder Gulch

Sheriff Henry Plummer sat down at his desk, removed his hat, and wiped the perspiration from his brow. "This damn weather around here," he said with disgust as he swatted his hat at a pestering horse fly, "it'll roast your balls in summer and freeze your rear end off in winter."

George Lane placed his clubfoot on a nearby chair to ease the throbbing pain. He grimaced and leaned back. "Hell, you're lucky. It's a hell of a lot worse with a bum foot...swells in summer and aches like a case of the piles in winter."

The sheriff stared unsympathetically at George. George was a whiner, one of the many things that irritated Henry about him. But the sheriff tolerated George, knowing he was an important piece to his developing operation. With George running his shoe repair shop at Dance and Stuart's store, he would have access to information on gold shipments, and which miners were finding dust and trying to leave unnoticed from the camp. No one would suspect a crippled shoe repairman.

"Well," Henry said impatiently, holding out his hand to encourage George to speak. "What's this big news you were so all fired anxious to tell me?"

"I'm getting to it," George said, wiping his mouth. "Hell Sheriff, you make me sit around here waiting for you, and now you're in an all fired damned hurry all of a sudden."

"I've got other business besides you," Henry said, gritting his teeth. "Now what the hell is it you've got for me?"

George's eyes flashed with anger, but he dropped the argument. "This morning, I overheard Oliver...you know, the stage line owner...He told Stuart that he was personally going to accompany the stage leaving in the morning and that he was also going to take along an extra man to ride shotgun." George stopped, looking disappointed at the sheriff's calmness of the news. "It sounds like a big gold shipment..." The door opened and Jack Gallager, one of the sheriff's deputies, entered.

Henry glanced at his deputy and looked back at George. "What the hell you so damned nervous about, George? Its only Jack."

"Yeah, well you can't be too careful. Ears listen and mouths talk."

"Yeah, like yours, you little weasel," Jack growled, taking insult to George's remark.

George grimaced with pain as he shifted his foot again. "This damn foot," he groaned, ignoring Jack's remark.

"Did Oliver say there was gold?" the sheriff asked, ignoring George's complaining.

"No," George answered curtly, " but why else would he put extra guns on the run to Salt Lake?"

Sheriff Plummer turned to Jack. "Where are Ray and Stinson?"

"Over at Sadie's Palace, I suppose. That's where they usually are. You want me to go roust them?"

"No! Those drunken bastards!" the sheriff shouted as he quickly rose to his feet. "I'll personally go drag their worthless asses out myself. I regret ever deputizing them. Someday, they're going to get us all hung if they don't straighten up." Henry pulled his hat firmly down over his long, sandy colored hair and slammed the door behind him as he left.

6

Jack grinned triumphantly. "The sheriff is going to have their ugly asses bouncing around the saloon like Sadie's big tits."

****

Sadie Campton carefully examined herself in the mirror. It was a ritual she enjoyed and followed each day. She liked the way she looked...silky auburn hair...white smooth skin-void of wrinkles and just enough freckles to add character...liquid green eyes...and most of all, a figure rich with curves. "Pretty good Sadie for thirty-two," she said aloud. She smiled as she jiggled her breasts beneath her red, silk, low cut dress. She had always been careful not to let the rugged West harden her exterior like it had her interior. Her two offsetting characteristics had always provided a perfect combination to deal with the men in the mining camps...They wanted to screw her, but never daring to screw with her.

Sadie picked up her pearl handle, colt .22 caliber revolver, and strapped it to her right thigh beneath her petticoat, being sure to stroke the softness of her skin as she did. Everyone knew she carried the revolver and where she carried it. It kept problems minimal, and she always enjoyed displaying it at the men's request.

She could hear the noise in her busy saloon below her small living quarters. She glanced at the clock on the wall opposite her bed, which she used to insure her customers never had fun on her time. It was two o'clock.

Sadie was in no hurry. Many of the customers, this early in the day, were freeloaders with empty pockets looking for free whiskey or a quick feel. Some were late arrivals in camp missing out on the good claims and were waiting for word of a new strike somewhere else. They would just as apt to be gone as here by this time tomorrow. They were always in every camp and this one was no different.

Sadie felt sorry for these poor souls, but the freeloaders who had no intention of working a claim or working for a living, only working those who did, were the ones she despised. She paid close attention to her establishment, watching for the shifty gamblers or crooks working in her saloon on the unsuspecting miners. She was quick to rid those leeches from her establishment.

Sadie decided it was time to make her appearance in the saloon and bring some excitement to the poor, deprived bastards' lives.

As Sadie descended the stairs and entered the saloon, she thrust her breasts forward like a soldier in review, fully aware of the watchful eyes of those around her. Tantalizing the men was the most fulfilling reward she could give herself. She knew there was not a man with a yearning eye that did not crave to put their hands on her. She smiled playfully and spoke to each as she passed.

Sadie carefully surveyed her establishment. She took great pride that it was the best saloon in town. When she first arrived in the camp, she immediately found a woodcrafter to build her bar. It glistened from its smoothness and a splinter could not be found on its well-structured body. Behind the bar was a large, well-crafted mirror. Above the mirror in large letters was a sign, 'Anyone doing harm to this mirror will find his jewels hanging from the rafters'. The patrons did not take Sadie's warning lightly. The rest of the saloon was clean and bright as lanterns hung abundantly from the rafters.

Only two of Sadie's girls were working the tables this early. Dorothy had been with Sadie since San Francisco. Dorothy was in her late forties, and the hard life of prostitution and working in the saloons was prominent on her face. But Sadie would never consider casting her into the street like so many others would. Dorothy had been loyal and Sadie was one to return that loyalty.

Christina was her other girl serving drinks. Usually Sadie's girls preferred later hours when the men with the gold laden pockets arrived after a day of working their claims; Christina, not participating in the sale of her body, preferred the earlier hours.

Sadie stood behind the bar watching Christina. Although Christina had worked for Sadie for over two years, she was obviously out of place in a saloon. Sadie had found Christina wandering helplessly in the streets of a mining camp in Colorado-broke, alone, and frightened. Her man had deserted her. She had taken Christina in out of sympathy, but since, Christina had become an important asset to her business. Whether she was out of place or not, Christina was the most popular of Sadie's girls.

Christina was considered by the men as 'a real looker'...light brown hair, slender face, soft brown eyes that danced flirtatiously when she laughed which drove the men crazy; and Sadie had to admit, a figure that challenged her own. Christina was kind and courteous to her customers, but Sadie was convinced that it was her innocence that was the most tantalizing feature to the sex deprived men.

The other girls never befriended Christina. They would refer to her as 'Sadie's saint'. But they tolerated her, never having to compete with her on the sale of their wares.

Sadie never tried to persuade Christina into selling her sought after body. Sadie felt it was Christina's choice and Sadie respected her wishes. She only considered Christina as foolish...missing such a golden opportunity.

As Sadie scanned the room sizing up her clientele, her eyes became fixed on a figure standing in the bright sun-lit doorway. It was not a particularly large figure, but it carried a sense of dominance. Sadie squinted her eyes, trying to recognize the man. He moved inside allowing her to recognize him as Sheriff Henry Plummer. He paused momentarily, casting a look around the saloon until he located his two deputies, Buck Stinson and Ned Ray, at the far end of the room. Sadie watched as the sheriff pushed his way through the crowd towards them. She found him to be a handsome man and from rumors, other women apparently did too. But despite his handsome features, Sadie found his eyes to be cold and hard. She had seen eyes like his before, and always on men who were evil and dangerous.

An argument quickly ensued when the sheriff arrived at the table of his two deputies. Sadie was convinced that the sheriff was trouble as were his deputies who were nothing more than street thugs. Shortly, the two intoxicated deputies rose and followed the sheriff. The three men arrogantly pushed their way towards the door and left.

Sadie curiously followed them outside, watching their continued disagreement until they disappeared inside the sheriff's office a block away. She paused for a moment before returning inside, looking up and down Wallace Street. Every day the streets of Virginia City were becoming more crowded with new arrivals. Even though the discovery of gold at Alder Gulch had only been three months earlier, she had heard that miners were strung along the gulch for fifteen miles, and new towns were springing up all along the way. But she also knew that in two or three years, the boom would be over. She had seen it happen, camp after camp. She had always had the foresight to know when to sell and move on, making a sizable profit each time. Those who were greedy and stayed too long to make another dollar eventually lost. It would be no different here...except this would be her last mining camp. She had accumulated enough wealth to allow her to go east, and live amongst high society that now scorned her. The thought humored her. A pretty future from such a meager beginning, she reasoned.

Her attention turned southward as she watched a billowing of dust rise slowly into the cloudless sky from an approaching wagon train. Wagon trains usually meant families, which did little for her business. Some freight wagons of whiskey replenishing her dwindling supply would be more beneficial, especially with winter coming in a few short months. Snow would close the passes and there would be no new supplies until spring. She knew a miner without whiskey would be an irate miner, something she did not want to encounter.

CHAPTER 2

The short train of ten wagons crested the rise and began their descent into Virginia City. Sam Templeton's wagon was the third in the train. Sarah, his wife, was seated next to him. Their daughter, Cynthia, inside the wagon peered between her parents at the new surroundings that would soon be the Templeton home.

Cynthia squeezed her mother's arm. "Mother, I'm scared," she said, her pale green eyes opened wide with fear. Her face could barely be seen beneath her bleached bonnet.

"I know dear," her mother replied trying to be brave for her.

Sam turned to his frightened daughter and rubbed his hand gently on her brown curls that rested on her back. "I know it seems frightening, honey, but there is nothing to be frightened about. You're safe here with us...I promise." Her strained face showed that little comfort had been taken from her father's words.

****

Sam felt unsettled and concerned that his wife and daughter were having such difficulty adjusting to their new life style. He hoped they would be more comfortable once they were settled in their new home. It had been his dream for many years, and he had been certain that all his family would find the West to their liking once they had arrived.

Sam, at the age of eighteen, and Daniel, one of his older brothers, left their home along the North Fork River in Wythe County, Virginia in 1846 to travel west to the Oregon Territory. They left with no money and few provisions...only a dream. Working their way west, it had taken them six months to arrive in St. Louis. Feeling their progress was too slow, they decided to stay in St. Louis, then a small community, and work until they could save enough money to continue their journey to Oregon.

They found work at a boatyard that built riverboats that traveled up and down the Mississippi River. They had been working there a month when one day, the owner, Mr. Bruner, brought his family to the yard. Sam immediately became infatuated with Mr. Bruner's youngest daughter. Somehow, Sam was determined to meet her. At first he kept his feeling to himself, but one evening he told Daniel his desire. Daniel laughed at his younger brother. "We're common laborers. Even if by some remote chance she found you to her liking, her father would have you hanged. Mind you I'm not saying it's right, but if you got these overwhelming desires, go down to the waterfront and find one of those women who take care of things like that. Put your head back on, Sam, before you get us both fired."

But Daniel's advice did not dampen Sam's hopes. Then one day, as though Sam's prayer had been answered, Mr. Bruner came by the yard looking for a volunteer to drive his wife and two daughters north to St. Charles to visit Mrs. Bruner's family. Ceasing the opportunity, Sam immediately volunteered.

That evening, Sam packed his small bag for his trip the next morning. He could sense Daniel was watching him. Daniel had not said much about Sam's interest in the boss's daughter since that first time, but Sam knew his brother was not happy with Sam's decision to drive the Bruner women. He knew Daniel was about to have plenty to say...he was being much too quiet, and it was not his character to withhold his feelings.

"So you say you're going to be gone three days," Daniel said, breaking the uncomfortable silence. The powerful looking man leaned forward, resting his large hands against the back of the wooden chair.

"Yeah. Three days," Sam answered, only glancing momentarily at his brother.

"So if she shows an interest in you, what's that going to do to our trip to Oregon?"

"I don't know. You're getting a little ahead of yourself," Sam answered as he began unbuttoning his shirt. He was in a hurry to get in bed and perhaps cut the conversation short.

"We've had this dream for some time, Sam. There's no way I'm giving up on it...with or without you. I'm moving on when I get my money saved." Daniel's eyes were intently staring at Sam.

"I know. I still have the dream too. But I can't help the way I feel."

"How can you feel anything? You don't even know her. You don't even know her name, do you?"

"No. But I know how I feel. I can't get her off my mind."

"You're being a big fool, Sam, but I'm not going to argue with you any more...at least not tonight. I'm going to read the Bible for a while."

Sam crawled into bed. He understood how Daniel felt. They both talked about their dream of Oregon for over a year. They talked of little else. Sam would never have believed he would feel this way about a woman when he had never spoken to her. And he wondered what he would do or how he would feel if it did come to a decision to go to Oregon or stay behind for ...for...he had to find out her name.

Early the next morning, Sam arrived at the Bruner's luxurious home. Sam hitched the horses and brought the carriage around front. He began to understand what Daniel had been saying. If the young Miss Bruner had become accustomed to such a lavish style of living, his meager offerings would never satisfy her.

Sam waited out front with the carriage for half an hour until he was summoned inside to help carry out the luggage. He was amazed at the massive amount of luggage that had been assembled for a three-day journey, but he eagerly carried it to the carriage and waited for the women's arrival.

He asked the estate's caretaker the names of the women he would be escorting to St. Charles.

The caretaker eyed Sam suspiciously. "You must never call them by their first name," he answered firmly. "They must always be referred to as Mrs., Miss, or Ma'am."

"I know," Sam, responded, "I just wanted to know, that's all."

"Okay, but you never heard it from me. Mrs. Bruner's name is Harriet. The daughter's are Jane and Sarah."

"Which one is the youngest?"

"Sarah."

"Is she spoken for?"

"No, but I don't see how that concerns you. You better be careful or you'll be asking for trouble."

"Thanks. I'll keep that in mind."

The caretaker grunted something undetectable to Sam and walked away.

Sarah. Such a lovely name, he thought. It was so befitting for her.

In a few minutes, the front door opened and Jane and Mrs. Bruner stepped through the massive doorway. Sam's eyes remained glued to the door, waiting for the arrival of Sarah. Then she appeared. She looked as radiant as Sam had remembered. She was smaller in stature than her mother and sister. Her golden brown hair was pulled back, and then dropped down her neck in ringlets. They danced vibrantly as she walked. As she approached, Sam could see her soft green eyes as though they were smiling at him. But it was her mouth, her lips, so softly set on her slim face that was most appealing to him.

Sam tipped his hat as the three women approached, but only Sarah seemed to notice him as she smiled politely. He helped each of

14

them into the carriage. He could feel Sarah's soft hand. He did not want to let go. He could smell her empowering fragrance, making his knees weak.

To Sam's disappointment, Mrs. Bruner seated herself in the front next to him and the two daughters sat in back.

The July day soon became quite warm and humid as the carriage made its way along the dusty road. Mrs. Bruner was soon complaining about the heat, dust, and the smell of the horses as she briskly swished her fan. Sam agreed that the front was the most uncomfortable and commended Mrs. Bruner for her generous sacrifice by letting her daughters have the more comfortable, shaded, rear seat. Now he only hoped she would take the hint that he had carefully placed.

At noon, Sam was told to stop along the road so the women could have a picnic lunch. He found a shady, grassy spot, and stopped. They took their basket and sat near the road as Sam stood by the carriage. He had not even thought about bringing something to eat along the way, and he could feel his stomach gnawing with hunger as he watched the women eat their chicken and soda bread.

He had turned away so not to increase his hunger and was surprised when Sarah suddenly appeared at his side. "We have far too much for us to eat," she said bashfully. "Please take this chicken so that it won't go to waste."

"Are you sure?" Sam said. "I'm fine."

"Yes. Please. I hope you find it to your liking. I made it myself."

For a moment, their eyes met. He wanted to reach out and touch her. "Thank you, Miss Bruner. It looks wonderful," Sam said politely as his heart beat rigorously inside him. "I'm sure it's delicious."

He wanted to continue their conversation, but she quickly handed him the chicken and left. He hurriedly ate each tender piece. Not only was she beautiful and charming, he thought, but she was a wonderful cook, too. He guessed she was perfect.

Shortly, the women were ready to resume their trip. Mrs.

Bruner informed her daughters that she was going to sit in the back the remainder of the trip and one of them would have to sit in front. Sarah quickly volunteered. Sam smiled. How clever he had been.

Although the afternoon sun beat down on the travelers, Sam found the heat soothing, the hillsides greener, and the road smoother and not as dusty with Sarah sitting in the front. Sarah did not speak to him during the remainder of the journey, but he was certain he caught her glancing at him. He wondered if she chose to sit in front to appease her mother, or whether she wanted to sit next to him. Sam wanted to believe she wanted to be there. But how was he ever going to find an opportunity to talk to Sarah with her mother sitting behind them? He could feel the watchful eyes of the elder Bruner woman staring at them.

It was late afternoon when they arrived at their destination in St. Charles. Sam was surprised to find the home here more elegant than the Bruner home in St. Louis.

Sam brought the carriage to a stop, and quickly rushed to the other side to help the women from the carriage. He held out his hand for Sarah. She graciously accepted it and stepped down. "The chicken was wonderful," Sam said in a quiet tone, hoping the other Bruner women would not hear.

"Thank you. I'm glad you enjoyed it," Sarah said with a courteous smile and for a brief moment she looked into his eyes, then glancing towards her mother and sister as though fearing she would be caught looking at the help.

Sam looked at the two women. Mrs. Bruner seemed unaware of their conversation, but Jane was inquisitively watching them.

Sam watched the women until they were inside, and then quickly began carrying their luggage to the house. Before he could enter, the butler took the luggage and informed Sam where the stables were located. Feeling disappointed he would not have another glance at Sarah, Sam acknowledged the old, gray haired man and drove the carriage around to the stables.

Sam unhitched the horses, brushed and fed them. When he was finished, an old black man showed him to his room. "It's not much, sir, but I think you'll find it comfortable."

Maybe to some people it might not have been much, but to Sam, it was fit for a king compared to the quarters he and Daniel lived in. What elegance Sarah must be accustomed to, Sam thought. The thought was depressing to him. Daniel's words were becoming more convincing. How could he ever win Sarah's heart? Maybe the infatuation of a beautiful woman was clouding his better judgment.

After supper, Sam sat at the door of his room and whittled on a willow branch. He wondered what Sarah was doing. Was she thinking of him? The thought was absurd. He knew he should forget about her and prepare to go on to Oregon with Daniel, but still, he could not stop thinking about her. Having been so close to her, he knew she was the woman he wanted. If she were only poor like him, maybe then she would find him more suitable. How selfish, he concluded, wishing her poor to better fill his needs.

While he sat idly thinking about his dilemma, he saw Sarah and Jane come out the back door of the mansion, and stroll leisurely through the garden. They stopped and glanced in his direction. He could see them talking, and as they conversed, it appeared Jane was upset with Sarah. Shortly, they returned inside. Had they been discussing him? He was thinking foolishly again.

****

The next morning, Sam rose early, fed and groomed the horses. He cleaned the carriage and spent the rest of the day walking about the grounds where he had been told that he had permission to be. He could not go near the house or garden, but the rest of the grounds were permitted, which still left a considerable area on the large estate.

It was late afternoon when Sam had finished feeding the horses and was on his way back to his room. He saw Sarah, by herself, come out the back door and began strolling in his direction, occasionally looking over her shoulder. His heart began to beat rapidly until he thought his head would burst. As she passed, she smiled. Sam was sure she hesitated for a moment. He wanted to speak to her, but his mind was empty and all he could do was smile back. He was angry with himself. At least he could have said a polite good evening to her. He watched Sarah return to the garden, stopping to smell some roses, and then return inside. He had ruined his one chance. He might never have another.

The next morning he brought the carriage around to the front of the house for the return trip to St. Louis. Sarah was the first one outside. She had already taken her place in the front seat before the others had arrived at the carriage.

Mrs. Bruner seemed not to notice her younger daughter's anxiousness, but Jane, again, gave her a suspicious glance.

Sam remained silent during the return trip, listening to the gossip about the family. There was that lazy Charles who drank too much, and poor Mary who had to put up with it. Sarah rarely entered the conversation-only when asked a question or was asked for her opinion. He wanted to speak to Sarah, but he understood his role as being the lowly help. If he did speak, he might risk making Mrs. Bruner angry and he would never have the opportunity to drive again. Sam was sure Sarah would not mind, but he had to be careful. Driving for the Bruner women would probably be his only chance of ever meeting Sarah.

When they arrived back in St. Louis, Sam helped the women from the carriage, and watched Sarah until she entered the house. He wondered if he would ever see her again. He could only hope that fate would someday bring them together again.

****

Although it seemed an eternity to Sam, it was only a week later that fate gave Sam his second chance. Sam was called upon to drive Sarah and Jane to a dinner engagement at a friend's home.

Sam was again breathless when he saw Sarah. Her radiance seemed to filter through his body. This time, her hair was curled into a bun with curls dangling down the side of her face. Her gown elegantly molded her slender figure. Her eyes glistened in the evening light. He knew he was surely in love...a love that perhaps would never be realized.

Jane again eyed him curiously as he stared at Sarah, but he no longer could help it. Sarah smiled politely as he helped her into the carriage. He wished he had better clothes to wear so that he would not look like a pauper to her.

As they rode to their destination, Sam could hear the women discussing an upcoming wedding. For a moment, Sam's heart leaped into his throat, thinking perhaps it was Sarah's, but he soon realized it was Jane's wedding they were discussing. He sighed with relief. However remote, there was still a chance.

The two women went inside while Sam waited by the carriage. The evening progressed slowly as Sam anxiously waited for Sarah's return. He tried to visualize what Sarah was doing. Was she talking and dancing with all the gentlemen inside? The thought gnawed at Sam's insides. Other drivers, waiting for their riders, tried to converse with Sam, but his mind was on Sarah and he was not interested in their casual chitchat.

It was some three hours later before Sarah and Jane returned to the carriage. He drove them home, listening to their discussion of the party. He clinched his teeth as he heard Jane trying to convince Sarah that a Mr. Henry Warren would be a perfect catch for Sarah. The only comfort Sam felt, was that Sarah did not seem to agree with her sister.

When they arrived at the Bruner's home, Sam helped the ladies from the carriage and watched them enter into the house. He was ready to leave when he noticed Sarah's parasol sitting on the back seat. He debated what he should do, but before he had made a decision, Sarah came running from the house.

"I forgot my parasol," she said bashfully. "I'm glad you're still here."

"I was about to bring it to you," Sam said excitedly. He was alone with her. Now was his chance. But what could he say? Without giving his mind a chance to rationalize what he was saying, he blurted out, "Sarah...I mean Miss Bruner...may I be so bold to say how lovely you look tonight."

"Why thank you," she said, her eyes dancing bashfully. "And you can call me Sarah. I feel terrible, but I don't know your name."

"Sam. Sam Templeton."

"Sam. It is nice to meet you."

"Sarah...I..."

"Yes, Sam"

"I think..." Sam could feel his ears burning. "I know I shouldn't be saying this, but I think you're the most beautiful woman I've ever seen. I've thought that from the first time I saw you at the mill."

"Well, thank you. That's so kind of you."

"Sarah!" a voice called from the front door of the house. "What on earth are you doing out there?" It was Jane. "The neighbors will talk to high heaven."

"I have to go, Sam. I hope you will always be the driver."

Sam nodded. "Good-night, Sarah."

Sarah smiled and ran for the house. Sam could see Jane scolding Sarah as they went inside. He only hoped that Jane would not put an end to his driving.

****

Sam was relieved when he was again summoned to drive the Bruner women. For whatever reason, Jane had decided not to squelch the growing interest between he and Sarah.

Jane was married a month later, and often times after that, he and Sarah would be alone when he drove her somewhere. They would talk and laugh. Sam was convinced they were perfect for each other, but he was still hesitant to try and advance their relationship any further. Perhaps he was only assuming that Sarah thought as much of him as he of her. Perhaps he only amused her.

Weeks passed. Daniel was becoming impatient and was ready to start for Oregon. Sam remained reluctant.

"Either you're going or not," Daniel said irritably. I'm going in a week...with or without you, so you'd better make up your mind."

It was two days later when Sam was summoned to drive Sarah to a friend's house. It was dusk when he picked her up. She was cheerful and friendly as usual. It was time to speak his feelings. He could not go on indefinitely the way it was. Besides, he knew she was popular with several men, and if he waited, he would surely lose any chance he had with her.

They had been traveling for several minutes, talking mostly about the weather when he reined in the horses along a quiet spot on the road.

"Sarah...I know I shouldn't say what I'm about to say. I know I am nothing...and you're such a beautiful lady of society. But I must say it." Her eyes were carefully studying his face. He had never seen her expression so serious. "I've fallen in love with you, Sarah. I've felt this way for a long time. I'm sorry if it offends you."

She smiled bashfully. "Not at all, Sam. I'm really quite honored. I was afraid you might think me a snobbish prude."

"Never, Sarah. Never until my dying days would I ever think that of you. You're so kind and gentle."

"Why thank you." Sarah's voice suddenly sounded uncertain, her eyes fixated on his. "Honestly, Sam, I have to confess I'm in love with you. I think I felt this way since that day we went to St. Charles when I brought you that chicken. It was the first time I had looked into your eyes. I felt I could honestly see your soul and I liked what I saw. I told Jane how wonderful a man I thought you were."

"She didn't object?"

"Yes, of course. But then, that's Jane. Now she is snobbish and prudish. But she finally accepted my feeling and even as prudish as she is, she wished me well."

"I know I'm pushing my luck, Sarah, but I want to marry you."

"Sam, that's the most wonderful words I've ever heard. I want to marry you...more than anything."

Sam brought her into his arms as their lips met. He could not believe what was happening. All this time he had feared how she would feel, how she would react, and now she said she loved him and wanted to marry him.

He looked seriously into her eyes. "What about your mother and father?" Sam asked. "I'm sure they'll disapprove of us."

Sarah smiled and clutched his hand. "They will disapprove. But after Mother has a hysterical fit, she'll come around. And for Father, he will resist a little longer, but I must admit, I have a way with him. A few tears and his crusty outer structure will melt and then he'll never be able to resist my wishes."

"Gee, maybe I'd better be careful, considering you know how to bring people around to your way of thinking."

Sarah covered her mouth and giggled, "You're too late, Sam. You already have."

****

Sarah had been right about her parents. They did resist the wishes of her and Sam. Then as Sarah had predicted, they finally consented. But Mr. Bruner insisted that if his daughter were going to marry Sam, then Sam would be promoted to at least foreman. Sam reluctantly consented. He would rather had remained a laborer and work with his hands, but he would do anything to have Sarah.

Daniel although disappointed, wished Sam and Sarah well and left for Oregon. As Sam watched his older brother disappear over the horizon, Sam knew he would never see him again.

Two months later, Sam and Sarah were married, and against everyone's belief, Sam and Sarah were happy. They lived in a modest home in a part of St. Louis that the Bruners thought to be barbaric, although Sam thought it to be rather nice.

Both Sam and Sarah wanted a large family, and a year later, happiness filled their home when Sarah gave birth to a son, Hezekiah.

A year later however, their joyful home was filled with sadness when their second son, Sam Jr., died three days after birth. But Sam and Sarah were set on a large family. The third pregnancy was extremely difficult for Sarah and she had a miscarriage six months into her pregnancy. The doctor was concerned for Sarah's health and tried to convince her not to attempt at having any more children, but Sarah would not listen. The next pregnancy, she again had a miscarriage. Sam would come home and find Sarah crying. "I'm a failure to you, Sam. I know how much you want children."

Sam tried to assure her that Hezekiah brought enough joy to him and that her health and well-being were far more important. She begged Sam to try one more time. Although her pregnancy was difficult, she gave birth to a daughter, Cynthia.

Sam was finally able to convince Sarah that the two children were enough, and finally Sarah reluctantly agreed.

Sam could not have been happier with his family, but as the years passed, the urge to go west began to build inside him like a prairie fire that was beginning to burn out of control. Hating his work only intensified his feelings. But whenever he mentioned moving west to Sarah, she would flatly reject the idea. She felt the West was too dangerous and was not the place to raise the children.

Several years passed and Sarah's mother passed away, and two years later, her father died. Jane's husband, Frank Stratton, took over the operation of the business. Sam had no desire to participate.

After the death of her parents, Sarah no longer had the will to resist and began to listen to Sam's reasoning to move west. It was two years later that Sarah finally agreed.

****

The journey west had been difficult for Sarah, but she never complained. Sam watched her struggle through each day, yet she would always greet him with a smile. He knew she had sacrificed her family, friends, and a comfortable home for him, and he was determined to make any sacrifice necessary to make her happy.

Now at last they had arrived at their new home. Sam looked out over the bustling mining camp of Virginia City. He was amazed at the number of buildings already erected and number of new ones in process. It had been such a short time since the discovery of gold in the area. The dusty streets, lined with the crude structures, were crowded with people.

"Hezekiah, get back into the wagon," Sarah shouted. "It's too dangerous out there."

"Mother," he called out with an air of disgust and humiliation.

"You heard your mother," Sam said in defense of his wife. "Now do as you're told."

Sam watched his son mumbling something as he crawled back into the wagon. Sam was sure Hezekiah had grown six inches since they had started their journey from St. Louis. Although barely fifteen, he was half a head taller than his friend, Isaac, even though Isaac was almost a year older.

Once Sam was assured Hezekiah was back in the wagon, he turned his attention back to the raw mining camp before him. "Up there, Sarah. See that dip on the hillside over there," he said, pointing to the west. "That's where we're going to build our home. It might seem a little rustic at first, but I promise you in a short time I'm going to make it a mighty fine home- one that you deserve. I promise you, Sarah."

Sarah smiled, patting his arm. "I know you will, Sam...And I know we'll be happy. As long as we're together, we'll always be happy."

24

CHAPTER 3

Sarah Templeton's Letter to sister in St. Louis

D *1863, September 15*
earest Jane,

I pray this letter will find its way through the wilderness to your home, and that it finds all of you well.

As I mentioned in the letter I sent to you from Fort Bridger, we are taking up residence here in Alder Gulch in a camp they call Virginia City.

We have been at our new home for three weeks now. It is more frightening than I could possibly have imagined. Although Sam has never mentioned it, I have overheard the other women discussing the horrible stagecoach robberies and killings that are common place here. One such robbery took place the day after our arrival.

There is little relief from the work required since we have arrived. Water must be hauled from such a long distance. Wood must be chopped for cooking and stored for the long winter that awaits us. Hezekiah has toiled hard with all the chores. I am so proud of him. He has never complained once to me. But I worry about him. I see the fever in his eyes. I fear that somehow his thirst for adventure will lead to terrible things. I pray each night for him.

Cynthia, bless her soul, is trying hard to be helpful. She is more frightened than I of this terrible land. She is afraid to leave my side, which I must admit is a comfort. I wish Hezekiah were a little more fearful.

Sam works so many hours. He starts at dawn and works until after dark. He has already found several carpenter jobs around town. After he comes home in the evening, even with the long hours, each night he takes me in his arms and holds me tight. All the fears that I have accumulated during the day seem to melt away in his arms. I am so thankful for his strength and tenderness. Perhaps it is the only thing that saves me from certain insanity.

Please write as often as you can. I anxiously wait to hear news from civilization.

> *With Sincerest Love,*
> *Sarah*

****

Hezekiah placed the two buckets of water on the ground that he had just carried from the stream a half-mile away. He flopped to the ground and leaned against the wheel of the wagon. It had been his third trip and his legs were so wobbly that he could not take another step, and his arms felt like they were on fire. This was not the adventurous life he had been expecting. Hezekiah removed his hat and dipped his hand into the bucket and splashed the cold water on his face. The coolness of the water felt good against his warm skin. He sat with his eyes closed, wishing at that moment he could take time from his busy afternoon to take a nap. He opened his eyes with a start to the sound of an approaching horse. Hezekiah rolled over on the ground and looked beneath the wagon to see who it was. The rider dismounted, but Hezekiah could only see the man's feet. His voice was unfamiliar as he spoke to Hezekiah's father who had been chopping wood on the other side of the wagon.

"Good afternoon," the stranger said casually. "Welcome to Virginia City."

Hezekiah could see his father set the ax down as he returned a friendly reply, "Afternoon, neighbor."

26

"The name's Sidney Brewer.

"Sam Templeton."

"Been here about two months now," Sidney continued as the two men shook hands. "Came up from Nevada. Originally from Iowa."

Sam quickly responded. "I brought my family out here from St. Louis. We had planned on going to Oregon, but in Fort Bridger we heard about the new strike, so we changed our minds and came here."

"I hope you made the right decision. I don't envy you, having your family and all. Tough enough surviving around here alone and not having to worry about a family."

"I suppose. But I think in time it'll be well worth it."

Hezekiah slid further beneath the wagon, but he still could not see the stranger.

"Just be careful, Sam. I reckon you've heard about the stage robbery that happened just the other day."

"No, as a matter of fact I haven't. I've been so busy around here since we've arrived, I haven't heard much news at all."

Hezekiah strained to hear the exciting news. A real stage robbery, his friends back in St. Louis would never believe it.

"It's not the first, you know. There's been two now in the last month. Been a lot of other holdups too. There are definitely some varmints at work around here. They seem to know every time someone is leaving with any dust. Seems as though you can't even trust your neighbor anymore."

"That is bad. Being able to trust your neighbors is too important. I just hope my wife doesn't hear about these robberies. She's half frightened out of her wits as it is."

"Well she won't hear it from me," the stranger said as he mounted his horse. "I reckon you've got nothing to fear though. They seem to be after the miners with gold...at least for now anyway. Have a good day, Sam. It was nice meeting you."

The stranger rode off. Hezekiah lay under the wagon, absorbing the exciting news he had just heard. There was so much going on around him and never a chance to see any of it. He could hardly wait to relay the news to Isaac.

****

Over a month passed after their arrival in Virginia City before Hezekiah and Isaac had their first opportunity to search out the highly anticipated adventures that surrounded them. It was decided by the new residents of Alder Gulch to have a day of celebration with prayers, conversation, and a Sunday dinner. After dinner, Hezekiah and Isaac, after a great deal of pleading, were permitted to roam the nearby hillside. "You two stay away from town," their mothers ordered. "It's no place for God fearing children, and don't wander too far from home."

"Yes, Mother," they answered and hurried off.

"Damn. It gripes me," Isaac said, once they were out of earshot of their mothers. Isaac spit angrily. "When it comes to working, we're old enough to do men's work, but when it comes to something we want to do, we're helpless children." Isaac wiped the spit from his chin.

"I know," Hezekiah responded, beating his hat against his leg in disgust. "I guess they figure work won't kill us, but having some damn fun will. My Mother has always been so damn protective. Father keeps telling me it's because she loves me. Can you believe that stupid reason?"

Isaac only shook his head as though it was impossible to believe.

"So what shall we do, now that we have a little time to ourselves?" Hezekiah asked, his eyes squinted as he surveyed the surrounding countryside.

"I don't know. You think there might be any Indians out here?"

"No. I think we're too close to town," Hezekiah quickly answered, his eyes carefully studying every boulder, bush and tree.

Isaac pointed. "Let's follow along that gully so our mothers can't see us."

Hezekiah looked over Isaac's suggestion. From his observation, the gully led straight to the main street at the edge of town. He wondered if Isaac had realized that. "Okay," Hezekiah said. "What are we waiting for?"

Hezekiah had been right. They soon found themselves at the southern end of the main street.

Not wanting to disobey their mothers, they remained at their disadvantaged location, inquisitively watching the bustling activity further down the street. But in time, after an elaborate discussion, they determined that it would be much easier and quicker to return home if they passed along the main street, rather than the roundabout way from which they had come.

They moved cautiously at first, stopping momentarily to fill their nostrils with the tantalizing smell of the pleasant aromas of bread baking in the Mechanics Bakery. But the delightful aroma of the bakery was soon replaced by the stench of the livery stable. Next came the blacksmith shop. They watched Jacob Avery, or so the sign above the door read, beating forcefully with his giant hammer on a glowing red-hot piece of iron.

As they moved further down the street, it became louder and more rowdy as the numerous high-spirited patrons of the eateries and saloons mulled about the dusty street. The boys' inquisitive eyes absorbed everything around them as they moved slowly forward, uncertain of the new and strange surroundings.

Hezekiah suddenly stopped. He blinked his eyes in wonderment. Before him was the most beautiful woman he had ever seen coming out of the saloon called 'Sadie's Palace'. She was wearing a shimmering bright blue dress cut so low that Hezekiah could see her soft white neck, shoulders, and the rising mounds of her breasts. Her face, gentle in feature, exhilarated a warm smile. Her soft green eyes glistened in the warm afternoon sun, radiating a gentleness as her eyelids fluttered playfully.

She smiled and spoke to some men near the doorway, who called her by name...Christina. What a pretty name, Hezekiah thought. She turned and quickly walked down the alley next to the

29

saloon. Hezekiah stepped back for a better view. Her hair pulled up, had curls dancing vibrantly down the back of her delicate white neck. He could hear Isaac shouting in his ear, but at that moment, nothing was going to break his trance. He did not want to miss one tantalizing moment of heaven as he stared at Christina. Then as quickly as she had entered his life, she disappeared from view. Hezekiah stared helplessly where she had been. Were all miracles so short in time? It had all happened so quickly, he wondered if she had only been a mirage.

Isaac was now tugging with exuberance at Hezekiah's sleeve. Hezekiah, feeling irritated that Isaac was interrupting an important moment of his life, turned to face his pestering friend. "What is it?"

But Isaac was not interested in Hezekiah's feelings. "There's a gun fight about to start. Let's get the hell out of here."

Hezekiah turned his attention to the middle of the street where Isaac was pointing. Two men were facing each other, both obviously angry. One, with his hand resting on his revolver tucked in his pants, was shouting at the other man. "You bastard! I'll blow your damn head off if I ever catch you around my claim again." Hezekiah did not wait for the other's response as he raced after Isaac already some distance ahead of him.

After Isaac had made his way to a distance he presumed safe, he stopped and waited for his friend to catch up with him. Isaac's eyes looked like they belonged to someone possessed by the devil. "Damn, that was close," he said, gasping for breath. "What the hell were you doing?"

"Didn't you see her?" Hezekiah responded with excitement.

"See who? You damn near got us killed."

"I did not. Hell I don't even hear any gunfire."

"Well, there could have been," Isaac responded angrily. "I guess the one guy must have been one of those claim jumpers I've heard about."

Hezekiah shrugged his shoulders. As exciting as the near gun battle had been, Hezekiah's thoughts were on Christina. He never had a woman make him feel the way she had. It was confusing, both physically and emotionally.

"You really didn't see her?" Hezekiah asked, no longer able to contain his feelings.

"Who in the hell are you talking about?" Isaac answered, showing his irritation.

"She was absolutely perfect, Isaac. I didn't think a woman could be that darn beautiful."

"So who is she?" Isaac was growing more impatient with his friend's absurdity.

"I don't know. I know her name is Christina and I saw her come out of the saloon back there."

"She came out of the saloon?" Isaac laughed. "She must be one of those floozies that works at those places...And this is what you damn near got us killed for?" Isaac was feeling confident that he was about to rid Hezekiah of his foolish notions about the woman. "So how was she dressed?"

"Really nice. She had on this pretty blue dress that came down to about here," Hezekiah answered, showing Isaac with his hand.

"Definitely a floozy." Isaac began to laugh more boisterously. "Boy, you really picked a good one. She's a hurdy-gurdy girl."

Hezekiah could feel his face flush with anger, but he couldn't think of a good reply. All he wanted to do now was get Isaac to shut up about her. Besides, what made him such an expert about women.

"We better get back before our folks come looking for us," Hezekiah said, hoping that would end of the conversation about Christina.

"I guess," Isaac responded with disappointment in his voice.

They circled around behind their houses not to create any suspicion. When they arrived a short distance on the hill above the houses, Hezekiah flopped on his back in the tall, brown grass. Isaac quickly followed his lead. They lay there quietly for some time. Hezekiah closed his eyes and listened to the sounds around him. He could hear a bee nearby and nervously listened to determine if it was coming closer. In the distance he listened to the saddened sounds of a bagpipe. An irritating cry of a baby below them broke their spell.

"I heard they're looking for a schoolmarm to teach us," Isaac said with disgust.

"Yeah, so I heard." Hezekiah digested the thought for a moment. "I also heard they're looking for a preacher too... and a place to hold church services."

"Damn. You know, we came out here for some excitement and we spend our whole damn time working, schooling or going to church."

Hezekiah sat up. Isaac was lying with his hat over his face. "Does your mother know you swear so much?" Hezekiah asked.

"Hell no. She'd kill me," Isaac answered without moving. "Does your mother know you swear so much?"

"You've met my mother. What do you think?"

Isaac peered from under his hat showing a broad grin. I've met your mother."

Hezekiah stood up. "I guess I better go. I've got to haul water yet."

Isaac sat up and flung his hat across the tall grass. "Hells bells! Me too."

CHAPTER 4

Mid-October had brought with it the first signs of an early winter. The pre-dawn cold stung Jack Robert's face as he quietly led his rust-colored mare through a thick brush covered gulch that led out the western edge of Virginia City. Even with the cold, he could feel the nervous sweat run down his sides. He and his horse jerked as a frightened jackrabbit scurried in front of them and disappeared into the underbrush. Jack cursed the rabbit under his breath.

Once out of town, Jack mounted his horse and made his way along the gulch. The frost covered leaves crunched beneath the horse's feet. Jack gritted his teeth. The threat of danger surrounded him and he knew each sound could alert the wrong people and death would be a certainty.

After two miles, Jack rode through a grove of cottonwood trees and then into open terrain. He was more vulnerable here, but he felt relieved that the darkness was still with him. He could see no one, and hoped no one could see him. He figured he had almost two hours before the late dawn would begin to lighten the sky.

He pulled the collar of his coat snugly around his neck and reached back and patted his bulging saddlebags filled with gold dust.

It had taken almost eight years to finally make his strike and there was no way that any damn road agents were going to take it from him. Once he arrived in Salt Lake City, he would cash in his finds and head for Ohio...home, or at least it was at one time many years ago.

He wondered if his mother and father still owned their little farm, or even if they were still alive? He had never written since he left, embarrassed that he had not made his fortune like he had so absolutely assured them he would. How could he tell them he was no more than a vagrant? Besides, he was never in one place long enough to receive a reply.

He wondered what his two older brothers were doing? Maybe they had joined the Union Army to fight the Confederates. Hell, maybe they had been killed. He had heard the horror stories from people arriving from the East of so many men dying on both sides.

And then there was sweet Samantha. All she had wanted was for him to be by her side. But he had insisted he wanted her to have the luxuries of life that she deserved. "I'll be back before you know it. A year, two at the absolute most," he promised her. "Then we'll have everything we could ever want for the rest of our lives."

But good fortune never came. The years continued to pass as he moved from one mining camp to another...one fleeting dream to the next. Time became lost. Then one day, he suddenly realized it was too late. He wondered how long Samantha had waited for him? How long had she carried the hope of his return?

He tried not to think what his life would be if he had stayed in Ohio. Was the gold in his saddlebags worth everything that he had lost so long ago? It no longer mattered; he had chosen his destiny that now seemed an eternity.

****

A darkened silhouette of a man stood silently on the edge of the bluff. The man looked out over the vast terrain below him. He took a long drag from his cigarette. A grin appeared as he let the smoke roll lazily from his lips. He squinted as he watched a shadowed lone rider appear in the darkness, and move northwest across the barren plateau. "Stupid son-of-a-bitch. He thinks he can sneak out of town without being seen," he mumbled. Leaving at night and staying off the main road only assured him that the rider was obviously carrying treasures ripe for the picking. He waited, watching the rider for some time, determining the route he was taking-northwest around the foothills and then south towards the pass, staying within visual distance of the road to insure not getting lost. Others had tried the same route and failed. Now, their bones were strewn along the desolate landscape.

The watchful observer took a final drag from his cigarette and crushed it with his boot. He swung into the saddle, and spurred his horse into a gallop towards a nearby ranch house to arouse the others.

****

As Jack Roberts moved along the foothills, the first light of daybreak was beginning to appear behind him. It soon became obvious from the clouded sky that a storm was moving in, and with it would bring snow-a sure fire enemy to him. Snow would make the terrain more difficult to travel and even worse, it would leave his tracks. He cursed at another run of bad luck.

He had planned on resting by day and traveling at night, but this storm would require a change of plans. Jack only hoped if he continued traveling that perhaps the snow would cover his tracks. He had no choice...he had to keep moving, trying to put as much distance as possible between he and the road agents.

He moved as swiftly as the rugged terrain allowed. By noon, the first snowflakes began to fall. How gentle and innocent the snow seemed...how deadly it could become. He paused for a moment viewing his surroundings for signs of anyone following. In the distance to the west, he could see the Point of Rocks where a stage line station was located. By this time tomorrow he figured he would be out of the road agents territory. How important the next twenty-four hours would be.

Snow was falling heavily by late afternoon. He wanted to keep traveling, but the combination of snow making the ground unsure footing and the oncoming of darkness made it too difficult. He had to make camp for the night. With any luck, it would continue snowing, covering his tracks and leaving him secure...at least for now.

He found a dense grove of willows with a stream nearby and made camp. There would be no fire tonight, not wanting to chance that it might be seen. After feeding and watering his horse, Jack crawled into some brush to help protect him from the cold. In a few days, he could bathe in luxury, but for now he would have to do without. He chewed on some jerky as he thought about Ohio.

****

Jack awakened at the first light. His body was frigid. Slowly he crawled from the underbrush and began slapping his body briskly to regain circulation. Four inches of snow covered the ground. The sky was still overcast, but no new snow was falling. If someone picked up his trail now, he would be easy to follow, but he had to continue. He only hoped that somehow he had passed unnoticed through the bandits' deadly web.

Travel proved difficult and slow, but he remained determined to stay off the road. It was mid-morning when he suddenly pulled in the horse's reins. He stood in his stirrups, poised like an animal listening for its predator. He thought he had heard something. Was it only his frayed nerves? No sound. He eased back into the saddle, hearing only the creaking of the leather. He could only see a short distance around him following along the river, but if he moved to higher ground, he could be seen as well as he could see. The crisp air was still silent. He edged his mare cautiously forward, listening for a sound of danger.

Then the sound came again. This time he was certain he had heard something. His body tensed. More sounds. Now he could distinguish the sound of horses moving rapidly towards him-at least two.

Without hesitation, Jack spurred his horse. The horse lurched forward, stumbling, but Jack's spurs never left the horse's flanks. The branches whipped at his face as his horse moved with precision through the trees.

He reached a small clearing. A frightening chill surged through him...two riders with revolvers drawn were waiting for him. He quickly yanked at the reins to retreat back into the trees, but two more riders appeared in the clearing behind him. He was surrounded.

Jack stopped, carefully observing his four captors. All had revolvers drawn. None were masked, but he didn't recognize any of them. He tried to reason a possible escape, but it appeared hopeless.

"Morning," the one bandit said. Jack never responded, but the outlaw seemed unconcerned. "We were wondering why you slipped out of town so rudely without saying good-bye." The others laughed. "You're not trying to hide anything from us are you?" he continued, his darkened teeth showing as he displayed a broad grin. The two men behind Jack moved to his front.

"What do you want?" Jack said angrily. "I don't have anything."

"Yeah, and my mother's a virgin," a second one said. They all laughed again.

"Slipping out in the middle of night sure seems mighty suspicious to me," the first outlaw said. "I gotta give you credit though. You damn near slipped by us." He leaned forward. "So what might you be carrying in those saddlebags?"

Jack knew his time was short. If they had not bothered to mask themselves, they were not intending on leaving a witness. He figured the only reason they hadn't killed him thus far was because they were entertaining themselves at his expense. It was over. He knew his run of bad luck was preparing for its final encore. The best he could hope for now was to take one of them with him.

"I told you I had nothing," Jack grumbled, reaching back, unhooking his saddlebags, and letting them slip to the ground. "Take a look for yourself."

"I think I might just do that," the apparent leader said as he slid from his horse.

For the moment, all eyes were greedily looking at the saddlebags. Jack knew this was his only chance. His hand moved swiftly to the rifle strapped on his saddle in front of his right leg. The rifle had just cleared the holster when the air rang out with gunfire.

Jack slumped forward in his saddle, but his horse reared, throwing him to the ground. Jack lay motionless in the red stained snow while one of the gunmen continued to unload his revolver into the luckless miner.

"Damn, Zeke! Take it easy," Red Yeager shouted as he watched the gunman's hand shaking. A frightening satisfied grin was frozen on the gunman's face.

"Look at him, Red. I think Zeke gets his thrills in killing," Haze Lyons said, staring at his fellow bandit.

Zeke's face became flush with anger as he turned to face his challenger. "You think you're so damn saintly," he shouted. "I didn't see you having any problem squeezing the trigger.

"I do what I have to do. That's all. I don't get any kicks from it," Haze angrily responded.

"Drop it!" Red shouted. "Take a look at what's in these bags." Red smiling victoriously, displayed the bags filled with gold.

The joyous foursome, once finished in delighting over the cache, prepared to leave.

"Want to find his horse, Red?" Haze asked.

"Let it go. I'm too damn tired to look for it," Red answered. "Wolves or coyotes will take care of it anyway."

A light snow began to fall on Jack Robert's body as the four bandits headed north.

****

Zeke Clemens watched the other three men enter the ranch house. He lit a cigarette and walked towards the barn. His anger had not subsided during their return from the killing of the miner. They would pay someday, ridiculing him the way they did. What made them so high and mighty? When he got his share of the gold, he would kill all of them.

Zeke had left Tennessee at the age of fifteen in a hurry when he was nearly hung for stealing horses. He had been on the move ever since trying to avoid the law. He had stolen horses and pulled some minor robberies.

After his near capture for raping a young girl in Illinois, Zeke headed west, fearing someone would be tracking him. Zeke eventually arrived in Oro Fino, in the Idaho Territory. There he met Dalton Williams. One night while they were drinking, Dalton told Zeke about his intentions of coming to Alder Gulch where he knew Boone Helms, who was part of an outlaw gang operating in the territory. The word was business was booming for them and it was easy pickings. Zeke convinced Dalton to let him ride along.

Business was good, but to Zeke's disappointment, the gold cache was not being split up until the bandits were ready to disperse with their operation.

One of Zeke's first jobs when he joined the gang was to kill the rancher where the bandits had taken over the ranch for their hideout. He had never killed any one before and was uncertain whether he was capable of murder, but that night when he led the rancher a short distance from the house to kill him, he quickly realized the enjoyment he found in murdering someone. Seeing the rancher's pleading eyes and hearing his begging words, gave Zeke the enormous feeling of power that he held over the doomed man. Pulling the trigger was the easiest and most thrilling thing he had every done. Even taking his pleasure with the young girl as she begged him to stop, could not match the pleasure he felt killing the rancher. He had only regretted not killing the girl now that he realized how pleasurable it would have been.

Each killing became more exciting to Zeke. The fire inside him grew with each one as his sense of power and control grew.

He would enjoy killing these bastards who had humiliated him. His time would come and he would watch their pleading eyes, their begging words not to kill them. He promised himself... they would pay.

CHAPTER 5

W ith all the tell tale signs of an early winter, the people of Alder Gulch began to hastily make preparations for the oncoming cold weather. The miners, who had all summer been satisfied with their rustic living quarters of tents, wickiups, and drafty cabins, soon began to realize that more adequate shelter was needed. Sam Templeton, a builder and carpenter, and Harvey Kyle, a logger and saw man, were ready for the surge of new business.

Some of the residents left for warmer climates. With each arrival of a freight wagon, wagers were being made whether it would be the last until spring.

Hezekiah and Isaac's thoughts were more short term as they anxiously waited for another adventurous afternoon to themselves; but it was not until late October before it came. Then near disaster struck...some of the younger children wanted to tag along.

"Please, Mother," they begged, "We deserve time to ourselves. We shouldn't have to baby-sit."

Finally, both mothers, more from fear that the younger children would be neglected than consideration for the boys' freedom, agreed not to send the smaller children with them. Fearing a sudden change of heart, Hezekiah and Isaac wasted little time in departing.

They followed the same path as the first time, which once again, soon led them to the edge of town. Hezekiah was anxious to return to Sadie's Palace where he had seen Christina. Hardly a day or night passed that he did not think of her.

Isaac was reluctant, recalling the near disaster the last time; and besides, he did not have the motivation Hezekiah had. Isaac stopped in front of the livery stable.

"Come on, Isaac, it stinks here," Hezekiah said, feeling irritated that his friend was betraying him.

"I don't know," Isaac said, sitting on a nearby log. "We damn near got killed last time."

"We did not. Besides, you said you would go."

"I did not. I just never said, I wouldn't."

Isaac seemed determined. Hezekiah sat down next to him. He figured eventually Isaac's uncertainty would give way to his curiosity. Hezekiah would just have to be patient.

"How much could you really see?" Isaac asked after a few seconds had passed.

"What are you talking about?" Hezekiah asked, looking inquisitively at his sidekick. "How much of what?"

"You know, the floozy you saw the last time. How much of her could you see if she had on a low cut dress?"

Hezekiah was about to correct Isaac for calling Christina a floozy, but realized this was an opportunity to heighten Isaac's curiosity.

"I guess you mean Christina," Hezekiah said firmly. "A lot, I'm telling you," Hezekiah added, flickering his eyebrows to emphasize his statement. "You could see all the way down to where her bosoms begin to rise and separate." Hezekiah licked his lips. "They looked mighty pretty. Prettier than anything I've ever seen."

"Cleavage," Isaac added.

"Cleavage?" Hezekiah said, confused by Isaac's response. It was not the reply he had expected.

"Yeah. That's what they call that space between a woman's breasts."

"How do you know that?"

42

Isaac sat up straight, looking proudly at Hezekiah. "Back home...I mean the old back home, Johnny Hertz brought a book to school that told all kinds of stuff like that. It even had some pictures drawn of naked women."

"Wow. And he let you look at it."

"Yeah. He let all the guys look at it." Isaac was busily drawing an outline of a woman in the dirt at his feet with a stick to emphasize he was knowledgeable on the subject. "Nobody really liked Johnny, but I must admit, for a while he was the most popular guy in school. Then one day, somebody tore a couple pages out of the book, and it really made Johnny mad. After that, he wouldn't let anybody look at it."

Hezekiah, having a sudden interest in women since seeing Christina, was listening intently, hoping to learn more. "So, what else did it say?"

A voice behind them suddenly interrupted their intriguing conversation. Fearing they had been caught, both boys jerked with a start. They whirled to find an old Indian standing behind them. They scampered to their feet, fear gripping them as they stood face to face with him.

He was wearing a faded, baggy shirt and buckskin pants. A leather band encircled his long, mostly white hair. A slight smile softened his wrinkled, leather skin face. "I'm sorry. Did I frighten you?" he said, taking a step closer.

"Hell no," Isaac answered, stepping back. Hezekiah wanting to keep a united front quickly stepped back alongside Isaac.

"Good," the Indian said, his grin becoming broader. "You boys watching all the action?" Neither answered as they stood with mouths open. "Down the street," he continued, pointing towards the main part of town. "You've been watching all the excitement?" Still neither answered. "Is there something wrong?" he said, raising an eyebrow inquisitively.

"Are you an Indian?" Isaac asked, wanting to confirm what he already knew.

"I am. They call me Joe around here."

"That's not an Indian name," Isaac said defiantly.

"No it's not. My tribal name is Eagle Feather."

"Gee, that's great," Hezekiah said excitedly.

Isaac's inquisitiveness was beginning to conquer his fear. He propped his hat to the back of his head. "So, if you're an Indian, why do you live here in town and they call you Joe?"

"Ah, a young brave with a lot of questions. Are you asking me to learn something, or to challenge me?"

Isaac shrugged his shoulders. Hezekiah, not wanting to upset the old Indian, quickly intervened. "Can we call you Eagle Feather?"

He smiled again. "Sure. It would please me if you did. What shall I call you?"

"How about an Indian name?" Isaac asked.

"Maybe someday."

Isaac frowned. "Why not today?"

"If I were to give you a name now, it would be 'Running At The Mouth'."

Hezekiah burst into laughter. Eagle Feather grinned. Isaac glared at both.

"Can you tell us how come you're here in Virginia City?" Hezekiah asked.

"Yes, if you'd like to hear." Eagle Feather seemed pleased by the request. "But later. I still have some work to do in the stables. When the sun reaches halfway to that peak," he said pointing behind him, "I'll be on the bluff over there." He turned and pointed to a plateau on a hill to the east of town.

****

"How long do you think it'll take the sun to get there?" Hezekiah asked, once they had left.

"I don't know. I'm wondering if we should go," Isaac said.

"Why?"

"Maybe he wants to get us alone so he can kill us and take our scalps," Isaac said, patting his head.

"No he wouldn't. He's a nice old man."

"Maybe, and then again...maybe not. I heard one of the men on the wagon train say you can't trust an Indian, even a dead one."

"Well I'm going," Hezekiah, said, feeling irritated at Isaac for being so suspicious...but none-the-less, Hezekiah was relieved when Isaac finally agreed to go.

****

The youths climbed to the rocky crest before the sun had reached its destined place in the sky to assure their early arrival. They were surprised to find Eagle Feather already there. He stood motionless, gazing towards the eastern horizon. He never turned to acknowledge their arrival, only continued staring silently eastward.

"Maybe he doesn't hear us," Isaac commented.

"He had too. We were making too much noise. Besides, Indians can hear everything.

"Maybe he's too old," Isaac said.

About then, Eagle Feather raised his arms to the sky and slowly lowered them to his side. "You're early," he said before turning to face the boys.

"Yeah. Sorry if we interrupted," Hezekiah said apologetically.

"What were you doing?" Isaac asked as Eagle Feather approached.

"Listening to the Spirits."

"I didn't hear anything," Isaac said suspiciously.

"Maybe you didn't listen."

"All I heard was the wind in the grass," Isaac responded assertively.

Eagle Feather seemed undisturbed by Isaac's argumentative attitude. "The Spirits speak in many ways. Sometimes through the wind...sometimes in the shriek of an eagle, or the howl of a coyote, or sometimes through silence."

"How can you hear silence?" Isaac asked confidently.

"By listening and not talking."

"Can you teach us to hear the Spirits?" Hezekiah asked, embarrassed by Isaac's rude questioning.

Eagle Feather squatted cross-legged on the ground. The boys quickly followed, sitting in similar fashion. Eagle Feather stared for a moment at the boys before speaking. "Before one can hear the Spirits, a brave has to become part of everything around him. The sky...the grass... all the animals. Everything." He moved his hand across the horizon as he spoke. "You have to become a part of all creations and it a part of you." He paused, watching the boy's faces. "That is the only teaching I can give you." The boys listened in awe. Even Isaac had become quiet. Eagle Feather continued, "Does not your God speak to you?"

"I don't know," Isaac answered, "I don't think I ever heard him."

Eagle Feather raised his eyebrow signifying he doubted Isaac. "When you are about to do something wrong, but you don't because you know its wrong, is it not your God speaking to you?"

"Hmm, I never thought of it that way," Hezekiah said.

"I get it," Isaac added. "Well sort of."

Eagle Feather smiled.

Any remaining fear of Eagle Feather was now gone. "Tell us more," Isaac requested, scooting closer.

"Tell us why you're living here in Virginia City," Hezekiah said with excitement.

Eagle Feather nodded and became silent as he looked out over the horizon beyond Isaac and Hezekiah. They waited patiently, having already learned that Eagle Feather did not proceed until he was ready.

As he began, he seemed to be somewhere far away. His eyes continued to stare solemnly into the distance.

****

"Many winters have passed," the old Indian began, a distant sadness in his eyes, "when I was a young brave... younger than you. I lived in my village much distance from here, along a mighty lake to where the sun rises. Our village was part of the proud and peaceful Erie Nation. We had tried to live in peace, to nourish and hunt our land. But for generations our forefathers had been under constant attack by the Cayuga, Mohawk, Oneida, Onondaga and the Seneca, who formed the mighty Iroquois Nation. My people fought bravely, but could not match the Iroquois numbers or the weapons they had acquired from the white man. Most of our villages had been destroyed or had become small in the number of warriors. Many of the women and children had been captured by the warring nation to serve as slaves or to bear children.

Then the white man began to take our land. The animals grew scarce and our people grew hungry. We were small in numbers and could no longer resist. My village and another nearby village sadly decided we had to leave the land and Spirits of our ancestors and search for new land where we could live in peace.

When the new buds came to the trees, we left our land and the Spirits of our brave ancestors. We were sad, but our elders felt this was our only hope. We followed the setting sun, passing through the land of other nations-the Miami, the Potawatoni, the Sauk and the Dakotas. They felt anger and fear of the white man coming as their food and land were already decreasing, so they let us pass, but we could not stay on their land. Many of the older people and children of our village could not endure the difficult journey and died.

We arrived in the land of the Ojibway as the frost covered the ground and the leaves fell from the trees. They were kind and let us stay. A third of our village had died on the journey, including my grandfather and grandmother. Those of us that survived the journey were tired and starving.

Winter came early to our village. Because we had been moving, we were not prepared for winter. Food and skins were scarce. We felt the hunger and cold. Many more of our people died. Then, two white trappers passed through our village. Soon after, the white man's burning fever came.

Death became a part of life to us as whole families often died within a few days. Within the same night, both of my brothers died.

47

Shortly thereafter, my father and sister died. Everyone was weak and sick. The bodies lay where they had died. The only food we had was chewing the few hides we had for warmth and the bark of trees.

Then one night as a storm raged outside our wigwam, my mother closed her eyes. They never opened again. That night was the first time I heard the Spirits. They gave me strength through that night as I sat resting my mother's head on my lap.

By morning the storm had subsided. I left the wigwam in search of others, but no one answered my frightened call.

Alone, frightened, cold and hungry, I returned to my wigwam. I covered my mother and asked the Spirits to take her to be with her ancestors. Not knowing where I was going or what I was going to do, I left the village.

For two days I wandered the frozen barren land. I could feel death near as I lay half frozen in the snow. As I lay there waiting for death, I heard voices. At first, I thought it to be the Spirits coming for me. I looked to the sky to meet them, but instead, I saw the grizzly face of a white trapper.

He and his friend brought me to an isolated farmhouse where an elderly couple lived. She was Sioux Indian; he was white.

They nourished me back to health. They were kind and good to me, but I hated them...he because he was white, she because she married him. I had decided I would leave when the time was right. But I found their kindness begin to melt the hate inside me.

I stayed. I helped them work the poor soil of their farm. I found happiness and considered them my new mother and father.

Then the fall as I reached my manhood, Yellow Flower died. By spring, from a broken heart, Zachary died.

I stayed and worked the soil. One evening, the following summer after their death, I sat on the porch looking at my ruined crops from the locust. I decided I could stay no longer...The Spirits had spoken.

Feeling isolated from both the white man and Indian, I came West into the mountains and began a solitude life of trapping.

Life was content for many years. But in time, with the discovery of gold and the intrusion of the prospectors, life for the trapper became difficult.

A trapper friend, Ross Norton, started the livery stable here. He asked me to help him and I reluctantly agreed. However, shortly after, a bear killed Ross. The Spirits had led me here, so I stayed.

Now you understand why I live here."

****

As Eagle Feather finished his story, he smiled as though pleased. Hezekiah wondered how anyone could smile with such a sad life. He did not even seem bitter with all that had happened to him.

Eagle Feather looked to the sky. "It is getting late. You must hurry or you'll be late for your supper."

The boys rose and started to leave. Isaac paused and turned back towards Eagle Feather. "I'm sorry for being so rude and asking so many questions," he said, staring at the ground.

Eagle Feather smiled. "You were just inquisitive. If I make the answers to your questions too easy, you'll never learn how to think. That would be bad. You will be faced with many questions in life and there will not always be someone there with the answers."

"Can we visit you again," Hezekiah asked.

Eagle Feather nodded, smiling at his new friends.

CHAPTER 6

Sadie's Palace was half empty as many of the miners had already left knowing that dawn would begin another day of grueling work.

Christina moved among the tables serving drinks to those that remained, cleverly avoiding their grasping hands. With each near miss, she would politely scold them and force a flirtatious smile. She did not like working the later hours, but Sadie was short-handed tonight so Christina had volunteered. She glanced at the clock on the wall behind the bar as it slowly ticked away the minutes...almost ten. She sighed with relief. She would soon be able to leave and return to the solitude of her small cabin. She only wished that someday this would all end.

It had been almost four years since she had first met Yantsey Dalton, a smooth talking, and handsome gambler. Christina, at the unsuspecting age of nineteen, became enchanted with his debonair, romantic lifestyle. She soon found herself uncontrollably in love with him.

Yantsey, not accustomed to staying very long in one place, was soon ready to leave for new surroundings. He asked Christina to come with him. She accepted. Her parents distraught and embarrassed by their eldest daughter, informed her that if she left with the unscrupulous gambler, she would never be welcome in their Philadelphia home again. Her love for Yantsey prevailed.

The first few months were filled with the excitement, adventure and love that she desired. The couple weaved their way west, never staying but a week or two in one place. Although Christina dearly missed her family, she was sure she had made the right choice.

But in time, Yantsey began to change. Christina was becoming a burden to his carefree lifestyle. She was becoming more aware of other women in Yantsey's life. At first, he would not return all night, then it became days that he would not return to the room where Christina waited, crying until there were no more tears.

One morning, after Yantsey had been gone for two days, Christina confronted him. He became angry and went into a rage, slapping her so hard that she fell helplessly to the floor.

"I can't take anymore of your damned jealousy," Yantsey shouted as he grabbed his bag and began to pack. "I'm leaving. The room is paid for tonight and then you're on your own. Maybe next time, you'll learn to mind your own damn business." Christina pleaded with him, begging his forgiveness, but shortly he was gone.

Christina spent most of that day lying on the bed, crying over the loss of her love. But by evening, fear began to grip her. What would she do? She knew no one and she had no money. Even if she had a way to return, she knew she could never return to her home in Pennsylvania.

The following morning, she packed her bag and left the safe confinements of her room. She found the streets frightening as she wandered hopelessly in disarray.

By nightfall she had grown weary and hungry. Her fear was mounting. She had used all the daylight hours and still had no answers. The chilly, night, Colorado mountain air was beginning to enclose around her. She fought back the tears that kept trying to emerge. Her life was ruined. She began to wish for her death. The tears she had bravely held began to pour from her eyes. She desperately tried to wipe them away, but they kept streaming down her cheeks.

Suddenly, she was startled by a woman's voice. "It looks like you could use a friend about now."

Christina looking through her clouded eyes saw a woman standing before her. At first, Christina was somewhat frightened by the woman's exuberant dress and appearance. But the woman's gentle voice and sincere smile eased Christina's anguish. The woman handed a handkerchief to Christina.

"I must look foolish," Christina said, wiping her tear stained eyes and cheeks.

"Not at all," the woman answered. "We all need a good cry from time to time."

"Thank you for being so understanding."

"I bet this is all over a man."

Christina nodded, her face showing her embarrassment.

It usually is," the woman said, resting her hand on Christina's shoulder. "I'm Sadie. I own the saloon over there." She pointed across the street to a well-lit establishment. "I saw you standing here and I thought you looked like you could use a friend."

"Thank you for being so kind. I'm Christina." The tears began to flow again.

Sadie put her arm around Christina. "Come with me. I'll get you a hot bath and something to eat. You can stay with me until you have a chance to straighten things out."

That had been the beginning of Christina's association with Sadie. With no other alternative in Christina's future, she soon began working for Sadie in her saloon. Sadie was always kind to Christina as she was to all her girls. Christina had soon discovered that a saloon was only part of Sadie's business, but Sadie never tried to persuade Christina into prostitution. "We each do what we wish, and that's the way it should be," Sadie would always comment.

A few months later Sadie sold her thriving business in Colorado at a lucrative profit, packed up and moved to the Idaho Territory to open another saloon and brothel. All her girls were eager to follow. Christina frightened at the thought of being alone, decided to follow Sadie.

After only a year, Sadie heard of the new strike at Alder Gulch. Once again, all of Sadie's girls, including Christina, followed.

Someday Christina hoped she could leave the lifestyle she had by chance been thrust into so long ago. Sadie was truly the only friend she felt she had, but she longed for the quiet family life and she knew as long as she worked for Sadie, it would never come.

Christina's attention returned to the saloon as she felt a hand patting her behind. "Hey there, sweet thing. We need a fresh bottle of your best whiskey and whatever else you might be offering."

She quickly turned to the voice. It was Buck Stenson, one of the deputy sheriffs. Sitting at the table were two other deputies and Sheriff Plummer. Her eyes immediately came in contact with the sheriff's penetrating stare. She quickly turned away and went after the whiskey. The stare had frightened her and she could still feel his watchful eyes on her.

She delivered the whiskey, while listening to the deputies' rude remarks, but it was the sheriff's silent stare that bothered her most.

She returned to the bar and breathed a sigh of relief. It was ten o'clock. Her shift was over. She called to Sadie, who was sitting with a table of patrons at the far side of the saloon that she was leaving. Sadie waved goodnight and returned to her business at hand.

Christina hurried from the saloon and began her short walk home. Her body felt tense. Never before had she been frightened walking home after work, but tonight, she did as she headed down the alley.

Her fear heightened as she heard quickened footsteps coming from behind her. She felt a chill race through her and she quickened her pace, but the steps were coming closer. She turned to face the intruder. It was Sheriff Plummer.

"Sorry, Christina. I hope I didn't frighten you." A smile curled on his lips.

"Well, a little," Christina answered, trying to force a cordial smile.

"I wanted to walk you safely home. I know you were upset when you left the saloon tonight."

"Oh, that won't be necessary. I'm fine. Besides I'm almost there." Christina had felt safer alone than with the sheriff.

"No, I insist," he answered sternly. "Besides I wanted to apologize for my deputies' actions. They had no right to be so rude."

"I guess it comes with the job. Besides I'm fine. Thank you for your concern." Christina continued to hurry her pace, but Sheriff Plummer remained persistent as he continued to walk with her.

"This is my place here," she desperately commented as she pointed to her cabin. "Thank you for seeing me safely home." She unbolted the lock on her door.

The sheriff stepped forward and pushed open the door. "Maybe I'd better check inside for you. You never can be too careful." He stepped past her and once inside found her lantern on the table. He very deliberately lit it and slowly strolled around her small cabin, sometimes stopping to slowly stroke her clothing hung about the room.

Christina stood by the open door, becoming increasingly nervous with each passing moment. After the sheriff had encircled the room, he gently pushed the door closed.

"I guess it's safe enough," he said, watching Christina's nervous eyes.

"Thank you again," she replied. "But I am awfully tired, so if you don't mind." He stood quietly, staring at her. "Please, Sheriff," she pleaded.

"You're a real pleasure to the eyes," he said, his voice low but demanding. "I've wanted you since the day I first saw you." His hand reached towards her.

"I must insist you leave at once," Christina said, her voice filled with fright.

A sneer appeared on his lips. "A whore should feel honored that I'd desire her."

Terror gripped Christina. She was looking into the most evil eyes that she had ever seen. She stepped towards the door, but he grabbed her arm and threw her onto the bed. Before she could recover, he had thrust himself on her, knocking the breath from her. She gasped for air as she tried to scream but found it impossible.

An agonizing pain filled her body. She tried to push him off her, but his overpowering grip held her helplessly to the bed. She could feel his ruthless hands grabbing violently between her legs. She closed her eyes trying to shut out the pain and terror as he tore away her clothing. She felt her strength draining from her. She pleaded, but he was beyond reason as his hand began to penetrate her.

Then suddenly, he stopped. Christina bewildered, opened her eyes. Standing above them was Sadie with the barrel of her pearl handle revolver shoved against the side of Sheriff Plummer's head. The expression of hate on Sadie's face was almost as frightening as the attack itself.

"Get your goddamn ass up, you son-of-a-bitch!" Sadie's voice shook with anger. "I ought to blow your crotch off where you lay!"

Slowly the sheriff pulled himself away from Christina. She quickly leaped from the bed and stood behind Sadie.

"Why don't you mind your own business, you old whore!" the sheriff shouted.

"I should do the town a favor and put a bullet between your beady little eyes you worthless bucket of horse dung."

"That might not be wise killing the sheriff," he answered with a sneer frozen on his lips.

"I would guess the town would make me a heroine if I shot your ass off. Now get the hell out and I don't ever want to see you bothering any of my girls again."

For the moment, the sheriff seemed somewhat in doubt whether Sadie would restrain herself or not, and slowly backed towards the door. He tipped his hat as he opened the door. "It was a pleasure, Christina. We'll finish our business another time and maybe there'll be a big tip for you...And oh, Sadie, you do understand...we're not through." He burst into laughter as he slammed the door behind him.

****

Electra Plummer read from her favorite book of poetry. She felt weary, but chose not to retire yet, hoping her husband would soon arrive home. She had difficulty concentrating as she continually went to the window, peering through the shutters into the darkened night, hoping to find Henry arriving home. She knew she clung to a small hope. Often he would not come home, claiming it was his duties as sheriff that kept him away. In hopes of being able to be with him more, she had recently moved to Virginia City from Bannack, but it had not helped her dire situation.

Electra recalled the distant memories when after supper Henry would take her tenderly by the hand to his favorite chair. He would carefully select a book, often times the one that was now resting in her lap, and read to her as she sat on the floor at his feet, resting against his legs. His voice seemed to penetrate her very soul. Then without warning, he would set the book down and make love to her. When they finished, he would sit back in the chair and resume reading to her.

Electra clung to those precious moments when their love seemed like ocean waves crashing to shore, retreating, and then came crashing again.

She remembered when she and Henry would stroll along the streets. She would proudly cling to his arm, knowing the passing women would watch with envy.

Electra knew of the rumors of other women, but she could never believe that there were other women in his life. Not the way they loved each other.

Electra also knew her husband had been in trouble before she met him. He had even been wrongly accused once of murder. But how could a man so gentle as he do anything so wrong. She loved Henry, and he loved her. That was what was most important.

But in recent months, Henry had begun to change. He was becoming moody. He no longer held her gently. Sometimes Electra felt frightened by his sudden temper. And now the loneliness was the worst of all.

Electra realizing the late hour decided she would wait no longer for her husband's return. Still hoping he might return later, she selected Henry's favorite nightgown. As she let the silky garment slide over her body, she critically studied herself in the mirror. She saw no reason for her husband's sudden lack of interest. She had been careful to retain a youthful look. Her skin was soft and smooth. She slid her hands gently down her sides, momentarily arousing herself with the smoothness of the silk against her skin. She felt her figure was still vibrant. She would match herself against other women. Why did he seem to no longer desire her? It was only the strain of his job as sheriff. It had to be...not other women.

Suddenly, the door opened behind her. It was Henry. Electra jumped at his sudden entrance. She turned to face him, feeling embarrassed by being caught observing herself in the mirror. "You startled me," she said, giggling.

Henry glanced at her and without speaking, sat in his chair. He sat motionless staring at the wall.

He didn't even care what I was wearing, she thought. Although hurt by his action, Electra forced pleasantries. "Can I fix you supper?" Henry only shook his head. "Shall I read to you while you relax?" Again he shook his head.

"I was just preparing to retire for the evening. You look tired. Why don't you come to bed with me like old times?"

He sat motionless as though he had not heard her. The delay was making Electra feel uncomfortable. Slowly Henry turned his stare towards her. Anger filled his face, leaving Electra frightened. His voice was slow and deliberate as he spoke. "Why do I want to do that? You don't excite me anymore."

Electra stood in the middle of the room in shock. She couldn't move. She couldn't speak. Then as suddenly as he arrived, Henry left.

Total despair swept through Electra's body as the door closed echoing the emptiness in the room. Her whole world, in one agonizing moment, had crumbled. How could he have been so cruel?

Electra fell to her knees and then slumped to the floor, sobbing. Never had she felt or imagined a pain so terrible as she felt now.

CHAPTER 7

Sarah Templeton found the first months in her new home painfully difficult. She missed her family in St. Louis, her home and friends. She found the lifestyle hard and dramatically different. She feared traveling beyond the confines of her home, even to a nearby neighbor's house.

But Sarah was determined to adjust. She would have to accept the hardships, begin acquiring new friends and make the best she could of her new life. She knew the most difficult transition would be to overcome her fear of the unruly west.

Sarah sat quietly staring out the window watching for her husband. Sam had promised her he would come home early to take her to the mercantile store. She suddenly rose, almost without thought and prepared to leave. She had made the courageous decision to go shopping alone.

Sarah started along the snow covered, rutted road towards the mercantile store. With each new step, she thought about turning back, but continued forward. She soon found herself on Wallace Street, the main street of Virginia City. She hurried along the street, fearing at any moment coming face to face with one of the many undesirables in town.

She tried to control her shaking body as she entered the store. She was relieved to find it near empty. Henry Taylor, the owner, was behind the counter, conversing with two men. He smiled warmly and spoke to her as she nervously passed them.

As Sarah began to collect her items in the back of the store, she noticed a pleasant looking woman nearby. They nodded and smiled. The woman's eyes radiated a sadness that immediately made Sarah feel close to her. Sarah felt an overwhelming need to befriend the woman.

At first, Sarah repelled the idea and resumed her shopping, but her mind could not forget the forlorn eyes of the woman. Sarah, almost without realizing her actions, found herself approaching her. Sarah barely spoke above a whisper. "I'm sorry, but I don't believe we've ever met. I'm Sarah Templeton."

The woman smiled politely, but the sadness in her eyes remained. "I don't believe we have," she answered, "I'm Electra Plummer."

Sarah recognized the name. "Plummer. Are you Sheriff Plummer's wife?"

The woman nodded she was. The sadness remained in Electra's eyes, and Sarah wondered if she had done the wrong thing by introducing herself, but she continued the conversation. "We came here from St. Louis a few weeks ago and I'm embarrassed that I hardly know anyone here."

"Me too," Electra said, her eyes brightening somewhat. "I came here to Virginia City recently from Bannack. I'm so glad you introduced yourself."

****

Sam returned home early from work as promised to take Sarah to the mercantile. He was surprised to find the house empty and a little irritated that he had left work early and Sarah was at a neighbor instead of ready to go shopping.

Shortly, Cynthia returned from the Kyle's and informed her father that her mother had left the Kyle's much earlier. Sam was becoming concerned, wondering where Sarah could be. It would be getting dark soon and she wouldn't intentionally be out alone after dark.

He put on his coat to start looking for her when Sarah arrived. Her face was bright and cheery. Sam stared in disbelief at his wife as she began removing the staples from her basket.

"You were shopping alone?" he said.

"Yes. I'm sorry supper isn't ready. I'll get to it right away," she said, kissing him and then hurriedly began preparing supper.

"I don't understand, Sarah. Why did you go alone?" Sam said with a half confused, half delighted look on his face. "You knew I was coming home early to take you."

"Sam, can't a woman do anything for herself?" she answered, giggling.

"But weren't you frightened?" Sam said, sitting at the table, still in disbelief, watching his suddenly changed, exuberant wife.

"Of course I was," she said turning to face him, "or at least at first." She moved towards him, wiping her hands on her apron. Sam could not remember the last time he had seen his wife with such youthful vitality. She sat on his knee and put her arm around him. "I'm so glad I went today, Sam. I met the most wonderful woman at Taylor's. We hit it off so well. It was like we had been friends all our lives."

"So, who was this wonderful woman?" Sam asked, smiling as he wrinkled his forehead in bewilderment.

"Electra Plummer. Sheriff Plummer's wife. We talked for the longest time at the store, then she invited me to her home. We talked and talked. I just lost track of time. I'm sorry about supper." She kissed Sam's forehead, then hurried back to the stove. "Tomorrow she's coming here. You know, I guess it's strange, us hitting it off so well. She's so much younger and doesn't have any children. Of course, she wants children." Sarah's back was still towards Sam as she continued to talk. "She said so herself. She actually envied me for having children." She turned towards her confused husband, who was leaning his elbows on the table. "I'm being silly, aren't I?" she said, showing her embarrassment.

"Not at all, Sarah. I'm just pleased you're so happy."

"I am," she said. "Until now, I never felt at home here. Mary Kyle and the others have been so good to me, but I just felt so alone. I've missed my friends and family so much."

Sam patted his knee. "Come here and sit on my knee again. I forgot how much I enjoyed it."

"Sam, the children may come in at any moment."

"I don't care," he said, pulling her onto his lap. "They'll only see how much I love you."

Hezekiah opened the door. He stood frozen in the doorway, uncertain whether to enter or quietly retreat.

CHAPTER 8

A week had passed without incident after the sheriff's attack on Christina, but Sadie knew all too well that Sheriff Plummer would carry out his threat. She concluded the only reason he hadn't sought his revenge more swiftly was his desire to increase her anxiety or wait for her to ease her guard.

Sadie had learned to be cautious. Her many years of working and living in the raw, uninhibited mining camps had taught her well. She had taken extra precautions since Sheriff Plummer's threat, not so much for herself, but for her girls, particularly Christina. The girls were not to travel alone at night, and she also insisted that she knew whom they were seeing. They were all loyal to her and in return it was her job to protect them.

Shouting from outside awakened Sadie as she slept in her room above the saloon. She slipped her revolver from under her pillow and made her way through the darkened room to the door. As she opened it, she choked from the heavy smoke in the stairwell leading down to the saloon. Panic griped her as she gasped for air. She began blindly feeling her way down the narrow stairs. Through the smoke, she could see flames at the front of the saloon. Unable to see, she searched for the back door. Her eyes stung and she could hardly breath. At last she found the bolt to the door. It was stuck. A renewed fear rushed through her. She was uncertain how much longer she could maintain consciousness. She searched for something to break the latch. Near fainting, she found a wooden club that she kept to break up any brawls in her saloon. She beat frantically on the latch over and over. With little strength remaining, she gave one last blow. The latch gave way. She threw open the door and stumbled into the alley, coughing uncontrollably. Wiping the tears from her eyes, she made her way to the front of the saloon.

Sadie was surprised to find half dozen men already trying to douse the fire, and within a short time, the fire was extinguished. The men had saved her saloon. Thankful for their early arrival and effort, she offered them free whiskey anytime and quickly began to survey the damage of her establishment in the early morning light. She had been lucky by the early arrival of the miners, and figured she could be back in business in one day. She knew the sheriff had kept his promise.

****

Sadie wasted no time. By noon, she was standing in front of her saloon, supervising workmen busily making the repairs. She was not surprised by the arrival of the sheriff, only that he had not come sooner.

He cocked his hat to the back of his head with an air of satisfaction. His sneering smile chilled her. "I understand you had some trouble last night, Sadie."

"And I suppose you know nothing about it," Sadie snapped. The hate was building in her.

The sheriff's reaction was calm, but direct. "I hope you're not implying anything, Sadie. I just dropped by to see what I could do to help. I carry no grudges." His smile became more prominent showing his teeth.

Her eyes became hardened as Sadie stared directly into his eyes as she spoke, "I'm only saying that snakes should beware. I've handled enough in the past to know how to deal with them."

The sheriff's composure lessened; his eyes began to flicker nervously. He had approached her expecting a woman submitting and fearful, instead he found a woman confident and ready to fight. "Life can be ruthless on a woman in these parts," he said. "Even an old whore. Just a reminder to manage your own affairs and leave others to be." He tipped his hat and started to leave, then slowly turned back to Sadie. "And by the way, say hello to the lovely Christina for me."

Sadie's insides churned with anger as she watched him leave. She no longer feared the son-of-a-bitch for herself. He was through with her. But Christina's safety was of great concern to her. He would be determined to finish his dirty business with Christina. She regretted not killing him that night.

Sadie turned her attention back to the repairs of her saloon. Christina was standing in the doorway watching Sadie with sad and apologetic eyes.

"It's all over, Christina. Everything will be fine now," Sadie said, wishing it were true.

Christina hesitated as though to speak, but silently returned inside.

****

Christina had only arrived at the doorway to hear the sheriff's last remark pertaining to her. She knew that she was the cause of Sadie's problem, but she didn't know how to resolve it. She could leave town, but Sadie had taken her from the streets and if she left, she would probably return to the streets. The thought frightened her. She had some money saved, but not enough. Besides, where would she go?

She could try talking to the sheriff, pleading for his understanding, but she knew him well enough to know he would do as he chose. Besides, what if he insisted that her succumbing to his wishes was the only option. The thought was revolting to her. If she said no, it might make the situation worse, and if she did say yes to

65

help Sadie, he might feel his wishes could be granted at every opportunity he chose.

There was no sense talking to Sadie. She would strongly reject any of her ideas. Christina would have to make the decision and take action alone. Sadie had saved her, and now she had to find a way to return the favor.

****

By evening, Christina had made her decision. Whatever the risk, she would try to reason with Sheriff Plummer.

After Sadie had escorted Christina home and lectured her 'to be sure and keep your door bolted as a precaution', Christina began to struggle with herself to find enough courage to go through with her plan.

She reluctantly made her way along the darkened street towards the sheriff's office. The evening air was chilly, but the frightening cold inside her was far greater. Ahead she could see the light in the lone office window. Her body began to shiver.

She approached the door, paused, listening for a moment to the silence within, took a deep breath trying to control her quivering body, and knocked lightly. There was no answer. She knocked louder.

Christina heard a muffled voice inside call out, "Hell, come in, the door's unlocked."

She opened the door just enough to peer inside. She could see no one. She slowly stepped inside. There was still no one visible to her. A whiskey flask sat on the desk. She heard a rustling sound coming from the back. A knife like chill tore through her as she fought the urge to retreat back into the darkened night.

Momentarily a figure strolled into the dim lit room. It was the deputy, Buck Stenson, still buttoning his pants. Christina bit her lower lip, trying to remain calm. She already regretted coming.

Buck looked up. His eyes were glazed from too much whiskey, but they opened wide with surprise when he saw Christina. "Well.

Well. Fancy this," he said, wiping his mouth as he staggered to the middle of the room.

"I was looking for Sheriff Plummer," she said, proceeding immediately to her business.

"I bet you are," he remarked, his grin showing his yellowed teeth. "I guess you have a little unfinished business with the sheriff."

"Is he in?" she said, avoiding his remark.

Buck turned a complete circle, stumbling with each step as he looked around the room. "I'll be damned. I sure the hell don't see him. Maybe I can help you? Why the hell should Henry have all the fun?"

"My business is with the sheriff," she firmly insisted, backing towards the door.

"Wait!" he said, holding up his hand. "He'll be right back."

Christina suspected he was lying. She felt she should leave, but she feared if she left, she would never have the courage to return. She decided to wait. She had to try and help Sadie.

Buck relaxed when he saw Christina hesitate. "Have a chair," he said, pointing to one nearby.

"I'll wait here."

"Want some whiskey," he said pointing to the flask on the desk.

Christina shook her head, no.

"Suit yourself, honey," he said in disgust. He sat in the chair at the desk, grabbed the flask and threw his feet on the desk. He slowly sipped the whiskey as his gaze roamed over Christina.

As the minutes passed, Christina grew more uncomfortable from Buck's seductive stare. She could see he was becoming more impatient. "I'll come back another time," she said, turning towards the door.

Buck jumped from his chair. Panic raced through Christina as she fumbled with the door handle. From the corner of her eye she could see Buck quickly moving towards her.

Suddenly, the door swung open knocking Christina backwards. Sheriff Plummer stood in the doorway. Christina felt helpless with nowhere to retreat standing between the two men she feared most.

Sheriff Plummer stood silent, jaws clenched, his eyes glazed with anger as he glared at Christina, then at Buck and back to Christina. She could tell from Buck's expression that he feared the sheriff's sudden entrance almost as much as she did.

"What the hell do you want?" he questioned Christina, his voice filled with anger.

"She says she's got some business with you, Henry," Buck answered immediately.

"I asked her," the sheriff responded, his stare remaining on Christina.

Christina thought she would vomit. Her heart was pounding so hard, she was afraid he could hear it. Tears welled in her eyes as she attempted to contain her composure. "Like he said," but that was all she could answer.

"Let me tell you, and you can tell Sadie. I'll say where and when I'm ready to do business with her whores."

As much as she wanted, she could no longer speak. She felt the tears gushing into her eyes. She pushed past the sheriff and rushed into the night.

His silhouette in the lighted doorway loomed out beyond her like a giant beast. The door slammed and the night closed in around her. She could hear the sounds along the street, but it was as though they came from another world, another time. All her emotions shot through her like a hot fire, making her feel as though she would explode-anger, fear, humiliation, and frustration. She had sought help for Sadie, a problem Christina felt she had caused, but instead she had only made it worse.

Christina didn't remember how she got home. She threw herself on the bed. The tears continued to come late into the night until she finally fell asleep exhausted.

****

Christina was awakened by first light filtering through the curtains. It produced eerie shadows throughout the room. She sat up with a start, fearing someone was there. Once she was convinced she was alone, her thoughts returned to the prior night. Tears began to fill her eyes again, but now her mind began to rationalize what had happened. Why had the sheriff been so angry? Surely he couldn't have been so angry because she was there. He had appeared upset before he had even entered the office. Something else had happened before he had arrived that had angered him. She had only been the recipient of his anger. The look on Buck's face made him think so, too. She curiously wondered what it could be.

CHAPTER 9

Robberies and stagecoach holdups were becoming a common occurrence along the roads leaving Alder Gulch. Also, the increasing disappearances of men after leaving the gulch were becoming alarming to the residents.

Hezekiah and Isaac were anxious to find out more details about the robberies and waited with anticipation for an opportunity to return to town. The fire at Sadie's Palace had heightened their curiosity even more. Although hearing no one was injured, Hezekiah was particularly concerned about the well being of Christina. He had begun to wonder if Christina was still in the territory, having seen her only that one time that now seemed so long ago.

Two days after the fire at Sadie's Palace, an opportunity came early in the morning for the two adventurers to slip away from the confines of their mothers. They wasted no time and headed directly for the Palace, not even stopping to see Eagle Feather at the stables.

When they arrived at Sadie's, they were surprised to find the saloon open for business as usual. Except for occasional places where charred wood still appeared, there was no evidence a fire had even taken place.

"Hell, it couldn't have been much of a fire," Isaac said, sounding disappointed.

"Yeah, well that's good," Hezekiah answered, feeling relieved about Christina.

Isaac finding little to interest him at Sadie's, quickly became impatient hanging around the saloon. "Come on. Let's go over to the stage office and see if we can find out anything about the robberies."

"Wait. Just for a minute," Hezekiah pleaded.

"Come on, damn it. I have to be back pretty soon and I don't want to waste all my time here."

Hezekiah took one last hopeful look at the saloon door. Would he ever see Christina again?

"Hurry up, will you. Look, there's a bunch of men gathering near the sheriff's office," Isaac shouted as he ran down the street. Hezekiah reluctantly followed, still glancing back towards the saloon.

As they approached, they could see the crowd was angry, so they cautiously stopped a safe distance away. But unable to hear what was being said, their curiosity slowly began moving the boys closer.

"What are they saying?" Isaac whispered.

Hezekiah shrugged his shoulders. "Something about finding somebody's horse."

"Come on, let's get closer," Isaac said, motioning Hezekiah to follow.

"I don't think we'd better. They look pretty damn mad."

Isaac stopped, placed his hands on his hips and stared at Hezekiah. "You just want to go back and watch for that floozy."

"I do not...and she's not a floozy." Hezekiah said angrily, moving quickly past Isaac.

They had just arrived at their closer vantage point when the sheriff's office door opened. Sheriff Plummer appeared and confidently strolled towards the dozen men. Two of his deputies followed closely behind.

"That's the sheriff," Isaac whispered.

"I know. I can see," Hezekiah responded, still somewhat irritated by Isaac's earlier remark about Christina.

The sheriff stopped a few feet from the irate crowd. His stare was hard and penetrating as he slowly looked from one face to the next. His voice was deliberate as he spoke, "What seems to be the problem here, men?"

The apparent appointed spokesman hesitantly stepped forward from the group. "A freight driver brought in Jack Roberts' horse last night. He found it wandering on the road south of Bannack. We reckon Jack was robbed and killed and we reckon there's been several others having the same fate. Along with all the stagecoach robberies, it isn't safe around here anymore for an honest man to make a living." His voice became softer with uncertainty, "we're wondering what you're doing about it."

The crowd voiced their agreement.

"We're doing the best we can. There's a lot of territory out there," Plummer said without changing his expression. "Secondly, we don't know that Jack Roberts was killed. The weather was pretty damn bad when he left. He probably had an unfortunate accident."

"Accident, my ass!" the miner shouted. "Why were the saddle bags missing? Maybe we need to take action on our own."

Without warning, the sheriff drew his revolver and placed the barrel to the miner's forehead. His voice was cold. "No son-of-a-bitch is going to interfere with my job if he wants to live. Is that understood?"

Hezekiah could not see the miner's face, but from his rigid stance, it was obvious the sheriff's words had been well taken. The grumbling crowd quickly became quiet. The sheriff dropped the revolver to his side. Both deputies had their hands resting on the butts of their guns.

"Good," the sheriff said, his eyes glaring at the men. "Now get your asses back to work so we can do our job."

Slowly the men began to disperse. The boys, frozen with fear, had watched with bewilderment. As the sheriff turned to go inside, his glare rested momentarily on Hezekiah and Isaac. A frigid chill raced through Hezekiah's body. The sheriff glanced back at the men to insure they were leaving and went inside.

As the door closed, Isaac, big eyed, looked at Hezekiah, also big eyed. Both of their faces were pale with fright.

"Damn, that was close. Let's get the hell out of here," Isaac said with a squeaky voice. Hezekiah was not about to argue with his friend's decision.

****

When all three lawmen were inside, Sheriff Plummer threw his hat on the desk. "Damn it, Buck. Didn't I tell you last night, finding that horse was going to be trouble?"

He kicked a chair and stood motionless staring at the wall. "Buck, I want you to go find Red, and you tell that son-of-a-bitch I want to see him at the ranch tonight." He swung around quickly, startling his two deputies. "And you tell that bastard, he'd better have some answers."

****

Later that same day, Sam Templeton was working on a job adding on to Crenshaw's Wagon and Buggy Shop when Arthur Hanover paid him a visit. Arthur and his family had arrived on the same wagon train as the Templetons. Arthur was quick to get to the matter of his visit. "Sam, I remember you telling me you were a Masonic brother."

Sam nodded. "Sure am," he said, removing his hat and wiping his brow.

"Several of us are having a meeting tonight above Carter's store at seven. Thought maybe you'd like to join us."

Sam looked into Arthur's nervous eyes. "Sure, Arthur, I'll be there."

"Great. See you then," he said, and quickly left. Sam inquisitively watched Arthur, knowing there had to be more to it than a lodge meeting. He wondered what was making Arthur so nervous. Deciding he would have to wait for his answer, Sam resumed his work.

****

Red Yeager paced nervously in the ranch house until he could no longer take the confinement of its walls. But he soon found himself pacing to the same methodical rhythm in the barn. Buck had told him what had happened in town and that the boss was damn mad. An error in judgment, that's all it was. Hell, anybody could make a mistake. He worked his rear-end off, not like Ned and Buck sitting on their lazy behinds in town, drunken most of the time. That should be worth something.

Red could hear an approaching rider. His jaws clenched as he nervously felt his revolver in his holster. Hell, it wouldn't come to that, he thought as he opened the barn door and looked out into the dark night. He watched the sheriff enter the house and momentarily return outside.

"Over here, boss," Red called nervously as he slowly made his way from the barn to meet the sheriff half way. Buck had been right. The boss was obviously upset.

"What the hell was you thinking about, Red, letting Jack Roberts' horse go. The whole damn town is up in arms about that horse."

"It spooked when we shot the miner, boss. By the time we recovered the gold, he was gone. I figured some damn hungry critters would take care of it for me."

"Well, you figured wrong. Now I've got to deal with a whole town that wants blood. They're ready to take matters into their own hands." The sheriff kicked the dirt in disgust. "You know what that means, Red? Our boots could be swinging from some tree if they get to damn inquisitive. A few more months, Red, and we'll be

74

filthy rich. But if we botch this up, we'll be dead. It's your choice...worms eating your carcass, or being so damn rich you can stick a different whore every night until your cock falls off. You've got to think, damn it."

The sheriff stared at Red. Red only nodded he understood. The sheriff paced back and forth. Convinced he had made his point, he was ready to discuss other business. "How are your two new men working out?"

"I tell you, Henry, they make me nervous," Red answered, anxious to change the subject. " I haven't had a good night sleep since they up and joined us."

The sheriff frowned. "You think they'll grab what loot they can and skip out?"

"Hell no, it's not that. They're missing something in their belfry, especially that crazy Zeke. He gets some kind of thrill out of killing and then watching them die. It's like he goes into some kind of trance. And he'll sit and stare at you. I expect any night to wake up with him over me, ready to blow my damn head off." Red could see his boss was not convinced. "I'm telling you, he scares the living hell out of me."

The sheriff burst into laughter. "Damn, Red, you're getting as soft as a woman's tit. Maybe you need to get into town and get a good lay. You know, calm your nerves. Haven't you dipped your stick lately in your old squaw you've got in Deer Lodge?"

Red became irritated by the humiliation. "I don't give a fired ass damn what you think. I sleep with my gun under my pillow, and you would too if you were around the creepy bastard."

"Forget it, Red," the sheriff said, tired of listening to Red complain. "Remember, Red, a few more months and we'll be the richest men this side of the Mississippi."

The sheriff, not waiting for a response, walked to his horse. As he mounted, he laughed again. "Red, I'm going to do you a favor. I'm not going to tell anyone what you just told me."

Red listened to the sheriff's laughter as he rode away. "Laugh now you son-of-a-bitch," Red mumbled as he headed towards the house.

****

While the sheriff was at the ranch with Red, thirty men were filing into a small room over Carter's store. The room had no furniture, only a small wooden box sat at the front. Sheets hung over the two small windows.

Each man entering the room was verified that they had been invited. Arthur Hanover nodded to the guards when Sam and Harvey Kyle arrived.

Sam knew only a few of the men and recognized only a few others. He felt edgy and uncomfortable not knowing what to anticipate and was relieved when a short stout man in his fifties stood on the box and called for order. After a prayer, the man stroked his long grayish beard; his gaze moving slowly across the room as though doubting the guards had done an adequate job. The quiet room waited for him to speak.

"Before I begin," he said with a firmness in his voice, "we all are brother Masons here in this room. It is of absolute importance that outside this room, there will be no discussion of this meeting. Either what is said at this meeting, or who attended this meeting. Discussing this with your wives is the only exception." He paused briefly before continuing. "I'm Paris Pfouts. As I'm sure you're all aware, there have been an increasing number of robberies in recent weeks on the hard working citizens in this territory. We can also be relatively assured that a large number of other robberies and murders have been committed that we're not even aware of. The sheriff has absolutely refused any support, and he's done nothing to protect us or bring any of these ruthless outlaws to justice. For those of you who are willing to participate, you will become a part of our 'Citizens Committee for Law and Justice of Alder Gulch'. We will unite with a similar committee being formed in Bannack." He waited until the crowd quieted. "We will not act out of impulse or anger. To do so, would make us no better than the bandits. We will challenge and react accordingly to those who do. You will be contacted in the next couple days. If any of you choose not to join, it will be understood and accepted with no questions asked. From here on, all contact will be made individually. For safety and secrecy, this will be our last meeting unless an emergency warrants it. The meeting is now adjourned. May the Lord guide you in your decision."

****

Sam and Harvey never spoke as they walked home. The words of Paris Pfouts repeated over and over in Sam's mind. No matter what name was given, it all came down to being vigilantes. He had heard of vigilantes before that had turned into rioting mobs. Would the committee truly act responsibly once they were formed?

Sam had never imagined that he would ever consider participating in such an organization. He recalled the words of the wagon master on their trip west. 'The west is rugged and cruel at times. It will change you. You'll do things that you would never have imagined doing, just to survive.' Sam, at the time, had given little thought to those words, but now he was faced with that very warning.

Sam knew Paris was right. Something needed to be done. If the outlaws were left unchecked, their uncontrolled actions would spread. No one would be safe. The most important thing to him was the protection of his family. But was the threat real enough to justify his participation in the committee. At sometime it probably would and with time, the committee would have more difficulty regaining control. What about Sarah? She was just beginning to adjust to her new lifestyle. What would this do to her? She would hate the thought. Could he ever make her understand? Particularly now that she had befriended the sheriff's wife.

****

Hezekiah pretended he was asleep when his father returned home from the meeting. After his father had checked to insure he and Cynthia were asleep, Hezekiah opened his eyes.

His father walked to the table and sat across from his mother. Hezekiah strained to hear what his father was saying. He could not understand what was being said, but he could see his mother's face. As his father spoke, a horrible look of shock and fear covered her face, and then she began to cry. Hezekiah could hear her pleading voice, "No, Sam. Oh Lord, it hasn't come to this."

His father reached across the table for her hands, but she pulled away. Hezekiah desperately strained to hear his father, but all he could understand was, "they've got to be stopped, Sarah. I don't like it either."

"I'm so afraid, Sam, " she said, still weeping.

Hezekiah's stomach was in knots. Something bad was going to happen. He wished he could have heard everything. He watched his father walk to the other side of the table and put his arms around his mother. At first, she tried to reject him, but then, still sobbing quietly, she stood and threw her arms around him. Hezekiah watched them for sometime as she laid her head against his father's chest. Neither spoke.

Hezekiah lay awake long after his parents had gone to bed. He hoped Isaac would know more, but he would have to wait until morning, and right now that seemed like a long time.

****

As soon as Sheriff Plummer returned from the ranch that evening, Ned and Buck were waiting for him at the office with the news of the secret meeting.

"Nobody may want to talk willingly," the sheriff said angrily, but damn it, somebody's going to talk. I want you to find out who attended that meeting. Check with George. I want some names."

****

George Lane awoke by a banging on his door. Grumbling, he crawled from bed, shivering from the sting of the cold air. He cringed as he stepped on his clubfoot. "Wait a damn minute," he yelled as the banging persisted. "Who is it?"

"Ned. Hurry up, it's cold out here."

"You better not be drunk, again," George grumbled as he opened the door.

"The boss sent me," Ned said, entering uninvited and began slapping himself to try and keep warm.

"At this hour? Hell, he's getting as dimwitted as the rest of you."

"Stop your bitching. He wants to know who was at the secret meeting tonight."

"Hell. Couldn't it wait 'till morning?"

"The sheriff wants to know tonight. Would you rather he come over here and ask you?"

"All right. It's the only way I'll get any sleep," George said, shoving a log into the stove. He grabbed a poker and stoked the few remaining hot coals. "I was on my way home from a poker game when I saw some men leaving from above Carter's store. Mind you, it was only by accident I saw them."

"How many?" Ned asked impatiently.

"I reckon I saw ten, maybe a dozen. There may have been more, but I didn't want to hang around looking suspicious."

"Who in the hell is going to be suspicious of a cripple," Ned said, chuckling.

Anger filled George's eyes as he pointed the poker at Ned. "Go to hell, Ned. At least I'm not the town drunk."

"All right. Damn, take it easy," Ned said raising his hands in self-defense. George slowly lowered the poker. "So who were they?" Ned asked.

"I only recognized a couple of them. One was Paris Pfouts." George rubbed his forehead as he thought. "That lawyer--Sanders-- I think Wilbur is his first name. Uh, Robert Patterson. I suppose Carter was there, beings it was his place. His helper. What the hell is his name? Thalbt. Yeah, Nichols Thalbt." George closed his eyes for a moment. "I guess that's about it."

"That's all?" Ned said, irritated by the short list.

"I said that's all."

"Damn. The sheriff's not going to be happy about this. Anyway keep your eyes and ears open." Ned opened the door, then turned back towards George. "By the way, George," Ned said coldly, "don't ever threaten me again or I'll kill you." He closed the door.

"Tell the sheriff he's welcome," George grumbled.

****

His father wakened Hezekiah the next morning. "You going to sleep your life away? You're going to be late for Mrs. Herman's class."

Hezekiah groaned at the thought of another morning listening to Mrs. Herman. This was only the second day and already he was sick of it. Suddenly, he remembered the previous night. He had to meet Isaac early to find out what he knew.

Breakfast was unusually quiet as Hezekiah watched for a sign or word that would give him a clue as to what had happened, or was about to happen. There was nothing, only Cynthia's usual complaining. "Bobby Hanover said I was ugly. I'm not, am I, Mother?"

Hezekiah snickered.

"Mother, make Hezekiah stop."

"You're not ugly, Cynthia," his mother said sympathetically. "You're a beautiful young girl that will someday grow into a beautiful woman. Bobby probably says that because he likes you." Sarah ran her fingers through Cynthia's curls. "Boys have a funny way of showing a girl that they like them. And Hezekiah," she said glancing at him, "you had better be behaving yourself at Mrs. Herman's. She's doing us a wonderful favor."

Hezekiah looked to his father for support, but he was staring into space, unaware of the conversation. No use arguing on this one, Hezekiah thought. Besides it would waste time and he had to find Isaac before school started. But to Hezekiah's disappointment, Isaac knew nothing. Hezekiah quickly relayed what he knew.

"You know," Isaac said, shaking his head, "I thought Mother was acting strange this morning, but I thought she was only mad at me, so I kept my mouth shut." Suddenly Isaac's face lit up. "The outlaws!" he shouted.

"What?"

"The outlaws have to be stopped. That's what your father was talking about."

Hezekiah looked at Isaac in amazement. "Our fathers."

"Yeah. What else could it be?"

"But you heard the sheriff. He said he would kill anyone that interfered."

Isaac was determined to prove he was right. "That's why they're so secretive."

Hezekiah could not believe what Isaac was telling him. His father would never participate in such a thing...yet Isaac made sense. That was why his mother had been crying. She was frightened...And now he was too.

****

After Sam and the children had left for the day, Sarah sat at the table trying to understand what was happening. There were no more tears left, only a sickening and frightening feeling inside. She feared for her husband's life. She feared losing the gentle and kind man she had always loved. Was the west changing him...taking him away from her? He had always been a man so strongly against violence and now he, for whatever reason, was becoming a part of it.

She wished she had someone whom to share her feelings, but she had promised not to mention the committee to anyone. She could not endanger her husband for her own selfish well-being.

And what about Electra, who had become her dearest friend? Sam and the others were acting against the sheriff's orders. What would this do to their friendship? Sarah suddenly remembered Electra was coming to her house that very afternoon. How could she pretend nothing was wrong?

Sarah rose and began clearing the breakfast dishes. A skillet fell from her shaking hand and grease spilled onto the floor. She stared at the mess she had made. Without warning, newfound tears gushed from her eyes.

****

Two days after the Masonic meeting, Arthur Hanover delivered Sam some frightening news. Nichols Thablt was missing.

CHAPTER 10

A frigid Arctic storm bore down unmercifully on Alder Gulch abruptly halting the isolated mining camp's activities. Miners, temporarily leaving their claims, scrambled for warm surroundings....the saloons being the overwhelming choice.

With whiskey in their gut and ample time at hand, speculation on the disappearance of Nichols Thbalt became a dominant conversation piece. It was common knowledge that Nichols Thbalt had left on an errand to acquire some mules for Carter from the ranchers in the valley, and he never returned. As the whiskey flowed freely, arguments and wagering ensued...."I'll bet my left ball and Sadie's right tit, he took the money and is laid up in some whore house in Oro Fina"..."You keep your left ball, but I say it's the work of those murdering road agents"...."Hell, he probably got caught by some jealous husband and is hanging by his balls in some rancher's barn."

After two weeks, the cold relinquished its tight grip, and the mining camp began to resume its normal activities. As the miners resumed working their claims, their thoughts returned to their dreams of finding the big strike, and the whereabouts of Nichols Thbalt began to drift from their minds.

But the miners were soon reminded of the danger they faced daily. It was the seventeenth of December, when William Palmer rode into Virginia City with the frozen body of Nichols Thbalt strapped to a horse. A bullet hole protruded above Nichols' left eye. A nearby rancher, while rounding up stray cattle, had found the frozen body and the carcass of Nichols' horse.

The town was besieged with shock. A man carrying little money had been killed and left to rot on the barren countryside. How many other bodies were out there? No longer could anyone feel safe.

****

The snow glistened as the sun crested the peaks on the southeastern horizon. The land left a misleading sense of tranquility with the crisp morning air solemnly quiet. Only the sounds of twenty-nine horses moving briskly down Wallace Street could be heard.

No longer was the committee hiding behind covered windows and latched doors. They now rode with determination, signaling, 'road agents beware-we will soon cast your fate'. Whatever reason the townspeople thought to be the motive for the killing of Nichols Thbalt, the committee members knew it had been the work of the outlaws, either for information about the committee, or a warning to them. The reason no longer mattered, only the ruthless action that had been taken.

The twenty-nine riders moved silently north from town, passing miners busily at their claims. As they passed, the miners would stop work, lean against their shovel and curiously watch the riders. No one spoke to the riders; the riders spoke to no one.

Shortly, the riders arrived at Nevada City, one of the numerous small towns along Alder Gulch that had sprung up overnight after the gold strike. By now, the streets were filled with an abundance of activity, but the committee continued to ride silently past the curious onlookers.

North of Nevada City, the committee split into three pre-determined groups. Sam Templeton and Harvey Kyle rode with Wilbur Sander's group.

Each group had been assigned an area of land to cover. They were to question anyone they found in their area, including all ranchers, looking for anything suspicious or information from anyone that might help find the killer, or killers of Nichols Thbalt.

****

Wilbur Sanders leaned over in his saddle, calling out to Sam and Harvey, who were riding to his right, "The last place up ahead is Hal Dodge's according to the map. If we don't stir up something here, it looks like we've wasted the day."

Sam nodded. "Maybe the others had better luck. I'd hate to think we're no better off than we were this morning."

Tom Burtsey rode alongside the three in front. "It looks pretty damn strange to me, Wilbur," he said, slowly shaking his head. "Hal had a nice little herd of longhorns, and I don't see a one of them."

"You know Hal?" Wilbur asked, tightening his reins.

"Yeah...well at least a little," Tom said, shifting in his saddle. "You know another thing bothers me. See the corral," he said, nodding his head in its direction. "It looks like a piss ant could knock it down. If there's one thing I know about Hal, he takes pride in the looks of his ranch."

"Maybe he hasn't gotten around to repairing it with the bad weather," Harvey said.

"Yeah, maybe," Tom answered, sounding doubtful.

Sam had to agree with Tom; the place looked almost deserted except for some horses he could see through the open barn door.

As they stopped in front of the ranch house, the door opened and a slender, unshaven man stepped from the doorway; his eyes glared at the men on horseback.

"Good afternoon," Wilbur called out, but the man, without speaking, only continued to glare at the riders. "We're looking for Hal Dodge," Wilbur continued, ignoring the unwelcome reception.

"He's not here," the man responded gruffly and was prepared to return inside.

"When do you expect him back," Wilbur said, being persistent with his questioning.

"Spring, I reckon. He left me in charge for the winter."

Two more men appeared in the doorway, but Sam was unable to see their faces because of the shadows. Sam was beginning to feel nervous, and from the expressions of the others in the committee, they too sensed danger.

"I see." Wilbur's voice sounded reluctant to believe the man's answer. "I'm Wilbur Sanders. We're checking with all the ranchers in the area to see if they've seen anything suspicious. A young man was murdered out this way a couple weeks ago."

"I ain't seen a damn thing. The only thing suspicious around here is your lot nosing around where you don't belong." A burst of laughter came from the doorway.

Wilbur remained calm. "If you suddenly remember anything, I'd appreciate you letting us know." The man never responded as he watched the committee ride away.

"He's lying through his teeth," Tom said as soon as they had left the ranch. His jaws were clenched with anger. "I bet they murdered Hal just like they did Nichols...those bastards."

"When's the last time you saw Hal?" Wilbur asked, trying to approach the situation more logically.

"Early fall. He never made mention about leaving for the winter."

"Did he have any hands helping him work his ranch?" Wilbur continued to inquire.

"Nope. He worked it alone," Tom answered, his frustration becoming more evident. "And the one that did the talking is George Ives. There's no way in hell he'd be working as a ranch hand. I think we should go back there and bring the whole damn bunch of them in."

"Wait a minute, Tom. I know what you're feeling, but they seemed pretty damn confident. They're probably prepared for us and if we rode back in there now, we'd sure as hell get some of us killed. I don't want to live the rest of my life knowing I made some woman a widow."

Sam, listening to the conversation, spoke, "Paying an unannounced visit may not be too easy. A person up on that bluff to our left could track a jackrabbit for miles around here, and I'd guess it'd be only a five to ten minute ride from up there to the ranch house."

"Those damn heathens! I wouldn't be surprised if they used that bluff to watch for men leaving the gulch," Tom said, then leaned to the side and spit. "Those poor damn souls wouldn't have a chance."

****

Upon their return to Virginia City, Wilbur asked Sam and Tom to come with him to report their findings to Paris Pfouts and discuss their strategy.

Paris paced about the room as the three men explained what they had found and their suspicions. He continued to quietly listen until they finished. His eyes expressed his concern.

"Sounds like you discovered something, all right," Paris commented, slowly stroking his beard. "If the man at the ranch was George Ives, then I know there is something no good taking place. I know his reputation. The story goes he left Colorado in a hurry when he got into trouble with the law. Also, it might interest you to know, I've seen him here in town, drinking on several occasions with Buck Stinson, one of Sheriff Plummer's deputies." Paris paused to watch the reaction of the men in the room. "I see you seem surprised by what I've just said. To be honest with you, I've had bad feelings about the law around here for some time. I just never had any proof to link the law with the bandits. Now I think I do." The men shifted nervously as they listened to Paris' observation. "I feel we'll have to use extreme caution from here on out."

Sam felt a deep sickness boring inside him. If Sarah knew the committee expected her best friend's husband to be involved, it might destroy her already fragile existence here in the west.

Sam tried to concentrate as the men began laying out the plans for their return to the ranch, but the thought of Sarah made it difficult. Yet he knew with or without him, the plans would continue. He just hoped Paris was wrong about the sheriff.

****

By evening, each member of the committee had been notified of the plan. Ten men, lead by Wilbur Sanders would leave before dawn and circle in from the back of the ranch to serve as a surprise attack. Ten more men, lead by Paris Pfouts, would approach from the front. If the bluff were being used as a lookout for the bandits, the ranch would be warned of the approaching committee from the front. When they attempted to escape, Wilbur Sander's men in hiding would be waiting. The remaining men on the committee would be posted outside of town to insure the committee members at the farmhouse would not be assaulted by a surprise attack from the rear.

Sam was assigned to Wilbur Sander's group. He joined the others south of town in the pre-dawn cold. He could feel the cold nip at his face and fingers, but beneath his clothes he could feel the nervous sweat. He had never imagined ever being faced with a gunfight. It had never been part of his dreams for he and his family. Once again, doubts plagued him about his decision to come west. The frightened and saddened eyes of Sarah as he kissed her when he had left, still haunted him. He could not find the courage to tell her about the committee's suspicions of the sheriff.

Wilbur Sanders silently motioned the men forward into the quiet darkened night. No one spoke, but each knew what the others were thinking-would any of them not return?

They moved cautiously through the draws and along the underbrush. As a silver hue began to show on the eastern horizon, the ten men had made their way behind the bluff and were approaching the ranch house. None had spoke during the ride.

Shortly, Wilbur raised his hand, motioning the men to halt. The distant outline of the ranch house could now be seen in the early light.

"We'd better go on foot from here," Wilbur whispered. We don't want our horses giving notice of our arrival."

The men dismounted and moved quietly by foot to a grove of cottonwood trees, some three hundred yards from the building.

"We'll wait here for awhile," Wilbur directed the others. "It'll give the others time to arrive for the frontal assault. Sam, when I give the orders to move out, take four men with you over by the barn and corral. They'll need their horses to get away. The rest of us will circle the house. If we can, we'll wait until it appears they have all left the house. I'll then give the order for them to throw down their weapons. If they don't, then we'll have to do whatever is necessary."

They had only waited ten minutes when the sound of a fast rider could be heard approaching from the direction of the bluff.

As the lookout arrived, he quickly dismounted and ran inside the house. Shouting and the sounds of confusion could be heard inside.

"He must have spotted the others coming," Wilbur said calmly. "Okay, Sam, move out.

Sam could feel his pulse pounding as he signaled for his men to follow him. They moved quickly through the shadows to fortified positions around the barn and corral.

Sam knelt behind a feeding trough near the barn door. He quickly surveyed the position of the other men. Satisfied with their cover, he turned his attention towards the house. He could no longer see any of the other committee members.

He took a deep breath and waited. He wondered how close Paris and the others were from the ranch. If the lookout had spotted them too soon, he feared their arrival might be too late. There appeared to be a dozen horses in the barn. Could there be that many men inside? Being outnumbered by the bandits was not a comforting thought.

The ranch house door opened. Two men quickly stepped through the doorway and headed directly towards him. Then two more appeared, then a fifth. All were headed his direction and in a hurry. How long could he wait? He had to be calm and wait for Wilbur's signal. The first two were now no more than one hundred feet away.

A sixth man appeared, apparently the lookout as he quickly climbed onto the saddled horse.

Wilbur's voice rang out, "You're under arrest by the authority of the Virginia City Citizens' Committee. Throw down you weapons."

The surprised outlaws froze momentarily, uncertain of their next move. "Go to hell!" one shouted as he drew his revolver and fired aimlessly in the direction of Wilbur's voice.

The two men closest to Sam started to run in his direction with revolvers drawn. "Stop or I'll shoot," Sam yelled. Both fired in his direction. Sam heard the thud of their bullets as they tore into the barn wall behind him. Sam squeezed the trigger of his rifle as the others around him opened fire. One of the outlaws groaned and fell to the ground. The other quickly found shelter behind some logs. Sam looked on in disbelief at the motionless figure on the ground. Had it been his bullet that had killed him? He hoped he would never find out.

The echoing of gunfire filled the cold air. Sam could see a second body near the house. He assumed there were only four left. But the rider that had been on horseback had disappeared. Sam also began to realize that there seemed to be firing from only one location held by the outlaws. He began to look around, fearing the bandits were circling behind he and his men. They were helplessly pinned down. Where was Paris with his men? The gunfire became less frequent.

Another two or three minutes passed when Sam spotted Paris and his men approaching from the front. They dismounted and began moving in on foot. The gunman behind the logs apparently aware of the reinforcements, called out, "Don't shoot!" The gunfire subsided.

"Throw out your gun and come out with your hands raised," Wilbur called out.

A gun landed on the ground in front of the logs and a lone bandit stepped from cover with his arms raised.

"Where're the others?" Wilbur shouted.

"Damn if I know. The sons-of-a-bitches deserted me."

Sam recognized the outlaw as the one that had been referred to as George Ives.

"You didn't see anyone as you came in?" Wilbur asked Paris.

"There was no one headed our direction," Paris answered, shaking his head with disgust.

Wilbur took a count of his men to insure everyone was okay. "At least, thank the Lord none of us were hurt," Wilbur said with relief.

"Only the one had a horse," Sam remarked. The other two can't be far on foot. I'll take some men and we'll get our horses and look for them."

But as soon as they arrived at the cottonwood grove, it was obvious two of their horses were gone. The two outlaws had circled behind them and made off with the horses. Sam returned to the others with the bad news.

"Damn it!" Sanders said, clenching his fist. "Okay, Ives," he said turning to the sneering outlaw. "Who are the three that left you here by yourself?"

"I would rather smother in ten feet of horse dung than tell you anything, but those cowardly bastards aren't going to get away with deserting me. I'll tell you who they are, but other than that you can go to hell."

"All right, Ives. Who are they?" Wilbur asked, anger filling his voice.

"The one was Red Yeager. The other two I don't know a damn thing about, other than they were strange ones. They were new here. One was called Zeke and I think the other was Dalton."

"Where would they go?" Sanders asked.

"Red talked about a squaw over in Deer Lodge. The other two bastards, I don't know. They probably high tailed it out of the territory."

"Who else is involved with your gang?"

Ives smiled. "Go to hell."

"You want to hang alone? You will you know."

"Then hang me, you bastards. I'll tell you where you can find a rope."

"Your choice, Ives. At least you'll get a trial. Not like the poor souls you and your ruthless friends murdered."

****

The following day after capturing George Ives, Paris took seven men and started for Deer Lodge in search of Yeager. The remainder of the committee stayed in Virginia City to place a heavy guard on George Ives while preparations for the trial was made. There were concerns that either an attempted lynching would be made or Ives' associates might attempt to prematurely quiet him or help him escape. The trial was set to start in two days.

The days leading up to the trial carried a carnival atmosphere around the mining camp. The town was booming as curious miners throughout the territory gathered for the event. Many, feeling more confident now, discussed other possible hangings. As much as Sam wanted the outlaws to be brought to justice, his concern for the situation to get out of hand became more prominent.

The search of the ranch house and surrounding area brought a gruesome discovery. A shallow grave was discovered with the presumed remains of Hal Dodge. Also, Nichols Thbalt's revolver, holster and coat were found.

****

The evening before the trial was to begin, Wilbur Sanders sat quietly in his office reviewing his case. The evidence for a conviction was strong. That was not his concern. He leaned back in his chair and lit his pipe. He watched the smoke roll aimlessly upward. The shadows flickered on the far wall in the dim lit room. He wondered if this would be his last moment of solitude. Tomorrow and the days ahead seemed uncertain. Always before, he had approached his future with confidence. He was concerned the trial would become a mockery. He also worried that a show of force by Ives' colleagues would intimidate the jury to give an acquittal verdict.

An acquittal could create mayhem in the camp. The miners, being frustrated, could react out of anger, endangering many innocent people. Also, the outlaws with a renewed air of confidence would step up their reign of terror. The men on the committee and their families would be in particular danger. Never before had he felt his abilities would affect so many people.

Wilbur gathered his papers and placed them in his folder. He blew out the lantern leaving him in a shroud of darkness as though symbolizing the uncertainty of the days ahead.

****

The December sun was slow at warming the crisp morning air. The territorial judge, Tom Bissell had arrived the evening before and was busily directing how the court was to set up. Due to a lack of a building capable of holding the trial, it was decided to hold court outdoors. The judge would direct the proceedings from a buckboard wagon. He had also ordered no gallows to be built prior to the trial, fearing it would render a preconceived verdict.

Two blocks away, Sanders was giving instructions to two-dozen men where the sentries should be posted. Two men were placed at each end of town, and another ten men strategically around town, particularly at the saloons that were to remain closed by order of the judge. The remainder of the men was posted around the court to insure order.

With Paris Pfouts away, and Sanders busy in court, Sam was placed in charge of the sentry.

By mid-morning, a twenty-four man jury was selected. George Ives was led from his guarded cell to the street where the trial was being conducted. Shouts of "hang him" came from the crowd, but the judge quickly threatened to ban anyone with any more outbursts.

The day progressed without further incident and by day's end, Sanders had concluded the prosecution's case. The judge ordered the jury to confinement for the evening and allowed the saloons to be reopened for the evening to the crowd's enthusiastic response.

After determining the sentries were adequately posted, Sam went directly to Sanders' home to discuss the coming day. The early winter darkness had settled about the camp by the time he arrived.

Sam stood facing the fireplace, letting its warmth ease the chill in his cold body. The flames danced methodically in front of him, soothing his frazzled nerves.

Sam turned as Sanders spoke, "Pretty quiet today, wouldn't you say, Sam?"

"Better than I had hoped," Sam answered, taking a hot cup of coffee from his host.

"I'm afraid tomorrow may be different, Sanders said, his face taut with concern. "The jury should go into deliberation by noon, and one way or another, I don't think it'll take them long."

"Do you think we'll get a guilty verdict?"

"We damn well should," Sanders quickly replied, and then he lit his pipe and puffed on it defiantly. "However, I am worried the ruffians out there may try to intimidate the jury. There seemed to be quite a few seedy characters hanging around there today."

"I noticed. I also noticed the absence of the sheriff and the deputies."

"Strange isn't it," Sanders added with a raised eyebrow. "In the past, the sheriff has demanded complete control of law and order, and now, the biggest event yet, and he's nowhere to be seen."

"What's the plan for tomorrow?" Sam asked.

"Ives' friends may try to make a show of force, particularly if Ives is found guilty. We need to make a heavy presence at the trial to assure the jury that they will be protected. And if the verdict is

94

guilty, I'll ask Judge Bissell for an immediate sentencing and hanging. No sense in taking any added risks by delaying it. I also want to make sure Ives is fully protected until he is hanged. I'm hoping he will talk once the noose is around his neck."

"I agree, but we don't even have a gallows."

"We do," Sanders said, a smile forming on his lips. When the judge wouldn't allow one built before the trial, I did some checking around. There's an unfinished building at the corner of Wallace and Van Buren near where court is being held. One of the rafter beams should do nicely."

Sanders watched Sam for a moment and could see the nervousness in his eyes. "So you can rest tonight, Sam, I'll put your mind at ease. I'll serve as the hangman."

Sam forced a meek smile. "Thanks."

****

The chilly December morning did not dampen the enthusiastic crowd that gathered at the court site. Hezekiah and Isaac, forbidden to go anywhere near the main streets of town, found the best possible site on the hillside overlooking Wallace Street to watch the proceedings.

The trial proceeded rapidly and by early afternoon the jury was sent away for deliberation. In fifteen minutes the judge was informed they had reached a verdict.

The crowd became unusually quiet as the jury returned. The jury foreman rose to his feet as the judge asked for the verdict. The foreman paused, scanning the crowd as though to dramatize the moment. He cleared his throat. "We, the jury, find George Ives guilty of murder and should be hanged by the neck until dead."

The crowd burst into a roar of jubilation. Sam immediately motioned the guards to the front as the ruffians began to push their way forward through the crowd. When Ives' cohorts saw the show of force by the committee, they stopped. The trouble had been diverted.

Wilbur Sanders motioned for an immediate hanging. The motion was granted. Sam looked at the convicted killer. Ives' face remained expressionless as he was quickly led away to the makeshift gallows. The festive crowd followed, expressing their satisfaction each step of the way.

When they reached the partially constructed building, Sanders immediately led Ives inside. Ives seemed almost humored by the proceedings.

Ives was placed on a box and the noose was dropped around his neck. "Any parting words, Ives," Sanders asked. His voice was raspy. "You don't have to take this alone."

A snarl formed on the doomed man's lips, but he never spoke.

"May your soul be saved," Sanders said softly. Sanders, for the first time since Sam had known him, sounded unsure and weak.

Sanders glanced for a moment at Sam and then back at Ives. Without saying another word, Sanders kicked the box from beneath Ives' feet.

Sam watched in disbelief as the killer jerked when he hit the end of the rope. The creaking sound of the rope against the rafter was all Sam could hear as Ives' body swung lifeless in the noose.

The cheers of celebration rang out in the street. "That's one bastard down," someone shouted outside. Sam could only feel a sickness inside. "I'm going home now," he said to Wilbur as George Ives' body was cut loose from the rafter.

Sanders nodded. "I can't think of a better idea."

****

Hezekiah and Isaac could not see the actual hanging from their vantage point, but neither had to be told when it happened. They looked at each other silently. Hezekiah knew he would never forget what had just happened.

That evening, the Templeton house remained quiet. Hezekiah watched his father as he sat at the table reading the Bible. Hezekiah never mentioned the hanging…nor did his father.

CHAPTER 11

The morning after the hanging of George Ives, Sam was summoned to Paris Pfouts home. The committee members that had gone in search of Red Yeager had returned.

Paris offered Sam a cordial greeting, but it was evident to Sam that he had not been requested to Paris' home for pleasantries.

Wilbur Sanders, Tom Burtchey, Eziekel Turner and Sidney Brewer were already there. Paris immediately asked the men to be seated and began to unfold a piece of paper. He seemed unusually unsettled for a man who had always displayed confidence in all of Sam's prior meetings with him. "I was glad to hear that everything was successful here at the gulch while we were gone." He cleared his throat as he studied the paper in his hand. "Our trip proved successful in its own right, although at first it looked bad for us. We traveled all the way to Deer Lodge to find that Red Yeager was not there. On our return however, we received word that Red Yeager had been seen at Rattlesnake Ranch, just north of here. The information proved to be correct. We caught him by surprise, and he immediately confessed to his part in the robberies and killings." Paris paused, carefully studying the face of each man before continuing. "Although I would have preferred otherwise, from the information he told us, I saw no other choice. We hung him there at Rattlesnake Ranch."

Paris' words hung in the air like smoke from a stale cigar, choking at Sam's thoughts. Sam could not believe what he had just been told. They had all committed themselves to justice by trial and would not tolerate any lynching. Now the committee was doing the lynching. Anger began to consume him. He had been tricked into being a part of it.

Paris raised his voice over the unsettling sounds of the men. "I know what you're thinking," he said with a firm voice. "But before you hold judgment, listen to what I've got to say. Maybe then you'll more fully understand our action." Paris waited until the men had quieted. "Red Yeager not only confessed to his part in the road agents activity, but he also told us the names of all those who are part of the gang, how their operation works, and where their hideouts are located. I hold the list of these ruthless bandits here in my hand," he continued, holding the paper up so that everyone could see. "I guess Red wanted to go out with a clear conscious. He told us that perhaps as many as one hundred men had met their deaths from the work of the ruthless road agents." He watched as the men stared at him in disbelief. "I wasn't surprised by any of the names on this list, but I must tell you I was extremely surprised by its length. Red said the gang operated all the way from the Gallatin to the east, through Alder Gulch, Bannack, Deer Lodge and west as far as Hellgate." He paused, and then with a dramatic slowness, raised the paper to begin reading the names. "My suspicions were correct. Henry Plummer is their leader." He gazed curiously over the paper at the men seated around him before continuing. "Plummer had seven lieutenants. Yeager was one of them. The others still out there are Haze Lyons, Frank Parish, Boone Helm and the sheriff's three deputies-Stinson, Ray and Gallagher."

Paris continued reading the list. Sam quickly began to understand Paris' concern. The list seemed endless. "The last two," Paris concluded, "are two men that Red only knew as Zeke and Dalton. Red, himself, seemed frightened of these two. He felt they

98

would kill just for the enjoyment. I believe these were the names that Ives gave us that had slipped through our fingers at the ranch. I'm sure they're half way to Nevada by now."

Sanders whistled. "How many names are on that list?" he asked.

"Thirty-four. Thirty are still out there. Whether you agree with my decision or not, now you at least know the reason I chose to hang Red without a trial. By the time we put each one of them on trial, every one of us would probably be dead. If we gave them a chance to regroup, we would be no more than a turkey shoot for them. We still have an element of surprise. We know who they are and where they operate and they don't know we know." He looked around the room. "Sam. You look quite concerned. What are your feelings?"

"My heart says, no. An action like this has always been something I found deplorable. But I'm also a reasonable man. None of us are gunslingers, and many of us are family men only trying to protect our loved ones. I believe Paris is right. They wouldn't hesitate to kill any one of us just as they did Nichols. And I believe they wouldn't hesitate to bring harm to our families. I can't believe I'm saying it, but I vote, yes."

Voices of agreement filled the room. "I had hoped you would understand my action," Paris said as he rose to his feet. "Christmas is day after tomorrow. After Christmas we'll begin to lay out our plan. Now all of you go home and enjoy your families. You all truly deserve it. We'll contact you in a few days."

****

Electra Plummer prepared for another quiet, lonely evening as she gazed from her window, watching a gentle January snow fall outside. Its peaceful existence was so contradictory to her life of turmoil. She had made a decision to return to Boston in the spring. As much as she still loved Henry, she could no longer accept his vial actions toward her. She brushed her eyes, closed the curtain and selected her favorite book of poems from the bookcase. She sat with the book opened on her lap for a considerable period of time, but never a word reached her eyes.

The door abruptly opened, startling Electra. Henry entered, brushing the snow from his sleeves. Electra's body tensed, uncertain of his mood or actions. She had grown to fear him. He removed his hat and holster, turned and momentarily looked at her before walking towards her. Without a word, he took her by the hands and gently pulled her into his arms, kissing her with a gentleness that she had not felt for so long. She thought her body would melt as he held her in his arms.

He picked up the book that she had left sitting in the chair. "Would you like me to read to you?" His voice was gentle as she had once remembered.

"More than anything," she murmured, her words seemed to be caught in her throat. She tried to reason his sudden change. She felt tears of joy fill her eyes, where only moments before they had been filled with tears of unhappiness. She was like a lantern to him...he could adjust her burning flame to whatever level he desired. She knew she could never resist him. If he wanted her, she could never leave him. One moment of his love was worth all the anguish she had felt. She only prayed that this moment would never end.

The words of poetry flowed softly from his lips, tingling every part of her body. She gently stroked his leg as she sat at his feet, watching each word that formed on his lips. His face looked so gentle and calm now.

After reading several verses, he slowly closed the book and sat it on the table next to the chair. He smiled warmly at her, rose from the chair, lifted her into his arms, and carried her to their bed.

****

It was still dark when Electra wakened. She could see the silhouette of her husband fully clothed. "What time is it?" she called from the bed.

100

"I'm sorry I wakened you," he said moving to her side. He sat on the edge of the bed next to her. "I'm sorry, Electra, for a lot of things I've done." His voice sounded saddened.

She reached up, placing her hand on the back of his neck and pulled his willing body to her until their lips met.

"You go back to sleep," he said, rising to his feet.

"Must you go, Henry? I never want you to leave me again."

"I have to," he said, brushing her cheek. She kissed his hand. "I love you," he said. "I always have."

She watched him leave. Shortly, she heard the hoof beats of his horse as he rode away.

As she lay there, an uncomfortable feeling began to absorb her. His parting words had almost sounded like a good-bye.

She was uncertain how long she had laid there in a drowsy slumber when she heard a knock at the door. She sat up with a start. The first signs of dawn filtered through the window as she quickly searched for her robe. It wouldn't be Henry, she thought. He would never knock. But who would be calling at such an early hour?

She opened the door. Although she did not know the man personally, she recognized him as Paris Pfouts. A short distance away were a half dozen men on horseback.

"I'm sorry to disturb you, Mrs. Plummer, at such an early hour," Paris said, tipping his hat. "Is Sheriff Plummer at home?"

"No. He left much earlier. Is there something wrong?"

"Nothing, ma'am," Paris said without expression. "Did he happen to say where he was going?"

"He didn't say. Please tell me if there's something wrong," she pleaded. A terrible fear began to grip her. Why did they want Henry at such an early hour?

"I'm sorry we disturbed you, Mrs. Plummer," Paris said, tipping his hat again, and quickly walked to the other men waiting on horseback. He said something to them that was undetectable to Electra, and then mounted and they rode away at a gallop.

Electra watched them disappear. Her body shivered as she wrapped the robe more tightly around her, but the chill did not come from the winter cold, but a feeling that had settled in her heart.
Electra quickly dressed and went to the sheriff's office, but found it empty. She returned home and waited for news from her husband. The morning passed, but Henry never returned.

In the afternoon, Electra again returned to town, but everything still seemed normal. She passed by the sheriff's office again, but it still remained empty. The stove was cold. She assumed no one had been there all day.

The day passed into evening, then night. Around midnight, she went to bed, but was unable to sleep as she listened for the sounds of her returning husband. They never came.

****

The committee had been taken by surprise that Sheriff Plummer had slipped away during the night. They feared the road agents had received word of the committee's plan and had left the territory, or worse, they were re-grouping to counterattack the committee and community.

The committee's plan had been to capture the sheriff first, hoping it would leave the rest of the bandits in disarray without a leader. They still wanted to proceed with the plan. It was decided that Paris would take some men and go to Bannack in hopes of finding the unsuspecting sheriff there.

The rest of the committee would stay in Virginia City and proceed as usual so not to arouse any suspicion. The men staying behind would also be able to monitor the activity of the outlaws around Virginia City. Sam, Harvey and Wilbur were among those that stayed.

During the first day, Wilbur Sanders sat in his office watching from his window. He saw Electra Plummer about town, stopping by the sheriff's office. It was obvious she was unaware of what was happening, but Wilbur wondered if the sheriff would even tell her if he knew. What confused Sanders was why the sheriff spent most of the night at home and then slipped away before daylight. Why would he take such a risk if he knew? But why did he leave in such a hurry if he didn't know?

Later that same day, Sanders saw Deputy Gallager come into town and head straight for the sheriff's office. His casual arrival and not in any hurry to leave eased Sander's mind that at least Gallager, one of the gang's lieutenants, was not aware of anything unusual.

****

Darkness had fallen over Virginia City late on the fourth day after the disappearance of Sheriff Plummer. Sanders sat near the dim lit lantern in his office reviewing the long list before him. He ran a line through the names of Red Yeager, George Ives and the two men killed at the ranch, Bob Grover and Cass Haven. He tapped his pen at the name, Henry Plummer. When could he scratch the name? He hoped it would be soon. As more time passed, the more apt the bandits would become suspicious and run.

He leaned back and slipped his watch from his vest pocket. He popped open the cover. Six-thirty. Feeling disappointed, he decided he would have to wait another day for word from Bannack.

He leaned forward to extinguish the light. A knock sounded at his door, momentarily startling him. He took a deep breath. Was this the long awaited word he had been waiting to hear?

Sanders opened the door sending a blast of cold air into the room. Bob Carter, one of the men that had gone to Bannack, stood bundled in the doorway.

"Get in here, Bob," Sanders said, motioning him inside. "You look frozen to death."

"Death right now sounds pretty damn good compared to my frozen limbs."

He stepped inside and pulled the collar of his coat down. He smiled at Sanders. "We got him, Wilbur," he said excitedly.

"The sheriff?"

"Yeah. Plummer, Stinson, and Ray. Hung 'em shortly after daylight, yesterday."

"Sit down and give me some details. I've been going out of my mind waiting to hear."

"It was almost too easy to believe," Bob said, sitting with his legs stretched. He cocked his hat back. "We arrived night before last. Got word the sheriff was there and about an hour before daylight, we knocked on his cabin door." Bob leaned forward. "I swear, Wilbur, he acted as though he was waiting for us."

"No resistance?"

"None...or at least from the sheriff. The other two we caught by surprise and they cursed us 'till they were swinging."

"I don't understand," Wilbur said, suspiciously raising his eyebrows. "If the sheriff had wind of what was going on, he'd been out of the territory. Did he say anything?"

"Strange. We asked him if he had anything to say when we slipped the noose around his neck. All he said was 'I've already said what needs to be said'."

"Guess I'll never figure the man out," Sanders said, squinting his eyes in thought. "So when are the rest due back?"

"Tomorrow. Paris said to be ready, because all hell is about to break loose. The next few days is going to be mighty busy and exciting, I reckon."

"I can well imagine, and I can tell you, we'll be ready. You'd better get home and take care of any frost bites you might have."

Bob left, leaving Wilbur alone. Wilbur stood for a moment staring at the darkened sheriff's office. Maybe the next one will bring a little dignity to the office, he thought. Wilbur returned inside, scratched the three names from the list, blew out the lantern, and headed for home.

****

The committees of Bannack and Alder Gulch acted swiftly with expedience and without hesitation during the days following the hanging of Sheriff Plummer. The road bandits, without a leader and unaware of the list held by the committee, were in disarray and offered little resistance. As the bandits were methodically captured and hung, the remaining bandits began to run and hide. The bandits, unaware that their names were on a list, were also unaware that the same list stated all of their hideouts. The bandits trying to find refuge at the hideouts, soon found themselves surrounded by the relentless committee.

****

When told about the hanging of Sheriff Plummer, Sarah immediately went to Electra's home to try to comfort and console her best friend. But Electra was not answering the door. Each day, for four days, Sarah would call on Electra with no response.

Sarah's heart was heavy. She wanted to help her grieving friend, and she wanted somehow to apologize, feeling she had been a part of causing her husband's death. Sarah wondered if Electra hated her, which only added to Sarah's sadness. Electra's friendship had given Sarah a renewed hope and happiness in this unforgivable land. She could not, or would not, abandon Electra.

Sarah poured a cup of broth, wrapped a loaf of bread, and began her daily ritual to Electra's home. With each passing day, Sarah was becoming more concerned about Electra's well being. Only the smoke from the Plummer's chimney assured Sarah that Electra was even alive.

As she approached the house, Sarah could see only her footsteps from the previous days. No one else had come, and Electra had not left.

Sarah took a deep sigh and knocked. She called out, "Electra. It's Sarah. Please answer the door. Please let me help."

She waited, listening for some response inside. Her heart leaped as she heard the door being unlatched. Slowly the door opened.

Sarah gasped at the frail woman standing before her. Electra's face was pale and drawn. Her soft brown eyes, that Sarah had so admired, were swollen and red. Electra forced a meager smile.

"Oh, Electra," Sarah murmured as she grasped her mourning friend and helped her to a chair. "I've been so worried about you."

"Thank you for caring," Electra whispered. "I'm sorry about the other days. I just couldn't force myself to see anyone."

"You poor thing," Sarah said, clutching her friend. "You look as though you haven't eaten in days, and you must be half frozen, it's so cold in here." Sarah quickly placed the last log on an almost diminished fire. "I brought some broth and bread. You must eat to keep your health, dear."

After Electra had finished taking some broth, Sarah sat next to her, holding and patting her hand. "Electra, you must hate me, but please let me help you. You are so dear to me, it pains me to see you like this."

Electra looked softly into Sarah's eyes. "I don't hate you. I don't hate anyone. I only regret everything that has happened."

Electra's eyes were dry, but Sarah knew Electra was still crying inside. Her saddened look was overwhelming. Sarah bit her lip, trying to retain her composure.

Sarah sat quietly watching Electra, patiently waiting for her to let out the pain that was stored inside her.

"That last night," Electra began, "Henry was the gentle man that I used to know. He had always treated me with love and compassion. I know he had another side, but never with me. I couldn't understand what was happening to him these last few months. I thought it was his job as sheriff. Now, I believe he had regretted what he had become. I think he knew what was about to happen. That is why he went to Bannack to wait for the committee. He didn't want me to see it. I think he was prepared to pay the consequences...perhaps he wanted it to happen. I only wish he had realized it before it was too late."

Sarah never spoke, only listening to the desperate words of her heart broken friend.

106

Except for a quick trip home to request Hezekiah to bring plenty of firewood for Mrs. Plummer, Sarah spent the remainder of the day and the entire night with Electra. She wanted to be assured Electra was returning towards recovery before she left her alone. It was good for Electra, but it was also good for her.

****

Sam sat quietly at the table watching his family. Sarah wiped her hands on her apron, gazed into the small mirror nearby and began tucking the loose strands of hair into her bun. Cynthia had already crawled into bed, leaving her blankets pushed down so that her mother would tuck her in. Hezekiah sat on the bed half-heartedly pulling off one of his boots, trying to delay the inevitable.

Sam felt both a sense of relief and despair. He had received word earlier in the day that some of the committee had returned from the Gallatin, hanging what was believed to be the last of the remaining outlaws still in the territory. The total number of road agent dead was now twenty-nine. Only five men on the list had escaped the relentless hunt of the committee. The word was given...the committee was through.

As Sam watched Sarah and the children, he wondered whether his participation in taking twenty-nine lives, killers or not, was justified. Had he really provided safety for his loved ones? He had to believe he did or the horrifying memories would surely bring him insanity. He knew he would never forget seeing so many men die. Some had died silently, some cursed to the end, and others cried and pleaded for their life, but at the moment of impact, they all had the same horrified look, and always the same horrifying sound. Perhaps it was best if he could not forget. Maybe it would be all that would save his soul.

Sam rubbed his face with his hands as though trying to awaken himself from a horrible dream.

"Are you tired, Sam?" Sarah asked. She had been watching him in the mirror.

"No. I'm fine, Sarah," he answered, although inside, he knew he was not fine.

"Thank the Lord it's over," she said, walking behind him and she began rubbing his neck. "Thank the good Lord it's over."

Sam straightened up with a start. He could hear someone approaching rapidly on horseback. His only thought was that some of the remaining outlaws had returned for revenge. It had to be bad news-someone this late approaching in such a hurry. He could see the frightened look on Sarah's face as he hurried to his revolver hanging near the door.

A loud knock sounded on the door that seemed to echo throughout the house. Then they heard the familiar voice of Sidney Brewer. "Sam, are you there?"

Sam quickly opened the door. Sidney's face was tense. "Sam, we've got problems," he shouted. "Some men at one of the saloons have been drinking too much, and they've decided they're going to hang Joe, the Indian from the livery stable."

"Are any of the men from the committee?"

"I don't think so. Wilbur and some of the others are already on their way down there. I've got to go tell the others."

Sam stood for a moment in shock as he watched Sidney mount and ride off. He went inside, grabbed his coat, and strapped on his holster.

"Oh, Sam, please be careful," Sarah pleaded, her voice trembling.

"I've got to go, Sarah. It was part of our agreement on the committee to protect innocent people. Maybe for once I can save a life. I promise I'll be careful."

Sam looked at Hezekiah. There were tears in his son's eyes, his face racked with fear. "We'll save him. I promise, son," he said, before heading into the darkened night.

****

Hezekiah could not believe what was happening. His thoughts were jumbled as he watched his father disappear. How could anyone

108

hang his friend...a kind old man who would harm no one. Eagle Feather had never done anything wrong. Somehow he had to help his old friend.

Hezekiah pulled on his boot, grabbed his coat, and raced out the door. He could hear his mother screaming and pleading for him to return. He never hesitated. This once, he had to directly disobey his mother. He did not care what the consequences would be. He had to warn Eagle Feather.

He ran as fast as he could towards Isaac's house. The dark overcast night and rough ground made his progress difficult. He stumbled and fell, but immediately rose and continued running. The cold air ripped at his lungs, and he could feel the cold of his tears on his cheeks. He could still hear his mother calling him.

As he approached Isaac's house, he could see Isaac standing in the doorway, his face distorted with torment. "We need to warn Eagle Feather," Hezekiah shouted, gasping for air.

Isaac, never hesitating, raced after Hezekiah. Hezekiah could hear Isaac's mother pleading for their return.

Isaac's mournful shouts kept filling Hezekiah's ears, "They're going to kill him!"

As they crossed Wallace Street, Hezekiah could see a crowd gathered some two blocks away. Hezekiah and Isaac never hesitated as they ran down the slope past the livery stable towards Eagle Feather's small cabin, which was located a short distance behind it.

Hezekiah pounded on the door. "Eagle Feather!" he shouted, "It's Hezekiah and Isaac. Hurry! Open the door!"

The time seemed eternal until the door opened. Eagle Feather looked confused as he stared at the two boys. "What is it my friends?" he said, staring blankly at them.

"You have to hide," Isaac shouted, his voice shaking.

"Some men are coming to hang you," Hezekiah shouted at the same time. "You have to get away!"

"Wait. Slow down," Eagle Feather said, calmness in his voice.

"Some men in town are drunk, and they're coming to hang you," Hezekiah responded, trying to calm his voice. "Our fathers and some other men are trying to stop them. You must hide."

Eagle Feather's face remained expressionless as he listened to the two boys. When they finished, he walked to the rear of the cabin and removed his rifle from the wall. Hezekiah glanced around the small cabin. There was only a small stove, and a couple blankets on the floor. Hezekiah was amazed at the basic living quarters of Eagle Feather.

Eagle Feather checked his rifle and walked back to the door. "You young braves must return home now," he said sternly. "It is too dangerous for you here."

"You've got to go hide," Isaac pleaded.

"No. I cannot hide while brave men endanger their lives to protect me. I must stand beside them." His eyes softened as he looked at the frightened boys. "It is not bad," he said, a smile coming to his lips. "It is good to know that one does not stand alone."

They watched Eagle Feather move swiftly up the incline and onto the street. The boys moved along the shadows following Eagle Feather down Wallace Street towards the unruly, noisy mob.

Hezekiah and Isaac stood along the shadows of the building. A crowd of about twenty men stood facing their fathers, Eagle Feather, and a half dozen other men. Hezekiah's body was shivering uncontrollably.

"He's only an Indian," one of the men in the mob shouted. "Hell, I figure he was probably a lookout for those damn outlaws anyway, with Indians being so damn sneaky and all."

"Unless you have proof to back what you're saying, he's considered by all of us here to be innocent." Hezekiah recognized the man speaking as Wilbur Sanders.

"He's a blood thirsty renegade. What the hell do you care?" a voice from the mob shouted.

"Frank, you seem to be the leader here." Wilbur Sanders' voice remained calm. "I'm telling you right now, if anybody harms Joe, I will personally insure they will be hanged. Frank, I'm also making you responsible for Joe's well being. Any harm comes to Joe, you'll be hanging too."

"What makes you so high and mighty, Sanders, that you can say who's to be hung and who's not?"

"I'm telling you for the last time, Frank. Call off your wolves if you want to see another sunrise."

Frank momentarily studied Wilbur's face. He turned to receive support, but found his supporters beginning to retreat from him. He threw his arms in the air with disgust. "All of you can go to hell," he said, and walked away without looking back.

Hezekiah sighed with relief. Eagle Feather had been spared. He looked at Isaac and caught him hurriedly wiping his eyes. At that moment, Hezekiah completely understood his friend's feelings.

****

Hezekiah had anticipated the worst for disobeying his mother; but he found his father, and, to his extreme amazement, his mother, very understanding. The subject was dropped with only a severe scolding and lecture from his father and an apology to his mother for disobeying her.

The words of Wilbur Sanders were apparently well heeded by the townspeople. After the incident with Eagle Feather, Alder Gulch began to return to normalcy. Traveling no longer carried the fear it had, a new sheriff was elected, and although winter still prevailed, mining resumed to its expedient level.

Hezekiah was relieved and excited as he began seeing Christina around town again. His enchantment for her had never wavered. With each opportunity, he would wait patiently in the cold for a mere glimpse of her. He was absolutely sure there was no woman more beautiful and enchanting, and someday he would find the courage to meet her.

In the spring, Electra Plummer returned to the east. Sarah, sadly missing her dear friend, resumed the struggle to find her own happiness in an angry land.

CHAPTER 12

As Christina prepared to leave for work, she hummed cheerfully studying herself in the mirror. "I think this will do," she said to herself. It was a pleasant day in May. But it was not the pleasant day that made her feel so happy. She had a young admirer.

Christina had first noticed him two or three months earlier. At first, she thought it was only a coincidence that he often appeared where she was; but she began to realize it was more than fate. Although he tried to be inconspicuous, his gaze was always following her.

Christina found his boyish innocence humorous at first; but in time, she found herself caught up in the enchanting game. She even began selecting her wardrobe with the explicit purpose of pleasing him. Sometimes at night, she would lie in bed, wondering who he was and what he was thinking. On her days off, she would go for strolls, hoping to catch a glimpse of him. She felt like a schoolgirl flirting with a first love. Somehow he had entered her life, giving her a sense of importance-a feeling she had not felt for a long time. Christina often considered approaching him, but feared she would frighten him away and end the delightful game.

Christina closed her door and stood for a moment with her head raised, letting the warm sun radiate against her skin. She shook her head gently, letting her curls bounce playfully on her neck before proceeding down the alley towards the saloon. She chuckled. What would Sadie think about the way she was acting over a young boy? Her admirer could not be more than fifteen or sixteen years of age.

As Christina approached the street, she slowed her pace, her eyes in search of her admirer. She could feel her heart beating rapidly with anticipation. Goodness, how silly, she thought, but still it felt good.

Christina smiled. He was waiting for her...across the street...nervously pawing at the ground, pretending to be looking in the window of Garrad's Clothiers. He glanced in her direction, then quickly towards the window, then back towards her. She stopped and watched him. The longer she stared in his direction, the more he shifted towards the storefront. How enchanting he was...bashfulness in a man had always been intriguing to her.

An urge to meet him swelled inside Christina until she thought she would burst. She knew nothing about him, but she knew she had to find out who he was. She could no longer retain her pent up urge to meet him. With a deep sigh, she nervously stepped into the street and started towards him...hurrying her pace in fear that at any moment she would lose her courage. The closer she came towards her young admirer, the more he turned away.

****

During the previous months, Hezekiah had become familiar with Christina's time schedule...knowing what time she went to work...which days she had off...when she went shopping or went for strolls. He worked diligently to set his schedule so he would be available to watch her come and go. He had worked out all the details...well, except how he was going to meet her. Each time after he had seen her, he made a promise the next time he would approach her and introduce him to her. Her charming beauty possessed his very being. Each time he saw her, a funny feeling filled his stomach until he thought he would go crazy, but he did not want it to stop.

Isaac did not seem to understand and was always quick to speak his disgusted disapproval. Hezekiah did not understand Isaac's feelings either, but he knew how he felt. Each time he saw her, all the reasons why he should not introduce himself rushed to his head. Surely she would think he was merely a strange boy. Why would someone like her, so radiant and beautiful, ever want to know him? But still he continued to practice...someday he would find the courage and he had to be ready to meet the woman of his life.

Today was no different for Hezekiah. He had hurried to finish his chores so that he would be able to watch Christina going to work as usual, shortly after noon. He waited patiently for her arrival. His eyes remained riveted on the alley except for an occasional glance up and down the street to be certain no one he knew was nearby. He would only have a moment, and then she would disappear into the saloon.

There she was...more beautiful than ever. The funny feeling in his stomach started as usual. She was wearing her sky blue dress...his favorite...the one she was wearing the first time he saw her.

His throat tightened. What was she doing? She had stopped at the entrance to the alley and was looking in his direction. Why was she looking towards him? This was not part of the ritual.

Hezekiah could feel his ears burning and the heat sweltering under his collar. He shifted his body away from her so as not to draw her attention. He glanced her direction. She was still looking in his direction! He looked away. Was she gone yet? He looked again. Suddenly he felt as though all the blood in his body was rushing to his head...she was crossing the street and heading straight for him! His body was on fire. He completely turned away from her. He wanted to look back but feared she would notice him...that would be disaster.

"Hi." He almost collapsed at the sound of a woman's voice. He glanced up. Christina was talking to him!

"Hi," he whispered. He thought he was going to be sick.

"Is there something in the window that interests you?" she asked.

He looked at her eyes that seemed to smile. "P-pardon, ma'am," he stuttered.

"I thought maybe you had found something to your fancy in the store window."

Hezekiah looked in the window where she was pointing. He wished he could die at that moment. On display in the window was an assortment of women undergarments. How could he have been so stupid? Such terrible thoughts she must have of him. "No, no, ma'am," he stammered. He could feel his face red with embarrassment. He dropped his gaze from her eyes. He realized he was looking directly at her cleavage. He quickly looked back at her face.

She continued to smile at him. "I thought maybe you were choosing something for your girlfriend," she said.

"Oh no, ma'am," he said, trying to remain calm. "I don't even have a girlfriend." So why was he looking at the undergarments, he thought. She'll surely ask me.

"A handsome young fellow like you with no girlfriend. I bet several girls would like to be."

He felt relieved she had dropped the subject of the window. "I don't think so," he answered sincerely. She raised her eyebrows. "Really," he assured her.

"I understand. I don't have any men friends either."

How could that be true, he thought. She surely could if she wanted.

Hezekiah suddenly feared someone might be watching. He quickly glanced up and down the busy street. If his mother ever found out he was talking to a woman who worked at a saloon, she would yank every hair from his head.

"Are you waiting for your friend?" Christina asked.

"My friend?" he said puzzled.

"The one I've seen you with on numerous occasions."

"You've seen me before?"

"Indeed I have. Many times. I had thought perhaps in time you'd introduce yourself, but alas, to my disappointment, you never did, so-o-o I took it upon myself to do it. I hope you don't mind?"

Her eyes seemed to melt everything inside him. She was not only the most beautiful woman he had ever seen, but the kindest too. Hezekiah wiped his face with his sleeve. "I'm sorry. I just thought...well..."

"That's all right. I understand." Christina extended her hand. "I'm Christina."

"Hi. I know." He felt the softness of her hand as he shook it.

"So now you know my name. May I have the pleasure of knowing yours?"

"Oh, yeah. Sure. I'm Hezekiah."

"What a handsome, strong name."

Hezekiah wiped his face again. "My parents gave it to me." How stupid, he thought. Of course they did. He had waited and practiced all this time how he would act and what he would say when he met Christina...How he would impress her...leave her breathless. And now, look at him, acting and talking stupid like a blubbering fool. She would surely have a good laugh about this.

"I have to go to work now," Christina said, motioning with her head towards the saloon. "I guess you know where I work."

Of course she had to leave. She would find any reason to leave. He had made a mess of everything.

"If you would like, maybe one day soon, you could be my guest for tea." Her voice sounded sincere. "Do you like tea?"

He didn't know if he liked tea. He had never had it. But he would drink kerosene to be with her. "When?" he asked without hesitation.

Christina looked surprised by his sudden assertiveness. "Well," she said, "Sadie has given me tomorrow off. Would that be too soon? You know, if your social calendar is open tomorrow afternoon."

"I'm sure it's open," Hezekiah quickly insisted, fearing she would change her mind. "I know it's open."

"Good. Tomorrow at twoish.

116

"Twoish it is...I mean two. I'll be there. I promise."

"See you then, Hezekiah. I'm glad we met," she said with sincerity in her voice.

Hezekiah's body shivered with excitement. He watched her as she flowed across the street. Tea with Christina. It would be the most wonderful moment of his life. She turned and waved. Life could never be better than this. Never!

****

The following morning, Christina rose early. She began preparing cinnamon cookies for her afternoon guest. Her mood was one of cheery excitement as she cleaned her cabin and chose the dress she would wear. She wanted the day to be perfect. She giggled. She was acting as though having tea with a young boy was the biggest social event of the year. How sad, she thought, it was.

She removed the cookies from the oven and sat them on the counter to cool. She thought of the days when as a girl in Pennsylvania, her mother would have social tea parties with the neighborhood women. The women would sit in the parlor rendering gossip, while the girls would gather around the kitchen table. The girls' discussions would ultimately lead to, and be dominated on the subject of boys. They would discuss who was the cutest, and whom they were going to marry. Their voices would lower when the sensitive subject of who they had kissed, or would like to kiss, came up.

One such day that Christina would never forget was when Judith Bolten, smiling proudly, whispered to the other girls, "Last Friday after school, Timothy Johnson took me behind the school fence and put his hand under my skirt, and he touched me."

Everyone squealed, cupping their hands over their mouths. Judith looked at Christina, knowing Christina had a crush on Timothy. Christina bravely fought back her hurt and anger. She was determined not to let Judith know she had been hurt.

"Tell us what it was like," Mary Peters said, giggling bashfully.

"Where'd he touch you?" Margaret Cassidy asked, her eyes wide with shock and excitement.

"Where do you think," Judith answered proudly, casting another glance at Christina. "Has he ever touched you, Christina?"

All the girls squealed again. "Has he?" Mary whispered.

"If he did, I would never be so bold to say so."

"I bet he's never kissed you," Judith replied as she turned to the other girls and made a face.

"Was it exciting?" Margaret asked, her eyes still open wide.

"It's no big deal. I'm not sure why it's so hush-hush. That is unless there's no boys who want to kiss you."

That night Christina lied in bed unable to sleep. Judith had successfully hurt and embarrassed Christina. Angered by Judith's remarks, Christina promised herself to seek revenge. She was not going to be outdone by Judith when it came to Timothy. Timothy would want to touch her...any boy would. She would show Judith...and show her good.

A few evenings later, Christina was given her opportunity. Judith's mother was having a sixteenth birthday party for Judith. Judith spent the evening flirting with Timothy, always being sure that Christina was watching, but later in the evening, Judith disappeared for a moment giving Christina her chance. She grabbed surprised Timothy by the hand and led him out the back door and to the nearby deserted Miller's barn.

When they arrived at the barn, she turned and gazed into his eyes. She, like all the other girls, always practiced at gazing into boys' eyes. They had found it far more useful than the ancient tools their mothers had taught them-like sewing and cooking.

Timothy began to nervously kiss her as their mouths roughly bumped together. Inside her, Christina wanted to stop, but the smug face of Judith kept appearing. She could feel his hand moving about her body. She flinched, but forced herself to relax. He pulled her down onto a pile of hay, his hand moving more forcefully. She wanted to scream for him to stop, but she did not. His hand was under her garments and against her skin. It was too late now. She had to go through with it. She closed her eyes. Please let it be over soon, she thought.

She had outdone Judith that evening, but she did not feel like she had won.

She was sixteen...about Hezekiah's age. She wondered if he had ever touched a girl or even kissed one. She shook her head in bewilderment. Why would she even think such a thought?

****

Hezekiah quickly discovered that Isaac did not take the news of having tea with Christina with the same level of enthusiasm that he had. In fact, Isaac became more cynical than ever. What kind of friend would not be happy for him, Hezekiah wondered. But whatever Isaac's feelings, Hezekiah was not going to let it spoil his day.

Hezekiah quickly set about his chores that morning to insure they would be done. After forcing some food into his nervous stomach at the noon meal, he walked to a quiet spot on the hillside overlooking the town and began waiting for the destined hour of two o'clock. He wanted to be sure that no last minute projects from his mother would disrupt his rendezvous with Christina.

He wondered what Christina would be wearing. He knew whatever she wore, it would be perfect.

What would they talk about? He hadn't given it much thought. There was nothing interesting about him that she would want to know, but still, he could not just sit there. She would never invite him back. He suddenly began to regret he was going. Maybe Isaac was right. She would hate him by the time the afternoon was over. It would be a disaster. Why did he say yes? He would bore her to death. He could ask questions about her. Yeah, let her talk about herself. Still, what would he ask her? Why do you work in a saloon? She would think he was terrible. He was doomed.

It was almost time to go. He still had no idea what he would say. He began to feel sick. Maybe he would get sick in front of her.

It was going to be terrible. Maybe he should not even go. She probably would not care anyway. She probably only asked him for tea because she felt sorry for him. What excuse could he give her? Yet, he had waited so long to be with her, and if he did not go, he would always regret it.

Hezekiah stood up, still debating which direction to go. Slowly, he began moving down the hill towards Christina's. With each step, he was uncertain which direction the next step would take him. Then, before he realized it, he was standing at her door. He had no choice now.

Hezekiah's hand nervously tapped lightly on her door. He had knocked so quietly, maybe she had not heard him. He was afraid to knock again. If she did hear him the first time, it would make him look too anxious and rude...but he did feel foolish standing there.

His dilemma soon ended when the door opened. As Christina stood before him, he no longer regretted coming. Even if the remainder of the day became a complete disaster, this one moment seeing her was worth it. He had never imagined someone could be so lovely. Her playful eyes and gentle smile left Hezekiah in a trance.

"I'm glad you came, Hezekiah. I was so afraid that you would change your mind and I would have been terribly disappointed."

She stepped back to let him enter. Hezekiah stood motionless staring at her. "Would you rather I serve you tea and cookies out here?" she said, winking at him.

"Out here?" Hezekiah responded, not fully understanding what she was saying.

"I'll have to if you don't come inside."

"Oh. No, ma'am, I'll come inside." Hezekiah wiped his face with his sleeve.

Christina directed Hezekiah to a chair. "If you'll excuse me for a moment," she said, "I'll get the tea and cookies. The maid has the day off." She laughed, throwing her head back. Hezekiah complimented her humor with a burst of laughter.

He watched her every move as she gracefully placed the teapot and cups on the serving tray. "I made these cookies this morning," she said placing them on the tray. "I hope they're all right. I never have the pleasure to bake for any guests these days," she continued, setting the tray on the low table in front of him.

As she bent over, Hezekiah's eyes immediately became fixed on the front of her low cut dress. He had never imagined breasts to be so tantalizing. Her skin looked so soft, he wanted to touch them. He did not want to stare, but his eyes would not move as though they were frozen there for eternity. Without realizing what he was saying, the words burst from his mouth. "You're so beautiful, ma'am."

Christina, suddenly realizing her precarious position, stood up straight with a start. "Well thank you, Hezekiah. It's always good for a woman's ego to hear such kind things from a gentleman."

Hezekiah was embarrassed by his remark. He could see the redness on Christina's cheeks. Still, he was glad he had said it...And she did seem pleased by the compliment.

Christina sat across from him. He tried not to stare at her cleavage, but his eyes kept darting back to it like a magnet. Hezekiah began to regretfully realize a bulge forming in his pants. He felt totally shocked as he shifted positions, hoping she would not notice. No woman had ever placed him in such an embarrassing predicament. Oh Lord, he thought, please don't let her see me. He tried to take his mind off Christina. What would Isaac be doing now? If Isaac knew about his awkward situation, Isaac would tease him for the remainder of his life.

"So, Hezekiah," she began, "I must learn everything about you. I've been so curious about you for the longest time." Hezekiah watched her mouth open, as the words seemed to flow effortlessly from it. If he wasn't so stupid, he could have started the conversation the same way by asking about her. She brought the cup to her soft red lips, waiting for him to respond. Everything about her seemed so soft and gentle.

"There's not much about me that's very interesting, ma'am."

"First, Hezekiah, please call me, Christina. If we are going to be good friends, I would much prefer Christina to ma'am."

She wanted to be good friends. At least everything was starting good, he thought. "Yes, ma'am...I mean, Christina."

She giggled. "That's better. You must have some cookies or you'll hurt my feelings," she said, leaning forward to push the cookies toward him. Hezekiah tried not too, but he couldn't help looking down her dress again.

"Thank you," he said, taking a cookie and biting into it. "Oh, they're great. I mean the cookies."

"Well thank you. Eat as many as you wish," she replied. "Here's a napkin for your lap. They're so..." She stopped and quickly looked away. Hezekiah looked down. His heart hit his throat. She had seen it. He quickly grabbed the napkin and placed it over his lap...his bulging lap.

"So, where did you and your family come from before settling here," she said quickly.

He could still see her embarrassment. He wondered if she could see his. "St. Louis," he said, trying to continue on. "We came here last summer by wagon train."

"What does your father do?"

"He's a carpenter around town."

"I don't believe I know him."

"He was one of the men who helped catch the outlaws," Hezekiah said proudly as he sat up straight, then quickly slouched again to better hide his situation.

"He must be a brave man."

"Yeah, I suppose so. I wanted to help him, but he wouldn't let me." That was stupid to say, he thought.

"I'm sure you would have been brave, too."

Hezekiah felt she was patronizing him, but it sounded good anyway. "Did you know Sheriff Plummer?" he asked.

The smile on her lips suddenly disappeared. "He was a terrible man, Hezekiah. He did some terrible things." She became quiet as though her thoughts were elsewhere.

Hezekiah quickly concluded the sheriff was a bad subject. "Where do you come from?"

She smiled. "Originally Pennsylvania."

"Is your family still there?"

"Yes, I believe so. The mail delivery between there and here isn't too good."

"Really. Mother writes to my..." Something wasn't right. He had picked another bad subject. For now he would avoid her family...and the sheriff. "I've got a sister, Cynthia. She's spoiled and doesn't like it here."

"You must be patient with her. Little girls don't like the same things as boys. I know. I was one once."

It sounded to Hezekiah like she was referring to him as a boy. Maybe he was...sort of, but he preferred her reference to him as a gentleman.

As the afternoon progressed, Hezekiah began to forget about her breasts...somewhat...and Christina talked about all the places she had been. She was not only beautiful, but kind and smart too. No doubt she was perfect.

Hezekiah was surprised when Christina mentioned it was after four o'clock. "I don't want your mother and father to worry," she said.

Hezekiah was embarrassed by her remark, making reference that he was a child, but he smiled politely. "Thank you for the tea and cookies. They were good," he said as he made his way to the door.

"Please come again," she said sincerely. "I haven't enjoyed an afternoon like today in a long time."

"I almost didn't come. I was afraid you would find me boring. I'm glad I did though."

"Just so you know, I was terribly nervous about today, too." She smiled. "I guess we were both nervous for nothing."

As he walked away, he knew she was still at the door watching him. She was perfect, but he hated to think she was also sad. He hoped he could change that someday.

****

Christina returned to work the next day after her tea social with her charming new friend. She cheerfully found her job more tolerable. The afternoon with Hezekiah had given her a refreshed outlook. It was her first encounter with someone outside of the saloon in years. She had almost forgotten how wonderful it was.

Christina had only been at work for an hour, when she received an unexpected message that Sadie would like to see her in Sadie's room upstairs. Christina could not imagine what could be so important that Sadie would want to see her during work. It was not like Sadie to take her girls away from their moneymaking duties.

When Christina arrived at Sadie's room, she found her cleaning her revolver. "Come in and kick up your doggies," Sadie said very deliberately. "Might as well rest them when you can."

Christina sat and watched Sadie continue to clean her gun. Whatever Sadie wanted, she seemed in no hurry to get to it. Christina was starting to become a little anxious, wondering if Sadie had bad news and was hesitant to tell her. "You wanted to see me?" Christina finally asked.

Sadie's head was still down when she spoke, "You don't mind me cleaning my gun while we talk, do you?" Christina shook her head. Sadie smiled. "You never know when this beauty will come in handy. I guess you already know that though." Sadie chuckled. "I bet that damn old sheriff is still shaking in his boots up on Boot Hill."

Christina forced a smile. As much as she disliked the sheriff, she found little humor in the remark. Sadie became silent again. Christina continued to become more uncomfortable.

"How's life?" Sadie finally asked as she continued cleaning her prize possession.

"Very well. Thank you for asking," Christina answered, still puzzled by Sadie's peculiar actions.

"I thought so," Sadie quickly responded, looking up.

"Pardon."

"I said I thought life was going well for you."

"I don't understand."

124

"Yes, you do. You've been acting like a school girl lately, particularly today."

"I'm sorry if my work isn't..."

"Oh balderdash. Your work is excellent as usual. I just figured you'd found a man and he's been sticking it to you on a regular basis."

"Sadie! You're terrible. You're...you're being so direct, you're embarrassing me."

Sadie laughed. "Hell, you've known me all these years and I still embarrass you because I'm so direct. All the crude comments you've heard in the saloon and you're embarrassed because I'm so direct. Every man this side of the Mississippi has asked you for a prod and you're embarrassed because I'm so direct." Sadie pushed the gun to the side and leaned forward. "Christina, I've watched you all these years live a life that most preacher's wives would find absolutely boring. Now something is going on. You don't have to tell me his name. All I want to know is, is he good?"

Christina could see the playful look in Sadie's eyes. Sadie was not going to let it go until Christina confessed. "It's nothing like that, Sadie. Honest."

"What is it like then," Sadie responded, her stare glued to Christina.

"I just had tea yesterday with a new friend."

"Male?"

"Yes, but he's just a boy."

Sadie's eyes opened wide. "Interesting," she said, slowly shaking her head. "Sometimes they're a little awkward from inexperience, but their enthusiasm more than makes up for it. So how old is he? Eighteen. Nineteen."

I don't know. I didn't ask. Besides we just talked. He's a real gentleman."

"A gentleman!" Sadie cried out, snorting as she laughed. "I find the only difference with a gentleman is that he'll say 'thank you' when he's done." Sadie was on her feet now, standing directly in front of Christina.

125

"It's nothing like that at all. He's only fifteen or sixteen." Christina knew immediately she had made a mistake on her emotional appeal. Sadie had the firepower she wanted and Christina knew Sadie would use it.

Sadie slapped her leg and stumbled back, cackling with laughter. "Oh, Christina," she blurted, "I never thought you would get one up on me...Sadie...queen of experiences. But, by hell, you sure did this time."

"Sadie, stop it or I'm going to leave." Tears of embarrassment filled Christina's eyes.

"Wait," Sadie begged. "I'm just so excited that you seem to be enjoying life for a change...for whatever reason you seem to want to give me."

Christina wiped her eyes. "Sadie, he's just a boy. It's nothing."

"Nothing! I think you'd better listen to someone with experience. Hell, experience. I know it all." Sadie's eyes were now dancing with delight. "When boys turn...oh, let's say fourteen, a caged bear awakens in them. Now mind you, you can well imagine a bear in hibernation for fourteen years is mighty damn hungry. The old bear begins to growl and starts clawing to get out. The longer it's in there, the angrier it gets. It knows as soon as it gets out it can start looking for honey. This bear, tearing at the insides of this boy, is driving the boy crazy. The boy quickly determines there is only one way to satisfy this bear and relieve his agony. Then one day, an innocent girl bee loaded with sweet honey, minding her own business, is suddenly faced with this furious bear. She screams 'Oh no, don't take my honey. I'm saving it for someone special'. Do you think that hungry old bear who hasn't eaten for fourteen years or more is going to give a damn about that poor little girl bee and her honey? Hell no. He's got that honey and is gone before she can even use her stinger. Now, do you think this sixteen year old boy you had tea with yesterday sat their prim and proper, sipping his tea, and his only thoughts were how delicious the tea was?"

Christina, with mouth open, sat in bewilderment listening to Sadie. "Well," Sadie clamored, one eyebrow raised.

Christina smiled. "To be honest," she said, knowing she was making a mistake, "I did see him looking down the front of my dress as I was pouring tea."

"See!" Sadie remarked, triumphantly shaking her finger. "One moment his eyes are looking down your dress, and the next, his hand will be up it. Now don't get me wrong. I think it all sounds pretty interesting. But I also think from the way you have been acting, that it would tickle your fancy if he did tickle your fancy.

Christina sat in shock. What was Sadie saying? Was Sadie implying she would be interested in some passionate love affair with Hezekiah? Sadie had let her imagination run away with her. That was absolutely the furthermost thing from her mind.

Sadie glanced at the clock on the wall. "Damn. I was enjoying myself so much I lost track of time. I'm going to be late for my rendezvous with Parson Blackwell out at Twin Buttes." Sadie began to quickly powder her cheeks while still talking. "You run into some strange ones in this business, Christina. None of the girls will have anything to do with him. The whole time he's humping you, he's yelling and damning you to hell. I don't know, I guess he's practicing his sermon for Sunday. Actually, I find it a pleasant change from the usual grunting and groaning. You know variety is important, Christina. If I ever get married, I'm going to make my husband pay every night. That way, he'll think he's getting it from a whore." Sadie smiled. "Hell, I guess he would be. Anyway, I gotta' go." She stood and smoothed the wrinkles from her dress. "I hope the church took up a nice collection last Sunday." She laughed and winked, then rushed out the door.

Christina sat dumbfounded. She had heard more about Sadie's perspective on life in a few minutes than she would care to hear in a lifetime.

CHAPTER 13

The summer of sixty-four had arrived. School was out. Life could now be filled with days of adventure...or almost. Hezekiah and Isaac's fathers both agreed that the boys needed to learn a trade and develop good work ethics. It was decided their sons would work for them each morning during the summer.

Isaac and Hezekiah found this to be acceptable. They were to be paid for their work, and except for their chores, they would have the remainder of the day to themselves.

Isaac immediately began figuring if he could earn enough money to buy a rifle. Hezekiah was trying to decide what to buy for Christina. Isaac thought Hezekiah was crazy...a rifle being far more sensible.

One afternoon in late June, with chores done and the remainder of the day to themselves, Hezekiah and Isaac went in search of Eagle Feather, a common ritual they had undertaken on many afternoons. Not finding their old friend at the stables, they made their climb up the now familiar ridge.

It seemed unusual to the boys that Eagle Feather appeared to be waiting for them rather than in prayer with the Spirits.

"Were you waiting for us?" Isaac asked.

"I was."

128

"I suppose the Spirits told you we were coming," Isaac commented.

"Perhaps. Perhaps it was your noisy arrival." He smiled.

"Do the Spirits tell you everything?" Hezekiah asked.

"Enough. They have told me something you two might be interested in hearing."

"What's that?" Isaac asked.

"The Spirits have chosen names for both of you."

"What are they?" they both hollered at the same time.

"Wait. Not so fast." Eagle Feather motioned them to sit. They hurriedly gathered around him. "Among my people," he began slowly, his eyes carefully studying the boys' faces, "this is an important time in the life of a young brave. The names are not given for fun. It is an important responsibility. It is important that you do not bring shame upon your name, or the Spirits who have chosen the name. It is a name given in honor. It is important you understand this and are willing to accept the responsibility that comes with it." He paused, gazing at the two young braves. "You have doubt," he said, nodding his head. "That is good. It means you do understand. But you must not fear-only respect. The Spirits believe you are ready, or they wouldn't have chosen your names."

Eagle Feather pointed to the sky. "The Spirits have been watching you. They know who you are and what you can become. This is how your name is chosen. First, Isaac."

"Yes, sir," Isaac responded eagerly.

"You are clever and intelligent. You move cautiously and will stay within the territory that is familiar to you. You may venture out alone, but you prefer to be with others. You will become a good provider and be loyal to your family. The Spirits have chosen your name, Gray Wolf."

"Great. I like it. Gray Wolf. I'm Gray Wolf. It's good, huh, Hezekiah."

Hezekiah nodded. "It's a good name all right."

Eagle Feather smiled at Isaac's jubilation, and then becoming somber again, he stared silently at Hezekiah. Hezekiah shifted nervously from Eagle Feather's silence.

Eagle Feather placed his hand on Hezekiah's shoulder. "You my young brave say little. You always are watching and listening. You are more independent and often times welcome moments alone. You are more adventurous, but also very patient. You see life with great seriousness. Your few words are spoken with the seriousness you see through your watchful eyes. The Spirits have chosen your name as Silent Hawk."

Hezekiah remained still after hearing the words 'Silent Hawk'. Eagle Feather carefully watched the young brave's expression before continuing, "Your reaction was as I had expected. A hawk is regarded highly by the Spirits. It is mighty like a great warrior, and swift like the wind. You have been honored by the chosen name. The Spirits have also told me you will be faced with many difficult decisions. You must turn to your inner hawk to help you. Your careful judgment will be crucial."

Hezekiah shivered at the words. Eagle Feather raised his hand. "You must not fear your name, but take great pride.

****

Eagle Feather watched somberly as his two friends left. He did not share the same joy of his two friends. He slowly turned to the eastern horizon, raised his hands to the sky, and spoke to the Spirits. "I ask you, Great Spirits, give the young brave, Silent Hawk, the inner strength he will need to endure the pain and sorrow that your wisdom has told me he will face."

CHAPTER 14

The haunting words of Sadie continued to disturb Christina. Not only had Sadie insisted Hezekiah had more than a friendship in mind, but had even suggested Christina would welcome it.

Sadie had a great perception of people. She had often stated she could read people's minds like an open book. Sadie claimed it had always given her an advantage in her successful business ventures. Had Sadie only been teasing Christina...or had she read Christina's thoughts better than Christina could read them herself? Had Christina's loneliness and lack of companionship allowed her to fool herself?

Christina knew all to well her loneliness and desire for companionship, and no doubt, she had found satisfaction being admired as a woman. But could that be wrong? Any woman felt exhilarated by a man's attraction to her. Of course, Hezekiah wasn't really a man yet.

Christina began to fear that somehow she had allowed herself to cross that forbidden barrier that even raised Sadie's eyebrows. No! Sadie was wrong this time. Christina knew she sought only a friendship. But then, even if Sadie was wrong about her, had she given a false pretense without consideration of Hezekiah's feeling? The last thing she ever wanted to do was hurt him.

By their next planned afternoon social, Christina had become more nervous than before their first social. How would Hezekiah act? How would she act?

She decided to serve cider because of the warm summer weather, and molasses cookies because of Hezekiah's comment about liking molasses. She chose her wardrobe more carefully, deciding on a dress with a higher neckline. It might be obvious, but much safer, she concluded.

Christina waited for two o'clock, uncertain if she wanted time to rush by or stand still. Then the knock sounded at the door. She jumped, almost as though it was unexpected. She felt her muscles tense as she moved with reservation towards the door.

Hezekiah stood bashfully in the doorway, hat in one hand and a colorful array of wild flowers in the other. As usual, she was the first to speak. "Good afternoon, Hezekiah. My what beautiful flowers."

Hezekiah wiped his face with his sleeve. "They're for you, ma'am, I mean Christina. I thought you might like them."

"I do. Thank you," she said, accepting the flowers.

Hezekiah sat patiently watching her as she scurried about looking for her vase to display them. She felt self conscious, sensing his eyes on her every move. What was he thinking? Was his bear raging wildly inside him?

"It's so seldom I get flowers, I never know where to find my vase."

"Don't worry about the flowers. I can always pick you more," he said as she continued her search. "Maybe I can help you," he added, rising from his chair.

"No. I'll find it," she answered curtly as she stretched to look in a high cupboard.

Hezekiah quickly sat back down. Christina quickly realized her rude tone of voice. She could see his troubled look. "I'm sorry," she quickly responded. "These flowers are so beautiful and I'm so

132

embarrassed by my lack of organization. Maybe you can help me. I think I see it on the top shelf and I believe you're taller than me."

Hezekiah quickly responded to her desperate call as he proudly reached the vase and handed it to her. "Gee, I think this vase is too pretty for these flowers," he said.

"Oh goodness, not at all. You're much too kind"

Christina arranged the flowers in the vase and placed them on the table to insure Hezekiah that she was pleased with them. She served the cider and cookies and soon she was seated comfortably across from him.

Hezekiah began to excitedly tell Christina about Eagle Feather and the Indian names that were chosen for he and Isaac by the Spirits.

"Silent Hawk sounds like a brave and important name," she commented with a smile. "Eagle Feather must think a great deal of you."

"Eagle Feather says Silent Hawk is a very proud and brave name. I'm not sure why he gave it to me."

"That's quite a responsibility to place on a young gentleman."

"Yeah. I've never done anything brave or important, but Eagle Feather says that the Spirits said that someday I would. I think he was just being kind though."

"I'll bet he's right. He sounds like an intelligent man. So what does your family think of your new name?"

"Oh, I haven't told them."

"You haven't?"

"My father would probably think it was all right, but Mother would think it was uncivilized. She thinks the west is no place to raise a family. She says there's too much violence and bad influences."

"Honestly, I would have to agree with her. I guess that's a woman's feelings. I would well imagine she would object to our friendship. She doesn't know, right?"

Hezekiah hesitated, nervously shifting in his chair. "If she knew you like I do, I'm sure she wouldn't mind."

Christina laughed. "You put that very diplomatically, Hezekiah...or should I call you, Silent Hawk."

Hezekiah grinned. "Hezekiah will do."

"The way you have a way with words, I don't understand why you don't have a girlfriend."

"No. Anyway, there's only a couple of girls about my age and they're both homely. Besides, they're usually acting stupid. My father says all girls go through that stage, but someday they'll become beautiful women."

Christina laughed. "I guess all of us girls were ugly ducklings."

Hezekiah became embarrassed. "Oh, I didn't mean you. Honest."

Christina could not resist the tease. "Do you mean the ugly duckling or the beautiful woman?"

Hezekiah's began wiping his face with his sleeve. "Oh, I mean the ugly duckling. You're the most beautiful woman..." He suddenly stopped.

"I'm sorry. I shouldn't have teased you so. Anyway, thanks for the compliment even though I forced it from you." They both began laughing, and suddenly, Christina found herself at ease, and enjoying their conversation.

The remainder of the afternoon passed without incident and as Hezekiah left later that day, Christina was convinced Sadie was wrong. Bear or no bear, they had a delightful friendship and no more."

CHAPTER 15

Hezekiah reluctantly let his mother finish knotting his tie. He hated ties, particularly when it was so hot. And he hated the wool, tweed coat he had to wear to church on Sunday mornings. The church would be unbearably hot. It was always hot or cold inside, and today, with a July heat wave, it would be a scorcher.

But what he disliked most about church was Parson Blackwell. Hezekiah would shiver when the Parson glared relentlessly through his beady coal black eyes while his tongue lashed out like a soldier's sharpened sword, ripping the helpless parishioners to shreds. One would think everyone was destined for hell as he bellowed out his damnation of fire and brimstone.

The sermon would reach a fever pitch as the donation plate was passed, and as the plate returned to the front of the church, the Parson's eyes would stare in absolute disgust at the insufficient offerings.

The Parson had arrived in Virginia City about three months earlier. He rode into town, dressed in his black coat and hat. The church not having a preacher, delightfully took him into their fold.

Isaac, not caring for the Parson either, had suggested because of his evil appearance, that he might be one of the outlaws returning to haunt the folks of Virginia City.

Hezekiah tugged at his tie as the Templeton family entered the sweltering church. As usual, it was standing room only for the men in the small church. Sarah and Cynthia made their way to the benches in front, while Sam and Hezekiah took their usual places in the back with the other men. Isaac and his father had already arrived and were standing slightly in front and to the left of Hezekiah. Isaac smiled and made a choking motion with his tie. Hezekiah grinned and nodded in agreement.

The women's fans were waving briskly as Parson Blackwell entered the side door and stepped to the podium. He slowly stroked his dark beard and stared ruthlessly at his parishioners. He looks more evil than usual, Hezekiah concluded. The heat must have him primed for a fiery sermon today.

The services began with a quiet prayer and two verses of 'Rock of Ages'. The sermon started slowly and began to build. And the higher the level of the Parson's voice, the faster the women swished their fans and the more the men shuffled their feet. The heat was almost intolerable as Hezekiah flapped the lapels of his coat.

Then without warning, Hezekiah felt something wet smack against his forehead. Startled by the sudden disruption, he grasped it. It was a spitball. He held the soggy wad of paper in his hand, looking in the direction of its flight. Isaac had his hand cupped over his mouth to retain his laughter.

Isaac is not going to get away with this one, Hezekiah decided. He would wait for the opportunity to seek his revenge.

It soon came. Parson Blackwell was in excellent form as he reached a booming pitch in preparation for the passing of the plate. No one would be watching. Hezekiah took careful aim and flung the wad at Isaac, but Isaac had been anticipating Hezekiah's move. As the soggy wad sailed through the air, Isaac stepped back. The misguided spitball sailed past its intended victim and landed directly on Mrs. Dalton's cheek. She screamed, bringing the church, including Parson Blackwell, to instant silence.

Mrs. Dalton pulled the slimy object from her face, gasped, and flung it to the floor. Her head turned in the direction of the assault. The eyes of everyone followed her stare as it stopped on Hezekiah.

Hezekiah felt the room become more intense with heat as he tried to slither out of view of the penetrating eyes, but it was too late. He had been caught like a beaver in a trap. From the expressions on everyone's face, it was apparent no one doubted what had been done, and who had done the wicked deed.

Hezekiah caught a glimpse of Parson Blackwell's glaring stare. Hezekiah, with ears on fire, stared helplessly at the floor, but he could still feel the penetrating eyes of the Parson.

An eternity seemed to pass. Why didn't the Parson resume his sermon? Hezekiah began to realize how it would feel to spend an eternity in the burning hell.

At last, the Parson's voice boomed through the church like a cannon that Hezekiah was sure could be heard throughout Virginia City.

"Satin is all around us!" The words echoed through Hezekiah head. The Parson continued to bellow, "He enters our church and disrupts the glorification of our Lord. He destroys the essential fibers of our families by entering into our children to do his evil work."

Damn, Parson, it was just a spitball, Hezekiah thought. He tried to shut out the words, but they kept coming. I'm not the devil, he thought. If anyone is evil, it's the Parson. Why can't everyone see that? The Parson's words continued their brutal assault. Hezekiah swore that someday he would prove to everyone that he, Silent Hawk, was good, not evil, and that Parson Blackwell was the one that worked for Satin.

After church, Hezekiah was promptly informed by his totally humiliated mother that she had never been so embarrassed in her entire life; and that her greatest fear of raising her children in this evil, horrible land was coming true.

Upon their arrival home, Hezekiah received a stern lecture from his father; although Hezekiah was convinced, by the look in his father's eyes, that his father truly did not think the church fiasco was so terribly wrong. Cynthia's smirk showed her enjoyment of Hezekiah's problem as she stood innocently next to her mother.

But the worst part, to Hezekiah's total dismay, was that he was restricted to home for three weeks except when he was helping his father. A beating would be far more appropriate, he thought. Then the horrible realization hit him. He would miss his scheduled social with Christina on Tuesday, and it would be three terrible weeks until he could see her again.

****

Isaac reluctantly came by to see Hezekiah the day after church. Hezekiah was in back chopping wood.

"Three weeks!" Isaac said when he heard the news, and expressed his dissatisfaction by kicking a block of wood. "Maybe if I fess up, it'll help."

"It won't help. It'll just get you in trouble too." Hezekiah tossed the ax to the ground. "But you can help."

"Sure. Anything," Isaac quickly offered, trying to ease his guilt.

"I'm suppose to see Christina tomorrow afternoon for tea."

"And," Isaac said, looking at his friend curiously.

"I need you to give her a message that I can't come."

"I don't think so," Isaac said, picking up the ax. "Besides, what would I say?"

"Tell her I can't come," Hezekiah said irritably as he grabbed the ax from Isaac's hand. "You got me in this mess. It's the least you can do."

"Would I tell her why?" Isaac asked, reaching for the ax again.

Hezekiah pulled the ax away. "No, you're not going to tell her why. Tell her I'm helping my father for the next three weeks, and I can't come." He swung the ax with all his force on a block of wood. Isaac danced out of the way of the flying chips. "So, will you do it?" Hezekiah asked, holding the ax in a threatening position on his shoulder.

138

"I guess. But why don't you write a note that I can give her. That way you can tell her exactly what you want to say."

Hezekiah dropped the ax. "Yeah. That's a great idea." He started for the house, but stopped. "Damn, Mother's inside. I can't go in there to get a pen and some paper. She'll wonder what I'm up too."

"I'll go home and get some. If my mother asks, I'll just tell her you need it."

"Yeah...but hurry up before Christina goes to work."

Isaac soon returned. "She didn't even notice me," he said smugly, handing the quilt pen, inkbottle, and paper to Hezekiah.

"Chop wood while I write so Mother doesn't get suspicious." Hezekiah sat down and began to think. Slowly and neatly, he began to write.

Dear Christina,

With much regret I cannot come tomorrow for tea. My father is very busy and I have to help him for the next three weeks. I shall see you then.

He stopped. Should he write 'with love'? Would that be too bold? He thought for a moment, finished writing and neatly folded the note.

"Okay. Here. Take it." He handed the note to Isaac. "Don't read it either."

Isaac nodded and left.

****

When Isaac reached the bottom of the hill, he looked back. He was out of sight. He opened the note and read it. "With love," he murmured, grabbing his mouth as he snickered.

Isaac knocked lightly on the door. No answer. Maybe she had already left for work, he thought. He knocked louder.

"Just a minute," a woman's voice called from inside.

Hell, maybe she's busy with a man in there, he thought.

The door opened. "Hi," Christina said, her face looking puzzled. He suddenly realized why Hezekiah was in love with her. She was beautiful with soft red lips, sparkling eyes and her hair raised, showing the gentle contour of her neck and shoulders above her low cut dress.

"I have a message from Hezekiah," Isaac whispered.

She bent forward. "I'm sorry. I didn't hear you."

Isaac's eyes immediately fixed on her breasts-softly curving together into a valley. He couldn't remember what that was called. He gulped. "I have a message from Hezekiah," Isaac repeated as he handed her the note.

"Thank you. You're his friend, Isaac, aren't you?"

"Yes, ma'am."

"I've seen you around, but I never had the pleasure of meeting you." Christina smiled and he automatically smiled back. She opened the note and began to read while Isaac stared at her breasts. He was surprised by the sudden tightness in his pants. He nervously began backing away.

"Wait," she said. "That is if you don't mind. I'll answer it and you can return it for me."

"No. I'll wait. Take a lot of time if you like. I have all day. I don't mind. Really."

"Oh, I'm sure a minute will do," she said with a smile. "Come inside."

Her smile only made the tightness worse.

Isaac stood by the door as Christina quickly wrote her reply. He could see the gentle jiggling of her breasts as she wrote.

"There," she said, suddenly rising to her feet, startling Isaac. She handed him the note. "Thank you for waiting, Isaac. It was very kind of you."

****

As Christina closed the door, she smiled, shaking her head and murmuring out loud, "Isaac's bear is certainly restless."

****

Once Isaac was out of sight, he stopped to read the note. No, he thought, Hezekiah was his friend. Besides he was already feeling guilty about his reaction towards Christina. He could still vividly see her breasts jiggling so delicately as though wanting to be touched. It was enough to drive someone crazy. And Hezekiah got to look at them all the time.

Isaac hurried on up the hill. Hezekiah was anxiously waiting his return. "What'd she say?" he quickly asked, then seeing the paper, "She wrote me a note?"

Isaac nodded and handed it to Hezekiah. He was glad the bulge had left.

Hezekiah walked a short distance away and began reading the note. He smiled and looked up. "What are you staring at?" Hezekiah said defensively.

"Nothing," Isaac said, shaking his head. "What'd she say?"

"Nothing."

"Why you grinning then?"

"'Cause."

Isaac shrugged his shoulders. "I'm going," he said with disgust. "I'll see you tomorrow if I'm not too busy."

Some friend, Isaac thought. He could have read the note if he wanted too. Maybe he would be too busy tomorrow having tea with Christina.

****

After Isaac left, Hezekiah quickly began re-reading the note.

Dearest Hezekiah,

I will miss our tea, but it will make the next one more special.

Fondest love,

Christina

'Fondest love'. He had only said 'with love'. 'Fondest' meant the most. She said she loved him the most. The world suddenly did not seem all that dismal. If he needed to wait, he could wait three weeks for Christina...forever if he had too.

****

Isaac came back the next day...and the next. A week passed and Hezekiah was once again faced with the dreaded arrival of Sunday and a renewed encounter with Parson Blackwell.

He watched Parson Blackwell take the podium. His dark eyes scanned the parishioners, stopping momentarily at Hezekiah before moving on.

As usual, he started the sermon slowly and began to build. Hezekiah soon found the Parson's words were directed towards him, only today the Parson had time to prepare. The Parson had found a sinner and he was going to make full use of it.

Another week passed, and the Parson continued his onslaught towards the church's lone sinner. Hezekiah was now certain he would be faced with his sin until he perished to hell.

Another week came, and another familiar sermon by the Parson. By now, Hezekiah was beginning to believe the Parson...he was surely destined for the burning fires of hell, which he was convinced would be a relief from the Parson's fiery sermons. The only sense of satisfaction Hezekiah felt: the restriction was over and he could see Christina again.

****

Tuesday afternoon, after reading his note for the hundredth time, Hezekiah carefully folded it, and proceeded down the hill towards Christina's. He was unaware that Isaac was watching him from a nearby boulder.

142

Christina seemed pleased to see him and to his delight, Christina invited him inside, informing him she had the day off...which Hezekiah already knew.

She sat the tea on the table. "So, your father has been busy. I bet he's glad he has you to help him."

Hezekiah could feel the guilt building for lying to Christina. He had never lied to her before, and he felt terrible. But if she knew the truth, she would laugh at him for being a child.

Then, almost as though his mind was being picked clean, the words burst from his mouth, "I wasn't helping my father. That's not why I couldn't come."

"Really," she said, her eyes open wide with surprise.

Hezekiah wiped his mouth with his sleeve. "I'm sorry I lied. I only thought you would think I was terrible."

She reached across the table, patting his hand. "You don't have to give me a reason."

"I got in trouble at church and my parents restricted me to the house." He felt embarrassed. He was sure she would burst into laughter at any moment, telling him to leave and never come back, and that she wanted nothing to do with an unruly child.

"My goodness. What happened?" she asked, her face showing concern. Once he had confessed, the words seemed to unravel from his mouth like a dropped ball of yarn.

Hezekiah conveyed his horrible story, and was pleased that she didn't laugh, but instead showed a sincere concern.

"...And Parson Blackwell, each Sunday, keeps looking at me when he talks about sin," he said finishing his story. "He'll never stop. I know it."

"Parson Blackwell," she said out loud, squinting her eyes. "Why does that name sound so familiar?" She stood. "Where have I heard that before? Let me get us some more tea," she said as she carried the cups to the stove. She soon returned, carrying the steaming cups. "Sadie!" she shouted, almost dropping the cups.

Hezekiah jumped from the chair. "What's wrong?" he called, hurrying to her aid. He took one of the cups and sat it down. Christina's body shook with laughter. Hezekiah watched her in disbelief.

She was still laughing as she seated herself. Hezekiah still dumbfounded, watched her every move, waiting for an explanation for her unexpected outburst.

"I may be wrong for telling you," she said, still giggling. She leaned forward, her eyes sparkling with excitement. "I know something about Parson Blackwell...well, that I guess only Sadie and I know." She raised her eyebrows, showing a look of satisfaction.

What could her and Sadie possibly know about the Parson? Hezekiah wondered. He was surprised they would even know him.

"Every Saturday afternoon," she began, leaning further forward, "Sadie meets Parson Blackwell out at Twin Buttes."

"What for?" Hezekiah asked innocently.

Christina appeared embarrassed. "You know. Messing around."

"You mean..."

"Yes. Every Saturday that I know of."

"Are you sure?...The Parson?...He and Sadie?"

"I swear. Sadie told me herself."

"Wow," Hezekiah said, shaking his head. "Boy, if the rest of the church knew, they would think I was a saint in comparison." Hezekiah fell back against the chair.

"I don't care what you do with the information, if anything, but you mustn't tell anyone where you heard it. Sadie would kill me."

"Oh, I won't tell...Can I tell Isaac?"

"Okay, Isaac, but no one else. Promise?"

"You bet. Wait 'till Isaac hears this."

****

It was unusual for Hezekiah to be glad when his social with Christina was over, but today he could hardly wait. He immediately began his search for Isaac. He found Isaac on the hillside, tossing rocks at gophers.

"I wish I had a gun," Isaac said with disgust as he flung a rock at a gopher, missing his target by several feet. The gopher, standing precariously on its hind feet, looked uncaring at Isaac. "I'd blow their damn, smug heads off."

"Forget the gophers," Hezekiah said, unable to contain his excitement.

"What are you so happy about?" Isaac said, looking at the broad grin on his friend's face. "Christina kiss you or something?"

"No," Hezekiah answered, not giving any thought to his friend's remark, "but she told me something you're not going to believe."

"Yeah. What?" he replied, not yet convinced.

As Hezekiah relayed the unbelievable news, Isaac listened with his mouth hanging open.

"Are you sure she's not teasing you?" Isaac responded when Hezekiah finished.

"No. It's true. But now I can't figure out what to do about it," Hezekiah said, flopping to the ground. "Any ideas?"

"Maybe we should just tell someone," Isaac offered, tossing another rock at a nearby gopher. "Scared that one," he said proudly.

"If we did that, no one would believe us. Besides, they'd want to know where we heard it. I promised Christina. Besides, they'd want to know how I know Christina." Hezekiah cupped his hands over his face, trying to think.

"We'll tell the sheriff there's a dead body out there," Isaac suggested. "When he goes out there, he'll see them."

Hezekiah frowned. "Yeah. Great. He goes out there and doesn't find a body, he'll tar and feather us, especially if the Parson isn't there."

"Okay. So we can go and watch anyway."

"I plan on that, but I'd like to get even with the old Parson and get him caught."

"We got a few days. We'll think of something."

"I hope so. I want to get even with that mean old Parson so bad I can taste it," Hezekiah said, spitting angrily, then quickly wiping his chin.

****

Each afternoon, Hezekiah and Isaac would meet to see if the other had come up with a plan for the Parson, and each afternoon they would part with no solution. Saturday arrived. Hezekiah, although excited by the day's event, felt frustrated by the lack of imagination of he and Isaac. They were letting the opportunity of their lives slip away.

After gulping down his noon meal to the dissatisfaction of his mother, Hezekiah quickly left to meet Isaac. They hastened along their two-mile journey to the north of town, staying off the road so as not to be seen. Hezekiah was relieved when they reached Twin Buttes to find that the Parson or Sadie had not yet arrived. They found a good observation point in some tall grass at the base of Twin Buttes where they could see the road in the distance and most of the surrounding area.

"I couldn't sleep last night," Isaac said as they patiently waited for the arrival of Sadie and the Parson.

"I just wish we had a plan," Hezekiah said, peering through the tall grass. "Look!" Hezekiah pointed to the south on the road. "That's got to be the Parson. He's all in black."

The two observers slid deeper into the grass as the rider looked cautiously around before turning off the road. He started coming straight for them. The closer he came, the lower the boys slid into the grass. He was only two hundred feet away when he finally stopped and dismounted.

"Whew. He scared me," Hezekiah whispered. "I thought for sure he was going to come right over us."

The Parson began to pace, mumbling something undetectable to the boys. With Hezekiah leading the way, they slid into a shallow gully and moved closer. The Parson was still pacing and mumbling.

146

They now had a poor view of the road, but they caught a glimpse of another rider coming. "It's a woman. It must be Sadie," Isaac said as he raised his head to get a better look.

"Get your head down," Hezekiah whispered nervously, poking Isaac.

Shortly, Sadie came into view. The Parson stopped pacing and stood motionless watching her.

"Hi, Parson," Sadie said, sliding from her saddle. "Nice day for a little sunbathing, wouldn't you say?" She laughed, but the Parson continued to stare, never answering. Sadie shrugged her shoulders. "Feeling a little grumpy today, Parson?" She slid her blanket from the horse. "I can see it's going to be one hell of a ride today." Still the Parson stood silent. She unfolded her blanket and carefully laid it on the ground and smoothed it. "I hope there aren't any damn rocks under here this time," she said as she began to unbutton her dress. "Of course, what the hell do you care, you're always on top." The Parson remained motionless watching her.

"I wish I could see his face," Isaac whispered.

"To hell with his face," Hezekiah answered, straining to get a better look as Sadie's dress slid to the ground.

She stepped from her dress and carefully laid it on a nearby bush. "This should damn both of us to hell," Sadie said, smiling as she began removing her undergarments. She slid the top down, bringing her breasts into full view. She cupped them in her hands and jiggled them.

"Damn hell. They're more beautiful than the picture in the book," Isaac said in a squeaky voice.

Hezekiah ignored his friend as his eyes, never blinking, were riveted on the unbelievable scene before him.

Sadie slid the remainder of her clothes from her well-endowed body and hung them carefully on the bush. She stretched out on the blanket, resting on one elbow. "Your move, Parson," she said and blew him a kiss.

After a short moment, the Parson removed his black hat and tossed it to the ground. "Damn you woman!" his voice thundered. "You're going to get me sent straight to the burning fires."

"My, my, Parson. Is that a proper thing to say to a lady?"

The Parson mumbled something and moved with disgust behind a bush. Partially hidden, he began to disrobe. When he reappeared, Hezekiah stared in astonishment. He had always feared the Parson hidden behind his black suit, but now as he looked at the same man naked, he no longer felt afraid. The Parson looked like a fragile, delicate piece of pottery that would shatter at the slightest jar.

Isaac was covering his mouth, his body shaking with laughter. The Parson strolled deliberately towards Sadie still lying on the blanket. He stopped in front of her, resting his hands on his hips.

"Come on, Parson," she said rolling her eyes tantalizing at him and patting the blanket. "I must say you look like you're ready. Tell me how bad I am."

"Damn you, woman. The fires are surely burning," he said, dropping to his knees and then falling on top of Sadie.

Hezekiah could hear Sadie giggling as the Parson began his sermon. All Hezekiah could see now was Sadie's legs and the parson's white butt bouncing up and down as it glistened in the bright sun light.

Suddenly, Hezekiah had an idea. "Isaac. The clothes. Let's steal the Parson's clothes."

Isaac's face brightened, then changed to concern. "Don't you think they'll see us?"

"Right about now, I don't think they'd notice a herd of wild horses coming through," Hezekiah said as he observed the hysteria below him.

Quickly, on hands and knees, they moved through the tall grass into the gully. They came in from behind the trees and bushes and grabbed the Parson's clothes, leaving only his hat. They took one last longing look and departed.

148

They ran the entire two miles back to town. Once they reached the edge of town, they slowed to a walk. They were panting so hard they could hardly speak.

"Now what the hell shall we do with them?" Isaac asked, laughing at each opportunity he could catch his breath.

"I don't know. Let me think." Hezekiah thought he would vomit from being so nervous. "If somebody sees us, we'll get in trouble. Wait, I know. We'll leave them at the front door of the church."

"But when he comes back, he'll see them and nobody will know."

Hezekiah smiled. "He'll know. Besides he has to come back through town."

Isaac agreed and they headed for the church. Being careful not to be seen, they left the clothes at the front door, and found a place to hide behind some rocks and waited.

Isaac was in deep thought as the time slowly passed. "How old do you think Sadie is?" he suddenly asked.

"I don't know. Maybe forty."

I always thought when women got older, they weren't as pretty anymore."

"Do you think she's pretty?"

"Yeah. Don't you?" Isaac asked, looking at Hezekiah in disbelief.

"I guess. I wonder if all women are that beautiful without clothes?" Hezekiah questioned thoughtfully.

"Geez, do you think so? We've waited here so long. I wish we had stayed longer," Isaac said sounding disappointed.

"The Parson was blocking our view anyway."

Yeah, I suppose," Isaac answered, disappointment still in his voice. "I didn't think it was supposed to take so long."

Hezekiah chuckled. "He's probably trying to figure out how to get back to town. Besides, you know how long the Parson's sermons are."

"He's coming now," Isaac said, pointing towards a small rise.

They both began chuckling. The Parson, sitting atop his horse, wore only his black hat and Sadie's blanket that was wrapped around him. He stopped in front of his cabin by the church and was about to enter, when he spotted his clothes. He looked around, rushed to the church door and bent to pick them up. The blanket came loose and fell to the ground. Isaac and Hezekiah grabbed their mouths, trying to hold in the laughter. Parson Blackwell quickly grabbed the blanket and clothes, and raced inside his cabin. The entertainment was more than Hezekiah and Isaac had hoped for as they rolled on the ground with hysteria. But now they would have to face tomorrow and endure the Parson's sermon.

****

The next day at church, Hezekiah took his normal place at the back of the building with his father. He rubbed his sweaty palms nervously waiting for the Parson's entry. Isaac was casting nervous glances his way. They had their fun, but what would the Parson have in store for them.

The Parson entered through the side door as usual. Hezekiah studied him closely as the man dressed in black headed for the podium. He seemed unusually nervous as his eyes quickly scanned the church, rather than his usual glaring stare.

He cleared his throat. As he spoke, his voice sounded soft and unsure. The rest of the congregation began to cast curious glances at one another. Hezekiah listened in shock to Parson Blackwell's words speaking of forgiveness, rather than damnation.

After church, Hezekiah walked quietly behind his parents. "The Parson's sermon was certainly different today," he heard his mother say.

"I have to admit it was a pleasant change, too," his father added. "I actually could say I found it enjoyable for a change."

"Sam. I hope you're not talking blasphemy."

"Sarah, I'm just speaking the truth. The Lord would appreciate a little more of it, I'm sure."

****

150

The following Sunday, the congregation waited for the arrival of Parson Blackwell, but instead of the Parson, Jack Summers, a deacon of the church, entered the side door and moved slowly to the podium.

"I have an announcement to make," he said, rubbing his chin. "Do to an unexpected emergency, Parson Blackwell has had to leave town and regretfully will not be returning. Now if you all will join me in singing 'Amazing Grace'."

Hezekiah suddenly did not feel well. He had meant no harm. As the words 'a wretch like me' filled the room, Hezekiah wondered if Deacon Summers had especially picked the song for him.

****

The next week when Hezekiah saw Christina, he told her what happened.

Christina rolled her eyes. "I know all about it from Sadie."

"Was she mad?"

"No. I think she was a little upset she lost a customer, but she said it was the funniest damn thing she'd ever seen. She said it was worth a fortune just to see it."

"It was funny and all. It really was. But I didn't mean to hurt anyone. I thought I would feel good about it, but I don't."

"Hey, don't be so hard on yourself. He was probably a good man that went off the straight and narrow. Maybe he learned his lesson and will be a good preacher somewhere else. Maybe you saved him."

Christina made sense. It certainly sounded good to Hezekiah. "Thanks, Christina. I feel a lot better now." Hezekiah took a deep sigh. Maybe Silent Hawk had done something good. Eagle Feather would be proud of him...except Silent Hawk was not about to tell Eagle Feather...or ever tell anyone.

CHAPTER 16

Parson Blackwell was gone, yet it seemed to Hezekiah as soon as one problem was solved, another appeared from nowhere. With the end of summer, school began.

It meant Hezekiah's time with Christina was now sorely limited. If that wasn't bad enough, school also meant monotonous hours listening to Miss Harrelson, the new schoolmarm. Miss Harrelson, somewhat in the same fashion as Parson Blackwell, had mysteriously arrived in town and was immediately accepted by the community. For whatever reason, Miss Harrelson quickly conveyed the first day of school that she considered the older boys to be troublemakers and was not about to tolerate their heathen ways. Although she never outwardly stated so, she also considered these same troublemakers to be her servants. "You will thank me someday," she insisted. "It will build your character. Make you useful in life."

Among the character building tasks she so generously assigned the troublemakers, consisting of Hezekiah, Isaac and Herbert Donaldson, were painting, cleaning and, by late September, chopping wood for the potbelly stove.

Herbert Donaldson was still another problem for Hezekiah, as well as Isaac, and all the other children in school. Herbert had recently arrived in Virginia City. Nobody liked him and that included Isaac and Hezekiah. He was large in size and used his size to bully everyone. Isaac and Hezekiah were no exceptions. Herbert had remained unchallenged. Only Miss Harrelson escaped his constant torment.

One day in early October, the three boys were assigned to chopping wood after school.

"This isn't fair," Isaac complained as he tossed the ax to the ground. "We have to do chores at home and here, too. At least she could let us do them during school."

Hezekiah was loading his arms with wood. Herbert was leaning against the schoolhouse wall, his usual position during chore time.

"Hell, it ain't so bad," Herbert said, stuffing a chaw of tobacco in his mouth. "If I thought it was, I'd tell the old hag to go to hell."

"You never do anything," Isaac said angrily, flopping himself down on the chopping block. "Of course you don't think it's so bad."

"That's right, runt. I do as I damn well please." Herbert spit. It landed only an inch from Isaac foot. "And that's the way it's going to stay."

Isaac stared silently at the spit at his foot. Slowly he raised his head. Hezekiah could see the anger in his companion's eyes and knew Isaac was about to speak his piece. Herbert was smiling in anticipation of the confrontation. "Damn, I missed," Herbert said, wiping his mouth.

Isaac with jaws clenched, slowly rose to his feet. "Don't ever do that again you blow hard...And it's your turn to chop some damn wood."

Herbert's smile disappeared as he stepped away from the wall. "Listen, you little runt, I ain't taking any guff off you. I'll kick your ass between your eyes."

Isaac was now out of control. "You're a bully and I'm damn sick and tired of it."

Herbert was moving closer to Isaac. "Oh, you scare me, you little twerp. Show me what you're aiming to do about it."

Hezekiah dropped his load of wood, and selected a nice size piece. He began moving around Herbert, until Herbert was directly between he and Isaac. "All Isaac said was that it was your turn to chop wood," Hezekiah said, hoping his voice would not give away the way he felt inside. "That's all."

Herbert, surprised by the confrontation from the rear, quickly turned to face Hezekiah. "This ain't none of your business. This is between the runt and me."

"I don't see it that way." Hezekiah was having difficulty controlling his shivering body. "I think it's your turn to chop wood too."

"Okay, if that's the way you want it. I'll kick your ass first then." Herbert began to slowly move towards Hezekiah.

Isaac picked up a piece of wood.

Hezekiah grinned. "I don't think you'll kick anybody's ass. Have you ever seen what a small, swift wolverine can do to a big, slow moving bear? He'll tear the bear to pieces."

Herbert laughed, but Hezekiah could detect the first sign of uncertainty on Herbert's face. "Okay," Herbert said, "you think you can whip me, Mr. Wolverine?"

"I know two can," Hezekiah answered, nodding towards Isaac.

Herbert glanced at Isaac, and then looked back at Hezekiah. It was becoming more obvious that Herbert's confidence was shaken. "Two against one don't make for a fair fight."

"Fair." Hezekiah forced a confident laugh. "Who said anything about fair. In the end, winning is the only damn thing that counts around here."

Herbert took a step towards Hezekiah testing his determination, but Hezekiah held his ground as he raised his stick of wood.

"Damn, you guys are crazy." Herbert glanced to Isaac, then back to Hezekiah. Everyone stood poised. Herbert spit and wiped his mouth nervously.

They stood like two armies...neither wanting to attack...neither wanting to retreat...a standoff that Hezekiah wondered if it would ever end. It eventually took a third, more powerful army to end the standoff.

154

"For heaven's sake, what are you boys up to?" Miss Harrelson's voice rang out. She was standing at the corner of the building, hands on hips, her face scrunched into a frightening scowl.

"Nothing, Miss Harrelson," Hezekiah said with a squeaky voice. He cleared his throat. "Isaac and I were just bringing in a load of wood we chopped. Herbert insisted he wanted to chop another load."

"That's right, Miss Harrelson," Herbert said, glancing angrily at Hezekiah. "They thought we had enough, but I wanted to chop another load."

Way to tell the old hag to go to hell, Hezekiah thought as he began loading his arms with wood.

"Well, hurry up and quit wasting the day. You boys act like it was a devilish sin to do a little work."

Herbert's big mouth had caused him to chop another load of wood. Hezekiah tried to contain his laughter as he and Isaac finished loading their arms with firewood.

Hezekiah and Isaac quickly unloaded the wood in the wood box and left. They could hear the sound of the ax out back as they raced from school.

"Do you think he'll try to get even with us?" Isaac asked, obviously still shaken.

"No, I don't think so. He knows we'll stand together now. Unless he has a sure thing, he'll back down." Hezekiah could only hope he was right.

CHAPTER 17

Hezekiah reluctantly crawled from his warm bed. A northern storm was moving in, and although a raging fire burned in the fireplace, he could still feel the sting of the cold cutting at him in his curtained off corner of the room. He shivered as his bare feet touched the cold floor. He quickly dressed and stood in front of the welcoming warm fire. Only the anticipation of breakfast diverted him away from the fire.

Hezekiah sat down to a breakfast of flapjacks and salted pork. His nostrils flared at the pleasant aroma of molasses syrup as he abundantly poured it on his flapjacks under the watchful eyes of Cynthia.

"Mother. Hezekiah is using all the syrup." Hezekiah scowled at his sister sitting across from him. "Well, you are," she emphasized smugly.

"There's plenty left, Mother," he called out, holding up the jar, trying to divert her attention from his plate filled with syrup.

But the diversion failed. "Hezekiah, you know supplies will be short this winter," his mother said, scolding him as she took his plate and poured the excess syrup onto Cynthia's flapjacks. "With this storm coming, we surely won't see another freight wagon until spring," she continued, setting his much emptier plate in front of him.

"Cynthia, I want you to take some cough medicine. You were coughing quite a bit last night." She felt Cynthia's forehead. "You have a little fever, too. Maybe, you should stay home today."

"No. Please, Mother. I want to go to school. Miss Harrelson promised I could read today."

Miss Harrelson. All the more reason to stay at home, Hezekiah thought, staring with disgust at Cynthia. How irritating. She's just trying to be Mother's pet. Why would anyone go to school if they could stay home? But he knew Cynthia would get her way. She always did.

But it did give him an idea. Maybe he could make being sick work for him. With his sickest face, he hoarsely pleaded his case. "Mother, I'm not feeling good either. Maybe I should stay home."

He glanced at his mother. Her silent stare quickly convinced him it had been in vain.

After finishing breakfast, Hezekiah and Cynthia bundled warmly, and headed into the crisp morning air. A cold wind slapped with annoyance at Hezekiah's face. He was still irritated by Cynthia telling on him, and once outside, quickly confronted her. "You're a tattle tale and a spoiled brat!"

"I am not!" she said, looking confidently at him. "You're just jealous because Mother likes me better."

"She does not! She just feels sorry for you because nobody likes you."

She smiled arrogantly at him. "She does like me better. I'm her favorite."

Hezekiah angered by Cynthia's remark, quickly walked ahead of her. The worst part, he felt she was right.

He could hear her voice singing behind him, "Mother likes me better. Mother likes me better."

He hated her. How come he had to be stuck with such a spoiled brat for a sister?

By the time they had arrived at school, Hezekiah felt numb from the cold and welcomed the comforting warm fire in the potbelly stove. He felt relieved that plenty of wood had been cut and stored.

As the morning progressed, Hezekiah could hear the storm building outside as the wind whistled around the cracks in the door. The raging storm left him feeling uneasy. He could not remember one so bad during the previous winter.

By noon, the full force of the storm had arrived. The lone window in the school rattled from the driving force of the wind. Everyone seemed on edge, even Miss Harrelson.

Hezekiah had also become concerned about Cynthia's increased coughing and her face had become quite flush, so when Miss Harrelson asked him take his sister home, Hezekiah anxiously agreed. He was glad to get out of school, but he also had to admit, he was more concerned about his sister.

Bundled, they headed into the blizzard. Hezekiah never imagined a storm could be so violent. He clutched tightly to his sister as they struggled slowly along, heads down, into the driving snow. Hezekiah had difficulty keeping his direction. Cynthia was sobbing. "We'll be home soon," he kept repeating. Any other time, he would have only felt disgust by her crying or complaining, but today he felt sorry for her. He only wanted to hurry home, so he could make her feel better.

They arrived home covered with snow frozen to their clothes and face. His mother, with a sense of urgency, immediately undressed Cynthia and put her to bed. Cynthia's face was bright red now, and her coughing had grown worse. He watched his mother move with precision, her face distorted with concern as she prepared some broth. "I knew I should have kept you home today. What was I thinking?"

As she began feeding broth to Cynthia, she looked with pleading eyes at Hezekiah. "I hate to ask you, Hezekiah, with the weather so bad, but I need to have you find Doc Stogner and your father."

"Is she going to be all right, Mother?"

The concerned look of his mother gave Hezekiah a frightening chill "Yes, but please hurry," she answered, trying to remain calm.

158

Hezekiah went back into the blizzard. His heart was pounding inside him. No matter what his mother said, Hezekiah knew Cynthia was very sick.

Hezekiah first went by Doc Stogner's house. His wife said he was on another call, but assured Hezekiah that she would send him to their home as soon as he returned. Hezekiah found his father building some new shelves at Pritchard's store.

Doc Stogner had just arrived at the Templeton home when Hezekiah and his father arrived. Doc Stogner was already examining Cynthia as his mother watched attentively. She immediately threw her arms around Sam when they arrived. "I'm so frightened, Sam. Her fever is high." She glanced at Hezekiah as though regretting that he had heard.

Doc Stogner stood up and looked at the anxious onlookers. "I'm afraid she's got pneumonia. We need to break the fever as soon as possible."

Hezekiah stood by helplessly as the day progressed into evening, watching his mother, father, and Doc Stogner as they diligently worked to break Cynthia's fever. Hezekiah studied their faces for a sign that she was getting better, but their expressions remained taut.

Well into the evening, Hezekiah was sent to bed. "Is she going to be all right?" he asked again, one of several times.

The answer was always the same. "We're sure she will be, but she needs your prayers."

Sleep averted Hezekiah for some time. He hated himself for being mean to Cynthia. He wished he could take back the terrible things he had said to her. "Oh, God," he whispered, tears in his eyes, "if you make her better, I promise I'll be nice to her. Don't punish her because you're upset with me. God, I promise. Please make her better."

With the strained weariness of the day, Hezekiah at last fell into a slumber, and for the moment, was relieved of his agonizing fear.

****

During the night, Hezekiah was awakened by the mournful cries of his mother. He sat up with a start. He could see her through the crack in the curtain, slumped over in a chair, her hands clutched to her face. His father stood solemnly beside her, his head down and his hand resting on her shoulder.

Hezekiah leaped from bed. "Mother, what's wrong?" he shouted. His heart was pounding.

His father immediately rushed towards him. "Son," he said, his voice cracking, "Cynthia is...". He was unable to finish as tears flooded to his eyes, but he did not need to say any more.

Hezekiah knew. "Cynthia's dead!" Hezekiah screamed. "God, how could you?" he shouted angrily. "I promised."

****

Hezekiah could not look at the small wooden coffin before him. He could hear the voice of the preacher, but he had no idea what was being said. He glanced at his father next to him. His father's eyes were damp, but he was not crying. His face, usually strong and sure, now sagged and was expressionless. In St. Louis, Hezekiah had once seen a black man flogged. Hezekiah had always remembered the beaten man's face, rendering an expression of hopelessness and despair. His father's face had the same tortured look.

Hezekiah could hear the tormented sobbing of his mother. He was afraid to look at her. He wondered if she hated him for being mean to Cynthia. Maybe she even blamed him for her death. She had hardly spoken a word to anyone since Cynthia died.

If he could just go back in time to change things. He remembered the saddening sound of Cynthia crying as he had helped her home from school. He could have said he was sorry, or even that he loved her...but he had said nothing. Now he never could.

Life had been so much fun...now there was only pain. It would never be the same again. The tears rushed from his eyes. He felt the soothing arm of his father around him.

160

****

Hezekiah returned to school a few days after Cynthia's funeral. He was actually glad to leave the house, even for school. His home had become dark and empty. Rarely were any words spoken, the mere few were without feeling. Although his mother had resumed her usual functions, it was as though she was not there. His father would sit, watching her, but rarely speaking. Hezekiah had never felt so alone. He feared it would always be the same.

Isaac never mentioned Cynthia's death, trying to pretend everything was the same. Hezekiah, not wanting to show a weakness, pushed the pain inside him and tried to follow Isaac's lead.

Each day after school, Hezekiah would return home to the agonizing silence. He waited for change as he diligently did his chores and homework, trying to be as good as he could. He thought maybe it would help. But the distance among the three seemed to grow.

Christmas was only three weeks away. Christmas had always been exciting, his favorite time, but this year, he was dreading it. There would be no celebration.

Hezekiah felt he needed some answers. He had been uncertain whether to see Eagle Feather since Cynthia's death. Hezekiah felt he had become weak, and it would shame his friend. But everything seemed hopeless. He felt he could live with shame more than the emptiness that consumed his life.

After school, he told Isaac that he would like to see Eagle Feather alone. It was a dreary overcast day. Hezekiah was nervous as he climbed the hill. How could he ever tell Eagle Feather how he felt without disappointing his old friend?

When he arrived at the top of the bluff, he found Eagle Feather watching him. "It's good to see you, Silent Hawk. Good friends should not be parted so long." He motioned Hezekiah to be seated.

Eagle Feather sat silently watching Hezekiah. Hezekiah sat with head down, uncertain what to say. How would Eagle Feather ever

161

understand how he felt? Eagle Feather finally spoke first, "Young brave, you hurt inside and don't know how to make it stop?"

"I guess...a little." Hezekiah watched Eagle Feather for a reaction.

"You feel it is weak to cry, even inside?"

"I guess. I'm not sure. I just know I feel terrible."

"Do you think I didn't cry when my mother died in my arms? I was sad. I was angry. I was frightened. These are not reasons to be ashamed."

"Really," Hezekiah answered, surprised by Eagle Feather's answer. "I thought with my given name, I was...well...I thought I wasn't being brave...a warrior."

"Perhaps, you didn't fully understand when I gave you your name. A warrior cannot be only a shell. He must be able to feel pain and fear to be a good warrior. I remember our best warriors crying when they lost a brother in battle. It should not bring shame. A warrior who feels nothing can only harm his village...bring bad spirits to the village. I hope you better understand now."

"I think I do. I was afraid to come to you."

"Good friends should never fear one another. A good friend will listen and try to understand."

"Thanks, Eagle Feather. I feel better...at least some."

"How are your mother and father?"

Hezekiah could see the look of concern on Eagle Feather's face. Somehow he knew there were problems. He always seemed to know.

"I think they hurt a lot, although they never say so. Nobody seems to talk. I hate it the way it is. My mother acts as though she died too."

"A part of her has died. When a mother gives birth to a child, a part of her goes with the child. As long as the child is with her, she remains whole, but if the child dies, then the part of her that is with the child dies also."

"She'll never change then? It'll never get better?"

"That part of her that died will never come back. But she will get better if you show her you care for her. Remember, a part of her is also in you. It is important that you let her know she will always have that part."

"I will, but I'm not sure what I can do."

"Patience. Be there for her. When you feel the time is right, go to her."

"But how will I know."

"You will know. Remember who you are."

"Silent Hawk."

"Yes, but far more importantly, her son."

****

Sarah watched Hezekiah leave for school. Once she was certain that he was gone, she went to the bedroom and opened up a drawer on the table next to the bed. She reached to the back and near the bottom, and pulled out a carefully folded kerchief.

Sarah carefully carried the kerchief to the kitchen table. She sat in front of it and for several minutes, just stared at the kerchief. Slowly she began to unfold it, carefully smoothing the kerchief as she did.

When the kerchief lay unfolded in front of her, Sarah stared at the picture inside. She gently picked the picture up and held it to her bosom. It was the only one she had of Cynthia, she had to be careful. Tears began to pour from her eyes as she rocked slowly in the chair, singing Cynthia's favorite lullaby.

Several minutes passed before she set the picture back on the table. As Sarah had done every day since Hezekiah had returned to school, she would recall a memory of Cynthia. Sarah feared that she would begin to forget those memories. If just one part of one memory left her, then there would be less of her little girl.

Today, Sarah began to recall the first day that she had taken Cynthia shopping. Cynthia was almost four. Sarah had carefully curled her sandy hair. Cynthia had such easy hair to curl. Sarah had dressed Cynthia in her....

Sarah felt a sudden rush of panic. She could not remember what Cynthia was wearing that day. Was she beginning to forget already? Renewed tears fell on Sarah's cheeks. "The pink velvet dress!" she cried hysterically. "You were wearing the beautiful pink velvet dress that you loved so much. How could I forget? I'm sorry, honey. I'll try to do better. I promise."

Mid-afternoon, Sarah began to carefully fold the kerchief around the picture of Cynthia. She returned it to the drawer, carefully insuring it hidden. "Tomorrow," Sarah said as she closed the drawer. "I promise I'll be back tomorrow and all the tomorrows I live."

****

Hezekiah was glad he had talked to Eagle Feather. He felt he better understood, and with his understanding, he now had hope that, at least one day, his home would once again feel the love it used to have.

But it was difficult being patient. As days passed into weeks, he began to doubt the encouraging words of Eagle Feather. His mother continued to be withdrawn. His father was not only having remorse for the loss of Cynthia, but carried the burden of his wife's broken heart.

Christmas Eve day, Miss Harrelson informed the children that she was dismissing them early, so they all could enjoy the full celebration of Christmas. Perhaps the others, Hezekiah thought, but he knew his home would have no joy or celebration. He only wished Christmas would be over.

Hezekiah reluctantly headed for home. When he entered the house, he found his mother sitting at the table, crying. He had not seen her cry since the funeral. He suddenly realized she had been crying all this time when she was alone. He saw her quickly fold a kerchief and stick it in her apron pocket.

Surprised by his early arrival, she quickly wiped her eyes and walked to the kitchen cupboard. Hezekiah watched her as she busied herself.

"You're home early," she said, her back still towards him.

"Miss Harrelson let us go early for Christmas." He wanted to mention she had said it was to celebrate Christmas, but decided against it.

"That's nice," she answered, sounding distant. Hezekiah wondered if she had really heard him.

As Hezekiah stood watching his mother, he decided he could not stand the torment any longer. He had to breakthrough to her, or at least try. Eagle Feather had said he would know when the time was right. It had to be now. He knew she was dying inside, just like he and his father. The longer he waited, the further she would withdraw.

Hezekiah placed his books on the table, and with determination walked up behind her. He took a deep breath, determined that his words would be firm. "Mother," he said, turning her towards him. "Father and I love you." He clutched his arms around her as he felt the tears come to his eyes. "Don't be angry with us. Please don't shut us out."

She never answered. She didn't have to. As Hezekiah clutched her to him, he could feel his mother releasing herself. He could feel her love returning. She was giving back that part of her that belonged to him. He knew the pain would not stop, maybe never, but he was getting her back. He could live with the hurt as long as he had her love. For him, that was what was important. Maybe in some small way, they could celebrate Christmas after all.

CHAPTER 18

By February, the bitter-cold winter had taken its toll on the isolated mining community. Critical food supplies were reaching dangerously low levels. The mountain passes had closed early, leaving sugar, flour, spices, and salt for curing almost gone. The prices had soared to extraordinary levels on what did remain. The ranchers had lost most of their livestock to starvation and the cold, and much of the wild game in the surrounding hills had succumbed to the same fate.

Hezekiah would see his father on many occasions return from hunting empty handed. Eagle Feather had taught Hezekiah many of the tricks he used for hunting and Hezekiah had asked his father if he could go with him, but his father had always said no.

As Sam prepared for another hunting trip one evening for the following morning, Hezekiah approached his father once more about going with him. This time, his father finally agreed.

Early the next morning, Hezekiah and his father headed west from Virginia City into the foothills. The sun was trying to break through the clouded sky on the eastern horizon behind them. The crisp morning air stung Hezekiah's face, but the cold did little to dampen the warm feeling he felt inside. Although they walked in silence, it had been a long time since Hezekiah had felt this close to

166

his father. An occasional glance and smile from his father told Hezekiah that his father also felt the same way.

They topped one hill, then a second larger one and moved along a gully, through a wooded area, and turned left into a clearing. The snow was deep, at times above their knees. After two hours struggling over the terrain and snow, his father suggested a short rest.

They sat on a couple large boulders, and both stared silently at the peaceful, surrounding country.

"Beautiful country isn't it," his father finally said. "So peaceful. Out here, it's hard to imagine that life couldn't be anything but perfect."

Hezekiah nodded in agreement.

"You like it here in Virginia City, don't you, Son?"

"I do, Father. A lot. I guess some people don't though."

"You mean your mother."

"Yeah. I wish she did though."

"Yeah, me too." His father's voice sounded saddened. "I thought she would eventually grow to like it, but I was wrong...terribly wrong. Cynthia's death only made it worse." His father continued to stare out over the countryside. "I've made a decision, Son." He looked at Hezekiah, his eyes dark with sadness. "Come spring, we're going back to St. Louis. I hope you can understand. It's important that I try and find some happiness for your mother. I owe it to her."

Hezekiah was not surprised by the words of his father; he had expected them, actually hearing the words, he felt like a giant weight was resting on his chest. "I understand, Father."

"Good. You're a good Son. I truly think living here in the west has done you good. I just wish Cynthia could be going with us. Somehow, if I could just go back in time. Poor Cynthia. I think she hated it here more than your mother. If I could only change the wrong I've done."

"Father, you didn't know. I don't think you ever did anything wrong. Sometimes I blame myself, too. I wish I hadn't been mean to her."

"Son, don't ever blame yourself for what happened to Cynthia or how she felt. What happened had nothing to do with you. I guess in some way, we all blame ourselves. I guess it's all part of trying to understand how such a terrible thing could happen."

They both became quiet again. Hezekiah watched his father's body tense as he stared out over the hills as though trying to glimpse Cynthia somewhere beyond. After sometime, he rose. "I guess we better get going. It looks like a storm's brewing." He pointed to a cluster of pine trees. "We'll head through there. Maybe we can stir up something."

"Father," Hezekiah said hesitantly, "if we cross over to the southern slope where there'll be less snow from the southern sun, we may have better luck. There should be more grass exposed for feed for the game."

Sam stopped and stared momentarily at Hezekiah. "Okay, son. That sounds like good advice."

"There's a wind from the north," Hezekiah continued. Sam looked at his son with raised eyebrows. "If we come in from the south, the deer won't be so apt to pick up our scent or sound."

"I suppose you learned all this from Eagle Feather."

"Yeah."

"Anything else?"

"No, I think that's it for now."

Sam smiled. "Okay, what are we waiting for?"

They moved silently north. They had traveled for another hour, when Sam raised his hand for Hezekiah to stop. He pointed to the edge of the clearing. A whitetail buck deer was feeding off some high grass protruding from the snow and a short distance further, two does were grazing. They stalked closer until Sam stopped. He leaned over a boulder and placed the butt of his rifle against his shoulder. He took aim and gently squeezed the trigger. The shot echoed through the canyon as the buck lurched forward a few feet and fell. He tried to get to his feet but fell silently back into the snow.

By the time Hezekiah arrived with the horse, his father had already slit the deer's throat and was cutting a slit along its underside.

"A storm's coming in," Sam said as he began preparing the buck. "I'd rather not be out here when it hits."

Snow soon began falling and the wind was picking up. They quickly hoisted the carcass on the horse. Sam paused and looked towards the sky. "It looks and feels like it's going to be a chiller."

"At least we won't go hungry for a while," Hezekiah said, feeling a sense of importance.

Sam nodded. "Thanks to you."

They quickly moved out. The snow was falling heavier as the gale force winds drove the snow into their faces.

They soon found themselves traveling along a narrow ledge with a steep embankment. Hezekiah was following his father and the horse. The horse suddenly slipped and stumbled under the weight of the carcass. Sam lunged to grab the bridle to help steady the horse, but instead the horse fell from the narrow ledge, dragging Sam with him. Hezekiah watched in horror as he saw both go over the side and out of sight.

"Father!" Hezekiah shouted as he raced to the edge of the embankment. He could only see the horse as it attempted to get up, and then slumped back into the snow, writhing in pain. Its mournful sound echoed through the gully, leaving Hezekiah with a dreadful, sickened feeling.

"Father! Father!" Hezekiah shouted as he slid down the steep slope, his eyes constantly searching for his father.

When Hezekiah arrived at the bottom, he found his father pinned beneath the horse. He quickly grabbed the reins and urged the horse far enough to free his father.

His father lie motionless, eyes partially closed. Hezekiah felt some relief when he could see his father still breathing.

"What should I do?" Hezekiah said, tears clouding his eyes. Fear knotted his stomach as he placed his hand under his father's head. "Please, Father. I don't know what I should do."

His father's lips quivered. Several agonizing moments passed before he spoke, his voice barely a whisper. "The horse's leg is broken. You'll have to shoot him, son."

"But what can I do to help you?" Hezekiah pleaded.

"First the horse," his father answered feebly.

Hezekiah began searching for the rifle. His tear filled eyes made seeing difficult as he frantically stumbled in the deep snow. He finally found the rifle and made his way to the horse, now lying still except for the heaving of his chest. Hezekiah looked into the tormented eyes of the helpless animal and wondered if it understood what he was about to do. Shaking, Hezekiah pointed the barrel at its head and fired. Its mournful sound tore at the insides of Hezekiah as he watched the horse writhe momentarily, and then lie motionless.

Still sickened by what he had just done, Hezekiah turned his attention back to his father. "Father, what's wrong with you. I don't know what I should be doing." He fell to his knees by his father's side. Hezekiah was trying to remain calm. He knew his actions might be the difference whether his father lived or died.

His father opened his eyes. They were glazed as though they were somewhere else. "My leg's broke and I feel like I'm busted up inside. After the storm's blown over, you'll have to go for help. Do you think you can find your way back?"

"I'm going now," Hezekiah said firmly, "I can make it."

"No. You'll have to wait. The storm's too bad."

"I'll be okay. The sooner I leave, the sooner I can get help."

"Wait, son. Not in a storm like this. You're liable to get lost, or freeze to death."

"I have to go, Father," Hezekiah said with determination. "You need help as soon as possible."

His father never answered. Hezekiah listened to his shallow breathing. He had to do something or his father would die.

Hezekiah quickly cut some pine branches and laid them over his father to help protect him from the storm.

When he finished, he knelt by his father's side. "I'm going now, Father. Is there anything else I can do before I leave?"

His father's eyes opened. "Be careful, Son. Don't take any chances."

"I'll be fine. I'm going to leave the rifle with you for protection from any animals."

Hezekiah rose. "Son," his father whispered.

"Yes, Father."

"Tell your mother that I love her...And Son, take good care of her."

A chill filled Hezekiah's body. His father's words sounded final as though he was saying good-bye. Hezekiah knelt and hugged him.

"You're a good Son," his father whispered.

"Hang on, Father. I'll be back soon." Hezekiah's voice began to break. "Just hang on for Mother and me." Hezekiah stood, taking one last glance at his father. He knew it might be the last time he would ever see his father alive.

"I'll be back soon," Hezekiah called out as he started out into the wind driven snow.

Hezekiah hurried as quickly as possible, but the snow was blinding, allowing him to see only a short distance ahead. He tried to concentrate on his route, recalling their earlier trip. It was his only hope not to become lost. He suddenly realized he could use the wind as his ally. With it blowing from the north, it would help him keep his sense of direction.

Hezekiah could not forget the parting look and words of his father. He had heard that someone dying knew better than anyone else that they were dying. If his father was dying, maybe he should have stayed so that his father would not be alone. But still, Hezekiah knew he had to try. He could not just watch his father die because he did nothing. His father would try to save him.

Hezekiah's body was aching from cold and fatigue. He covered his mouth to keep the cold air from burning his lungs. He was sure it was still afternoon, but already an early darkness from the storm was beginning to enshroud him.

Hezekiah wondered if this was the one that he was supposed to save. "Please make it my father," he cried out.

Hezekiah sensed he was reaching the crest of the larger hill. If he was on course, he had one smaller hill, then home. Feeling a renewed energy, he hurried onward.

The darkness continued to enclose around him. He could only see a step or two ahead of him now. He could walk over a ledge and never see it coming. He tensed at the thought, but never slowed his stride.

He began to feel the upward climb of another hill. Was this the last one? If only he could see.

Suddenly, a horrifying realization hit him. The wind was at his back, rather than coming from his side. Had the wind shifted without him realizing it, or, he stopped, had he changed directions? How long had it been at his back? He cursed himself for not concentrating.

He tried to get a sense of direction. He closed his eyes, visualizing the terrain. Maybe, this was the hill south of town, which would only be taking him away from home. Had he somehow drifted south? He had heard of people lost, who kept going in circles. How could he have been so stupid? He had let his father down.

He had to make a decision quickly-change direction, keep his course, or wait until morning. His stomach knotted. His father's life depended on his decision. He quickly wiped the angry tears from his eyes. He had to think clearly. Hezekiah ground his foot into the snow as he weighed his options. If he continued, he might drift further away from Virginia City and delay his arrival. He could even be lost for days, assuring his father's death. It would probably be too late for a search party to start out tonight. The thought sickened him, but he would have to wait until morning to be sure that he was headed in the right direction. Would his decision cause his father's death?

Hezekiah found a nearby cluster of bushes and slid into them. Waiting out the storm and darkness would be the hardest thing he ever had to do.

As he sat through the night, he kept visualizing his father dying, wondering why his son had not returned with help. From time to time, Hezekiah would crawl from the bushes to regain the circulation in his numb limbs. His eyes stayed riveted on the eastern horizon, or what he thought was the eastern horizon, watching for the first break of light. The night drug on endlessly as he listened to the wind howl outside his encampment.

Near morning, the storm began to subside as the wind lessened and only a light snow fell. Hezekiah crawled from the bushes. Daybreak began to outline the countryside around him. He began to evaluate his whereabouts. With all the freshly fallen snow, it was difficult to distinguish the landmarks, particularly in unfamiliar terrain. He began to realize he had in fact drifted south of Virginia City.

He quickly began moving northeast. The deep snow made his progress difficult. He would be home shortly but would it be in time to save his father?

The sun was struggling to appear on the overcast horizon as he crested the hill. He felt a sense of relief as he looked down over Virginia City and the early morning activity below with the lazy smoke drifting from the chimneys.

As he began his descent, he spotted four horsemen and two riderless horses coming towards him. He began waving and shouting to them. He soon recognized the front rider as Eagle Feather.

"Over here. Quick. Father's been hurt," Hezekiah shouted.

Eagle Feather quickly urged his horse forward through the deep snow. "Hawk, are you all right?" he called as he pulled in his reins and jumped from his horse.

"I'm all right, but Fathers' been hurt bad. I had to leave him to come for help." Hezekiah's voice broke, "I'm afraid...he may be dead. He was hurt awfully bad."

"Can you travel?" Eagle Feather asked as the other men arrived.

"Yes. I have too," Hezekiah said looking at the other riders, including Harvey Kyle. "I couldn't make it back before dark last night. I started to get lost. I'm afraid my stupidity may have killed my father."

Eagle Feather put his hand on Hezekiah's shoulder. "I don't know how you did this well, young brave. The storm was a bad one." Eagle Feather's eyes were soft and remorseful as he studied his young friend. "Are you ready to travel now? You can tell me what happened on the way."

Their progress was slow as Hezekiah carefully gave directions. Everything was covered with the white snow, and the sunlight, breaking through the overcast, glistened brightly off the snow-covered terrain. But Eagle Feather was patient. "If you need to, Hawk, close your eyes and feel your way," Eagle Feather suggested. "Remember, be part of the land around you."

Hezekiah felt relieved when they came into the clearing and spotted the rocks where he and his father had sat and talked. It now seemed so long ago. It would be easy from here, remembering the instructions he had given his father.

Hezekiah's heart was beating rapidly as they drew nearer to the fateful ridge. "There!" he shouted, pointing to the nearby hillside. "That's the ridge where Father went over."

Eagle Feather led the way, guiding his horse quickly through the terrain and along the ledge.

"Right here," Hezekiah called out as he rode close behind Eagle Feather.

Eagle Feather slid from his horse, and walked to the edge. He paused for a moment, staring down the steep embankment. "Wait here," he said and disappeared over the side.

Hezekiah sat on his horse, eyes closed, praying his father was still alive. The other men dismounted and stood by the edge, looking into the ravine.

Eagle Feather reappeared. Hezekiah slumped in his saddle as he saw Eagle Feather slowly shake his head to the others. They were too late. His father was dead. He had failed the most important task of his life. He wanted to die.

Hezekiah felt Eagle Feather's hand on his leg. Hezekiah stared ahead.

174

"I'm sorry, brave one. There was nothing you could have done. He's been dead for sometime."

Hezekiah nodded, continuing to stare ahead. He did not want to look at Eagle Feather. He never wanted to see anyone again.

"He probably died shortly after you left," Eagle Feather said, trying to comfort his mourning friend. "You did well. You tried."

Hezekiah found little comfort in the old Indian's words. He had felt closeness to his father that he had never felt before the accident. For the first time, he seemed to know what his father felt and was thinking. Now his father was dead. Was he being punished for something? All these terrible things were happening to him.

Hezekiah could not watch as they brought his father's body from the ravine. Suddenly his body felt all the cold and weariness it had endured. He could hardly sit in the saddle.

Hezekiah began agonizing about facing his mother. How could she ever be able to deal with another death? It had taken so long after Cynthia's death for her to show him any love. Maybe this time, she would never return from the half death that she lived after Cynthia's death. Maybe she would blame him for his father's death. He wished he were dead and not his father. Then and only then, maybe the punishment would stop.

Two of the men rode on ahead to inform his mother what had happened so that when the body arrived, it would not be so shocking.

Hezekiah was unaware of their trip home, except he knew Eagle Feather was watching him. How disappointed Eagle Feather must be of him. He had failed to live up to his name.

Hezekiah's body tensed as they began the descent down the hill towards home. He was afraid what he might find. He wanted to turn his horse around and ride into the wilderness, never to be seen again.

Hezekiah reined in his horse in front of the house, his eyes fixed on the door. As he was dismounting, his mother rushed from the doorway. "Hezekiah!" she screamed. "Thank God you're alive."

Tears poured from her eyes, and Hezekiah could feel tears fill his. She threw her arms around him. "I was so afraid I had lost both of you."

Hezekiah hugged her, not wanting to let go. He had been so self-centered, thinking he was the only one being punished. His mother had suffered so much. He knew then that he must fulfill his father's wish and return his mother to St. Louis. He would try to save what was left of her shattered life.

CHAPTER 19

The unforgiving winter passed and the first signs of spring began to appear around Virginia City. The first glimpses of green grass combined with sprinkles of colorful wild flowers were appearing on the hillsides. The miners resumed their vigorous search for their fortune, and new arrivals were beginning to flock to Alder Gulch. People walked more briskly and laughter was more prominent in the air. It seemed to Hezekiah that everyone was in a joyful mood; but to him the terrible memories of the winter still haunted him, and he wondered if they would ever pass.

Hezekiah had informed his mother of his father's last wish to return her to St. Louis, and he insisted he wanted to fulfill the wish of his father. His mother had written to her sister, Jane, in St. Louis of their plans and had recently received a reply from her. Aunt Jane and Uncle Frank had insisted on coming to Montana to accompany Hezekiah and his mother back to St. Louis. They would take a riverboat up the Missouri River to Fort Benton, and follow a freight train to Alder Gulch. They planned on arriving in early June, and June had already come. They could be arriving most any day.

Although Hezekiah wanted to return some happiness to his mother's life, he felt a great sadness leaving Montana, the land he dearly loved. He could not imagine resuming his life in St. Louis.

Eagle Feather had once told Hezekiah and Isaac that a person's soul was like an acorn. Once planted, a tree would grow. If the tree were removed from the ground where it had been planted, the tree would die. Hezekiah felt he was that acorn, but he could not break his mother's heart again. She had already suffered too much, and he felt she could not endure any more setbacks.

Since his father's death, Hezekiah had quit school, to his mother's objection, and had taken up odd jobs, using his father's carpentry tools. He wondered if many of the jobs, given by the town folk, were more from sympathy than need, but he took the jobs and worked hard at doing them well.

During the morning, he had done such a job, but his afternoon was free. He knew Isaac was helping his father and he knew Eagle Feather would still be working at the livery stable. Knowing Christina was off for the day, he decided he would pay her a visit. He had seen her only on occasion since his father's death, deciding he did not want to bring his sadness to her, who already had too much of her own. But today, he needed to talk to someone. He could not tell his mother how he felt about leaving; it would only pain her more.

He knocked on Christina's door, remembering how nervous he had been the first time he had come for their social. Christina opened the door and smiled. He immediately felt better.

"Hezekiah. I'm so pleased you came." She reached out her hands and grasped his. "You're almost a stranger around here and I don't like that one bit."

Christina closed the door and turned to him. "How have you been?" she asked, carefully observing his face.

"Fine," he answered, trying not to show his feelings.

Christina lifted his chin with her forefinger. "You look so sad, Hezekiah. You know it makes me sad to see you so unhappy."

He felt a surge of panic as he felt his eyes dampen. He quickly turned away as though gazing about the room. "Oh, I'm fine, Christina," he answered hurriedly. He glanced her direction. She was still staring at him.

"I'll make us some tea," she said, not wanting to embarrass him. She hurried off to the stove. Her back was to him as she heated the water, but continued talking. "How is your work?"

"Very good. I'm getting a lot of jobs. I just hope my work is satisfactory."

Christina removed the pan of water from the stove and set it to the side. She turned, paused for a moment as she looked at him, and then walked directly towards him, her gaze remaining riveted on him. Hezekiah, somewhat confused, watched her as she came towards him, and then without warning, she slid her fingers through his hair and gently put her lips to his.

At first, his lips and body tensed, but as the kiss lingered, his body began to relax. Her lips sent a raging fire through his body. He felt as though he was being lifted into the clouds. Not even realizing what he was doing, his arms were around her, pulling her soft warm body to his. He could feel her hand inside his shirt as her gentle fingers caressed his chest. Higher into the clouds he went, each moment more passionate than the last. His hands began to move about her body as though being directed by an uncontrollable force outside him. How wonderful you are, Christina, he kept thinking. The clouds enclosed around him as they fell to the bed. He no longer felt his pain, only the perfect world of Christina.

****

Hezekiah stood at the door, glancing back one last time before departing. Christina sat on the edge of the bed, her gentle eyes watching him as a smile of uncertainty came to her lips.

"Hezekiah," she said softly, "I just want you to know that I will never forget you. Not only this moment, but every moment I've spent with you in the short time we've known each other."

"I know I'll never forget you. I just wish I didn't have to go back to St. Louis."

"You're doing the right thing. I guess our destiny didn't intend for us to be any more than friends. You need to give life in St. Louis a chance. I know you'll be happy."

Hezekiah nodded and left. His body ached and his mind was filled with anguish until he thought his whole being would burst.

CHAPTER 20

Zeke Clemens sat quietly at a table in the far corner of Sadie's Palace. He and Dalton Williams had decided that it was safe enough for them to return to search for the gold stashed by their fellow road agents. The vigilantes had long since abandoned and everyone had mostly forgotten about the killings and robberies.

Dalton Williams sat across the table from him, talking, but Zeke's attention was elsewhere as he carefully eyed a tantalizing saloon maid, who was waiting on the tables of other patrons. He licked his dry lips as she moved ever closer to their table.

"I want that, bitch," Zeke said coldly, interrupting Dalton.

Dalton turned to where Zeke was looking. "I'd like a piece of that myself," Dalton replied, smiling arrogantly.

Like hell," Zeke answered defiantly. "I want her for myself. Besides, when I finish with her, she won't be for the taking, anyway. I can just see those eyes as she begs for her life. Her life will be at my mercy. She'll be totally helpless, and she'll know as her last thought, how powerful I am. I'll have total control. Damn, that bitch is driving me crazy."

Dalton studied Zeke's face as he listened, but never responded. Zeke had grown to hate Dalton, but had allowed him to follow along. He had decided Dalton might be useful in searching for the hidden gold of the road agents. Besides, he knew Dalton feared him, and it added to Zeke's feeling of power, something Zeke needed. Once they had found the gold, Zeke would rid himself of the pestering Dalton.

The saloon maid approached their table. "Anything for your table?" she asked. Zeke sensed a fear in her voice, which only added to his desire for her.

"Not now," Zeke answered, trying to keep his voice calm. His eyes slowly scanned her delicate body, carefully absorbing her into his mind.

"Not for me, either," Dalton added. "By the way, what's your name?"

The maid hesitated momentarily before answering. "Christina," she finally answered, then hurried off.

"Christina," Zeke mumbled, watching her leave. "Christina, soon, we'll get to know each other better...much better." A smile formed on his lips. "Guess we'd better continue our search for that damn gold, so I can get back here. I don't want to keep my Christina waiting."

Dalton nodded. "We find that gold, we can have a hundred like her."

Zeke continued to stare at Christina. We find that gold, he thought, you won't be around, Dalton. "We better see if we can find an unattended smokehouse to replenish our supplies," Zeke said, rising to his feet. "We should be through here by tomorrow and we'll need supplies for our trip to Bannack."

Zeke gave one last hungry glance at Christina as they left Sadie's. Gold or no gold, he thought, I'll be back soon, Christina.

Zeke and Dalton turned off Wallace Street as soon as they left the saloon, and rode up the hillside toward the edge of town, looking for an isolated smokehouse.

As they neared the outskirts of town, Zeke reined in his horse. His body suddenly filled with an uncontrollable desire. It raged through him like a prairie wild fire.

"Well, I'll be," Zeke said, a twisted smile appearing on his lips. He pointed to a nearby smokehouse. "Look at that gorgeous lovely coming out of that smokehouse, Dalton. She looks mighty lonely, I'd say. Maybe we can get more than just supplies for our saddlebags."

"I reckon, I'm for that," Dalton quickly added, leaning forward in his saddle for a better look. "No sense letting a pretty thing like her go to waste."

Zeke watched the unsuspecting prey close the smokehouse door and disappear inside the house. He slowly urged his horse forward as he carefully scanned the surrounding area for anyone nearby. All clear, he thought. She would do nicely until he could return for Christina.

****

Hezekiah strolled slowly across the western ridge above Virginia City. His hat was cocked to the back of his head, allowing the warm June afternoon sun to fall gently on his face. He had his afternoon kill-two jackrabbits tied by their feet and slung over his right shoulder. The holster, carrying his Colt revolver, hung over his left shoulder. His rifle, still carrying a shell in the chamber, pointed skyward as the barrel rested against his right shoulder.

He paused and gazed back over the horizon behind him. The terrain looked gentle and peaceful now. How different, he thought, from that day when his father died. Green grass lay like velvet on the hillside where the blinding snow had been. Now only occasional protected snow banks on the higher peaks remained as a reminder.

His gaze swung back to the east. He stared solemnly at the familiar plateau, where he and Isaac had spent so many hours and had learned so many things from their old friend, Eagle Feather. He could see no one there now.

Hezekiah wondered what Isaac was doing. He hoped he had not hurt Isaac's feelings, but Hezekiah felt he needed to be alone today. There were so many thoughts on his mind. There were no decisions to be made; they had already been made by the events that had already taken place. He just wanted a chance to think things over...perhaps for one last time be a part of the land.

Hezekiah knew his remaining days in Montana were numbered. Any day, Aunt Jane and Uncle Frank would be arriving from St. Louis to take he and his mother back east with them. The thought of leaving the land and his friends sickened him, but he had no choice. He was determined to fulfill his father's last wish.

Hezekiah scanned north towards the cemetery. How lonely it appeared. He knew his mother, as he, would hate to leave Cynthia and his father behind. He knew how excited Cynthia would be returning east if she were still alive. He could almost hear her words. "Mother, how many more days? Do you think Aunt Jane will still think I'm pretty? Will we be going to any parties?" Her pestering questions always irritated him, but now he yearned to hear them.

Hezekiah studied the town below him. Virginia City was changing. There were more formidable structures being built all the time, and the streets were filled with more women and children. It was no longer filled with the excitement that it once had when he and Isaac, wide eyed and innocent, would roam the streets, overwhelmed by all the adventurous activities around them. It was such a short time ago...yet it seemed an eternity.

Perhaps, Hezekiah thought, it was not Virginia City that had changed so much, but he had changed. Life, a year ago, seemed simple and happy to him. How quickly he had learned that life could be cruel and that things did not always remain perfect.

Hezekiah could see Sadie's Palace. So many hours he had patiently waited across the street for a moment's enchanting glance at Christina. He wondered if she was working. Was she thinking of him? He had not seen her since that wonderful day, almost a week ago now. Hezekiah wanted to rush to her and tell her how he felt, but it did not really matter anymore. He would be gone soon. Destiny had already played its cruel trick.

A quick glance at the sun made Hezekiah realize the late hour and decided he had better start for home. He did not want to worry his mother.

As Hezekiah approached the house, he caught a glimpse of two saddled horses in front. His heart sank. Had Aunt Jane and Uncle Frank already arrived? He moved around to the front of the house. His heart was pounding. He was sure little time would be wasted in departing for St. Louis.

Hezekiah could see the door slightly ajar. A man's voice and laughter rang out from inside. From what Hezekiah could remember, it did not sound like Uncle Frank. He quickened his pace and pushed open the door.

As his eyes focused into the dim lit room, he looked on with disbelief and horror. A stranger, with his back to the door, had one foot resting on the seat of a chair, and was laughing and shouting across the room. "Hurry up, Zeke. I want a turn."

Hezekiah quickly looked beyond the swarthy stranger to the bed in the corner of the room. Another man lie on top of his half clad mother. He could not see her face, but her tormented cries and pleading ripped through Hezekiah like a sharpened sword. His body became filled with rage.

The stranger with his back to Hezekiah, suddenly realizing their fun was being interrupted, quickly turned to face Hezekiah, his face showing his surprise. "What the hell!" he shouted. The stranger's right hand was already reaching for the revolver strapped to his hip.

Hezekiah's response was spontaneous as he jerked the rifle from his shoulder and squeezed the trigger without aiming. The roar of his rifle fire reverberated through the room. The shot fired true as the bullet ripped unmercifully into the surprised victim's neck. He squealed as he grabbed for his wound. He staggered back, falling against the wall and slid to a sitting position on the floor. His open eyes stared vacantly as the blood gushed from the fatal wound. The revolver unfired, remained clutched in the dead assailant's hand.

Hezekiah froze as he stared in shock at the dead man. The second man, quickly realizing the fate of his partner, had already rolled from the bed and was grasping wildly for his revolver.

Hezekiah, returning from his trance, suddenly became aware of the second attacker, and spun to face him. Hezekiah reached for his pistol. He could see and hear his mother screaming.

Hezekiah's momentary delay had been critical. The stranger's revolver sounded with a roar before Hezekiah could remove his pistol from the holster. He felt the agonizing pain rip into his chest. He stumbled and fell helplessly to the floor. His ears were ringing, but he could still hear his mother's pleading screams, "Oh, Lord, don't let him die. Please, oh please, Lord." Then Hezekiah heard another shot, but he could not open his eyes. The room was spinning...then silence and darkness.

****

Zeke rode as fast and as far as he could until his horse was ready to collapse with exhaustion. From a bluff, he reined in his horse and carefully scanned the terrain behind him, looking for anyone that might be following. Convinced he was safe, he dismounted and sat against a rock.

His body was shaking with excitement. A smile formed on his lips as he began to carefully relive each vivid detail of his conquest. He had never felt so exhilarated from any of his other killings. And very important, he had left no witnesses. Even Dalton was dead. He had known someday Dalton would be a problem for him. Dalton had a big mouth when he was drinking and would have eventually been Zeke's downfall. It would only have been a matter of time. The boy had done him a favor. Zeke only regretted the boy had arrived so soon, spoiling the wonderful moment with the woman and his delight in killing her. He had wanted to be able to savor the moment. There was no greater thrill than to watch the pleading eyes of someone just before he killed them. He never had a chance to see her eyes, her begging eyes, pleading for life as he stood masterfully in control of her. At least, he was still free to pursue his pleasures. Another chance would come. Soon, he hoped as he felt the fire continue to burn inside him at a feverish pitch.

Zeke was disappointed that he had not found the cache of gold from the road agents while he had been in Virginia City. He was sure it was still hidden someplace, but for now he would have to wait. He could not risk going back to Virginia City for a while. He would have to let things cool down, and then he would return. He could. He had left no witnesses. He smiled...He would have another chance..but another time. He would return.

CHAPTER 21

Jane Stratton clung tightly to her husband's arm as their wagon bumped along the rutted main street of Virginia City. Sadness consumed her as she realized her younger sister and nephew were stranded in such a God forsaken land. She wondered how Sam could have uprooted his family from the civilized confines of St. Louis and move them to a place so backward and ruthless. With each letter she received from Sarah, Jane would cry as she read the fear and anguish in her sister's words. Now Sam was dead, and beautiful little Cynthia was gone at such a tender age. She knew how poor Sarah must be devastated.

The freight wagon in front of them pulled to a stop. The wagon driver pointed to a small building with a sign marked 'Sheriff'.

"They should be able to tell you where you can locate your folks," he shouted.

Frank Stratton nodded to the driver and offered his thanks. The driver grunted and commanded his team of mules forward. A common response out here, Jane thought.

Frank turned to Jane. "I'll find out where Sarah and Hezekiah live."

"Not without me, you won't," she scolded, clinging more tightly to his arm. "I'm not staying here by myself."

Frank nodded and smiled. "Okay, dear. We shall find out together."

As they walked towards the sheriff's office, Jane could see two small buildings in the rear with bars on their small single windows. She shivered, wondering what heathens might be inside the crude buildings, staring at her.

Frank opened the door of the sheriff's office and stepped inside with Jane close behind him. As she stepped through the doorway, the stench smell of stale cigar smoke momentarily choked her. The office was small and basically furnished with a crude desk, three straight back chairs, a potbelly stove, and a cot in the far corner with a rumpled brown blanket lying on top. Three men occupied the chairs, but they quickly rose and tipped the brim of their hats. Perhaps some of these frontier heathens do have some manners, Jane thought.

A husky man, with a large bushy mustache, stepped forward to greet them. "Good afternoon, folks," he said with a deep voice. Jane made a mental note how well the voice of the man fit his physical character. "I'm Sheriff Hank Bowers," he continued. "How may I help you?"

"I'm sure you can," Frank responded. "We've traveled all the way from St. Louis to escort my wife's sister and our nephew back east with us. We'd appreciate it, if you could inform us where they live here in Virginia City."

"Reckon I can," he said, glancing confidently at his two companions. "What might their names be?"

"Templeton. Sarah and her son, Hezekiah," Frank answered.

Sheriff Bowers' smile faded, his face became taut. The other two men shifted nervously as they withdrew further from the new arrivals.

"Please be seated." The sheriff's voice had suddenly taken on a quiet and uncertain tone. He pointed to the chairs.

"What's wrong?" Jane asked, fear filling her voice. "Please tell me."

The sheriff persistently pointed to the chairs again. Jane sat tensely on the edge of one chair as she watched the sheriff slowly

189

remove his hat and place it on the desk. He sat on the corner of the desk; his eyes glancing from Jane and Frank to his two companions, and then back. Jane could feel Frank's grip on her shoulders as he stood behind her. She knew he also sensed something was wrong.

The sheriff now focused his eyes on Jane. Jane felt a sickness swell inside her. Something was wrong...dreadfully wrong. "Are they all right?" she stammered with a pleading voice.

The sheriff spoke slowly and with a gentleness that sounded so different from his voice moments before. "I reckon I wish you folks had come a few days sooner. I have news that isn't good about your family."

Jane was becoming light headed as she tried to listen to the sheriff's words. "Three days ago," he continued, "we had a terrible misfortune...I'm sorry, folks...but...but your sister, Mrs. Templeton, and your nephew...were shot."

"Oh, my Lord," Jane gasped, leaning further forward in her chair. "Are they...?"

"I'm sorry, ma'am...your sister is dead, God rest her soul. Your nephew is still alive, unconscious, fighting for his life."

Jane began to topple forward. Frank grabbed her. Her body felt numb as the room began to spin.

"Quick. Put her on the cot," the sheriff commanded. "Get her some water," he ordered his two companions.

"No," Jane said. "Please tell me what happened. I want to see Hezekiah."

Frank held Jane as she sat limply on the chair. "How could such a terrible thing happen?" Frank asked, hardly able to control his own emotions.

Sheriff Bowers waited for a moment until Jane had taken a sip of water. Hesitantly, he started. The sheriff had been in his office when word came that there had been a shooting at the Templeton home. When he arrived, he found three bodies-Sarah, Hezekiah, and one of the intruders. Sarah and Hezekiah were on the floor together. Sarah's hand was clutching Hezekiah's arm. At first, the sheriff thought all three were dead, but when he bent over Hezekiah, he was shocked to find Hezekiah was still alive. He quickly summoned Doc Stogner.

Doc Stogner had been hesitant to try and remove the bullet from Hezekiah, because it was so close to the heart. But by the next morning, he decided he would have to remove the bullet if Hezekiah was going to have any chance.

"Apparently, Hezekiah killed the one intruder before he was shot by the other," the Sheriff said dryly as he slowly stroked his bushy mustache. "A neighbor had seen a man riding away rapidly when he came to investigate the shots. He didn't recognize or get a descent look at the man.

"And where is Hezekiah now?" Frank asked.

"He's over at Doc Stogner's"

"I want to see him," Jane said, still sobbing. "The poor child...what kind of wretched heathens do you have out here?"

"I'm sorry, ma'am. There are some bad ones, but there's also a lot of good, kind people here, too."

"Could you take us to Hezekiah?" Frank asked.

"Certainly. I'd be glad to...but please remember, he's in pretty bad shape. I don't want you to be shocked when you see him." The sheriff grabbed his hat and started for the door, then turned. "Also, I think you should know. Your nephew hasn't been alone. It's the strangest combination of friends I've ever seen." The sheriff shook his head in bewilderment. "There's a freckle faced boy, and old Indian, and a pretty young lady that works at one of the saloons. There has hardly been a moment that all three haven't been there, particularly the lady. Doc Stogner said she had assisted him during the operation, and she just won't leave his side. She even sleeps there by his bed."

****

Christina gently squeezed Hezekiah's hand. "You're going to be all right," she whispered. "I know it. You've got to keep fighting."

Hezekiah's eyelids flickered and then were still once more. He has to make it, she thought, he has so much to offer. She felt she knew this better than anyone.   She gently brushed his matted, dark hair. He had entered her life so quietly, bringing her new hope and a reason to go on with life. So gentle, yet it was that gentleness that developed a renewed strength in her.

Christina recalled their last time together. Hezekiah had come to her, his eyes filled with pain and his voice with despair. He was filled with so much torment with the deaths of his father and sister, and the return to St. Louis. Her feelings, secretly stored inside her, suddenly without warning, had swept over her.   She still felt confused, but she knew, right or wrong, she loved him. Although he was so young, she had never regretted that day or what she had done.

Christina wiped her eyes with a kerchief. She became aware of voices in the outer room.   She could see Sheriff Bowers and a distinguished couple talking to Doc Stogner. She did not recognize the couple, but knew it had to be Hezekiah's aunt and uncle from St. Louis. "Your family is here," she whispered.   Hezekiah remained motionless.

****

Jane listened intently to the doctor, but her eyes remained fixed on the opening in the curtain that led to the back room. She could only see the foot of the bed and a young woman sitting quietly next to it.

"There hasn't been much change in the boy," Doc Stogner commented after the introductions. "I do feel he's gaining a little strength, though.   And the fact he's still alive after these three grueling days is certainly a good sign. However, you must realize he's still in serious danger. I honestly felt the first day or two that he wasn't going to make it. He's tough. He certainly has that in his favor."

"May we see him now?" Jane asked. She was anxious to make her own evaluation of Hezekiah. She had to find out for herself that he was going to be all right.

"Certainly. The young lady with him is Christina. Quite a woman. She assisted me during the operation and has been at his side almost ever since. The only sleep she's had is in the chair by his bed. Maybe with you folks here, she'll go get some rest."

Although her eyes reflected her lack of sleep and indications of crying, Jane was amazed at Christina's beauty and gentleness, something Jane had not imagined in a woman who worked at a saloon.

Jane forced a cordial smile and immediately moved to the bedside of Hezekiah. Her heart ached at the sight of her nephew. His complexion was a ghostly gray and his face was taut with pain. He looked far beyond his youthful age of sixteen. She recalled the last time she had seen him peering from the wagon as it rolled westward from St. Louis. His face had been an expression of innocence and excitement. It no longer showed the face of an innocent boy.

Tears spilled down Jane's cheeks as she gently kissed his cheek and stroked his matted hair. "Hezekiah, it's your Aunt Jane." She watched his motionless face. "You poor child. No one in a lifetime should have to go through the torment you have." She stood upright and turned to Frank. She could see the tears in his eyes as he pulled her to him and hugged her firmly.

Jane gently pulled away. She did not want to be rude and turned to offer her sincere appreciation to Christina, but to Jane's surprise, the mysterious woman had quietly left. Another time, Jane thought. She must let Christina know how wonderful she had been to watch over Hezekiah.

Jane and Frank sat quietly next to the bed the remainder of the day. As evening came, Jane insisted that Frank should find a room and get some rest. Frank was hesitant at first, but decided it might be best for them to take turns, knowing it might be a long ordeal.

When she was alone, Jane's tears flowed freely as she sat and held Hezekiah's hand. At least for now, she thought, he doesn't feel the pain of his mother's death that would surely torment him when he awakened.

When there were no more tears left to give, she fell asleep still holding Hezekiah's hand.

****

Jane awoke with a start to the sunlight in the eastern window. Its warmth on her face felt soothing. She stood to open the curtains wider, hoping it would also feel good to Hezekiah. She was startled to find Christina, an old Indian, and a freckle faced boy standing quietly behind her.

Christina stepped forward and spoke. "We're terribly sorry if we frightened you. We didn't want to disturb you." Christina extended her hand. "I'm Christina."

"I'm Jane. Hezekiah's aunt."

"I'm sorry about your sister," Christina said. "We're glad you're here, though. It'll help Hezekiah when he awakens."

Christina's sincerity made Jane feel better immediately.

"And these people are also good friends of Hezekiah," Christina said, waving her hand towards the others. "This is Eagle Feather." Eagle Feather nodded politely and smiled. "And this young man is Isaac," Christina added. Isaac waved bashfully.

"It does my heart good to see my nephew has such dear, caring friends."

"He's a wonderful, young man. You can be very proud of him," Christina said.

Jane was somewhat surprised by Christina referring to Hezekiah as a man. He had always been a child to her, but now realized he could hardly be anything but a man, considering all that he had encountered. "He's changed so," Jane said, sadly shaking her head.

"I'm sure the change is shocking to you," Christina said, her eyes shifting to Hezekiah. "He's been through so much. More than any of us will ever be able to understand."

"He is strong," Eagle Feather said, tapping his chest. "Inside, he is strong."

194

Christina smiled. "Eagle Feather says Hezekiah will live, and Isaac says Eagle Feather is never wrong."

Eagle Feather and Isaac looked at each other, nodding their agreement.

"I feel so much better already," Jane said. "I just wish we had come sooner so this terrible tragedy would not have happened."

"You must not blame yourself, Mrs. Stratton," Christina said, taking Jane's hand.

"We were told the river and the passes around here often times remain closed to travel until June," Jane said apologetically, " and that the weather sometimes was not suitable for travel. We should have come earlier."

"Travel is difficult around here," Christina said, trying to ease Jane's guilt. "With the terrible winter we had, I'm surprised you made it through this soon."

"I admit the river was horrible with high waters, and the road here was certainly not very suitable for travel. The freight driver said our boat was one of the first to arrive in Montana."

"See, there was nothing you could have done. It was an unfortunate tragedy."

"Look!" Isaac called out.

Everyone looked to the bed where Isaac was pointing. Hezekiah's eyelids were fluttering as he tried to open his eyes. Everyone rushed to his side.

"He is strong," Eagle Feather said proudly, rubbing an unexpected tear from his eye.

But as Hezekiah struggled for consciousness, Jane's heart sank, realizing that soon she would have to tell him the terrible news of his mother.

Grasping Hezekiah by the hand, Jane gently kissed it and held it against her damp cheek. "Oh, Hezekiah," she whispered, "I'm so glad you're back with us."

He momentarily opened his eyes. He stared blankly at the ceiling, unaware of those around him. "Mother," he murmured before closing his eyes again.

Jane's lip quivered uncontrollably as she looked helplessly at her nephew. How would she ever be able to tell him? "Rest, darling," she whispered needlessly, for Hezekiah had already returned to a deepened slumber.

Jane looked at the others. Their expressions reflected her feelings.

For the next forty-eight hours, Hezekiah lingered between consciousness and unconsciousness. The only words Hezekiah spoke were "Mother." Jane began preparing for the horrible task she would soon have to face. Christina and Jane spent their waking hours by Hezekiah. Jane would take an occasional rest, but finding rest fleeting, would soon return. Isaac would come as often as he could and Eagle Feather came by regularly.

During the wait, Jane heard the stories relating to Hezekiah and the family. As the stories unraveled, Jane was amazed at the courageous acts of Hezekiah. All the things that had happened, could he take the pain of any more agonizing news?

On the morning of the third day after Jane's arrival, Hezekiah awoke. Jane approached to his side with mixed feelings. Hezekiah's confused eyes slowly turned to Jane. "Aunt Jane," he whispered, "you're here. Mother will be pleased."

"I'm here," she said, forcing a smile as she kissed his cheek. Christina and Eagle Feather quietly moved to her side.

"Where is Mother?" he said suddenly, trying to rise.

"Silent Hawk, you must lie still," Eagle Feather said sternly. Hezekiah immediately responded to his friend's command.

Christina quickly summoned Doc Stogner from the next room.

Hezekiah slowly looked at each face around him. "Where's Mother?" he asked again.

Jane bit her lower lip as she struggled to tell her nephew the horrible news.

"She's dead, isn't she," he said. His calmness surprised Jane.

"I'm sorry, dear Hezekiah," she said, putting her arms around his neck as she tried to control her tears. Hezekiah stared silently at the ceiling until his eyes closed.

Jane looked at Doc Stogner. "Is he all right?" she asked, her body shaking.

Doc Stogner listened to Hezekiah's chest, and then rose to face the others. "Physically, he's doing fine," Doc Stogner answered. "I'm afraid his body will heal much faster than his tortured soul."

****

Hezekiah awakened to silence and darkness around him. Only a dimly lit lantern in the corner of the room gave off any light. A woman, with her head resting on his bed, slept quietly. He thought it to be his mother. He wondered where he was and why she was sleeping by his side. Except for the pain in his chest, his whole body and mind seemed numb. Had he only been dreaming? He had remembered seeing Aunt Jane, but he couldn't seem to remember anything else. Then out of the darkness in his mind came the realizing truth. His mother was dead. He tried to sit up, but the pain in his chest was too great.

The woman stirred and raised her head. It was Christina. "Hezekiah," she said with surprise. "How long have you been awake?"

"I don't know. Everything is so confusing."

Christina gently stroked his cheek. "I'm so glad you're going to be all right. You frightened us."

"Mother is dead, isn't she?"

Christina's eyes filled with tears. "I'm sorry, Hezekiah. But you're alive. For now, that's what's important."

"How'd she die? I can't remember anything. Tell me what happened."

Christina placed her hands to his cheeks and kissed him. "You must remain calm," she said, her eyes gazing into his with soothing warmth. "Get your strength back. We want you to get well." She held him to her until he began to feel a shroud of darkness envelope him.

CHAPTER 22

Zeke Clemens had ridden hard for several days. He was somewhere in the Wyoming territory when he pulled in the reins of his horse. From his unobserved position among a grove of birch trees, he could see an unattended horse and buggy in the meadow. Nearby, a young couple lay on a blanket, embraced and unaware they were being watched.

The fire, that had burned inside him since he had left Virginia City, began to rage with renewed desires. He licked his dry lips as he stared intently at the delicate figure of the woman. Remembrances of Virginia City raced through him. How exhilarated and powerful he had felt. He craved for that feeling again.

He urged his horse slowly forward, his eyes never leaving the tantalizing woman.

He was within fifty feet of the couple before they suddenly realized he was there. They pulled away from each other, looking embarrassed. But their expressions quickly changed to nervousness as they looked into his hardened eyes.

"Howdy," Zeke said dryly. Already he could feel the power and control he had over them.

"Afternoon," the young man answered nervously.

Zeke, without another word, slipped his revolver from his holster.

"What are you doing?" the young man shouted. "I don't have a gun." Zeke only looked at him. "If it's money you want," the young lover pleaded, "you can have what little I have." The helpless man's eyes were set with fear.

"I reckon I will have what you have," Zeke replied, a wry smile appearing as he stared with burning desire at the young woman. Zeke raised his revolver and without hesitation pulled the trigger. The bullet hit center in the man's chest. The young man groaned, his hand reaching helplessly towards Zeke. Zeke fired again. The young man fell back, lying silently on the blanket.

The woman screamed, clutching her lover. Still sobbing, she raised her head, her eyes staring at Zeke in disbelief. "Why'd you kill him?" she screamed.

A smile continued to show on his otherwise expressionless face. His penetrating stare remained on her. "He was in the way," he said without feeling. He rolled a cigarette and lit it. Her face of grief and anger changed to fear. How helpless she looks, he thought as he continued to smoke his cigarette. He now had absolute control of her. The burning desire continued to rage inside, but he wanted the moment to linger. This time he was not rushed. Savoring the moment was so important.

Slowly he slid from the saddle, his eyes never leaving her shaking body. She looked so perfect now. She was his. He crushed his cigarette with his boot. Her pleading eyes continued to feed his fire.

"Take your clothes off," he said deliberately. She hesitated. "I said take them off. Now!" he shouted, angered that she had questioned his total control and power.

Sobbing, she fumbled at the buttons on her dress. "Hurry up, bitch," he said moving towards her. She gasped as he ripped part of her dress from her.

When she had finished disrobing, she stood helplessly with her arms across her chest, her body shaking from fear. Zeke's fingers began to lightly touch her shoulder, then moving slowly down to her breasts. He wanted to savor the moment, but the fire inside was beginning to rage out of control. He could wait no longer. He smiled. "You're lucky, honey. You get my other gun." He laughed. Her pleading eyes stared helplessly at him. Suddenly, he smashed her face full force with the back of his hand. She screamed, falling helplessly to the ground.

He watched the blood ooze from her mouth. She no longer showed any desire to resist him.

"You're all mine, pretty one," he said as he fell forcefully on her. "You're mine for as long as I want."

When Zeke had finished with her, he mounted his horse. He sat watching her as she lay sobbing on the ground in a curled position. She was so weak; he was so powerful. He smiled as he slowly removed his revolver.

"No!" she screamed. "I did everything you wanted."

"It just wasn't enough," he said dryly. He watched the horrified woman plead for her life, but her eyes only increased his desire. He began laughing. His hand trembled as he slowly squeezed the trigger. The bullet sounded with a thud as it hit her chest. Her eyes looked at him, pleading one last time before she fell motionless. His body was shaking so violently he could hardly hold his revolver. Slowly he fired the remainder of rounds from his revolver into her motionless body.

Now he was safe and free, he thought. No witnesses...just like Virginia City. He could continue to feed his growing fire with no fear of being caught. There was no one to stop him.

He smoked a cigarette, staring at the dead couple. This time he could enjoy it. Virginia City had all happened too quickly. He wanted to carefully burn the images into his mind. He never wanted to forget the minutest detail.

He finished his cigarette, nudged his horse forward and slowly rode away.

CHAPTER 23

Hezekiah began his slow recovery. The pain in his chest from the bullet wound began to ease, but the agony of his mother's death worsened. His memory of his mother's death remained fleeting. No one would speak much about it, only that an intruder had killed his mother and had wounded him. He was sure there was more, but even Isaac avoided telling him.

Hezekiah was now able to get out of bed. Uncle Frank, assured of Hezekiah's recovery, left for St. Louis to attended to his neglected business. Hezekiah had tried to persuade Aunt Jane to accompany Uncle Frank, but she insisted she would remain behind and to return to St. Louis with Hezekiah when he was able to travel. Hezekiah had hoped to stay in Virginia City, but Aunt Jane would hear nothing of the sort. He had started to accept that he would have to return east with her.

Unable to move about, Hezekiah became bored, but his day was always brightened by visits from Isaac, Eagle Feather, and particularly Christina. One thing his memory had not forgotten was his memorable day with her. He wanted to ask her about her feelings of that day, but was always too embarrassed to ask, and she never mentioned it. He feared she regretted what happened, and he wanted to apologize.

Slowly the days passed and as his health improved, he would walk for short periods around the doctor's office. Whenever he asked to walk outside, Doc Stogner would always say, "Not yet. Be patient."

Hezekiah, although anxious to be better, also knew that the quicker his health returned, the sooner he would have to accompany Aunt Jane back to St. Louis. At least now, he was able to see Isaac, Eagle Feather, and the most beautiful Christina.

****

Hezekiah awoke with a start, his body shivering. Perspiration covered him. He had awakened from a horrible nightmare. He had dreamed of his mother's death. It had seemed so real and vivid. He lay there, reliving the nightmare. Slowly, he began to realize the nightmare had been a re-enactment of what had really happened. He could remember finding the two men attacking his mother when he had entered the house. He could remember the vacant look of the man he had shot. Then the look of the second man...Hezekiah sat up. His body began to shake again. The terrifying expression of the second man was almost as though he were laughing. He could remember the agonizing pain as he crumpled to the floor and the screams of his mother, then another blast from the killer's revolver. That had to be when the killer had shot his mother. Hezekiah started to vomit from the sickening thought. He had lain there helplessly while his mother was killed. Why had God let him live and let his mother die? Was God punishing him by leaving him alone with no family?

Anger filled his body. He swore he would take revenge and hunt the killer to the ends of the world. He could not let such a horrible man take his mother's life and not be punished. He would stay. Aunt Jane would have to return east alone.

****

The sunlight filtered through the window, but its warmth did little to relieve the agony that consumed Hezekiah. He had remained awake the entire night after his nightmare. Each time he relived his mother's death, the more vivid her screams and the more vivid the face of her killer.

He began preparing his speech to Aunt Jane. Somehow, he had to convince her that he should stay. He knew she would never accept his wish...but it no longer mattered. He was determined to stay so that he could seek just revenge.

****

Aunt Jane arrived early in the morning as usual. Doc Stogner had given her the good news that Hezekiah was well enough that he could move to her hotel room the next day. At the rate of his progress, he would be well enough to travel in about two weeks.

"That's good," Hezekiah said dryly when Aunt Jane relayed the message.

Aunt Jane cast him a curious glance. "You don't seem pleased by the good news."

"No...really, I am."

"Are you not feeling well?"

"I feel fine, Aunt Jane." Hezekiah prepared himself to give her the news of his decision to stay. "There is something you should know, though. I can remember now...what happened that terrible day...all of it."

Aunt Jane's mouth fell open. Her face grew pale. "Honey, are you sure?"

"Yes. It came to me in a dream, but I know it's real."

She clutched him. "I know how horrible it must be for you," she said, her voice erratic. "You must try to forget."

"How could I ever forget, Aunt Jane? I shall never forget the face of that beast that killed Mother...Never in a hundred lifetimes. And I can never forget the sound of Mother when I came into the house...her pleading and crying...it was the most terrible sound, Aunt Jane."

She looked at him, her eyes clouded with tears. "When you get away from here, it'll help. You'll start to forget. Everything here is just a reminder to you."

"I've been thinking, Aunt Jane...I've decided I'm not going with you to St. Louis. I made my decision last night. I'm sorry."

Aunt Jane's face became ghostly pale. Her eyes were filled with fear. "You must go with me. You're still a boy." Her voice quivered with panic. "Look at all the terrible things that have happened to you here already. I won't let you stay. Not on my life."

Hezekiah hated what he was doing to her, but he had to hunt down his mother's killer. Otherwise he would never find any peace within himself. "I can't leave things undone. It wouldn't be right."

"What things?" she said, her voice was near hysteria. "What things?"

"I have to find mother's killer and serve justice, just like father and the others did with the outlaws."

"Never!" she screamed, now sobbing. "I will never let you do that. He's a cold-blooded killer and I am not going to allow you to be killed, too. You're my only living reminder of my sister...Do you think she would approve, or your father for that matter?"

They became quiet, defiantly staring at each other. Hezekiah finally looked away. He knew it would be a long battle. Aunt Jane was obviously as determined as he was.

Although Hezekiah was not looking at her, he knew she was carefully studying him. He waited for the next frontal attack, but was surprised when she rose from her chair and spoke in a controlled tone. "We'll talk later. We're both too upset now."

Hezekiah nodded, but continued to look away from her until she had left.

****

Later in the morning, Isaac came by. They sat out front of the doctor's office. Hezekiah told Isaac of his nightmare and his decision to begin his search for the ruthless killer.

"Aunt Jane is determined for me to return east with her, but I have to find him and kill him. I'll never rest until I do."

"Maybe you can stay with us. Maybe your aunt will be satisfied with that," Isaac said, his face fixed in deep thought.

"Probably not. She seems determined."

"I'll ask anyway. Maybe I can go with you to hunt down the killer."

"No. Thanks anyway, but this is something I have to do." Hezekiah started to explain to Isaac that he had frozen after he shot the first man, and because of that, he had allowed his mother to be killed. But he chose not to, letting the thought of it continue to fester inside him. He would never know if he could have saved his mother. He wondered if he would ever be able to live with it. At the moment, he believed it would be impossible.

"I'll ask if you can stay anyway," Isaac said as he prepared to leave. "I have to go to the mill and help my father. He's been feeling poorly for a month now."

"Sorry," Hezekiah said, waving good-bye to his friend. Isaac nodded and left.

At least Isaac is on my side, Hezekiah thought. He wondered if Christina would understand.

Hezekiah was still sitting outside when Christina arrived. She was on her way to work and was dressed beautifully by Hezekiah's standards. She sat with him. Passersby' cast curious glances at them, but Hezekiah was no longer concerned with the thoughts of others. In fact, he felt proud to be sitting with her for others to see. She was better than any of them.

"Last night, I remembered everything about my mother's killing," Hezekiah said after a short while.

"Oh, my Lord, are you all right?"

"I guess. It keeps going through my mind. It was terrible, Christina."

"I'm sure it was," she said, taking his hand. "I want to help, but I'm not sure what I can do."

"Mrs. Dalton, from church, and her friend passed by them, their face's expressing shock. Hezekiah smiled at them and squeezed Christina's hand tighter. For the moment, it was a pleasant relief from his troubles.

After the women passed, Hezekiah turned back to Christina. "I've decided not to return with Aunt Jane. Instead I'm going to search for the killer."

Christina studied his face for several moments, making him feel uneasy. She squinted her eyes as she spoke. It reminded Hezekiah of his mother when she was preparing to scold him. "May I speak honestly?" she said, never taking her stare off him.

Hezekiah nodded. "Sure."

"I think you're making a big mistake. First, even if you killed him before he killed you, I don't think it will help ease your pain. Second, I know from experience, being young and alone, how this land and its people can devour you. I know you know that the west is not sympathetic to anyone. If you go with your Aunt Jane, you have a good chance to make your life good for yourself, even with all the tragedies you've had. Don't ruin it, Hezekiah."

Hezekiah only looked at her. He had hoped she would understand, but maybe nobody could really understand.

"I must leave for work now," she said, "but please consider what I said."

He nodded. "I will," he said, but he had made his decision and not even Christina could change it.

****

Late in the afternoon, Eagle Feather came by to see Hezekiah. Hezekiah quickly told Eagle Feather of his nightmare and decision, and waited for his old friend's reply. His response was confusing to Hezekiah. "It is very difficult," he said, his face somber. "You will never forget, my young friend, but you must learn to understand it.

206

It is the only way you will be able to face life with any happiness. All great warriors must learn to understand the agony of death. It will be a long difficult journey, but it will come if you allow it. Patience will be your greatest ally."

Hezekiah would have preferred a more direct answer. He was uncertain whether Eagle Feather supported him, but he was embarrassed to ask. After Eagle Feather had left, Hezekiah pondered the old Indian's remark. He could make the answer however he chose. It all depended on what he wanted. That would be easy enough. He would choose, yes. But in his heart, he was sure Eagle Feather had meant, no.

****

Isaac returned the next day with bad news. His parents would not consent for Hezekiah to stay with them. They agreed with his Aunt Jane.

"Maybe they're right, Hezekiah. They made a lot of sense. He's a professional killer. Next time you might not be so lucky."

His last ally had defected. Hezekiah had to stand alone. But it was not a matter of right or wrong, there was no choice. He could never live with himself knowing that maybe he could have saved his mother if he hadn't frozen. If they knew this, maybe they would understand, but he knew he would never tell them. The only reprieve he had from this horror inside him was to seek revenge and kill the murderer.

****

The days to follow were filled with arguments with Aunt Jane. She swore she would stay until her dying breath if he did not return to St. Louis with her. Living in the same hotel room intensified their continual arguments.

Hezekiah began to think about stealing some money and running away. It seemed to be the only solution.

One late afternoon after Hezekiah had another argument with Aunt Jane; he climbed the hill in search of Eagle Feather. Maybe Eagle Feather would give him some answers now. Surely his old friend knew what he should do. Hezekiah had to try again.

Eagle Feather was sitting in his familiar place, staring at the land before him. Hezekiah sat down next to him. Without turning, Eagle Feather spoke to his young friend. "You are confused."

"Yes." Hezekiah answered, angered and frustrated.

"You have learned well from my teachings," he said, still not looking at Hezekiah. "You give this old man great pride."

Hezekiah looked at him trying to read his face. Hezekiah was sure it looked saddened. "You think I should return to St. Louis, don't you?"

Eagle Feather ignored Hezekiah's question. "You have become part of this great land. You and the land and all its beings are now one...I know...The Spirits have told me." He looked at Hezekiah. "Do you remember when I told you that when you became part of the land, that then and only then could you hear the Spirits?"

"Yes," Hezekiah answered, recalling that day so long ago. He had listened with excitement and admiration to his new friend, but still he always had doubts.

Eagle Feather rose and rested his hand on Hezekiah's shoulder. "I shall wait for you in town," he said and left without another word.

Hezekiah watched in disbelief as Eagle Feather disappeared from view. Had Eagle Feather misjudged him? He would never be able to hear the Spirits. He really didn't even believe in them. If ever he needed his old friend, it was now. Why would Eagle Feather desert him?

Hezekiah felt anger and disappointment. He stared out over the rolling foothills. They looked no different. Feeling hopeless, he sat on the ground and leaned against a boulder. His gaze slowly shifted north towards the cemetery. The horrible agonizing feelings returned. He remembered the sickness he had felt, awakening to find Cynthia had died. The tormenting time after her death when the heavy remorse that seemed to crush their home. He could vividly see

208

his father going over the ledge, and the expression on his father's face when he left for help. He knew now that his father had known he would never see anyone alive again. He should have stayed with his father.

Suddenly before him, the face of his mother's killer. The face so frightening that a chill bore deep inside Hezekiah. The curled smile on the killer's face as he pulled the trigger. The haunting sounds of his mother's screams filled his head. He grasped his head, trying to shut them out.

Slowly, the screams began to subside. He could feel the dirt in his hand as he violently clawed at it. A breeze began to brush gently against his face, cooling it from the burning sun. He looked skyward. A few scattered clouds drifted methodically overhead. Silhouetted against the sun, a hawk soared with effortless precision. He watched the hawk circle patiently, floating downward and then effortlessly resuming its higher position, only to methodically begin his silent descent again. It felt as though Hezekiah's body was beginning to rise, floating skyward towards the hawk. The land lay below him in such detail as though he was looking through the hawk's eyes. Higher he went. His body felt so at ease. His mind was empty of everything but the land below him and the sky above him. He had never felt such calmness. He hoped it would never end. Higher he soared, so effortlessly.

****

Jane watched anxiously from her hotel window. It was getting late and Hezekiah had not returned. They had argued just before he left. She feared he had decided to take matters into his own hands and had left Virginia City. She breathed a sigh of relief to see his revolver and rifle still sitting in the corner of the room.

She could wait no longer. She had to go out and find him. She quickly grabbed her shawl and moved to the door.

As she opened it, she was shocked to find Hezekiah standing in the doorway. "Oh, Hezekiah," she said, taking a deep sigh. "You're all right. I was getting so worried."

"I'm sorry, Aunt Jane. I didn't mean to upset you."

"As long as you're okay." She took him in her arms and squeezed him.

Hezekiah slowly pulled away, and walked silently to the window at the opposite end of the room. Jane watched him for sometime as he stared out over the busy street below. Something had happened. He was acting strangely, giving Jane an eerie feeling. She decided to wait and let him break the silence.

After what seemed an eternity to Jane, Hezekiah turned to face her. His face was expressionless. "Aunt Jane, I've made my decision." His voice was calm, almost frightening to Jane. Her body tensed, awaiting his answer. "I've decided to return to St. Louis with you."

Tears rushed to her eyes. "Oh, Hezekiah, I promise I'll do everything in my power to make you happy," she said, unable to control her emotions.

"There's more," he continued, his eyes were sternly riveted on her. She wiped her eyes as she waited for him to continue. "When I decide I am ready, I'm going to return."

She hesitantly nodded. "I know I will dread that day. I hope it's not for some time." She raised her eyebrows. "May I ask, what made you change your mind?"

Hezekiah turned back to the window. His voice was raspy. "A hawk."

She looked at her nephew in bewilderment. She knew she would never understand, but for now, it was reason enough for her.

****

With Doc Stogner's okay for Hezekiah to travel, Jane immediately began preparation for their departure. She was anxious to leave the crude living environment; but most of all, she feared that if a simple reason like a hawk was reason enough for Hezekiah to agree to leave, then surely it would not take much for him to decide to stay.

By noon the following day, she had hired a wagon and driver to accompany a wagon train back to Fort Benton. From there, they would travel by boat down the Missouri River to the pleasurable confines of St. Louis and home. They would leave in three days.

Hezekiah spent the day with Isaac. He had another day to see Christina and Eagle Feather. The two friends walked about Virginia City, reliving all their adventurous times. They talked and laughed at all the good things that had happened, but both avoided conversations about Hezekiah's departure.

On the day before the departure, Hezekiah was up early. As the sun crested the peaks of the surrounding mountains, he climbed the hill to the cemetery. He sat cross-legged next to the graves of his family.

Hezekiah spoke softly, "Tomorrow, I'll be leaving with Aunt Jane for St. Louis. I know that'll make you happy, Mother. I just wish we were all going. It'd be different leaving. But I promise to return one day and I'll watch over all of you. I'll never forget you. I hope someday you'll all be proud of me. I know I've been a disappointment to you and failed you in so many ways. I wish I could change that, but all I can do is try to somehow make it up to you."

He rose and began gathering rocks and placed them at the end of their graves, until the words 'I love you' were formed. "This is to remind you each day 'till I return."

He quickly turned and left, never looking back.

****

It was not until the afternoon before Hezekiah could find the courage to say good-bye to Christina and Eagle Feather.

Christina answered her door immediately when he knocked. Hezekiah was surprised to see her eyes reddened.

"Come in," she said, a look of relief on her face. A forced smile formed on her lips. "I was afraid you might not come to say good-bye."

"Oh, I'd never do that. It's just...well...hard."

She nodded her head in agreement. "I know. It will never be the same with you gone." She stared silently at him as though in deep thought. She blinked her eyes as though bringing herself back. "How rude of me. Be seated. I made you some molasses cookies. What you don't eat now, you can take with you. I'm sure you'll get hungry along the way."

She hurried to the stove. "I have the water hot for tea. This'll be our last social, I guess." Her words trailed off.

As they ate cookies and drank their tea, they talked and laughed about all their good times like their first meeting and social. Christina confessed her concern about them after her discussion with Sadie. Hezekiah admitted Sadie was right. Christina admitted she was glad. They stared at each other red faced.

"And that incident with Parson...Parson...whatever was his name," Christina said, embarrassed by the lull in their conversation.

"Blackwell. Old Parson Blackwell," Hezekiah responded laughing. "You know, Isaac had a real interest in Sadie for sometime after that day."

"I guess he had first hand information about her...I suppose you, too," Christina said, laughing and blushing at the same time.

They were having such a good time, Hezekiah had almost forgot about his leaving. A sickness filled his stomach when it came time to say good-bye.

They walked to the door in silence. Christina opened the door. "I'm truly going to miss you," she said, her eyes clouded with tears. She hugged him tightly. "Such good friends like you are so rare. I know there will never be anyone more special."

"I'm glad we were friends," he said, nearly losing his voice.

He looked one last time into her face, one last time at her eyes, her smile. "Bye," he said. He was unable to say any more.

212

As he walked down the alley, he heard the door close behind him. It sounded so final...and he knew it was.

****

For the first time Hezekiah could remember, Eagle Feather seemed unsettled. They sat quietly for sometime before Eagle Feather gave one of his rare smiles. "It may be hard to believe, but Eagle Feather has no words."

Hezekiah nodded. "I guess we could use Gray Wolf about now."

Eagle Feather laughed. Hezekiah could never recall having seen his old friend laugh so boisterously.

Eagle Feather's eyes became serious. "Gray Wolf will miss you." He shifted uncomfortably. "It will not only be Gray Wolf."

"I'll come back," Hezekiah said.

"You will. This is where your soul is planted. This is where you must grow like the acorn that has fallen from the tree."

They became silent once more. "I guess I should leave. Aunt Jane will worry."

Eagle Feather nodded and rose.

"I will remember you every day," Hezekiah said as he began to back away.

"That is good. You will remain here with me," Eagle Feather said, tapping his chest.

As Hezekiah reached the crest, Eagle Feather called out, "Silent Hawk." Hezekiah turned. "You make me proud, young brave one," he said with a shaky voice.

Hezekiah was sure he saw a tear roll down his friend's cheek. Hezekiah waved and left.

****

The sun had just appeared over the eastern sky, when the luggage had been loaded onto the wagon. Aunt Jane and Hezekiah took their places on the lead wagon to avoid as much dust as possible. Aunt Jane sat up front with the driver, and Hezekiah sat in the back with his feet dangling off the end of the wagon.

Isaac said a quiet good-bye and watched the wagon as it began to rumble down the street. He stood motionless until it disappeared from view.

Hezekiah took one last look at the familiar hill where he spent so many happy hours. He could see a lone figure watching them.

"Good-bye, Eagle Feather," Hezekiah whispered. As the wagon was disappearing from view, the figure raised his arms and slowly let them drop, and then the figure disappeared. Virginia City, at least for now, was only a memory.

CHAPTER 24

U pon their arrival in St. Louis, Jane immediately set about her promise to make Hezekiah happy. She knew time would not be her ally.

She had hoped to receive more support from her three children, but only her youngest, Hannah, found delight in Hezekiah's return. Hannah was a year younger than Cynthia. Jane had always wished Hannah had been more like Cynthia, showing a desire for the womanly arts, but instead Hannah had become a tomboy. But now Jane found this to her advantage as Hannah had become infatuated with Hezekiah and his stories of the west.

Her two older children, Susanna, a year younger than Hezekiah, and Christopher, a year older than Hezekiah, found their cousin's rough edged ways revolting and embarrassing to them.

They particularly became unsettled when their mother insisted on having a welcome home party for Hezekiah so that he could meet their friends.

"Mother, he'll embarrass us to death," Susanna said, sobbing with her best theatrical performance.

"If he wants friends, let him hang around the river barges," Christopher argued, slamming a book on the table. "He's better suited for them anyway."

"I will not hear of such a thing," Jane said, determined to have the party.

"You've always taught us not to befriend riffraff and now you have one living in our house," Christopher retaliated.

Jane struggled with her anger as she stared at her defiant son. "Hezekiah is family and he's certainly not riffraff. How could you say such terrible things?"

"Mother, Hannah told me Hezekiah had an Indian for a friend," Susanna said with disgust. "What if our friends found out?" She grasped her forehead to dramatize her concern. "I would absolutely die."

"Yes, he did have an Indian friend," Jane responded defensively. "And I have to admit, I was a little appalled at first. But he was a kind, gentle, old man."

"And how many scalps did he carry as trophies, Mother?" Christopher said with a smug look.

"You're so...so different since you were out there," Susanna added.

Susanna's remark hit Jane as though she had been slapped. She realized her children were only echoing her feeling such a short time ago. It was she that had bestowed in them their resentful and hateful attitudes.

"I will not listen to any more of your arguments. The party will take place and if need be, I shall invite your friends personally...and knowing your friends, they'll never refuse an invitation to a party."

Jane immediately departed from her astonished children and went to her room. She lay across the bed and cried. How alone Hezekiah must feel, she thought. She began to understand his reluctance to come with her to St. Louis. She had acted and spoke terribly of his way of life. How awful it must have sounded to him. She knew how terrible the words of her own children sounded. She, without realizing what she had done, had only added to his unhappiness. She was determined to do everything in her power to make it up to him.

****

"Can I call you, Silent Hawk?" Hannah asked. "I think that's a wonderful name."

Hezekiah smiled at his younger cousin. Aunt Jane had dressed her properly in a pink and white lace dress, but now she sat, legs spread, her elbows on her skinned knees, and dirt smudges on her face. How different she was from Cynthia. Hannah would have loved the west. Poor Cynthia always wanted all the elegance that Hannah had and did not seem to want.

Hezekiah leaned back against the porch step. "I think it best you didn't. People around here wouldn't take kindly to it."

"You mean rotten old Christopher and Susanna."

"Well, I'm sure there's others too."

"Please," she pleaded, her innocent, brown eyes gazing at him and her hands cupped together as though in prayer.

"Okay, I guess, but only when we're alone...You promise?"

"Yes," she shouted. She looked around her and then back at Hezekiah. "Silent Hawk. Silent Hawk," she murmured, her face beaming with joy.

Hearing his given name did make Hezekiah feel good. It made him feel more at home while living in a strange place. The only time he felt comfortable was when he was with Hannah. Aunt Jane tried hard to make him feel at home, and Uncle Frank was always pleasant to him, but they were different. It seemed only he and Hannah was of the same blood.

"Can I have an Indian name?" Hannah asked, her voice filled with excitement.

Hezekiah smiled as he looked at her anxious, young face. He imagined it was the same expression Eagle Feather had seen on his and Isaac's when they were given their names. "Maybe...some day," Hezekiah answered her.

"When?" she asked, looking disappointed.

"You must first learn to be patient. I didn't get my name immediately."

"Don't wait too long."

Their conversation was interrupted by the arrival home of Uncle Frank. Everyone knew this meant supper would be served promptly.

Hezekiah seated himself at his assigned place at the table next to Hannah and across from Christopher and Susanna. Uncle Frank and Aunt Jane directed the supper from the two ends of the table.

Hezekiah immediately sensed an increased tension at the quiet table as Aunt Jane served a pork roast, potatoes and fresh green beans that he and Hannah had helped snap earlier in the day. The meal was to Hezekiah's liking but his unsettled stomach made eating difficult.

When everyone had finished, Aunt Jane spoke very deliberately. "I have an announcement to make." She smiled politely at Hezekiah, and then quickly glanced at Christopher and Susanna. "We're going to invite some of our young friends over for a party Saturday evening to welcome Hezekiah home."

Hezekiah's heart sank. The last thing he wanted was to meet his cousins' stuffy friends. He glanced around the table and caught the cold stares of Christopher and Susanna coming back at him.

"That's nice, Aunt Jane, but you really shouldn't."

"Maybe another time would be better," Christopher quickly intervened. "You know, when Hezekiah feels more comfortable."

"That's silly," Aunt Jane said politely to Christopher, but scowling at him at the same time, then looked back to Hezekiah, her smile reappearing. "He needs friends, too."

****

Hezekiah was nervously dreading the arrival of Saturday. With each day, he could feel the growing animosity of his cousins. Each day, he pleaded with Aunt Jane to cancel the party, insisting it would be too costly and too much work for her. But each time she became more insistent. Hezekiah began to accept defeat, having seen his aunt's stubbornness before in Virginia City.

Hezekiah would lie awake at night, envisioning Christopher, Susanna and their friends gathered around him like a snarling pack of hungry wolves.

Saturday came...even with prayers. Early in the morning, Aunt Jane took Hezekiah shopping for a wardrobe for the evening affair. Through a painstaking process, they returned mid-afternoon with shoes, a tweed jacket, britches, and a stiff collar shirt accompanied with a bow tie. Aunt Jane kept repeating how handsome he would be and could not wait to see him properly attired for the party.

Hezekiah went to his room and waited. As each half-hour passed, the startling sound of the chimes on the clock downstairs would push his tattered nerves ever closer to unraveling.

Evening came. Christopher came to the room, dressed and left without speaking or acknowledging Hezekiah's existence. And there's more fun like this to come, Hezekiah thought. He began to force himself to start dressing. As he stood before the mirror brushing his hair, he could hear the threatening sounds of voices and laughter downstairs. If it weren't for Aunt Jane, he would be able to stay in his room and no one would miss him...or at least care.

He paused and took one last hard look at himself in the mirror. It would have to do. At least once he had arrived and gone through the painful introductions, no one would notice him anymore.

Hezekiah entered the landing and started his descent down the stairs, then hesitated, debating a possible retreat to his room. But he suddenly realized the room had become quiet. Everyone's eyes were casting a curious stare his direction. Was he that much a freak? He carefully structured his best smile and continued his descent down the long endless stairs.

He saw Susanna with mouth open, staring at him. Was that good or bad? Her friends were also staring. Was that good or bad?

As Hezekiah approached the bottom of the stairs, Susanna pushed her way through the crowd and grasped his arm. She smiled at him and looked at the gathering. "This, my friends, is my handsome cousin from Montana, who will be staying with us for some time. May I present Mr. Hezekiah Templeton."

Hezekiah felt embarrassed by Susanna's introduction, but it felt good that she seemed to take a different attitude towards him. Maybe Aunt Jane knew what she was doing. He glanced to the back of the room. Aunt Jane's broad smile showed her approval. Hannah, standing next to her mother, was mouthing the words 'Silent Hawk'.

The party, at least in Hezekiah's opinion, had been a great success. Everyone had been cordial and showed a sincere interest in him. As the last of the guests left, Hezekiah stood in the middle of the room in bewilderment, and somewhat disappointed the party had ended. He had worried the whole week for nothing.

Apparently Christopher did not agree with the party's success as he hurried off to his room without speaking. However, Susanna seemed pleased with the outcome of the party and came over to him. "You were wonderful, Hezekiah. I mean it. All my friends thought you were wonderful, too."

"Thanks. I appreciate you being so kind tonight. I really had a good time."

"I must apologize for acting so terrible towards you. I wasn't very nice." Susanna looked sincere.

"That's all right. I think I understand. I'm sorry I've moved into your house and disrupted everything."

"That's what's terrible about the way I've acted. You haven't done anything wrong." She leaned over and kissed him on the cheek. "Welcome home."

"Thanks."

Susanna started to leave, but turned to Hezekiah. "One thing," she said. You remember meeting Jennifer?"

"Yeah."

"Be careful. She's got her eye on you and she's dangerous. She likes to see how many men she can keep under her spell."

"I'll keep that in mind. Thanks."

"Goodnight."

Jennifer found him interesting. Whether she was dangerous or not, the thought was intriguing and made him feel good.

Aunt Jane had been busy collecting dirty glasses, while Susanna and Hezekiah had been talking, pretending she was unaware of their conversation. But her joyous expression assured Hezekiah that she had been fully aware of them.

"Let me help you, Aunt Jane," he said as he busily began collecting the dirty dishes. "It was a wonderful party." He looked up at her. "Thank you."

She sat her glasses down and crossed the room to him. "You made it wonderful," she said, gently squeezing his chin with her thumb and forefinger, "but then I knew you would."

"How could you be so certain? I know I wasn't."

"Oh, let's say a birdie told me," she said with a grin. "I think it was a hawk."

CHAPTER 25

Hezekiah soon realized the bliss of the party was only to be temporary. The remaining days of summer quickly returned to a life of solitude for Hezekiah. Although Susanna now treated him pleasantly, the party seemed to only intensify Christopher's ill feeling towards him. Hezekiah became increasingly aware of the strain it was placing on his adopted family and hoped that with school starting soon, the situation would improve.

When school started however, the boredom and solitude was lessened for only a short time. Once the newness of Hezekiah wore off, his classmates ignored him. He became vividly aware that he had nothing in common with them. He felt even more isolated now that Hannah was also in school and they spent less time together.

Hezekiah began to spend more time thinking about Virginia City, his friends and the renewed desire to find his mother's killer. He would sit in his room, carefully sketching the horrid detail of the killer's face. He was determined to never forget it.

Then, he began to have the nightmare again of his mother's murder. He would awaken, his body shaking and wet with sweat. Each time the nightmare became more real, more detailed. He knew that one day he would have to return to Montana, and begin his search for his mother's killer. He was sure he would become insane unless he did.

His loneliness seemed to worsen as winter came. He found himself thinking of Christina most of the time. He wondered if she ever thought of him. One evening, while alone in his room, he decided to write her a letter.

21 October 1865

My dearest Christina,

I pray this letter finds you well and happy. It is important to me as it always will be.

Aunt Jane and Uncle Frank are very kind to me. I have no reason not to be happy. I am in school and I have many friends, but none can ever take the place of you, Isaac and Eagle Feather. I hope they are well too.

Someday, I shall return and life will be as it once was. If you see Isaac and Eagle Feather, tell them so.

If you have time and want to, please write.

I anxiously await your letter.

With Fondest Love,

Hezekiah

'With fondest love.' He grinned, remembering her note to him. How good it had made him feel. Maybe it would make her feel good when she received his letter.

****

The days passed slowly as Hezekiah anxiously awaited Christina's reply. He tried to determine how long it would take-a month there, a month for her letter to return. Surely she would not take long to answer...two months...by Christmas, at the latest. Why hadn't he thought to write sooner? He could already have a letter from her. It would have made time pass more quickly until his return.

He would lie awake visualizing her reading his letter. She would excitedly open it, and carefully read each word. She would read it again, just as excited as she was the first time she read it. She would immediately take her place at the table and begin her reply. He could visualize it all so well–each tiny detail...except the blurred words she would write on the paper. What would she say? Did she miss him? Fear that she no longer cared constantly stalked in the back of his mind, but Hezekiah was always careful not to open the door and let the frightful thought rush to his conscious mind. Christina still cared. He was determined to believe that. It was about all that kept his sanity as he moved through each day.

Christmas came and still no letter from Christina. His fears that there would be no letter began to grow. His loneliness was beginning to weigh on him like a giant boulder. Christmas morning, he sat in his room, remembering the previous Christmas. It had been a sad Christmas without Cynthia. He remembered his mother crying as she sat at the table in prayer before the Christmas meal. But this Christmas was worse. The loneliness without his mother or father and Cynthia was worse than he could imagine.

Eagle Feather had spent most of his life alone. Did Eagle Feather often feel the sadness that he now felt? How did his old friend seem to accept it and still go on finding the good in life around him?

And Christina...she was alone. If he could only be with her, he could see them singing Christmas songs as they decorated a tree that he had cut specially for her. It was a beautiful tree that she had decorated with colorful bows. Next year he would be with her. Everything would be different next year.

But now, he had to go downstairs, smile and show everyone he was happy. He couldn't spoil their joyful day. After all, it was Christmas.

****

The winter months trudged slowly into January. Hezekiah had wanted to quit school and find a job, but Aunt Jane would not hear of it. Finally, she agreed he could work an hour after school and on Saturdays. Hezekiah found a job helping Mr. Durkson in his grainery. Hezekiah knew if he was ever to return to Montana, he would need money. He would need a horse and saddle, and money for the trip.

Hezekiah wrote a second letter to Christina, thinking perhaps the first had been lost.

Hezekiah began to think more about his return to Virginia City. He would carefully count the money he had saved. He was surprised at the cost of a horse and saddle. He felt he would never save enough for his journey.

By the end of March, Hezekiah had given up on Christina's reply to his second letter. She had forgotten him. Would she even care when he returned?

****

Each day, Jane would look into the eyes of her nephew. Each day, she would feel the helpless frustration as she watched him drift further away. She knew that it was no longer a question 'if', but only 'when he would return to the west'. Only his body was still with them. His spirit had long since departed.

Spring was in the air, bringing a renewed life and color to St. Louis. But, it also brought the arrival of the day that Jane had dreaded for so long.

She was carefully studying a pattern for a dress that she was about to make for Susanna. She was startled by the voice of Hezekiah behind her. "Aunt Jane."

She turned to see his stern expression.

"Can we talk for awhile?"

His voice chilled her. She feared what he was about to say. She smiled, setting down her pattern and patted the spot on the sofa next to her.

Hezekiah gently grasped her hands in his as they momentarily looked into each other's eyes. Jane could feel the tears fill her eyes.

"I think you already know what I'm about to say," he said, squeezing her hands. "I have to go, Aunt Jane. I know you don't understand, but I do have to return."

She methodically caressed his cheek. "I'm so frightened. "You're all I have left of my sister's family."

"I'll be all right, Aunt Jane. I promise I'll be careful."

"You're still so young. Are you certain this is really what you want? Is there anything I can do to make you feel differently?"

"Aunt Jane, you've been wonderful to me. Uncle Frank has been so kind too. It has nothing to do with you. I can no longer live here in St. Louis. My soul is there. Please try and understand and don't be hurt."

"I know I promised to let go when you said you were ready, but I'm so afraid I will never see you again."

"That's not true, Aunt Jane. The road west is getting better all the time. Heck, it won't be long and they'll have railroads running from here to Virginia City." He paused, waiting for her to respond, but when she did not, he continued. "It would mean so much to me if I had your blessing."

She stared at him for sometime before she answered. "You must promise me one thing."

"What is it?"

"You must promise me that you will never hunt for your mother's killer. I must have that promise from you."

"Aunt Jane, I don't know if I can make a promise like that."

"If you are ever going to be happy, Hezekiah, you must forget about it. I would like to see him dead too, but I know if you don't forget about it and go on with your life, it will destroy you. If not in body, most certainly your soul, and that can be far worse than death itself."

"I don't know. I'll have to think about it. I feel it's something I owe Mother."

"I knew your mother as well as anybody, and I know that more than anything, she would want you to be happy and I know as long as that killer continues to fester in your mind and heart, there will never be happiness. Please consider what I've said. Please." She was somewhat relieved to see him in deep thought. Having him leave was difficult enough for her to accept, but if she thought he would

226

begin searching for the horrible man that had killed her sister, it would be more than she could accept. "When do you plan on leaving?" she asked.

"I think Monday."

"So soon," she said, gripping his shirtsleeve.

"If I go now, I can beat the heat. I still remember how bad it was the last time."

"You'll need money. I'll get your Uncle Frank..."

"No, I have enough saved for a saddle and horse. I've already checked."

"You'll need money for food and such."

"I have my father's revolver and rifle. I'll hunt for food."

"You will not. Do you want to put your aunt in her grave before her time? I insist you take some money for food or I'll never let you take one step off the porch. The issue is settled."

Hezekiah nodded. "Okay. Only a little, though."

"We'll see. Have you told anyone else?"

"No not yet. I wanted you to be the first."

"You know Hannah will miss you so."

"I know. I thought about that, but I think she'll understand. If it's okay, I'll tell her tonight."

Jane could no longer speak as she nodded her head in approval. She pulled Hezekiah into her arms and held him for sometime as she wept openly.

****

That evening after supper, Hezekiah reluctantly asked Hannah if she would like to go for a walk. To no one's surprise, she excitedly accepted.

At first, they talked about school as Hezekiah tried to decide how to tell her. But it was Hannah that spoke first about it. "You're leaving soon, aren't you?"

Hezekiah looked in shock at his young friend. Her eyes were riveted on him. "You're so perceptive at such a young age," he said. "How'd you know?"

"Easy. Mother looked so sad and then when you asked me to go for a walk, I knew for sure."

"You know I'm going to miss you," he said, putting his arm around her as they continued to walk.

"I know. And I'm going to miss you a lot, too. Of all my friends in school, you're still my best friend."

"Thanks. I guess without you I wouldn't have any."

She laughed, then he.

"Will you tell Eagle Feather about me?"

"Of course. I'll tell everybody about you. I'll be thinking of you all the time. And if anybody says anything bad about you, I'll punch them in the nose."

They began laughing as they skipped down the street towards home.

Aunt Jane, expecting the need to console her shattered daughter, was shocked to see them arrive in such high spirits.

"Well," she said when they arrived, "if I want to feel needed, I guess I'll have to make some ice cream. Anybody want to help?"

Everyone offered.

****

The remaining days were filled with both excitement and sadness as the preparations were made for Hezekiah's departure.

Hezekiah purchased a horse and saddle with the help of Uncle Frank's expertise on negotiation. Uncle Frank gave him money for food and Aunt Jane began to immediately lecture him on where he was to carry the money-not all in one place so to make certain, heaven forbid, if something should happen, he would not lose it all.

Aunt Jane was also busy deciding what he should take on his trip, which included the wardrobe that he had worn at the party. It

228

wasn't until the night before he left that he was able to convince her that it was much too bulky.

"But you look so handsome in it," she kept insisting. "The poor women out there shouldn't be deprived to see such a handsome gentleman."

****

Early on Monday morning, Hezekiah went to the stable to get his horse. Upon his return to the house, he found the entire family waiting for him, which included Christopher.

Hezekiah took a deep breath, preparing for his dreaded good-byes. It seemed as though he was always saying good-bye. He hated it.

Hannah held the reins of the horse as Hezekiah walked up the steps to the front door where Christopher stood. It was obvious Christopher felt uncomfortable as his eyes shifted restlessly and his right foot pawed at the wooden porch.

"I'm sorry, Christopher, for creating a problem for you while I've been here."

"Naw. It wasn't you. I was the one that created the problem. Many times I thought about making amends, but as time passed, it just seemed to become harder to do. I'm the one that should apologize."

"I'd like to part friends."

Christopher smiled for the first time that Hezekiah could remember. "Me too," he said extending his hand. "I hope you have a safe trip."

They shook hands and Hezekiah moved to Susanna. She stepped forward and kissed him. "Be careful," she said.

"I will. Thanks for your friendship. It meant a lot to me."

They hugged and Hezekiah turned to face Uncle Frank.

"You take care of yourself, son," he said, firmly shaking Hezekiah's hand. "We'll miss you around here. Be sure to write, because if you don't, your aunt will drive the rest of us crazy."

"I promise I will. Thank you for being so kind and generous towards me."

"I'm just glad we could help," he said, placing his hand on Hezekiah's shoulder.

Hezekiah could feel his stomach churning as he sighed and walked towards his horse where Hannah and Aunt Jane waited.

Tears were already flowing from Aunt Jane's eyes as he bent over and looked into the saddened face of Hannah. "Cheer up, little one," he said. "We'll always be friends." She forced a faint smile. "And because we're such good friends," he continued, "I have a gift for you."

"You do," she said, her face beginning to show excitement.

"Because you've been so patient, I have an Indian name to give you."

"Wow! What is it?"

"The name I have chosen is 'Mountain Flower'."

"Mountain Flower. I love it. Thank you, Hezekiah...I mean Silent Hawk." She threw her arms around him.

"Because it is tradition, I must tell you why you have been given the name."

"Because I'm beautiful like a flower," she said, her face beaming.

"That's part of it." Hezekiah watched her excited, curious eyes as he continued. "Each day, the hawk flies high overhead in the sky, looking down over the land below him. And as he looks down, the most beautiful thing he sees is the beautiful mountain flower. With me being a hawk and you being a mountain flower, each day I can look down and see you and always remember you, and you can look up into the sky and see me and always remember me."

"Oh, Silent Hawk, I promise I'll never forget you," she said, squeezing his waist tightly.

"And I shall never forget you." He kissed her hair as his eyes looked towards his Aunt Jane. She was busily wiping her eyes.

"Aunt Jane, there's so much I want to say to you, but my mind seems all mixed up."

"Me too," she said, forcing a smile. "Please write. I want to know everything you're doing."

"I will. I promise. Also, remember you asked me to make another promise." She nodded. "I thought about what you said and you were right." He removed a paper from his shirt pocket, ripped it in half and handed it to her. "I promise."

"You have no idea how much it pleases me. I suppose a hawk told you."

Hezekiah smiled. "No. This time it was me." He kissed her.

"I love you and I'm so proud of you," she said, squeezing him tightly.

"I love you, too," he said, then mounted his horse. "Thank you so much for everything. I don't know what I would have done without you." He nudged his horse forward as they waved goodbye. He rode off, afraid to look back.

****

Jane watched her nephew disappear from view. She slowly opened the paper Hezekiah had given her and placed the pieces together. She gasped. Never had she seen such an evil, cruel face in all her life. "Please keep your promise, Hezekiah," she whispered. "Oh Lord, please watch out for him for me."

CHAPTER 26

As the saddened farewell in St. Louis began to ease from Hezekiah's mind, an uncertain excitement of his journey began to increase. At first, the roads were bustling with activity and towns were numerous along the way, but as the first days began to pass, roads became no more than trails. Now it seemed the distance between farmhouses were as great as the distance between towns had been earlier.

Occasionally, he would meet a rider and suspiciously watch him until he had passed, remembering the road bandits of Montana.

The flatlands began to stretch out endlessly. Boredom started to set in. The towns often only consisted of a half dozen structures, and he would feel a sense of relief to see another living soul.

As he entered one small town, Hezekiah chuckled at its name on a small wooden sign-'Middle of Nowhere'. He decided to restock his supplies, but more than anything, he wanted to hear a voice.

Finding the mercantile store, which did not prove difficult among the dozen or so structures, he entered inside. Two older gentlemen were leaning on the far end of the counter playing checkers. They both looked up, eyeing him for a moment.

"Be right there, young feller," the one said and returned to concentrating on the board in front of him. Excitedly, he made a move, hopping over several of his opponent's checkers. "Got ya again," he said and then pompously walked towards Hezekiah. "I don't think Hank's beat me in five years," he said to Hezekiah, his broad smile showing his toothless mouth. "What can I get for ya?"

Hezekiah promptly placed his order and the old storekeeper slowly set about collecting the items.

"Clever name for your town," Hezekiah said upon the storekeeper's return.

The old man chuckled. "Yeah," he said as he turned his head and with precision, spit into a nearby spittoon. "A couple of years ago, a young feller, like yourself, came into town and asked where he was, and Arthur, he's our barber, grave digger and undertaker. He's had his eye on Hank and me for sometime. Right Hank," he hollered to his checker partner.

"He ain't getting no business here," Hank hollered back, poking himself in the chest.

"Hank's pretty deaf," the storekeeper said, "but healthy as a horse, otherwise. Anyway," he continued, "Arthur told him he was in the middle of nowhere. The stranger thought that was the name of the town. The story spread hereabouts and so at the next town meeting, we took a vote and changed our name."

"I reckon of the towns I've passed through, this is one I'll never forget," Hezekiah said to the obvious delight of the old storekeeper.

"So where ya headed?" Hank hollered, moving closer.

"Montana."

The storekeeper whistled. "Pretty dangerous territory out there for a young feller like you from what I've heard."

"I used to live there. Just returning there from St. Louis," Hezekiah said with a sense of pride.

"Ya got kin out there?" the old storekeeper asked.

"They're all buried there."

"Just be careful," the storekeeper said, shaking his head.

Hezekiah assured him he would and as he left, he could feel the two old men watching him. Even though they had only added to his anxiety, he was glad he had stopped. If only for a short time, somebody along the trail would remember him and that he had been

233

there. It somehow made him feel he existed, a feeling he had begun to question for sometime during his lonely trip.

****

The days continued to roll on endlessly like the rolling prairie in front of Hezekiah. Then one afternoon, before him like a mirage, he could see the distant outline of the Rocky Mountains. As he stared at them, his pulse began pumping vigorously from the overwhelming excitement inside him.

It seemed as though for the first time, he truly realized he was returning to Virginia City. He also began to realize that he was returning to an unknown. No longer would he be protected and surrounded by family. For the first time, he was on his own and suddenly, he felt frightened.

He also began to realize how frightened his father must have felt upon their arrival in Virginia City. His father had not only to worry about himself, but also his family. If his father had been frightened, he had never shown it. Hezekiah wished for a moment that his father were alive so he could tell him how brave he had been and how much he loved him.

At that moment, Hezekiah almost wished he had not made the journey and had stayed in the protected confines of his family in St. Louis. But he knew he must continue. Besides his family in Virginia City waited for his return. He had promised. When he arrived, he decided the cemetery would be his first stop to let them know he had returned.

"Soon," he shouted aloud. "Soon, I'll be home."

CHAPTER 27

Isaac stepped from the hot sun and took refuge in the shade of a nearby cottonwood tree. It was unusually hot for early June. He removed his broad brim hat and slowly wiped his brow with his sleeve. He carefully surveyed the structure before him. A sense of pride swelled inside him, bringing a smile to his lips. He was pleased with the workmanship on its almost completed outside. But as he stared at the house, the smile slowly melted as he begun to think about all the work remaining inside. He had only three weeks to finish before he would be carrying his beautiful bride through the doorway. His stomach began to churn at the thought of the approaching wedding day. Could he ever make the house worthy of Charlotte?

With a sense of urgency, Isaac was about to resume his work when he caught a glimpse of a lone rider moving along the ridge above town, heading towards the cemetery. Isaac squinted his eyes and tried to shield them from the sun with his hand, hoping to get a better look at the rider, but he could only make out a ghostly silhouette. It was not uncommon to see a horseman on the hillsides around Virginia City, but this rider gave Isaac an unusual feeling in the pit of his stomach. This rider seemed different...familiar. Was his imagination giving him false hope again?

The rider disappeared from view behind a knoll near the cemetery. Isaac waited, but the rider did not reappear. Isaac concluded that the cemetery would be Hezekiah's first stop when he returned to Virginia City.

Almost from the moment of Hezekiah's departure over a year earlier, Isaac had waited for his best friend's return. Isaac could painfully remember that early morning as he watched the wagon, carrying Hezekiah and his aunt, bump along the street and disappear from view. Isaac had spent most of that day wandering aimlessly along the streets, wondering if he would ever see his companion again. The streets suddenly seemed boring and unexciting to him, which always before had been filled with adventure when he and Hezekiah roamed the same streets together. Each day that followed seemed as empty. He would visit Eagle Feather and they would always talk about their friend.

However, by late summer that year, Isaac's father had become quite ill and Isaac found himself working more and more at the sawmill. By fall, his father could do little work and Isaac began to almost solely operate the mill and did not return to school in the fall.

Mid-October, his father died of consumption. Isaac's loneliness grew as he devoted more time to the mill. Conversations with Eagle Feather were his only source of friendship.

In November, both of Isaac's sisters married. Soon his mother moved in with his older sister, Beatrice, who had married Herbert. Isaac was asked to move in too, but he refused. There was no way he could live under the same roof with Herbert. Besides, Isaac found relief in his new solitude. He no longer had to hide his unhappiness from anyone.

December brought the full force of winter. Eagle Feather became ill, and as the days passed, he continued to grow weaker. Isaac begged him to see Doc Stogner, but Eagle Feather insisted if the Spirits wished him to be better, he would return to good health. Isaac accepted the wishes of his friend.

Each day, Isaac would bring food to Eagle Feather, but would return the next day to find it often untouched. Helplessly, he watched his old friend worsen. He would sit with the old Indian for hours at a time. Sometimes he sat silently as Eagle Feather slept; other times they would talk about life as it used to be. Isaac began to prepare himself for the death of his only remaining friend.

One particular night was disturbing to Isaac as he sat with Eagle Feather. Eagle Feather was particularly weak that evening. Isaac sat silently as his friend slept. Isaac had dozed off for a few minutes and when he awoke, he was startled by the silent stare of Eagle Feather watching him.

"Are you all right?" Isaac asked.

"Yes. I am fine. I didn't mean to frighten you." Eagle Feather continued to stare at Isaac for a moment before he spoke again. "You are a good friend, Gray Wolf. You have made this old man's last days good. One cannot ask any more from a friend. I also know you are a good, loyal friend to Silent Hawk."

Eagle Feather's eyes closed, and Isaac, confused by his friend's words, thought perhaps Eagle Feather had fallen back to sleep. But soon, his eyes reopened.

"I never told you before," Eagle Feather said, his voice only a whisper. "I never told Silent Hawk either. I never wanted to worry him. There was nothing he could do. The Spirits had told me of the tragedies that Silent Hawk would face. I knew not what the tragedies would be, only that they would happen." He paused for a moment. His eyes looked sad as he continued. "The Spirits have also told me that there is still great danger for Silent Hawk that will come from his past. As his friend I thought you should know. I will not be here but maybe you can watch over him. I know it is a great burden to place on you, but I also know how good a friend you are to him."

Eagle Feather closed his eyes again and there were never any more words spoken on the subject.

The words of Eagle Feather sat heavily on Isaac's mind during the following days but he never mentioned it to Eagle Feather again.

The morning after Christmas Isaac came early after spending most of Christmas with his family. He was surprised to find Eagle Feather's cabin empty. Eagle Feather had been so weak Christmas when Isaac had visited that he could not imagine his friend going anywhere. He searched the surrounding area near the cabin. His heart was beating rapidly, unsure what he would find. Eagle Feather was nowhere to be found.

Isaac decided to check the familiar plateau where Eagle Feather talked to the Spirits although doubtful how the sick old man could possibly climb the hill. He raced up the familiar hillside. He did not see Eagle Feather when he arrived at the top and declared himself stupid for even having such a thought. Then he saw his old companion sitting, leaning against a rock and facing the rolling hills.

Isaac called out, "Eagle Feather. What are you doing up here? You scared me."

Eagle Feather was silent. He never moved. Isaac's throat tightened as he approached his old friend. Eagle Feather's eyes were closed, his head tilted to one side. Isaac stopped and stared. He had to come no closer. He knew his old friend was dead.

Isaac sat for much of the frigid morning next to the body, feeling a complete emptiness inside. Although he knew Eagle Feather had been very ill, he had never really brought himself to the conclusion that Eagle Feather would die. The old Indian had almost seemed immortal to him. He sat motionless, staring at the land that Eagle Feather loved. Isaac loved the land, but he was never able to see the same beauty that Eagle Feather had always been able to see. Now, the land looked even more desolate and dreary. Yet, he was sure Eagle Feather had still seen the same wonder as he closed his eyes for the last time.

Isaac knew that his loneliness would be far greater now without Eagle Feather. He wished Hezekiah were there... someone to talk to...someone who would understand. Eagle Feather, Hezekiah and he had found a powerful tie among them. It seemed as though something inside was taken from him each time one of them left. He felt empty...isolated from the rest of the world.

Isaac began to decide what he would do about burying Eagle Feather. He quickly eliminated the cemetery in town. Eagle Feather would not be happy there. The thought angered him, but he wondered if the townspeople would even permit it. He tried to recall everything Eagle Feather had told him about his people's burial ritual.

"I know you're listening, Eagle Feather. I hope you approve of what I'm about to do." Isaac hurried home, saddled his horse and returned with a blanket. He never bothered telling anyone about Eagle Feather. They had never cared about him while he was alive; they certainly would not care about his death. Carefully, he wrapped the body in the blanket and laid Eagle Feather across his horse. He made his way off the hill and across town, heading for the hills to the west.

Isaac traveled some distance from town. The snow and rough terrain made travel slow, but he wanted to insure Eagle Feather remained undisturbed and would have a beautiful place to watch over each day.

He came upon a ridge that looked out over a small valley with the mountains looming beyond. It was peaceful. It was a perfect place for Eagle Feather.

Isaac quickly set about building a platform for his friend. Isaac's body ached from the cold, but determination kept him going. When he had finished, he placed the body of Eagle Feather on the burial platform.

For some time, Isaac sat nearby, staring aimlessly over the land around him. He suddenly realized the sun was setting low in the western sky. He had to hurry to get back to town before darkness. He looked to his friend one last time. He was surprised by sudden warmth even though the temperature was frigid.

"You like it here, don't you, old friend? Me too. I promise I'll come visit you often, and when Hezekiah gets back, I'll bring him around. I know it'll make both of you happy."

****

January remained cold. The intensity of Isaac's loneliness worsened. Many mornings Isaac struggled to get out of bed not wanting to face another empty day before him. His work was tedious, but it was all he had to fill his days.

Then in late January life made a sudden change for Isaac. Isaac had gone to the mercantile store to order a new saw for the mill. As he left the store and headed back towards the mill, he passed two women. The younger woman's beauty left his heart pounding. Both women smiled pleasantly at him and he politely tipped his hat. He stopped and pretended to look in a store window so he could have another look at her. He had never seen her before that day. Who could she be? He watched the two women enter the bank. Isaac was aware that a new banker by the name of Mr. Richmond had moved into town during the fall. Could this be his family? Could this beautiful woman be the banker's daughter? The thought was demoralizing to him. What chance would he have with her? She certainly would not be interested in a common laborer who owned a meager sawmill.

Isaac retraced his steps down the street in hopes of seeing her again. He slowed his pace as he passed the bank. The two women were in Mr. Richmond's office. He had been right. His hopes were dashed. He would have to forget about her.

Isaac returned to the mill, but his mind was still at the bank. He could not forget about her. He wondered how he could find out more about her. How would he ever be able to meet her? Then what? He certainly had nothing to offer her that would win her heart.

Isaac remembered how Hezekiah had met Christina through sheer determination. Isaac had always been convinced that Hezekiah was being ridiculous as he patiently waited to meet Christina. But Hezekiah did meet her. If Isaac was ever going to meet this beautiful woman, he could not give up so easily.

Although embarrassed by the thought, Isaac decided he would ask his sisters for advice. Maybe they could help. After all, they were women.

That evening, he stopped by Beatrice's house. He hated going there, having to listen to Herbert's boasting conversation, but it was important. He figured it was his only chance. Somehow he would have to get his sister alone. Besides, he did owe his mother a visit.

To Isaac's disappointment, Herbert answered the door. "Well, fancy who's here, ladies," he called to Isaac's mother and sister. "It's our long lost relative."

It sickened Isaac with the thought of being related to Herbert, but chose to ignore the remark.

Both women rushed from the kitchen to greet Isaac. "Will you have something to eat?" his mother immediately asked. "You're becoming skin and bones. I knew I should have stayed with you."

"Mother, I'm fine. I'm not any skinnier than I've ever been."

"A mother knows when her son is too skinny, and I say you're too skinny. I'll fix you a plate."

Isaac nodded. He had more important things to do than argue with his mother.

While eating the heaping plate of food set before him, Isaac listened, or at least pretended to listen, to Herbert tell of all the amazing things he had accomplished during the last few years of his life. Isaac kept telling himself the sacrifice was necessary. But how would he ever get Beatrice alone without creating suspicion among the others.

After some long period of time, Isaac determined there was no clever way to get his sister alone. He decided to just ask her. "Beatrice, can I see you outside...alone?"

"Of course," she quickly answered. She draped a shawl on her shoulders and they stepped onto the front porch under the watchful eyes of his mother and Herbert.

"My goodness, Isaac. What's this all about?" Beatrice asked, looking at him with a curious expression. "This must be something important."

Isaac embarrassed, stared at the ground, not wanting to look his sister in the eye. "Beings you're a woman, I thought you might know."

"Well, thank you for noticing that I'm a woman," she said, her gaze never leaving him.

Isaac avoided her remark. If he delayed, he might never ask his question. "How does a man go about meeting a woman, particularly if she's in high society?"

"My goodness," she said, her eyebrows raised. "And are you this man?"

"Yeah...I guess...but don't tell anyone. Promise?"

"Of course I won't if you don't want me to. I have to admit, though, I'm awfully excited." Beatrice kissed his cheek. "I've been terribly worried about you, dear brother."

Isaac smiled. "Thanks. I admit, I haven't been very pleasant lately."

"So, who is she...or aren't you going to tell me, now that you've got me all excited?"

"To be honest, I really don't know for sure. I only saw her once. I guess she was with her mother. I saw them at the bank. Honestly, I think she's Mr. Richmond's daughter...You know the new banker."

"You must mean Charlotte."

"You know her?" Isaac could feel his heart leap into his throat.

"Yes. We're both on the town's social committee. I certainly do know her."

"So what do think?"

Beatrice's face was glowing. "She is a beautiful woman, Isaac, and very pleasant I might add."

"I know, but what chance do you think I have...not much, huh?"

"And why not? You're the most handsome man hereabouts. Any woman would love to have you for a catch."

"Beatrice, you're getting carried away. How would I meet her?"

"That's the easiest part. I'll introduce you."

"How? I don't want it to be obvious...You know, by accident or something."

Beatrice slipped her arm through his. "You're being silly, dear brother. I promise I won't embarrass you...I'm so excited, I can hardly stand it. Please let me tell Dorothy. She can help. Besides, it would hurt her feelings if we didn't include her."

242

"Okay, you can tell Dorothy, but no one else...And please don't embarrass me."

"I promise," she said, crossing her heart. "I'll have something set up in a couple of days."

They returned inside to the inquisitive stares of their mother and Herbert.

****

Isaac faced life with a renewed exhilaration. He waited anxiously for word from Beatrice. He began to memorize what he would say and how he would act when he met Charlotte. If he had any chance at all with a woman accustomed to men with refinement, he would have to make a good first impression.

Three days after his conversation with Beatrice, she contacted Isaac. The following afternoon, Dorothy and Charlotte were having tea at Beatrice's. He was to stop by unannounced and would be introduced to Charlotte.

Isaac spent a restless night, carefully rehearsing the following day. With each passing hour, doubt became more prominent. It would never work. Surely, he would be a blundering fool and leave embarrassed. He considered contacting Beatrice in the morning and cancel. But if he did, he would always wonder, and until he had seen Charlotte, life had only been one dreary day after another.

The following morning, he went to the mill as usual and methodically set about filling orders, continually counting the hours and minutes until his planned, but unannounced arrival.

At noon, he returned home, made himself presentable and quietly paced his ever-shrinking cabin. The hours had suddenly become minutes. He took one final glance in the mirror and with heavy feet began the walk to Beatrice's.

Today the distance seemed extraordinarily short, and Isaac was surprised to find he was standing in front of his sister's front porch. He felt lightheaded as he took a deep breath and ascended the steps.

He raised his hand to knock. It seemed frozen, unable to move. With an effort, he knocked lightly. There was no retreat now.

The door opened. Beatrice stood before him. "Isaac, what a surprise," she said, winking playfully. She stepped back. "Dorothy, our dear brother is here. Come in, Isaac. Don't be bashful." She grasped Isaac by the hand and led him inside. "You must meet our good friend."

Charlotte was sitting at the table, facing toward him. She was smiling pleasantly as he entered. His gaze nervously danced between her and Dorothy as his sister excitedly approached him and offered a big hug.

Beatrice quickly pulled Dorothy away and led him towards Charlotte. "Charlotte, this is our dear brother, Isaac."

"Hello, Isaac," she responded, extending her hand delicately towards him.

She was as beautiful as Isaac had remembered, even more so. He gently took her hand. He felt weak as her soft blue eyes gazed into his. Words rolled unconsciously from his mouth. She graciously smiled at whatever he had said.

"I remember you," she said. "Mother and I passed you on the street the other day."

She remembered him. Suddenly, he felt a surge of confidence. "I remember," he said, trying to be casual about it. "I believe I saw you and your mother go into the bank. I presume you're Mr. Richmond's daughter."

"I am. How observant."

"Be seated, Isaac," Beatrice said. "Dorothy, can you help me with the tea?"

As his two sisters suspiciously hurried away, Isaac sat down across from Charlotte. "Have you been here long?" Isaac asked.

"We came late October. It's been almost four months now. How long has your family been here?"

"Since sixty-three. Right after the strike was made. We originally came from Indiana. And your family?"

"Oregon. For almost as long as I can remember. I was only eight when we moved there. We were originally from Cincinnati in Ohio."

"So how do you like Virginia City?"

"Well, honestly, I'm not sure I'm that fond of it. Maybe when spring arrives, it will be more suited for getting out and about. I really haven't had much opportunity to meet any nice people...except of course your sisters and now you."

"You'll find spring beautiful here. The winter does get pretty bad...Maybe, I can show you around sometime. I know about every corner of the town and a lot of the area around here."

"I'd love that, Isaac. It would be very kind of you."

The door was open. Isaac had to be sure he did not let the door slam shut. He gazed into her face. She seemed to be waiting for him to pass through the doorway she had left open.

"Unless the weather turns bad, which it can in a hurry around here, maybe tomorrow afternoon we can go horseback riding or for a walk around town. A proper escort is usually advisable...you know, with so many ruffians around."

"I certainly can't let such a marvelous opportunity pass. I must accept."

Dorothy and Beatrice suspiciously returned with the tea at that convenient moment.

"How are we doing here?" Beatrice asked.

"Your kind brother has offered to show me around. He's being so generous."

"Wonderful," Dorothy said excitedly. "I'm sure you'll find it enjoyable."

"I'm sure I will."

****

Isaac left Beatrice's house that day with life suddenly filled with hope and excitement. How quickly everything had changed for him.

Isaac and Charlotte went for their ride the following afternoon. Isaac was surprised how much they had to talk about and was

245

amazed to find Charlotte was not at all stuffy like he had imagined a banker's daughter would be. She would giggle like a little girl, and on occasion, throw her head back as she laughed boisterously. He knew by day's end that he had found his love. He only hoped at least in time that she would feel the same way about him.

Soon thereafter, Isaac was introduced to Charlotte's mother and father. Although Isaac found Mrs. Richmond to be a little stiff and Mr. Richmond a little arrogant at times, they were always considerate to him and seemed to accept him graciously.

Charlotte and Isaac continued their relationship. They would spend considerable time talking. Charlotte never seemed to require anything special, only time with Isaac.

By the end of March, Isaac was convinced that Charlotte was the woman he wanted to marry. He had tried to be patient, not wanting to offend her by too short a courtship, but he could wait no longer. He decided he would ask for her hand in marriage.

A balmy evening in early April, Isaac attended dinner at the Richmond's. He had decided to ask Charlotte for her hand in marriage that evening at a convenient opportunity.

Charlotte and Isaac excused themselves from the table, deciding to go for a walk. The moon was full, giving ample lighting for Isaac to look into the face of the woman he loved.

They stopped by a grove of birch trees. He kissed her gently. He prepared his speech. He wanted it to be perfect.

"Charlotte, you know I love you."

"I had hoped so, although I don't ever recall you telling me so." Her eyebrows were raised precariously as though scolding him, but her eyes convinced Isaac she was only teasing.

"I'm sorry for that. I guess I'm not very good at such things...but I do love you very much. I guess I started falling in love from that first day we passed on the street."

Charlotte's eyes glistened in the moonlight as she lingered on each of his words. "Perhaps I fell in love at that moment too," she responded. " I must confess, I told mother that day I saw you that I hoped I would meet you."

"I must confess something, too," Isaac said, gently squeezing her hand. "Beatrice and I planned our accidental meeting at her place."

Charlotte smiled. "I know," she said, almost apologetically.

"You did. Beatrice told you."

"No. She never said anything. I just knew."

Isaac's mouth hung open.

"Don't be so shocked," she said. "You must understand. Women, from the time they are little girls, plan and prepare for the man they love. It all becomes so natural for us. Men, on the other hand, give little thought to love...or at least not until they actually fall in love. It's all so new to them, they are surprised by everything about love...Oh yes, I knew, and admittedly, I was very pleased."

"I guess I was surprised by it all," Isaac said, shaking his head.

"It was probably good you were surprised. If you had seen it coming, you would probably have avoided it like the plague."

"Never."

Charlotte raised her eyebrows in doubt. "I'm not so sure. But the important thing is, we did meet and we fell in love."

Isaac cleared his throat. "Charlotte...because I love you so much, I know my life would forever be empty if you weren't in it. It would be silly for me to delay any longer...Will you marry me?"

Charlotte stared blankly at Isaac. Isaac was sure she was trying to find a way to say, no.

"I guess I was wrong," she said. "Sometimes a woman can be surprised by love...Will I marry you...There could be no greater pleasure. Of course, I'll marry you, Isaac."

CHAPTER 28

Hezekiah mounted his mare and sat for a moment looking at his family's graves. It felt good to be near them again. He had promised he would return, although he knew his mother would rather have him stay in St. Louis. Realizing he had been at the cemetery for sometime, he urged his horse forward towards town.

The excitement began to fill every fiber of Hezekiah's body as he moved down the hillside. He was back. He wondered if everyone would be glad to see him or would they even care. He was about to find out. He reached the bottom of the hill, crossed the gully and made his way onto Wallace Street. Hezekiah startled by a commotion, reined in his horse.

"Hezekiah! Over here! It's me. Isaac." Isaac flung his hat in the air.

Hezekiah, once realizing it was Isaac, urged his horse into a gallop towards the welcoming committee of one. He leaped from his saddle and the two men began shouting, hugging and backslapping as nearby onlookers watched with amused curiosity.

"What took you so damn long to get back here?" Isaac shouted. "I about gave up on you."

"You saying you missed me?"

"Hell no. Who said anything about missing you?"

"Yeah, I bet."

248

"I'm glad you're back, though," Isaac said, placing his hand on Hezekiah's shoulder.

"It's good to be back."

"How was the trip?"

"Long. Long and weary."

"So I remember. Come on. Let's get off the street," Isaac said. "You look like you could use a beer."

"You're right there. I think I still have about an acre of Kansas dust in my throat."

Isaac directed his friend towards the Fairweather House, purposely avoiding Sadie's Palace. He knew Hezekiah would eventually inquire about it and Christina, but he wanted to tell the news in his own time.

As they approached the entrance to the saloon, Hezekiah stopped and faced Isaac. "Sorry about your father. I saw his grave at the cemetery."

"Thanks. His health just kept failing after you left. By fall, I was pretty much running the mill. Things were pretty tough for a while. Come on. Let's get that beer. This is a time to celebrate."

Isaac carried the beers to the table. Hezekiah peered curiously about the saloon.

"So how was St. Louis?" Isaac asked as they sipped their beer from the foam-laden mugs.

"Growing," Hezekiah answered as he wiped his lips. "Business is booming with the West opening up. People are saying St. Louis is getting just like the Eastern seaboard cities." He took another drink, leaned forward and spoke very deliberately, "I reckon it's not for me, though."

Isaac nodded. "I'm glad. It's good to have you back."

Hezekiah scanned the saloon again. "They were just starting to build this place when I left. I guess Virginia City just keeps changing with the times, too. A lot happens in a year."

"A lot," Isaac said, grinning as he shifted in his chair. "I got some big news to tell you," he said with a little boy look on his face.

249

"With the sheepish look on your face, you must have found a woman."

"I'll be damned. How did you know?"

"Look at your face. You look like a kid caught in the cookie jar...or one watching Sadie and the Parson. I'd say that's pretty amazing, considering when I left, you acted as though you were afraid of women."

"Like you said, a year can change things a lot. In fact, there's even more."

"Yeah. What's that?" Hezekiah's face was wrinkled into an inquisitive expression.

"I'm marrying her in three weeks."

Hezekiah fell back in his chair and then leaned forward. "I don't believe what I'm hearing. You're actually getting hitched? You've got to be kidding me."

"I know it's hard to believe, but I am. I've only got three weeks as a bachelor."

"I'll be damned. Do I know her?" Hezekiah's face was frozen in disbelief.

"No. Her name's Charlotte Richmond. She moved here last fall with her family. I met her in January."

"Well, congratulations. She must be quite the woman. I still can't believe it."

"You'll get a chance to meet her tonight. The Richmond's are having guests over for supper."

"Wait a second here," Hezekiah said, holding up his hands. "I'm not going to barge in unannounced and uninvited."

"You're going. I'll stop by later and tell them you're here. They'd run me out of the house in a second if I didn't bring you."

"My clothes," Hezekiah responded, pointing to his dirty and tattered wardrobe. "I look like a vagrant."

"I won't argue that, but we'll take care of that in a hurry. I'll take you over to Bob's Clothiers. That's another new place here since you've left."

250

Hezekiah scrunched his face. "I hardly have a plug cent left. It took everything I had to get out here."

"Hell, we're old friends. I reckon I can buy you some new duds. You're not going to talk me out of tonight."

"Okay. Hell, you're more stubborn than ever. But it has to be a loan. As soon as I get a job, I'll pay you back."

Isaac began to laugh. "Good. It's just what I wanted to hear. Tomorrow you start working for me so I can get my house finished."

Hezekiah shook his head in bewilderment. "If I didn't know better, I'd say you planned this whole damn thing."

Isaac presented his best poker face. "Maybe. Maybe not."

"So what does Eagle Feather think of you getting married?"

Isaac's jaws tightened. "Eagle Feather doesn't know." Isaac's eyes looked away. "Eagle Feather..." He paused to gain his composure. He had not wanted to rush the bad news so quickly. "Eagle Feather died in December."

Hezekiah, without a word, stared helplessly at Isaac.

Isaac waited for a moment to let Hezekiah absorb the tragic news, and then began to give the detail of Eagle Feather's illness, death and burial. Hezekiah stared at the table, quietly listening, only occasionally glancing up.

When Isaac finished, Hezekiah looked up, his face taut with sadness. "I wish I could have been here. Damn, it makes me angry, Isaac. Sometimes life just doesn't seem fair."

"I know how you feel. I felt the same way for a long time after my father died and then Eagle Feather. Thank God for Charlotte. I was about to go plumb crazy after Eagle Feather died, until I met her. She changed my whole life."

"It sounds like you did good by our old friend. One of these days I'd like to go up there where you put Eagle Feather to rest."

Isaac nodded. A slight smile appeared. "Sure. In fact, I've promised him I'd bring you. I go up there sometimes to think and talk things over with him. I guess I was wrong when I said Eagle

Feather doesn't know about Charlotte. I talk about her all the time and I know he's listening."

"Does Charlotte know about Eagle Feather?"

"She knows. I've never taken her there. Maybe one of these days."

Hezekiah sat quietly for a short period of time before he spoke, "How's your mother and sisters?"

"They're fine. You'll get to see my mother at the Richmond's tonight. Beatrice and Dorothy both got married last fall. You'll never guess who Beatrice married."

Hezekiah shook his head.

"Herbert!" Isaac shouted. "You remember Herbert."

"Damn. How could I forget? Why'd she go and do something like that?"

"That's what I feel bad about. I think she did it out of panic when father died."

"Too bad. I guess sometimes we do things without thinking through what's best."

"You know, I think she's happy, though. At least, I hope so," Isaac quickly added.

Both sat quietly staring at each other, both shaking their heads. Isaac could see the determination building in Hezekiah. He knew what his friend's next question would be. Hezekiah had asked about everyone but one person. Isaac began preparing himself.

"You ever go over to Sadie's?" Hezekiah asked as he shifted uncomfortably in his chair.

"No. It's not Sadie's anymore. She cashed in and headed back East during the spring thaw." Isaac looked at his friend's anxious face. "You're wondering about Christina?"

"How's she doing?"

"She moved away not too long after you left, I guess. Sadie said she had left and had no idea where she was going. I guess she had only mentioned that she had wanted to start over. Sorry. I know you'd like to have seen her."

252

Hezekiah's jaws tightened as he spoke, "I'm happy for her. I really am. She's a mighty good person that deserved something better."

Isaac could see the disappointment on Hezekiah's face. Isaac hated lying to his friend. He wanted to tell him he knew where she had gone. It was one of the hardest things he had ever done, but recalling Eagle Feather's warning about Hezekiah's past, he felt he had done what was best for his friend. He just wished he could feel better about it. Hezekiah was staring beyond Isaac. He had to get Hezekiah's mind off her...at least for a while.

"We better get started," Isaac spoke, breaking the uncomfortable silence. "I would hate to show up at my soon to be in-laws with you looking like this."

"Yeah. Sure," Hezekiah answered quickly. A smile came to his face. "It'll take a good week to peel all the trail dust off me."

CHAPTER 29

After a suitable wardrobe was purchased for Hezekiah, Isaac left for the Richmond's to inform them of Hezekiah's arrival. Hezekiah took advantage of the quiet moment and wrote a letter to Aunt Jane and the family.

The remainder of the afternoon was like Hezekiah and Isaac had returned to their childhood. The house was filled with laughter, and playing pranks on each other was commonplace. But by evening, Hezekiah was pacing the floor. "Are you sure I'm dressed okay? They sound like pretty important people."

"You're fine, and I tell you, they'll like you." Isaac paused, staring at Hezekiah.

"What is it? Is there something wrong?" Hezekiah began looking himself over.

"You're fine. It's just I forgot to mention something." A sly grin appeared on Isaac's lips.

"What do you mean?" Hezekiah looked distrustfully at Isaac. "What aren't you telling me? "You're trying to pull something on me, aren't you?"

"Well...Charlotte's friend from Oregon, her bridesmaid, is staying with the Richmonds, and you understand, she'll be there tonight."

"And I suppose I'm suppose to be matched up with her."

254

"Well it just kind of evens things out, that's all. Besides, when you get one look at her, you'll thank me...Honest."

Hezekiah grabbed Isaac in a bear hug. "Eagle Feather should have named you Sneaky Coyote."

****

When they arrived at the Richmond home, Hezekiah was sure he would not be able to hold his supper down. Their home was large and elegant. It reminded him of his grandparent's home in St. Louis, but then as a child, he had normally only been allowed in the playroom or the kitchen.

Isaac knocked, and shortly a very pleasant young woman answered the door. Hezekiah hoped for a moment that she was Charlotte's friend, but the hope was quickly dissipated as she and Isaac kissed and hugged.

Hezekiah waited patiently for them to finish greeting each other. He could obviously see why Isaac had fallen in love with her. Her blonde hair was tied neatly in a bun at the back of her head. Her soft blue eyes glistened with a flirtatious laughter.

She turned to face Hezekiah. Her warm smile helped to ease his tenseness. "So you're the famous Hezekiah I've heard so much about," she said, her eyes moving up and down, carefully surveying him

Hezekiah nodded, feeling very awkward. "Well, I'm Hezekiah."

Charlotte extended her hand to greet him, but before Hezekiah could counter, she dropped hers. "Oh what the heck," she said, placing her arms around him. After a warm hug, she stepped back. "I wouldn't want to be formal with someone I already know everything in the world about them." She giggled, glancing at Isaac. "You know, he never shuts up about you. If I were the type, I'd be jealous. Come on, I must introduce you. Everyone is anxiously waiting."

Hezekiah and Isaac, both red with embarrassment, followed her inside. They proceeded down a long hallway. Hezekiah stared in awe at its elegance-with its carved wooden trim and polished hardwood floors. He had never seen anything so fine, and to find it out here in the west was astonishing. He wondered what his father would think of the workmanship of the house. He was sure even Aunt Jane and Uncle Frank would be quite impressed.

As they entered the sitting room, everyone stood and moved towards the new arrivals. Hezekiah could feel the large room suddenly closing in around him as he nervously clutched the brim of his hat.

Charlotte began the introductions. She started with her father, Mr. Joshua Richmond. He was stout and bearded, and had dark penetrating eyes. His handshake was firm and confident. Hezekiah hoped that Mr. Richmond did not notice his sweaty palms.

Then came Mrs. Cynthia Richmond, her mother. She had the same blue eyes and blonde hair as her daughter. She pleasantly welcomed him. Hezekiah responded. "You have the same lovely name that my sister had."

"Thank you. How nice of you to comment. And I am sorry about your sister and family. Such a tragedy."

Hezekiah nodded politely. Not wanting to dwell on the subject, he moved down the line. At least they know, Hezekiah thought. Now it won't come up at an awkward moment.

Next were the Sorensons, friends of the Richmonds', polite but reserved. Hezekiah was pleased that the next face was familiar. It was Isaac's mother.

"Hello, Mrs. Kyle. It's so good to see you."

She smiled pleasantly. Her face showed the year of suffering she had encountered since he had left. "Oh, Hezekiah, I'm so glad you're home." She squeezed him tightly. "You've become such a handsome young man," she continued, cupping his face with her hands.

"Thank you, Mrs. Kyle. I'm terribly sorry about Mr. Kyle."

Thank you, dear," she answered and politely stepped back.

Charlotte waited, not wanting to interrupt, then grasping Hezekiah by the arm, gently turned him to his right. "And Mr.

Hezekiah Templeton, this my dearest friend in all the world. Miss Kathryn Darcy, this is Hezekiah."

Hezekiah was surprised that he had not seen Kathryn on his entrance. He wondered how he could have missed such a lovely woman. He tried not to stare, but he found that he could not help himself. Her soft sandy hair curled precisely into a bun atop her head with just enough loose strands to give it a softened look. Her thin lips were pursed ever so slightly apart as she smiled at him. Her face looked soft, yet her features distinct. Her soft green eyes were opened widely and danced playfully as they gazed at Hezekiah in a flirtatious manner. Isaac had been right. She was irresistible! He felt the knot in his stomach tighten.

Her voice was soft. "Pleased to meet you, Mr. Templeton. Welcome back."

"Thank you, and I'm pleased to meet you, Miss Darcy," Hezekiah responded, gently squeezing her extended soft hand.

"A brandy, Mr. Templeton," Mr. Richmond called out from behind him.

Hezekiah realizing he was still holding Kathryn's hand quickly released it and turned to the others. "A brandy is fine, Mr. Richmond." Hezekiah felt flustered. Had any of the others noticed his stare? He glanced at Isaac. Isaac was fully aware of Hezekiah's moment of enchantment.

"Maybe a young fellow like you would prefer a stout whiskey," Mr. Richmond inquired.

"No. A brandy is fine, sir," Hezekiah answered, not wanting to direct any unnecessary attention to himself.

"I'm sure he'd prefer a whiskey, Mr. Richmond," Isaac said with a quick intervention.

Why did he do that? Hezekiah thought. Doesn't he know I'm nervous enough? Of course he does. He did it on purpose.

While waiting for the call to supper, the women sat at one end of the room and the men gathered at the other end. Hezekiah had no idea of the direction of conversation of the women, but he found little interest in the men's conversation as they discussed business and news from the East or the Oregon Territory. Hezekiah attempted to generally listen to the conversation, fearing he might at any time be asked a question or opinion.

With every opportunity he would glance towards the women to have another look at Kathryn. He could see Charlotte making facial expressions at Kathryn, obviously looking for answers on her impression of Hezekiah. Kathryn was not responding as she listened to the other women.

How do you feel about me? Hezekiah wondered. She had seemed pleasant, but maybe she is pleasant and cordial to everyone.

The announcement came that supper was being served, and everyone proceeded to the dining room. Its elegance was at least equal to the rest of the house.

Hezekiah, convinced it was no accident, was seated next to Kathryn and across the table from Isaac and Charlotte. Hezekiah fumbled with his napkin as the maid began serving the soup. The basic understanding of eating soup was easy enough, but the actual undertaking was quite different. No spilling, slurping or bending. Hezekiah glanced across the table at Isaac. He seemed to be handling it quite well. Perhaps he had already become accustomed to the luxury that surrounded him.

Hezekiah began slowly. If he made a blunder it would ruin the remainder of the evening. To his joyous relief he finished the soup without incident.

He looked up and was astonished to see Isaac making facial expressions toward him as Isaac's eyes danced back and forth between he and Kathryn. Was he crazy? Kathryn would see him. Hezekiah quickly turned away. He could hear the conversation at the other end of the table. He realized he had not spoken to Kathryn since they were seated. She must think I'm terrible, he thought. What could he say to her that would break the ice? Surely he had questions he could ask her. He remembered how he had acted like an idiot the day Christina had come to him on the street to introduce herself. Here he was again, acting in the same stupid fashion.

Hezekiah remained silent as the main course was served. When it was finished, he was back to his same situation. What was he going to say to her? He would ask her how she liked Virginia City. He turned slightly towards her, his mouth pursed to speak. He could smell the sweet aroma of her cologne.

"Mr. Templeton," Mr. Richmond's voice boomed from the end of the table, causing Hezekiah to jump. Hezekiah turned to face him. "I must say I'm quite disappointed in you."

Everyone sat quiet, their eyes darting back and forth between the two men. Hezekiah's skin crawled from the penetrating stare of the host. His body felt drained. What terrible thing had he done wrong? Could it possibly deserve humiliation in front of everyone, particularly Kathryn? Was this going to be another Parson Blackwell moment?

Mr. Richmond continued, "Based on all theses stories I've heard about you from Isaac, I expected more from you-to be shrouded in gold perhaps, and as a banker, I was rather looking forward to that."

Everyone burst into laughter. Hezekiah, trying to conceal his embarrassment, joined in.

After dinner, the older guests accompanied Mr. and Mrs. Richmond back to the parlor, while the four younger people gathered on the front porch.

"I do believe my father likes you, Hezekiah," Charlotte said as she firmly pulled Isaac next to her on one side of the double-sided swing. "He teases the ones he likes. Isn't that right, Isaac?" she continued, clutching his arm.

Hezekiah realized how cleverly Charlotte had taken control of the situation by leaving the other half of the swing open for him and Kathryn. Kathryn had noticed the obvious also as she gave Charlotte a curious glance before seating herself. Hezekiah, feeling awkward standing alone, slid into the narrow seat next to Kathryn, being careful not to brush her or sit on her skirt.

"Do you have enough room?" Kathryn asked.

"I'm fine, thank you." Hezekiah smiled nervously at her.

"Goodness, you two act like you carry some dreaded, contagious disease," Charlotte said, glancing from one to the other.

Kathryn's face became flush. "You're horrible, Charlotte," she said. "Isaac, can't you contain her?"

Charlotte just smiled with a look of satisfaction. Hezekiah concluded it would be a long embarrassing evening if he allowed Charlotte to remain in control. He had to break the lingering silence. With all his inner power, he turned to better view Kathryn. "I'm not sure I understand," he said. "Are you visiting Charlotte for the wedding or are you planning to take up residence here?" He felt relieved. It was out and he concluded it had sounded quite good.

"Actually, I'm not sure," she answered, glancing at Charlotte as though expecting to be interrupted. "All my family is in Oregon. My original intention was to only come for the wedding."

"Pooh," Charlotte quickly sounded. "Hezekiah, tell her how foolish she would be not to stay. She's my dearest friend, and I know I would surely die without her." Charlotte dramatically pretended to wipe a tear from her eye.

"Well, it certainly is my favorite place. But I'm sure it would be difficult to leave your family in Oregon."

"But her friends are here. We're like family you know," Charlotte said with a persistent air.

"Friends are important," Hezekiah replied quickly. "I say you should stay."

"Wonderful," Charlotte answered joyfully. "Don't you agree, Isaac? You have your best friend here. Why shouldn't I have mine?"

"I certainly say yes," Isaac said, nodding his head. "You could help keep Hezekiah out from under my feet all the time."

Everyone laughed. The cheerful sound echoed from the porch and into the darkened night.

"I'd have to say these pair are two of a kind when it comes to teasing," Hezekiah said, shaking his head. "Kathryn, you have to stay to help protect me from them."

"We'll see," Kathryn replied. "It is nice to be wanted...for whatever reason."

"I guess I need to learn how to keep my foot out of my mouth," Hezekiah said, throwing his hands up in defeat.

The tension had subsided and everyone began enjoying the evening fully as laughter filtered through the evening air. Charlotte became quieter as she sat confidently smiling, watching Kathryn and Hezekiah, only adding to the conversation if she thought it might stall.

When the older guests said good evening to the Richmonds, Hezekiah and Isaac decided they should also leave.

Hezekiah paused and looked one last time at Kathryn's soft delightful eyes. He wanted to gently touch her face...to feel its beauty. For so long, he had never imagined anyone being this beautiful other than Christina...this desirable.

****

After Hezekiah and Isaac left for the evening, Charlotte and Kathryn retired to their room. Kathryn began preparing herself for an interrogation from Charlotte. She did not have long to wait.

As Kathryn sat at the dressing table, combing her hair, she could see Charlotte in the mirror closing the door. A curious expression covered Charlotte's face as she went to the bed and flopped herself across it. Kathryn could no longer see her friend, but she knew Charlotte was watching her. She chose to ignore Charlotte for the moment, knowing Charlotte's inquisitiveness would not restrain her much longer. Their years of friendship had taught Kathryn that Charlotte was not one to remain silent when she had something on her mind.

"I found Mr. Hezekiah Templeton to be rather disappointing," Charlotte began.

The remark caught Kathryn by surprise, but quickly realized Charlotte was only baiting her. Kathryn calmly continued to look into the mirror, still brushing her hair. "Really," Kathryn said dryly. "I thought he seemed rather pleasant."

"I found him boring and certainly not as handsome as I had imagined," Charlotte added, still lying across the bed.

"Perhaps you're right," Kathryn said, trying to refrain from giggling. Your move, Charlotte, she thought.

Charlotte became quiet for a moment. Kathryn wanted to see Charlotte's expression, but she knew she dared not look if she wanted to remain in control. She knew there was no one better at this game than Charlotte.

"Such a shame," Charlotte said with an air of despair. "I had so hoped." She paused, but when there was no answer, continued, "I did think he found you to his liking."

"I guess. It really doesn't matter, though," Kathryn said, still looking straight ahead. "I do believe I shall pursue the possibilities with Harold. He seems quite interested and I think he is quite handsome and interesting."

"You find him interesting?" Charlotte had now risen from the bed and was moving towards Kathryn.

"I do find him very charming," Kathryn answered calmly, although her insides felt as though they would burst. "I can't believe you don't find him charming," she added, casting only a quick glance at Charlotte.

"That arrogant, pompous ass. How could you, Kathryn?"

"Charlotte! Such language."

Charlotte was now along side Kathryn. Kathryn could now see the expression on her friend's face. She could hardly contain her laughter. Kathryn had a triumphant feeling of satisfaction, having defeated Charlotte at her own game.

"Hezekiah was absolutely wonderful," Charlotte stammered. "How could you not feel otherwise?"

"Really, Charlotte, I think you're exaggerating. You said yourself that he was boring and a disappointment."

Kathryn looked at the frustration on Charlotte's face. She could no longer control herself and began to giggle.

"Kathryn, I'm going to get you for this. You had me half-frightened out of my wits. I thought you had lost all your senses. Harold. Really."

"You asked for what you got. It's about time somebody returned your teasing."

"Okay. I admit I had it coming. Now, tell me, what did you really think of Mr. Templeton?"

"He's interesting and quite handsome, I'll admit that," Kathryn answered, feeling a little bashful.

"Interesting?" Charlotte asked excitedly.

Kathryn raised her eyebrows. "Very," she answered with a smile.

"I'm so excited," Charlotte said, throwing herself across the bed. "I just knew everything would be wonderful."

CHAPTER 30

"**D**o you think Charlotte will like it?" Isaac asked, critically examining the completed house.

"She'll love it," Hezekiah responded. "It was built by the hands of the man she loves. How could she not love it?"

Isaac continued to stare at the house, his head shaking slowly as though doubting his friend's opinion. "It'll be quite a change from the home she lives in now."

"Relax. What'll be most important to her is it'll be your home."

"I hope so. I want her to be happy."

Hezekiah cupped his hand to his ear. "Listen," he said mysteriously.

"What?" Isaac questioned, straining to hear the sound.

"Can't you hear it?"

"No. I don't hear anything unusual"

"The sounds of children coming from the house. Sounds like a dozen of them." Hezekiah was displaying a broad smile.

Isaac shook his head with an air of disgust. "You fool. I think you're a little premature there, friend."

"No...not at all. The spirits have spoken."

"I think you're listening to the voice of a lunatic," Isaac said, shaking his head.

Hezekiah's smile disappeared as he looked seriously at Isaac. "So how many do I hear?"

"I don't know," Isaac said, feeling awkward with the questioning. "We've never discussed it."

"You should have discussed that before you even became engaged. How could you not talk about how many children you wanted?"

"Damn, Hezekiah, it's kind of awkward talking about things like that."

Hezekiah was standing face to face with Isaac. "How'd you ever get up enough nerve to ask Charlotte to marry you? If you can't even discuss children, how are you ever going to get up enough nerve on your wedding night to …to…you know?"

"Why are you so damn concerned about how many children we're going to have? And I'll be fine on my wedding night." Isaac had become flush from Hezekiah's questioning.

"Damn! This is important. I want you and Charlotte to be happy more than anything. Maybe you should have read more of Johnny what's-his-name's book. There is more to it than cleavage, you know."

"Since when are you such an all fired expert? Do you have some experience you haven't been telling me?"

Hezekiah ignored the retaliating question. "Common sense should give someone a few clues," Hezekiah said as a grin began to appear.

Isaac, seeing Hezekiah's lighter expression, grasped the opportunity to change the conversation. "Hey, I got a pretty good lesson from Sadie and the Parson," Isaac responded with a chuckle. He was relieved that Hezekiah was relaxing on his interrogation.

"Yeah, I guess you're right. There were certainly some lessons to be learned that day. More than any book could teach."

They both laughed at their recollection of that fine day. Hezekiah threw himself to the ground. "I still can't get over how scary the Parson was with his black suit on, and how ridiculous he looked when it was off."

"His face...," Isaac shouted. "The look on his face when he dropped the blanket and was standing there naked as a new born babe."

"Those were the good old days, Isaac. Too bad they're gone forever."

"Yeah, they were good," Isaac said with a more serious tone, "but you know, as good as they were, I've never been happier than I am now."

"That's good," Hezekiah responded, sitting up.

"Are you happy, Hez?" Isaac questioned, a sincere concern sounded in his voice.

"I am." Hezekiah shrugged his shoulders. "There's some things I'd wish I could change in the past, but honestly, I think I'm happy."

"Good. I think Kathryn could make you happy."

Hezekiah raised his hand. "Hold on there. I think you're the one rushing things now."

"It was just a thought, that's all," Isaac quickly responded, throwing his hands up. "Now we're even, so let's go have a beer and celebrate the completion of this house."

Hezekiah agreed and they headed for the Fairweather Inn.

"You want to go to Sadie's old place," Isaac asked as they approached the saloon.

"No, the Fairweather is fine," Hezekiah replied without showing any expression.

They continued on in silence. Isaac watched Hezekiah from the corner of his eye. He hated lying to Hezekiah. Isaac knew his friend still had feelings for Christina, but he still felt he had done the right thing by not telling Hezekiah about her. He would never forget the haunting words of Eagle Feather, 'The Spirits have said there is great danger for Silent Hawk that will come from his past.' Isaac wished he could better understand the warning from Eagle Feather. If he had something more specific that would allow him to help protect his friend.

"Hey, you going to buy me that beer or not," Hezekiah said, bringing Isaac back to the present. "You must have been rehearsing your wedding night the way you were walking right on by the saloon."

"Yeah, well, practice makes perfect," Isaac answered, trying not to show his concern.

Once inside the saloon, they purchased their beers and found a table in the corner.

Isaac sipped the foam from the top of his glass. "You decided what you're going to do?"

"About what?"

"For work. Are you going to take up carpentry?"

"For a while I guess. Not sure what else I could do."

"Kind of like me I guess. If I gave up the mill, I don't know what I'd do either." Isaac took a long drink. "You're pretty good with carpentry. You'd do right well by it."

"It's a honest living. I'm just not sure if that's what I want to do the rest of my life." Hezekiah rubbed his forehead. "It'd be nice to have a choice." Hezekiah smiled. "Maybe I'll run for sheriff."

"Yeah. Maybe I'll run for governor."

Hezekiah squinted his eyes. "What? You trying to say I wouldn't make a good sheriff? I'm about half serious. You could be my deputy. We'd bring this town to its knees."

Isaac tilted his head and finished his beer. "Yeah, we'd bring them to their knees with laughter. I have to admit though, it does sound exciting."

"Maybe one of these days," Hezekiah said seriously, nodding his head in thought.

"Want another beer?" Isaac asked as he looked at their empty mugs.

"No. You know what I really want to do." Hezekiah was leaning forward as though ready to tell a secret. "I'd like to go to Eagle Feather's burial site. That's what I'd really like to do."

"A damn good idea. I should have taken you there sooner. Let's go."

****

The two men on horseback weaved their way through a grove of tall pine trees. Hezekiah was amazed at the distance Isaac had taken their friend to give him a proper burial. Hezekiah knew how alone Isaac must have felt, and how difficult it must have been for him. Hezekiah wished he could have been there. It had been an important time for both of his friends. There were so many things that just never seemed to come out right.

Hezekiah suddenly pulled in his reins. He realized the familiarity of the area.

"Isaac, can we swing down this draw. I think it was just over that ridge where father died."

A look of surprise came to Isaac's face. "I didn't know, Hez. I never knew where he died."

"I'm sure it is. I had often wondered if I would remember the place. Now I know I'll never forget it." Hezekiah carefully studied the surrounding land as they approached the ledge where his father had gone over. "It looks so peaceful and non-threatening now," Hezekiah said, almost sounding bewildered. "That day, the blizzard was so bad. I tell you, it was hell out here. I was so damn frightened. I often wondered what father's thoughts were as he laid there alone and whether he was frightened."

"I'm sure his thoughts were of you and your mother."

"I wish I had stayed with him. I should have. I know that now. You know, that day, I had never felt closer to him. It was like we really knew and understood each other for the first time. It was such a good feeling."

"I sort of know how you feel," Isaac said. "When my father became so ill, and I worked with him at the mill, we truly became friends then. We used to talk a lot. I never really knew all the dreams he had inside him before then. It's too bad we put things off until it's too late."

"A real shame," Hezekiah replied. "I so often wish I had another chance."

They became quiet as they moved along the ledge. Hezekiah reined in his horse, slipped from the saddle, and walked to the edge of the ravine. Isaac waited on his horse, allowing Hezekiah to be alone. Isaac looked away, wanting to give Hezekiah a private moment.

After several minutes had passed, Hezekiah was along side Isaac, mounting his horse.

"Okay, let's go." Hezekiah said. He showed no emotion other than a somber quietness.

They rode on, neither speaking.

****

Not until Hezekiah and Isaac had arrived at the burial site did either speak. "This is it," Isaac said, pointing to the hillside. "Eagle Feather is up there on the plateau."

Hezekiah nodded as his eyes focused first on Eagle Feather's burial platform, and then he slowly surveyed the surrounding area as he turned in his saddle from side to side.

"Nice out here," Hezekiah said, nodding his head in approval. "It really is beautiful. I'm sure Eagle Feather must be very pleased."

They both dismounted. "I'll wait here," Isaac said. "It'll give you a chance to be alone with our old friend."

Hezekiah climbed the hill to the small plateau. He stared momentarily at the platform before him, then turned and looked out over the valley. "Gray Wolf did good for you, old friend. Damn, I really wish I could have seen you. I miss having you to talk to. I thought about you a lot while I was in St. Louis, wishing I could be here...I've never had a better friend than you, you know. You helped me through some hard times."

Hezekiah looked down the hill where Isaac was waiting. He could see Isaac throwing rocks at some nearby gophers. "Someday, Isaac's going to hit one of those gophers, Eagle Feather. He'll probably end up feeling guilty about it when he does."

269

Hezekiah turned back to the platform. "I'm sure sorry I wasn't here for you. That's what friends are suppose to do."

Then suddenly a warming sensation began to fill his body. It was different than the heat from the hot sun. It was like it came from inside him. At first, it startled him, but slowly his body began to relax, almost to the point of losing his footing.

Then as mysteriously as it came, it left, leaving him light-headed.

"Whew. I think I better go, friend. I'm feeling a might funny. But I promise I'll be back soon."

Hezekiah stumbled down the hillside to where Isaac was waiting.

"You felt it, didn't you," Isaac shouted. "By damn, you did."

"I'm feeling something," Hezekiah answered as he removed his hat and wiped his brow.

"I thought all along, maybe it was just me. But now that I know you feel the same way, it's got to be Eagle Feather. He's letting us know his spirit is here."

"Wait a minute, Isaac. I think your imagination is getting carried away."

"Explain it then," Isaac said, his eyes wide with excitement.

"I can't...at least not now. Have you told anyone about this?"

"No. They'd think I was crazy. Besides it might cause some people to come sticking their nose around here and disturb Eagle Feather's peace."

"I just can't accept what you're saying," Hezekiah said, sitting on a boulder, staring at the platform above him.

"Damn, Hez. Didn't you believe any of the stuff that Eagle Feather used to tell us?"

"Yeah. Sure...At least, most of it. Back then, anyway."

"Didn't the incident with the hawk happen?"

"Yeah. But that's different"

"Is it? I don't think so."

"You know you make it hard to argue against...What you're saying and all, but when you're face to face with the thoughts of spirits being all around you, it's pretty hard to accept."

"I know. I can understand that," Isaac responded, nodding his head. "In time, you'll be more convinced. It took me a while too. In fact, until you came off that hill, I wasn't fully convinced either. But I sure in the hell am now."

CHAPTER 31

Hezekiah had remembered Mr. Richmond's words, 'We have but one child to marry and by damn this town...hell no, this territory will never forget her wedding'.

Saturday, a week before the wedding, was the beginning of the weeklong celebration with a buffet supper and dance. Hezekiah was pleased to have a reason to see Kathryn, but he did have a problem. His dancing skills were poor...In fact, he could not dance a lick, and he was sure Kathryn would be an excellent dancer. But if he did not dance with her, there certainly would be numerous other gentlemen awaiting her beckoning call.

Hezekiah had only one choice and the thought chilled him. He would have to ask Isaac to teach him. Surely Charlotte had taught Isaac how to dance. It was the afternoon of the dance before Hezekiah had accumulated enough nerve to ask Isaac for the unusual favor.

Hezekiah stood across the room, watching his friend dry the last of the noon meal dishes. Isaac hung the drying towel and inquisitively faced Hezekiah. "What the hell is wrong with you?" Isaac questioned. "You've been acting strange all day. I thought I was the one that was suppose to be nervous."

"Are you?" Hezekiah asked, delaying his real question.

"I guess a little, but hell, I have a right to be. I'm solid as a rock compared to you. You're acting like a dog that's cornered a porcupine."

"Yeah, well-l-l, I've got a problem."

"Sounds serious. I'm almost afraid to ask what it is." Isaac's face seemed stuck between a state of concern and laughter. "It can't be that bad."

"Well, it sort of is that bad," Hezekiah mumbled as he turned and looked out the window again. "I can't dance worth a plug cent."

"Did I hear you right? You can't dance...Not at all?"

Hezekiah looked at Isaac. Isaac tried to hold back a smile that was pushing outward to his lips. "No. Not at all," Hezekiah said, feeling a little irritated. "What's so damn unusual about that?"

"Hell, I thought you being in St. Louis for a year, you would put the rest of us to shame."

"Yeah, well there wasn't too many of those high flouting girls there in St. Louis that wanted anything to do with a backcountry hick. Will you teach me?" Hezekiah mumbled as he began looking out the window again.

"Teach you? You mean like us dancing around the room here?" Isaac no longer could contain the smile. Now he was fighting back the laughter.

Hezekiah looked sheepishly at Isaac. "I don't know. Whatever it takes."

They looked at each other, and both started laughing. Isaac slumped into a chair. "I must be half out of my mind. Okay. I'll teach you...now mind you, I'm not much of a dancer myself." Isaac slowly shook his head. "I sure hope nobody shows up here while were dosadoing around the room."

"Where do we start?" Hezekiah asked.

"I guess for starters on our feet," Isaac replied, rising from the chair.

"What are we going to do for music?" Hezekiah asked.

"I don't know. You think I've done this before? You know any tunes you can hum?"

"I know 'John Brown's body'."

That's great. Tonight we'll be the only damn fools that'll know how to dance to it. That should impress the hell out of everyone." Isaac again burst into laughter, immediately followed by Hezekiah.

Once Isaac regained control, he suggested, "Why don't I just show you the steps. Maybe it'll help keep you off poor Kathryn's feet."

After an hour of clumsy frolic, Hezekiah had memorized the steps to Isaac's satisfaction. Isaac fell back into a chair and with a look of concern, slowly leaned forward. "I have two request," he said deliberately.

Hezekiah sweating from the exertion, leaned against the wall and wiped his forehead. "What's that?"

"First, don't count the steps out loud tonight."

Hezekiah smiled. "I guess I can do that. What else?"

"Whatever you do, don't tell anyone that I was the one who taught you to dance."

"Okay. I also have one request."

"And it is?"

"Will you save a dance for me tonight?"

Isaac nodded. "Only if I get to lead, and you wear some perfume."

The lesson ended with a final burst of laughter.

****

Isaac and Hezekiah arrived early at the Richmond home so that Isaac could greet the guests with Charlotte. When they arrived at the back of the house, Hezekiah looked around in astonishment at the elaborate setting the Richmonds had prepared. Their well-manicured estate was gaily decorated with streamers and flowers. A long table at one side was busily being prepared with food. In the corner, a whole pig was being roasted over a hot bed of coals. In the center, boards were carefully laid to serve as the dance floor, and at one end, a platform awaited the musicians. Around the dance floor, numerous benches were placed to seat those who would observe the dancing rather than participate…a place where Hezekiah thought perhaps he should remain. Bottles of whiskey, brandy, and kegs of beer sat behind the bar that would make any saloonkeeper envious. Lanterns hung overhead, waiting to be lit at the first sign of darkness.

Hezekiah looked for Kathryn, but other than the help, only Mrs. Richmond was present as she busily directed everyone where to precisely place each item.

"Hi boys," she called out to them. "Charlotte and Kathryn should be out shortly. You know how women are about getting ready. One last cinch on the corset." She smiled. "Fix yourselves a drink. No sense waiting for the bartender." With that, she scurried back into the house to oversee the workers inside.

"Shall we?" Isaac asked, pointing to the abundantly supplied bar.

"I think we could both use one." Hezekiah's stomach was already churning from the anticipation of the unknown. "How come you don't seem nervous?" he asked Isaac.

"I am. Why are you so nervous? Dreading to dance with Kathryn?"

"The way I dance, wouldn't you?"

Isaac handed Hezekiah his whiskey, and sipped from his own before answering. "How could I forget? You do have a reason to be nervous." Isaac smiled triumphantly.

"Thanks friend for instilling some confidence in me," Hezekiah said, playfully punching Isaac's shoulder.

"Hey, Hey. No brawling," Charlotte called out from behind them. The two surprised men turned to find Charlotte and Kathryn standing on the steps of the porch. "This isn't a saloon I'll have you know," Charlotte playfully scolded.

"Honest, dear, I've been trying to control his unruliness," Isaac responded, "but I've deemed it hopeless."

But Isaac and Charlotte had little success embarrassing Hezekiah. His complete attention was elsewhere. "Good evening, Kathryn. You look mighty beautiful tonight." Hezekiah meant every word as he stared in awe at her radiant flowing hair resting on her bare white shoulders. He quickly glanced at her cleavage, then back to her face, remembering his embarrassing moment with Christina.

Kathryn smiled. "Why thank you, Hezekiah. I'm glad to see you are taking the horrible teasing of these two very well."

How could he ever be successful in winning the heart of such an elegant woman...particularly the way he danced? He quickly tried to remember the dance steps. His brain was dead. He felt a moment of panic. Maybe he could get Isaac to the side later to refresh his memory.

"Not that either of you care, but guests are arriving and Isaac and I must go to greet them," Charlotte said, casting a departing glance at Hezekiah and Kathryn.

"That's fine," Hezekiah answered as Charlotte grasped Isaac's arm and led him away. Hezekiah looked beyond them to the gate. No guests had yet arrived.

"I guess she was mistaken," Kathryn said, obviously noticing the empty gate, too.

"She's nervous I suppose," Hezekiah added, trying to cover up the obvious. "May I get you something to drink?"

"Yes, that would be nice. Punch please." She gently took his arm and they walked to the bar. He could smell the sweetness of her perfume. He had not smelled such a pleasant fragrance since Christina.

Hezekiah was so nervous he could hardly hold the ladle while pouring her drink. He was afraid she would notice his trembling hand.

"Maybe it's too bold of me, but may I write your name on my card for the first dance?" she asked.

As he looked up from the glass, he caught a glimpse of her soft bare shoulders. How could he refuse the opportunity to hold her, even at the risk of looking foolish?

"Yes. That would be great," he said hoarsely. "But I must warn you, I'm a terrible dancer and I'm sure I'll embarrass you."

"If you feel uncomfortable," she said, looking somewhat rejected.

Seeing her face, Hezekiah quickly recovered. "No. Really. I would love too."

She smiled. "You'll do just fine. Maybe the first one will be slow."

He had to try. Besides, it would be one less time some other man would be able to dance with her. The party had not even started and he already felt jealous.

The guests were now beginning to arrive and they were making their way to the bar and introducing themselves to Kathryn and Hezekiah. Somehow Hezekiah found himself separated from Kathryn in separate conversations, but his glances always assured him where she was and whom she was conversing with at all times. Although he never caught her looking, he wondered if she too was watching him.

As the evening progressed, his anxiety grew as he watched the musicians gather near the platform. He tried to eat, but found the food unsettling. He returned to the bar and ordered another glass of whiskey. The screeching of the fiddles warming up rang through the darkening night air as the sun began to settle in the western sky with a golden glow. The lanterns were lit and he could sense the excitement of everyone as they prepared for the gala evening of dancing. He quickly gulped his whiskey.

He began reviewing the dance steps he had learned earlier in the day...forward one, two, turn...no wait...one, two, back one, turn. Yes! That was it.

Hezekiah felt a gentle arm slide into his and a familiar sweet fragrance flowed pleasantly into his nostrils. Hezekiah turned and looked into Kathryn's sparkling green eyes.

"I didn't want to miss the first dance," she said.

"You may wish you did."

"Never. Even if you step on my toes." She smiled and gently patted his cheek.

277

The voice of one of the musicians sounded, sending a chill up Hezekiah's spine to the top of his head. "Gentlemen, grab your special dance partner."

He could feel Kathryn tug his arm as they moved towards the dance floor. He began to feel light-headed. He should not have drunk that last whiskey, he thought. He could see Isaac watching him as the musicians started up 'Buffalo Gals Won't You Come Out Tonight'. It certainly was not the slow one he had hoped for, he thought begrudgingly.

Kathryn flowed into his arms and they started to move. At first, his feet had difficulty moving to the sound of the music. He could feel nervous sweat on his forehead. The steps Isaac had taught him didn't seem to work worth a damn to this music.

Fortunately, his feet began to find their own movement, and he found himself relatively enjoying it...in a survival sort of way.

Kathryn was a perfect partner, moving gracefully to his lead. Her head moved with such a gentle flow, causing her hair to shine in the lantern light.

Although relieved, Hezekiah felt disappointed when the music stopped. As they stepped from the dance floor, he saw Isaac smiling and nodding his approval.

"And you were worried about dancing," Kathryn said, squeezing his arm with hers. "You were wonderful." But before Hezekiah could respond, a young gentleman was asking her for the next dance.

It's going to be a competitive evening, he thought, watching Kathryn step onto the floor with her new partner. He looked on in dismay as the couple floated around the floor with perfect grace and unison to 'Pop Goes The Weasel'. Even more unsettling to him, was that many of the other guests were also observing and commenting on their excellence. In his whole life, he could never match what he was watching.

"Pretty good aren't they." As Hezekiah turned, Isaac slapped him on the arm. "I think you need a new dance teacher with competition like that."

"Yeah. I was just starting to get a little confidence, but now...I feel stupid."

"Hey, you did pretty darn good. Besides Kathryn likes you. She could care less about Harold Tibbs."

"Who is he anyway?"

"Harold. He works for Mr. Richmond at the bank. A real smug, stiff-collar sort of guy."

"So what makes you think Kathryn wouldn't find him to her liking."

"Actually, I don't know. I guess you better get your wagon hitched old friend." Isaac chuckled and walked away.

Hezekiah looked back to the dance floor. Why wouldn't Kathryn be attracted to Harold? She would probably consider him handsome. He certainly was a fine dresser and excellent dancer...and she certainly seemed to be enjoying his company, he thought, watching them laughing as they precariously swung around the floor.

Hezekiah went to the bar after another whiskey. He had just been served when he heard the music stop. He turned to find the whereabouts of Kathryn. She was standing at the edge of the dance floor, politely listening to the boring small talk of Harold. She spotted Hezekiah and smiled. Hezekiah decided he had to take the risk of looking foolish on the dance floor.

Hezekiah sat his drink down and began to hurry through the crowd towards Kathryn. Suddenly, a hand reached out and grasped him by the arm. It was Mr. Richmond.

"Enjoying the party, son?"

"Oh yes, sir," Hezekiah answered politely. Mr. Richmond was now standing between he and Kathryn. Hezekiah wondered if he was purposely trying to keep Kathryn in the clutches of his understudy?

"Father, can I see you for a moment?" Hezekiah looked in the direction of Charlotte's voice.

"You may, my dear," Mr. Richmond said as he proudly strutted towards her.

Charlotte winked at Hezekiah. He realized she was freeing him to pursue Kathryn. She had been observing he and Kathryn as though they were actors in a play. He smiled and continued his struggle through the crowd. But it was too late. The music started and as he broke through the throng of people, he saw Kathryn and Harold move onto the dance floor. Damn, it was a slow one too, he thought. Kathryn glanced at him and smiled as she passed. Is she trying to make me jealous? Well she's doing a fine job.

Hezekiah watched them move around the floor. He decided Harold was holding her much too close. He waited patiently for the dance to end. He was not going to miss another opportunity, no matter how badly he danced. But when the music stopped, he watched in bewilderment as Harold coyly escorted Kathryn to the opposite end of the floor.

Hezekiah began to debate his counter move, but before he could make his decision, the music started again. Disappointed and not wanting the painful task of watching Harold and Kathryn again, he started back to the bar. But before he had made his dejected way through the crowd, he felt an arm slip into his, and heard Kathryn's pleasant voice, "Aren't you going to dance with me?"

"Of course!" Hezekiah shouted. Embarrassed by his sudden outburst, he looked around to see if anyone else had noticed.

As they began to dance across the floor, to his pleasant surprise, his feet seemed to move with ease. How much better could Harold be than he was, he proudly thought, looking longingly into Kathryn's playful eyes?

When the music stopped, he glanced around to strategically prepare himself for a sneak attack from Harold. "It's so warm," Kathryn said, diverting his attention back to her. "I must be glowing terribly from all this dancing."

"You look great to me," Hezekiah responded, "but if you'd like, we could go for a walk."

"That would be perfect," she said, quickly grasping his arm and began to gently pull him towards the garden gate.

As they left the floor, he caught a glimpse of Harold's watchful eyes following their every move. Hezekiah smiled and took a deep breath, trying to refrain his urge to bellow out a triumphant bull moose call towards Harold.

They walked along the road away from the house. Hezekiah could hear the music and voices from the party, but at that moment, it all seemed so distant and unimportant.

"It's so refreshing out here. Your idea to go for a walk was splendid," Kathryn said, pushing her head forward to allow the light, gentle breeze to brush her face.

Hezekiah watched her gentle movements. How could she adapt to the ruggedness of the west so well and his mother and Cynthia could not. There was no one more delicate than Kathryn.

"Mr. Richmond must be pleased with the success of the party," Hezekiah said, not wanting the conversation to lull.

"Yes, he must be pleased. It is so elegant and everyone seems to be having a wonderful time."

And what do you think of Harold? Hezekiah thought. Do you find him as disgusting as I do?

"Do you realize this is the first time we've been alone?" Kathryn asked.

"By gosh, you're right," he answered, fully aware that it was.

"There are so many questions I've wanted to ask you. Isaac has told us a great deal about you, but that's all second hand," she said, carefully studying Hezekiah's face.

"I'm not very interesting. Not much to know, I'm afraid."

"I know that's not true. What are you thinking right now?"

Hezekiah stopped and looked at her. "You really want to know?"

"Of course."

Hezekiah bent over and lightly kissed her. He expected a shocked reaction, but her eyes were looking softly into his. He gently brought her into his arms and their lips met. When the kiss ended, he whispered, "That's what I was thinking."

"I'm glad I asked."

Her eyes convinced Hezekiah that she meant what she had said. He kissed her again.

CHAPTER 32

"What do you mean, you're not going to participate in the horse race?" Isaac said, standing with his hands on his hips. "You have to. You're the best man."

"I can't win with my old nag. Besides, I'm not much of a horseman, anyway," Hezekiah argued. Suddenly, the sun seemed much hotter.

"So what. I don't expect to win either," Isaac said, tipping his hat to the back of his head. "Besides, Kathryn needs someone to cheer on, and if you don't race, that'll only leave Harold for her to cheer for."

"I know what you're trying to do."

"Damn, Hez. You've got to race. It won't be any fun without you." Isaac looked with pleading eyes at Hezekiah. "Come on. For an old friend. Remember who delivered a note to Christina for you. Remember who taught you to dance."

"Okay. Okay. I'll race," Hezekiah said with an air of regret.

"Good!" Isaac shouted with jubilation. "Besides, you have nothing to worry about. Remember you came out on top even though you couldn't dance worth a hoot."

"I beg to differ with you. I danced like I had a fiddle in my leg. I'll just be glad when this race is over so I can crawl in a hole. Whose damn idea was this anyway?"

Isaac was grinning ear to ear. "Mr. Richmond. You want to tell him what you think of his idea?"

"No thanks," Hezekiah said grumbling. "I can find a better way to shorten my life."

It was set. Hezekiah would participate in the afternoon horse race, one of the planned events in the weeklong celebration. It was as though all of Hezekiah's inadequacies were being tested-his dinner etiquettes, dancing skills, and now his horsemanship. He had been fortunate to skirt disaster thus far, but he was sure the race would be his downfall. He could already see Kathryn, along with all the others, which would include Harold, finding enormous humor as he and his old nag crossed the finish line long after the others had arrived. His only hope would be that they would be so far behind, everyone would have left before he even arrived at the finish line.

****

"Riders mount your horses," Mr. Richmond shouted. The crowd, gathered at the end of town, cheered with a burst of excitement.

A dozen men climbed atop their horses. Hezekiah's stomach churned as he guided his old faithful mare to the starting line.

Isaac came along side him. "Take a deep breath, friend, because you'll be eating my dust from here on." Isaac winked at Hezekiah.

Hezekiah returned a faint smile. "I'll probably be so far behind, I won't even see any dust."

Mr. Richmond called for the riders' attention. "Gentlemen," he shouted, "here are the rules. You will ride out to Twin Buttes. A short distance off the road, you will find a pole with red kerchiefs attached to it. You are too take one of the kerchiefs and return with it. The first to cross the finish line with a kerchief wins. Any questions?"

"Twin Buttes was my idea," Isaac said excitedly, grinning like a little boy. "The pole marks the spot in memory of Sadie. I thought one last hurrah was in order for me as a bachelor."

"In memory of Sadie," Hezekiah shouted, raising his hat.

284

"In wonderful memory of Sadie," Isaac responded, also raising his hat. "Hell, I might even hang around for a while for old times sake."

Harold came alongside Isaac, sitting atop a stallion that Hezekiah estimated was at least four hands higher than his mare. He sat confidently looking at the crowd. Hezekiah followed his stare. Harold was looking directly at Kathryn.

Kathryn's face was aglow with excitement. Hezekiah thought he was going to be sick.

The other horses were becoming restless, anticipating their adventurous quest, but Hezekiah's mare stood silently still. Hezekiah leaned over and whispered in her ear, "Come on, old lady, don't go to sleep on me now."

"Men prepare to start," Mr. Richmond shouted, holding a revolver skyward.

The gun blasted, and the air was filled with the sounds of shouting, leather and hooves as men and horses surged forward.

Within a short distance, Hezekiah found himself at the back, and the distance from the other horses was growing rapidly. "That's okay, old girl," he shouted, "we'll save it for the end." But in his heart, he knew there would be nothing for the end. She had brought him all the way to Montana; he wasn't going to kill her for some damn race.

Before Hezekiah turned off the road at Twin Buttes, some of the riders were already returning, which included Harold at the front.

As Isaac met him, he shouted, "To the glory of Sadie."

Hezekiah grabbed the lone remaining kerchief. He recalled the day he and Isaac had watched from the tall grass as Sadie and the parson had left them a memory they would never forget. It had been a great day...a great time. Life was exciting and innocent. Pain seemed to be something that did not exist. For a moment he wanted to go back. Isaac had said he was never so happy as he was now, but somehow Hezekiah had not found that happiness, even with Kathryn. Maybe someday soon, he thought.

As Hezekiah began his return towards town, old lady suddenly found a renewed life in her, and although Hezekiah tried not to push her, she began gaining on some of the riders. To Hezekiah's amazement, she passed one, and then two more riders. By the time Hezekiah and old lady crossed the finish line, they had passed four riders.

Hezekiah patted her neck. "Great job, girl. You kept us out of last."

Hezekiah was not disappointed that he had not finished near the front. In fact he was delighted with his finish. But what was demoralizing was that Harold had won the race. Of all the damn luck, he thought.

He watched as Harold received his trophy from Charlotte. Harold rode proudly in front of the crowd, arrogantly displaying his trophy. He slowed as he passed Kathryn and smiled at her.

Hezekiah watched Kathryn to see her reaction. She smiled and applauded. Was she jubilant with Harold winning, Hezekiah wondered, or was she only being polite. Hezekiah suddenly felt angered with Kathryn. He never had to compete for Christina. She had always accepted him as he was. He was suddenly glad he had raced and lost. If Kathryn did not accept his defeat, then she was not the right one for him. It was now in the hands of Kathryn where his fate would lead him. Why was he being so jealous?

"That arrogant ass," Isaac mumbled as he rode along side of Hezekiah.

"Hey, he won," Hezekiah said calmly. "If I had won, I'd be doing the same thing."

"Wow, you're taking this calmly. You must be pretty confident about Kathryn."

"No. Can't say that I am." A wry smile came to Hezekiah's lips. "But you're right. He is an arrogant ass." Isaac and Hezekiah roared with laughter.

****

That same evening of the race, as the women took over the Richmond home for a bridal shower, the men proceeded to the back room of the Fairweather for a bachelor party.

When Hezekiah and Isaac arrived at the inn, Mr. Richmond and Isaac's two brothers-in-law, Frank and Herbert, were the only ones there. Hezekiah was relieved Harold had not yet arrived. Maybe he won't come, Hezekiah thought, but knowing all to well that he would not be that lucky.

It was obvious Mr. Richmond had a head start on the others on the consumption of the whiskey. "You boys got some catching up to do," he bellowed as he quickly filled their glasses with the potent distilled whiskey. "I've been waiting for this moment for almost nineteen years and I don't have my little woman watching over my shoulder tonight."

They all toasted the occasion. Mr. Richmond placed his arm around Isaac and guided him away from the others. A little last minute advice...or warning, Hezekiah concluded.

Hezekiah had never met Frank. He was a small slender man that spoke little and when he did, quietly. Herbert, quite the opposite, had not changed from their younger days in school. Each time he spoke, his chest would swell like a proud rooster ready to crow. He always seemed absolutely sure he knew everything about everything, or at least everything about anything that was important enough to know.

Hezekiah was relieved when the other guests began arriving so he could divert his attention away from Herbert. Mr. Richmond, seeing the new arrivals, slapped Isaac on the back and strolled to the door like a victorious general after a battle. Isaac, looking confused, glanced sheepishly at Hezekiah and shrugged his shoulders. Maybe Mr. Richmond was informing Isaac how many children he and Charlotte were expected to have, Hezekiah thought. Well, somebody needed to make the decision.

Isaac followed Mr. Richmond to greet the newcomers. Hezekiah, humored by his friend's sense of disarray, watched Isaac following Mr. Richmond like an obedient pup.

Hezekiah looked to the front door and quickly focused on Harold standing pompously in the doorway surveying the room. Harold's watchful eye stopped for a moment on Hezekiah and, then without expression, turned his attention towards Mr. Richmond.

Hezekiah took a big swig from his whiskey glass. He did not want to ignore Harold. It would only give him a sense of satisfaction knowing that he was getting to Hezekiah. Yet, Hezekiah did not want to be particularly friendly towards him either. Somehow he would have to find a way to treat him like everyone else...a chore he did not welcome or was not sure how to accomplish.

While Hezekiah was pondering his dilemma, he was surprised to see another familiar face appear at the doorway. It was Wilbur Sanders. Hezekiah would never forget how his strong voice had helped spare Eagle Feather's life. Hezekiah had remembered how his father had always spoken so highly of Wilbur Sanders.

Hezekiah watched the distinguished gentleman enter the room with confidence, yet showing no arrogance. He smiled graciously to those he met.

Harold, quickly realizing the importance of Wilbur Sanders, moved in to be introduced. But about then, Mr. Richmond spotting Hezekiah standing alone, and to Harold's look of surprise, led Wilbur Sanders towards Hezekiah.

"Wilbur," Mr. Richmond said as they reached Hezekiah, "this young man has just returned to us from St. Louis. Hezekiah, this is Wilbur Sanders, someday to be our next governor. Wilbur, this is Hezekiah Templeton."

Wilbur, ignoring the remark of being governor, smiled pleasantly at Hezekiah. "Templeton. You wouldn't happen to be the son of Sam Templeton?"

"Yes, sir, I am," Hezekiah said proudly, shaking Mr. Sander's hand.

"Your father was a very fine man," he said as he continued to shake Hezekiah's hand vigorously. His smile dissipated. "I was extremely saddened on my return from Washington to hear of his death. It was such an unfortunate accident. I'm also sorry about the rest of your family. Such a tragedy," he said, shaking his head. "I offer my sincere condolences."

"Thank you." Hezekiah looked at his confident, but gentle eyes. "My father spoke highly of you, Mr. Sanders. It's a real honor to meet you."

Wilbur smiled. "Indeed, it's my honor to meet you." He turned to Mr. Richmond. "I guess you never had the opportunity to meet Sam and his lovely wife."

"No I didn't," Mr. Richmond answered, looking somewhat shocked by Wilbur's exuberant excitement on meeting Hezekiah. "From knowing their son, I'm sure they were wonderful people."

Harold was standing nearby watching in dismay at the attention Hezekiah was receiving from such a distinguished person.

Wilbur seemed in no hurry to move on, and resumed his conversation. "So you moved back East for a while. Family, I presume."

"Yes, sir. My aunt and uncle." Hezekiah was beginning to feel more at ease. "Mr. Sanders, I would like to personally thank you for helping save my good friend, Eagle Feather a few years ago. You were very brave and I've always wanted to thank you."

Wilbur raised his eyebrows. "Eagle Feather. He was that old Indian from the livery stable they called Joe. It would have been a big tragedy if those men hadn't been stopped. We were just glad we were able to help."

"Still it was brave and it meant a lot to Isaac and me."

"So you were friends with him?"

"Yes, sir. He was Isaac's and my best friend."

"An Indian as your best friend," Harold said with a notable sarcasm in his voice.

"I find it very commendable," Wilbur said without even looking at Harold. "I wish I had taken the time to know him myself. I heard that he died."

"Yes, sir. We miss him, but one thing for sure, he taught us a great deal about life," Hezekiah said with pride.

"I'm sure he did," Wilbur said with a somber voice. He seemed to be digesting Hezekiah's remark for a moment before continuing, "So what are your plans now that you've returned?"

"I'm not sure. I've been helping Isaac finish his house since I've been back. I guess I could continue as a carpenter like my father. I know that would please him, but I'm just not sure if that's what I want."

"Tell you what," Wilbur said, "when I get back from my trip, which will be about six weeks, and if you wish, stop by my office and I may have some alternatives for you."

"I'll do that," Hezekiah answered excitedly. "I'm open to any ideas."

Wilbur smiled. "Good...and welcome back. He turned to Mr. Richmond for more introductions. Harold tagged along, still waiting for his introduction.

Hezekiah was feeling jubilant. What could Wilbur Sanders have to offer him? Hezekiah was already anxious for the meeting. And to add to the beauty of the evening, Harold had heard the entire conversation.

As the evening progressed, Hezekiah felt relieved that he had not had to deal with Harold. He did not seek out Harold, and Harold did not seek out him.

Mr. Richmond seemed to be enjoying the party more than anyone as he moved from one conversation to another, toasting every chance he could find. The abundance of toasts was obviously showing their results.

Late in the evening, Hezekiah heard a commotion near the rear of the room. He turned to see Herbert, with bloated chest, standing face to face with Harold. Herbert's fists were clenched and his face reddened. Harold stepped back, but Herbert stepped forward, maintaining only inches between them. Herbert's huge frame towered over Harold, making Harold look like a dwarf in comparison.

There was no doubt that if Herbert unleashed his fists against Harold, it would be devastating.

"You arrogant pup," Herbert shouted, "don't tell me what I don't know."

Without a moments thought, Hezekiah moved quickly in between the two men that he despised the most. He tried to keep his voice calm. "Herbert. You don't want to do this. Come on and tell me what all you've been doing with yourself since I left." He knew if anything would divert Herbert's attention, it would be the opportunity to talk about him.

Hezekiah tugged at Herbert's sleeve. He did not budge. For a moment, he wished Miss Harrelson would suddenly appear and separate Herbert from him. He tugged again. "Come on. Don't spoil Isaac's party."

Herbert grunted and began to reluctantly move back. His jaw remained clinched as Hezekiah continued to move him further away. Hezekiah never looked back at Harold, but the last time he had seen his face, it had been a ghostly white.

It was sometime before Hezekiah was able to pull himself away from the tormenting fate of listening to Herbert. When he did, he noticed Harold was gone.

A few hours earlier, Hezekiah would never have imagined that he would have risked his own neck for Harold. In fact, he would have thought he would have enjoyed such a moment. Now of all things, he felt somewhat sorry for Harold.

When the party ended, Isaac and Hezekiah helped Mr. Richmond home. They quickly escorted him inside, and left him swaggering down the long hall, bumping one side and then the other. They did not want to participate in-or be a witness to-any upcoming events that might be looming at the end of the hall.

After they left the Richmond home, they had a good laugh about Mr. Richmond's condition. However, Isaac was quick to change the subject. "Well, you sure loused up your opportunity to see Harold get the hell kicked out of him."

"I know. I guess I reacted without thinking. Actually, I don't think I'd gotten much enjoyment out of it. I'd rather do it myself when the time is right."

"I think Herbert may have scared a little humbleness into Harold, if that's possible. Maybe we'll see a changed Harold."

"Yeah. Just like we'll see a changed Herbert. Once a horse's rear-end, always a horse's rear-end," Hezekiah said, shaking his head in disgust."

"Hey, you're talking about family here," Isaac said.

"I know, and I feel damn sorry for you, too. I'd rather have a bad case of the piles than Herbert for a relative."

CHAPTER 33

Zeke Clemens rode quietly out of Denver, unnoticed and unsuspected. He had stayed too long. He needed to keep moving. He had already killed three women in Denver and to stay any longer would endanger his freedom.

Besides, enough time had passed. He would now be able to return to Virginia City with no suspicion and resume his search for the gold that he was sure still remained hidden somewhere in the area. Those damn vigilantes had disrupted their operation and everyone that knew where the gold had been stashed was dead and buried six feet under. He deserved it. He had done his fair share. But he had other reasons for wanting to return to Virginia City. It was where he had discovered the excitement and power he felt from killing. It was where his memory burned feverishly from the killing of the woman and boy. The memory had remained most memorable to him and the desire to return and relive it had remained with him all this time. He had left in too big a hurry. There had been no time to savor the moment.

Also, it had been Virginia City where he had remembered the beautiful and tantalizing saloon maid. She had been so delicate and helpless. He could never forget her. He had often imagined her eyes pleading for her life. Christina, that was her name. "You will soon to be mine, Christina," he kept repeating as he felt the fire begin to rage inside him at a feverish pitch. Yes, it was time to return, he thought as he urged his horse into a gallop.

****

Hezekiah sat up in bed. He was covered with perspiration. The nightmare had returned. But why now? It had stopped since he had arrived in Virginia City. He was convinced Aunt Jane had been right. Once he had stopped thinking about revenge for his mother's death, the nightmares had stopped. But now, not only had the nightmare returned, they were different from the ones he had before tonight. His mother's killer was attacking a woman, but this time it was not his mother. He could not see the woman's face, but her voice was familiar. He was certain it had been Christina. He could hear her mournful cries for help, but he could not move. He was frozen with fear. All he could do was watch with horror as the ruthless killer attacked her; just like he had frozen the day his mother was murdered.

As Hezekiah lied in bed shivering, he could see the first light of dawn. He arose. Isaac was still sleeping. Hezekiah boiled a pot of coffee and quietly sat at the table, drinking the dark brew.

He could not stop thinking about the nightmare. Why had it returned...and why had it changed? Now it was more terrifying than ever. At least before, he had understood why he was having it.

Life had been a dream of splendor the past three weeks. He had been hesitant to admit it, but he knew he was falling in love with Kathryn. He had almost forgotten about Christina. But the nightmare had returned her to him.

He wondered if she was happy and did she ever think of him. He felt responsible for her well-being. It had been he that had convinced her to start a new life. Had he diverted her into a dangerous situation? Maybe the nightmare was a warning...or did it mean he was still in love with her? But how could he be in love with her and Kathryn? Could he be that terrible of a scoundrel? Surely no decent man could love two women.

****

When Isaac wakened, he found an empty cabin. A half empty cup of cold coffee sat on the table. It was not until late morning before Hezekiah returned. Hezekiah never mentioned where he had been and Isaac never asked, but a distant look in Hezekiah's eyes made Isaac fear that his friend was troubled. Was it something about Hezekiah's past? Eagle Feather had warned Isaac. Isaac felt helpless and uncertain what to do for his friend. He just had to be there...be ready to help when it was needed.

****

It was Friday, the day before the wedding. The plans for the day were a wedding rehearsal and a supper for the wedding party and family.

As usual, the Richmonds spared nothing. Prime rib was served in elaborate portions with all the trimmings.

After supper, the younger folks proceeded to the front porch. Hezekiah was relieved that Isaac's two sisters were there, and, of course, Frank and Herbert. With Herbert present, it made it easy for Hezekiah to remain silent, which he found to his liking. He was still feeling the affects of his nightmare.

"Just think, Isaac," Herbert said, his voice echoing through the night air, "this time tomorrow, your life of freedom and happiness will be over." Herbert chuckled at his self-proclaimed humor.

Hezekiah caught Charlotte's expression of disgust, but she remained silent, an unusual trait for her.

"I don't feel that way at all," Isaac responded. Charlotte gave a triumphant smile.

Herbert discouraged by no one else finding humor in his remark, changed the subject. "Hey, it's still light out, why don't we get up a game of horseshoes so these women can waggle their tongues."

"Great idea, Herbert," Isaac answered. Charlotte jerked her head and looked at Isaac with surprise. A familiar coy smile came to Isaac's lips that Hezekiah recognized as the beginning of a prank or joke. "Go find a horse and we'll be ready when you get back."

Everyone but Herbert burst into laughter. "You're a funny man, Isaac," Herbert said, his face flushed with anger as he glared from one person to another.

"He's just teasing you, Herbert," Beatrice said, embarrassed by her husband's action.

"I can see that, Beatrice," he said with gritted teeth. He stomped off the porch, rolled a cigarette, lit it and puffed angrily as he stared out over the town, ignoring those behind him.

Without Herbert, the conversation soon returned to normalcy and the wedding became the primary subject. Hezekiah stood opposite where Kathryn sat on the swing. He watched her listen to the others, her changes of expression, her quiet laughter, and the loose strands of hair that gently curled on her forehead. When she blinked, Hezekiah blinked. Occasionally she would look at him and smile, and he would smile back.

What if she knew about Christina and that he had dreamed of her, he thought? He was so afraid of hurting her, yet he seemed destined to do just that. Why couldn't he forget about Christina? Why had she reappeared in his nightmare? Only if he had met Kathryn at some later time when he knew what was going on inside him. But then, maybe he would never understand. Enough time had passed. He should be okay by now...unless he was never going to be better.

He suddenly realized everyone was staring at him. "Are we boring you, Mr. Templeton?" Charlotte asked, smiling cynically at him.

"Not at all. I'm sorry. Was I daydreaming?"

"It seemed more of a deep slumber," she replied.

Everyone was smiling except Isaac. His face was rigid as his eyes carefully studied Hezekiah. Isaac's look was far more disturbing to Hezekiah than the teasing of Charlotte.

"Maybe he's playing mental horseshoes with Herbert," Dorothy said, covering her mouth as she giggled.

"From the look on his face, I'd say he was losing," Charlotte added.

"Where is Herbert?" Beatrice asked, looking over her shoulder.

"He's over there by the tree," Dorothy said. "What's he doing?...Oh my Lord!" she screamed as a horrified look covered her face. Everyone on the porch looked. He was standing with his back to them, facing the tree, however it became quickly obvious to everyone that he was relieving himself.

The women were screaming and covering their faces, while the men burst into laughter. Herbert, realizing he had been caught, hurriedly moved behind the tree.

Good old Herbert, Hezekiah thought, he saved me from an awkward moment.

Beatrice quickly excused herself and began an immediate escort of Herbert towards their home. She was intently scolding him as they moved quickly down the street, her finger wagging vigorously at him. Hezekiah chuckled at the sight of a petite woman making Herbert bow his head and shuffle along like a little boy.

CHAPTER 34

The sun was shining in Hezekiah's eyes. A peaceful night's sleep left him feeling refreshed and relieved. The night had passed without the horrible nightmare. It had only happened once. He had to believe it was gone...hopefully for good this time.

Hezekiah could hear Isaac scurrying about in the next room. The wedding...today was the wedding. He leaped out of bed and went to check on Isaac. He found the groom busily checking his suit for lint.

"About time you were getting up," Isaac said, glancing at Hezekiah, "Damn, if you don't start getting ready, you'll end up looking like some drifter."

Hezekiah rubbed his eyes. "What time is it?"

"Almost seven."

"Hell, Isaac. The wedding isn't until two."

Isaac was now trimming his nose hair. Hezekiah could see his bath water heating on the stove.

"I don't want to screw up and be late for my wedding, and by hell you better not be either."

"About time you were getting nervous," Hezekiah said, trying to look serious.

"Who said I'm nervous?" Isaac quickly replied as he checked his water on the stove.

"Hell, you're acting like one of Zachery Tomlin's chickens when he chopped off their heads."

"You can think it's all funny if you want. Someday when you get married, assuming some woman will ever have you...aw damn, never mind."

Hezekiah decided not to push Isaac over the edge, so he poured a cup of coffee and went outside on the porch. If he did not stay out of Isaac's way, they both would go crazy in the next seven hours.

But peace was short lived for Hezekiah as he sat on the sunlit porch. Isaac appeared frantically at the front door, his eyes wild with anxiety. "Damn, I can't find our ties," he said, his voice sounding hysterical. "We've lost them."

"Damn, Isaac. Calm down. They're in our suit pockets. Did you check the pockets?"

"No."

"Well before you go crazy, check the pockets."

Isaac wheeled around and hurried inside. Hezekiah smiled and shook his head.

"Here they are," Isaac shouted from inside.

Hezekiah could imagine Isaac later that night with Charlotte. He only hoped Isaac had better control of himself. They would never have any children otherwise.

****

With the weeklong celebration, Hezekiah had concluded that the wedding itself could only be anti-climatic. He was wrong. When he and Isaac arrived at the Richmond home shortly before two o'clock, he found the place absolutely breathtaking.

The garden was decorated with ribbons, bows, and streamers, and wild flowers that were gaily displayed. Benches were carefully placed for the guests. A trellis fully decorated stood at the front.

Hezekiah picked a white daisy and gently touched its soft pedals. He thought of Hannah. Quickly he made a mental note to write to his family. So much had happened since his arrival. For a moment, he felt loneliness for them. He kissed the flower. "For you, Hannah," he whispered. "My little mountain flower."

The early arrivals were already being seated. Hezekiah moved to the aid of Isaac standing to one side of the garden, rubbing his hands nervously. His face was pale and drawn.

"Damn, Isaac. Are you all right?"

"Are you sure you've got the ring?"

Yeah, I'm sure. It's right here in my pocket." Unable to resist, Hezekiah reached in his pocket. "Damn! It's gone."

Terror filled Isaac's eyes. Hezekiah startled by his friend's look, quickly ended the joke. "I'm kidding, Isaac. It's right here," he said, pulling out the ring to show Isaac.

"Damn! Don't do that to me. I'm nervous enough as it is."

"Oh, so now you admit it."

"Yeah, I'm nervous. What time is it?"

"Do I own a watch? Look at yours."

Isaac fumbled in his pocket. "Ten till two. I wish it would hurry up and be over."

"Having second thoughts?"

"No. Not at all. I just wish it would get over."

Isaac was becoming paler with each passing second. Hezekiah decided he had better find a way to calm Isaac, or there might not be a wedding. "So you never told me who you were going to have as a best man, if I never showed."

Isaac shrugged his shoulders. "In all honesty, I don't know. I guess I just knew you wouldn't let me down. Look there's Reverend Murphy. Where'd you put the ring?"

"In my pocket."

"Are you sure? Oh damn, I think I'm going to be sick."

"Take a deep breath. Do you want to sit down?"

"No."

"Stop worrying. Everything is going to be fine."

Isaac nodded and smiled. "I know. I guess I'm just so damn happy."

Hezekiah looked at Isaac. He did not look very happy.

The garden was now filled with guests. Reverend Murphy had made his way to the front under the trellis and was patiently waiting for two o'clock.

Mrs. Kyle was escorted to the front and seated. She looked happy as she cast a quick glance at Isaac and smiled. Next came Mrs. Richmond. She was far more exuberant on her entrance, greeting everyone as she moved slowly down the aisle. The Reverend motioned for Isaac and Hezekiah to come forward.

"This is it, friend. Your moment has arrived," Hezekiah said, placing his hand on Isaac's back.

They moved into place and waited for the procession. Isaac's face had become stark white.

What if he faints, Hezekiah thought. "Isaac, relax your knees and take a deep breath."

The music started. The heads of the guests began to turn as everyone anxiously waited for the first in the procession to appear at the back door of the house. Soon a young girl carrying a basket of flowers appeared. 'A daughter of a Richmond acquaintance' Hezekiah had been told the night before. She hurried down the aisle, her eyes fixed firmly in front of her. Before she had reached the front, Hezekiah looked again to the back. He knew who was next. He gasped. Kathryn was standing in the doorway in a lavender full-skirted dress. Her hair sparkled in the afternoon sunlight. She was more beautiful and radiant than he could ever have imagined. Goosebumps covered his body.

Kathryn stepped forward and moved slowly towards him. She politely turned her head from side to side, smiling at each row as she passed. He imagined for a moment that she was the bride coming to stand alongside him. But how could he ever be so deserving? He could never give her everything she deserved.

Hezekiah watched her delicate frame move closer. He could see her eyes dancing playfully with the innocence of a little girl. She seemed so fragile...so vulnerable...so easily hurt.

Kathryn smiled at Isaac and Hezekiah, then the reverend as she stepped to the side next to the little girl. Hezekiah shifted his position to better view her. He tugged at his tight collar. The July afternoon sun was becoming very warm. It was almost like standing in church, awaiting the arrival of Parson Blackwell.

He heard murmurs from the crowd. He glanced to the rear where Charlotte and Mr. Richmond stood on the first step of the porch. Isaac shifted nervously. Charlotte was a beautiful bride in her long white-laced dress and veil. Mr. Richmond stood proudly next to her, clutching her arm.

As the bride and father moved forward, the guests stood, their eyes fixed on them. Isaac was grinning like the boy at Twin Buttes. Hezekiah bit his lip, having a sudden urge to laugh.

As the bride and father reached the front, Mr. Richmond raised Charlotte's veil and kissed his daughter. Hezekiah could see the dampness in the eyes of the man who normally only showed a tough exterior. Isaac took Charlotte's arm and they stood in front of the reverend.

It seemed as though for the first time, Hezekiah felt the full impact of his friend being married. He felt alone. It would never be the same. Life was rushing on before him, leaving him behind. He seemed frozen in time. Why did he feel that way? His life was going well. He had admitted to himself that he was falling in love with Kathryn, and he sensed she felt the same. His future looked good with a possible position with Wilbur Sanders. Only that one nightmare had dampened his life in recent weeks. He was sure it would never return. Why could he not accept his future and move forward with it? Life was going to move forward...with or without him.

The happy couple spoke their vows. Even the steadfast Charlotte seemed nervous. Then came the time for the ring. Hezekiah removed it from his pocket and handed it to Isaac. He wanted to remind Isaac that he had done his part.

Soon the ceremony ended and Isaac raised Charlotte's veil and kissed her. The crowd burst into applause as the couple walked down the aisle. Hezekiah stepped to the center and took Kathryn's arm. She smiled at him. He wanted to kiss her. He wanted to tell her he loved her and wanted to say 'let's us do this soon'. He only smiled back at her.

****

The wedding and reception was hailed a complete success. The bride was beautiful, the groom handsome, the food delicious, and the setting spectacular. Everyone said so. Mr. Richmond had kept his promise...the week would be remembered for a long time.

Hezekiah and Kathryn waved the newlyweds good-bye as they left the reception for their new home. Hezekiah once again felt the panic inside him. He wanted to shout to Isaac, 'Wait. Stay a while. Don't leave your old friend alone'. But he was not alone. Kathryn was by his side. She made him happy. Kathryn was the future; his and Isaac's childhood was the past. Somehow he had to cast the fear of the future aside if he was ever going to find happiness.

"They look so wonderful and happy," Kathryn said, bringing Hezekiah back. He felt a little embarrassed neglecting her.

"They do, don't they." He wondered if Kathryn felt abandoned by Charlotte. Did she fear the future, too? He wanted to ask her. Maybe what he felt was not unusual...selfish.

Shortly after the newlyweds left, the guests began saying their good-byes and congratulations to the Richmonds. Mr. Richmond tried to encourage everyone to stay. "You won't leave me, will you, son," he said to Hezekiah with pleading eyes. "I don't want this day to end and I'm sure Kathryn would love to have you stay."

Hezekiah had been prepared to ask Kathryn to go for a walk, but when he saw the begging eyes of Mr. Richmond, he could not say, no.

****

After two hours of intense and somewhat drunken conversation, Hezekiah excused himself due to the late hour. "I appreciate you staying, Son," Mr. Richmond said, vigorously shaking Hezekiah's hand. "You made a wonderful end to a wonderful day."

Kathryn walked Hezekiah to the garden gate. "I had intended to ask you to go for a walk," Hezekiah said, "but I couldn't say no to Mr. Richmond."

"You did the right thing. He enjoyed himself immensely."

"Maybe tomorrow afternoon we can go for the walk we missed tonight."

"That would be splendid."

"If you don't mind, I thought maybe we could go to the cemetery where my family is. We don't have too if you'd rather not."

"Oh, I think that would be wonderful. There's nothing I would enjoy more. I feel privileged you would ask me to go with you."

Hezekiah returned home feeling much better. There was no reason not to feel good. He knew Kathryn could only make it wonderful. Even with all his doubts, everything in his life was going well.

****

The next afternoon Hezekiah and Kathryn walked to the cemetery. They stood quietly for sometime, looking at the graves. "I should have brought a blanket so we could sit on the ground," Hezekiah said, feeling a little embarrassed.

"I don't mind a little dirt. It will brush right off anyway," she said, already beginning to sit.

"I come up here sometimes just to remember. They were all so wonderful. You probably think I'm foolish."

"Not at all," she said, taking his hand. "I think it's wonderful. Back home, I used to sit for hours at my little sister's grave."

"You had a sister. I always thought you only had brothers."

"Mary. I was nine when she died. She died the day before her seventh birthday."

Hezekiah squeezed Kathryn's hand as a tear appeared on her cheek. "Tell me about her," he said, trying to ignore a lump in his throat.

Kathryn smiled. "We were the best of friends. She was really my only friend. I couldn't seem to understand why she left me. Almost every day, even when it was raining, I would go to her grave and play. I would talk to her and tell her everything that was happening. I was so afraid she'd be lonely. Years passed, but I never stopped going. Perhaps I never would have stopped if it weren't for Charlotte. I was twelve then. Charlotte moved into a big house a short distance away down the hill from the grave. I would see Charlotte in her yard, always alone. I felt sorry for her not having anyone to play with. I always felt lucky having Mary even though she was dead. Then one day, I saw Charlotte coming towards Mary and I. She wasn't walking straight towards me, but she kept wandering ever closer to me. When she arrived, she asked who was buried there. I told her. I was afraid to tell her I talked and played with Mary, fearing she would think I was strange. She asked me why I played there and finally I told her. She asked if she could be Mary's and my friend. She was so kind and understanding. After that she would come almost every day. Then occasionally, we would go elsewhere to play. In time, I stopped going to Mary's grave except on rare occasions. Charlotte helped me. I will always be grateful for her being so understanding. I know sometimes Charlotte seems a little overbearing, but inside she is the most wonderful person. I'm so glad she's happy." Kathryn suddenly stopped talking, her face showing embarrassment. "Goodness. I'm sorry for rambling on. You must think I'm terrible."

Hezekiah leaned forward and kissed Kathryn. "Not at all. I'm glad you told me all this. I want to know everything about you. I just learned something very important about you and your life. I always knew how beautiful and how wonderful you were, but I never really knew what you felt inside."

"It feels so good sharing things with you, Hezekiah. I never imagined how good it could feel."

If there had ever been any doubt about his feeling towards Kathryn, they had vanished that afternoon. He knew there would never be any turning back.

305

"I'll tell you what," he said, "let me fix supper at my house tonight. I don't want our day to end."

"I agree, but I insist on one thing. I will fix the supper. I've wanted to cook ever since I've been at the Richmonds, but Mrs. Richmond, the dear heart, will not let me set foot in her kitchen."

"Okay. It certainly will spare you the agony of eating my cooking. Isaac would never let me do any cooking either. He always claimed he was too young to die."

Kathryn covered her mouth as she laughed.

"Don't ever cover your face. It hides your beauty."

"Hezekiah. You're embarrassing me...I must insist that you don't stop."

****

That evening after finishing the supper dishes, Hezekiah and Kathryn sat at the table.

"I have something to tell you," Kathryn said, her eyes carefully studying Hezekiah's face. "The Richmonds have generously asked me to stay here in Virginia City with them."

Hezekiah could feel his heart pounding. His throat grew tight, barely allowing him to speak. "Have you given them you answer?"

"I have," she answered without a hint of expression.

Hezekiah leaned forward and held her hands. "Well," he said intently. "You're teasing me, Kathryn. What did you say?"

"I sent a letter to my family yesterday. I told them of the kind offer of the Richmonds."

"Kathryn! What'd you say?"

"Goodness, Hezekiah. I'm coming to it." She paused, looking into his eyes. "I said, yes."

"Wonderful!" he shouted, jumping to his feet. He pulled Kathryn to her feet and began kissing her on the face.

"When he had finally stopped, she patted her cheeks. "Goodness. I had hoped you would find it to your liking, but I never imagined this."

"This calls for a toast," Hezekiah said excitedly. "Wait. All I have is whiskey...well, I have water too."

"Water is fine," she answered without hesitation.

"All I have are these old tin cups."

"Splendid. Only royalty uses tin cups," she said, giggling.

Hezekiah filled their cups. They laughed at the clinking sound as their cups met. They sipped from their cups, their eyes never leaving each other.

Hezekiah took her cup and sat both cups on the table. Their gaze continued to meet as Hezekiah gently took her hand. They moved towards each other until their lips met. He felt her softness, her gentleness against him. He was sure they had melted into one. He could feel his passion growing, her passion growing.

She suddenly pulled away, looking apologetically at him. "I'm sorry, Hezekiah. I promised myself. Even as a young girl, I made a solemn vow."

"I shouldn't have," he said, squeezing her hand. "I spoiled this perfect moment."

"Don't be silly. It was part of this perfect moment."

"And I never want it to end, Kathryn."

"Neither do I." She blushed. "But I'm afraid tonight it must."

****

For the next two weeks, Hezekiah lived in a fantasy. Every evening was spent with Kathryn, and except for a couple evenings that the newlyweds had ventured from their home, they had spent them alone.

Kathryn and Hezekiah began sharing their feelings, their dreams.

One evening when Hezekiah returned home from an evening with Kathryn, he was feeling particularly jubilant. They had discussed children.

"I always felt five or six children would be right for a perfect family," Kathryn had said.

"That's exactly my thoughts," Hezekiah had quickly added.

They looked at each other. Neither spoke, but their eyes looking into the others, said everything that needed to be said. They both knew that someday they would be married with five or six children. At that moment, when did not seem important.

But as Hezekiah walked home, he knew it would be soon. He wanted to wait for Wilbur Sander's return from the East so that he might have good news for Kathryn. But he knew even if nothing came of it, he would ask Kathryn to marry him. Maybe two weeks. It would not be long.

He refrained from skipping home, but as soon as he entered his house, he began singing 'I love you, Kathryn, I love you, Kathryn' as he danced around until he fell onto a chair exhausted.

He went to bed, but sleep was fleeting as he lied awake envisioning the rest of his life with Kathryn. When exhaustion finally succumbed his exhilaration, he fell into a peaceful slumber.

CHAPTER 35

The darkness was closed around Hezekiah like a tomb of the dead. He sat up, shivering. His body was covered with perspiration. He clutched his head. "Leave me alone!" he screamed. "Leave me alone." He fell back on the bed.

The nightmare had returned. Christina's mournful cries had returned. The horrifying face of his mother's killer had returned, even more vivid...more real than before. He could only watch and listen...unable to move as the tormenting attack took place before him.

Hezekiah jumped from his bed and stumbled to the table. His shaking hand lit the lantern. He sat, staring at the dancing flame before him. It resembled the feeling inside his head, the fire burning deep into his mind.

"Damn! Why'd you have to return," he called out desperately as he stood up and flung his chair across the room. "Everything was so perfect. Now you're spoiling everything." He began to sob openly.

It did not stand to reason why the nightmare had suddenly reappeared. He had not thought about it for weeks nor had Christina even crossed his mind. He feared the bad spirits that Eagle Feather had talked about had consumed him and there was nothing he could do to rid them from him. They were driving him insane. He could never have a life with Kathryn as long as he was like this.

Every time his life was going well, every time he felt happiness...something terrible would happen...and it always happened to those around him...never himself. It was like he was a danger to those he loved.

He paced the floor until daylight. He dressed and went to work. He was determined not to let the nightmares ruin his life. He would have to learn to live with it. The night might be controlled by it, but the days would remain his.

Although tired, he kept his promise to go to work and spend his evening with Kathryn.

That night the nightmare returned, but again he made the day his. The nightmare continued each night, and in time, it began to wear more heavily on him during the day. The horror that filled his nights began to fill his mind by day. If it did not stop soon, he knew it would eventually win and overcome his body, mind, and soul. His life was reaching an important crossroads, his future hopes with Wilbur Sanders, and most important, his future with Kathryn. All the while, his life was beginning to crumble around him...or worse, within him, and there seemed to be nothing he could do to stop it.

****

Hezekiah looked into the mirror, seeing the reflection of his drawn, haggard face. His eyes were glazed from lack of sleep. He dipped his hands into the bucket of cold water and splashed it on his face. He had to continue to hide his problem from everyone, particularly Kathryn. Eventually it would get better...he had to believe that. He could not tell anyone. No one would understand...why should they...he did not even begin to understand what was happening himself. He glanced in the mirror again. How could he hide it from anyone?

****

Kathryn sat on the porch swing waiting for the man she loved. The evening was balmy. It made for a perfect evening, one that should be filled with excitement and happiness for her, but it was not perfect.

Something had gone wrong. Without warning, Hezekiah had begun to change. He had become quiet and distant, and no longer attentive to her. It seemed as though he was always somewhere else when he was with her.

At first, she thought somehow she had offended him. But try as she may, she could not remember anything that she had done that would have made him change. She had begun to fear the worst...the most frightening to her. He wanted to end their relationship. He had grown tired of her...no longer wanting to share his life with her. The most confusing to her was that it had happened so suddenly. She felt helpless. The control of their future was in his hands.

Kathryn could see Hezekiah coming up the road towards her. She sighed, trying to regain her composure.

"Good evening, Hezekiah," she called out as he approached. "It's such a lovely evening, isn't it?"

Hezekiah smiled, but she could see his tired, tense expression. "Hi, Kathryn."

At first as they sat on the swing, Hezekiah seemed more at ease, but soon his thoughts began to drift, his body becoming tense. Kathryn was sure he had forgotten she was there. He returned his attention to her, but shortly, began to drift away again.

"You seem so tired," Kathryn said after Hezekiah had remained quiet for several minutes.

"I really am," he said, looking apologetically at her. "I just haven't been sleeping. I know I must be a bore."

"Is there something I can do to help?"

"No. I'll get over it."

"You need to get your rest. I'm afraid you'll become dreadfully ill."

"I apologize. I'll make it up to you. I promise."

Kathryn only smiled, fearing at the first word, her emotions would erupt into a waterfall of tears.

Hezekiah excused himself, apologizing over and over again. She watched Hezekiah walk down the road until her eyes had filled with tears. She quickly rushed inside, passing Mrs. Richmond in the hall. She tried to be polite by speaking before hurrying on.

"Is everything all right, dear?" Mrs. Richmond called out to her.

"Yes, I'm fine," Kathryn, answered, trying to control her voice. But everything was not fine, and Kathryn feared it never would be again.

Kathryn closed the door to her room and lay across the bed. The tears kept coming. The door of her emotions had opened wide and there was no way of controlling them. She had always feared falling in love, knowing the risk of a broken heart, but when she met Hezekiah, she could no longer control, or wanted to control her feelings. She had never been so happy since she had opened her heart, but now that it was open, and the pain that she had so much feared, was unbearably bursting within her.

If she could only understand what was happening. She had been sure Hezekiah had been as much in love with her as she was with him.

Unaware as to how long she had lain there, Kathryn was startled by a light tap on her door. She could hear Charlotte's voice on the other side, "Kathryn, may I come in?"

"Just a moment," Kathryn called back, and quickly rose from the bed and hurriedly looked in the mirror, trying to wipe away the tears.

When she opened the door, it was obvious from the expression on Charlotte's face that she had failed at her attempt to hide her emotions.

"Kathryn, what's wrong," Charlotte said, clutching Kathryn into her arms.

CHAPTER 36

Hezekiah laid down his saw, and held the board up to its destined place. He reached for his hammer. Sensing someone behind him, he turned to find Isaac standing in the open doorway.

"What brings you here?" Hezekiah asked, placing the board back on the sawhorse. He deemed it very unusual for his friend to take time away from his work so early in the day.

"I felt like a beer." His voice sounded urgent and unsure. "Thought maybe you'd like to join me."

Hezekiah knew what was on Isaac's mind. "Yeah, I guess so. What time is it?"

"Two-thirty. Everyone needs a break now and then."

"I guess married life is getting to you," Hezekiah said as he brushed the sawdust from his pants. Isaac smiled, but the urgent look remained.

As they strolled towards the saloon, the conversation was about work. Hezekiah waited for Isaac to change the conversation to him and Kathryn.

The saloon had only a few patrons. Quite different from the earlier years, Hezekiah concluded.

They sat at a table in the corner and were quickly approached by a saloon maid who took their order. She smiled and carefully scrutinized both men. They sat uncomfortably quiet until she returned with their beer.

"Can I get you anything else...perhaps me," she said, placing her hands on her hips and pushing out her chest for display.

"Oh, no thank you," Isaac answered politely, somewhat taken back.

"He's a newlywed. Still getting use to what he has," Hezekiah added.

"A little change of scenery never hurt anyone," she said, stooping so her customers could better view her wares.

"No, I...I can't do that," Isaac said with determination. "I like the scenery I've got."

"As you wish," she said with disgust and turned to Hezekiah. "And how about you?" She placed her hands on her breasts and slowly slid her fingers down her body. "Maybe you'd like to see where these mountains lead too. There's a lot of beautiful country to see."

"I'm sure there is, ma'am, but not today...really."

The maid's smile faded. "Your loss," she said coldly and left for another table.

Hezekiah watched her as she began her solicitation all over again. He visualized Christina instead of her. It angered him for even thinking such a thought, knowing Christina was not like that at all.

When he looked back at Isaac, a cold chill raced through him. Isaac was staring at him as though he had committed a mortal sin.

"So, is Charlotte carrying a child yet?" Hezekiah asked, trying to lessen the tension that was building.

Isaac's stare remained. "No, not yet."

Hezekiah cleared his throat. "You do understand what you need to do?"

"I have a general idea." Isaac's face remained tense.

"Good." Hezekiah's stomach was tied in knots.

The conversation faltered again. "Okay. I guess it's up to me," Hezekiah said, uncertain if he really wanted to hear what Isaac had to say. "Is there something bothering you?" he asked reluctantly.

Isaac cleared his throat. "It's kind of embarrassing, but I promised Charlotte."

"Okay, Isaac. We're friends. Ask."

"I hate to butt in, but we've all noticed." Isaac's stare was replaced by his eyes nervously glancing from Hezekiah to the table and then back to Hezekiah. "You seem to be...well...preoccupied with something. Distant...You know what I mean?"

"We meaning you, Charlotte, and Kathryn," Hezekiah said, emphasizing Kathryn.

"Yeah, I suppose...but even Mrs. Richmond asked Charlotte if something was wrong."

"Honestly, I don't know what's wrong, if anything." Hezekiah sighed and ran his fingers through his hair.

"Something must be wrong. To be honest with you," Isaac said with a tone that sounded like a lecture, "Kathryn is very concerned."

Hezekiah gritted his teeth. "Damn! The last thing I want to do is hurt Kathryn."

Isaac raised his mug, sipped slowly, his stare returning. "Is it something from your past? You know...like your mother's death."

"Maybe...some, I guess. I honestly thought I was over it." Hezekiah looked beyond Isaac. "You know, I promised Aunt Jane I would forget about Mother's killer...and I did...and it seemed to help...but lately, I've been having nightmares again." Hezekiah was firmly gripping his mug. "I must have visualized the murder a thousand times." Hezekiah looked at Isaac with helplessness. "Now recently, the nightmare is there every night...but it's different...worse. I see the killer attacking a different woman and I can't move because I'm frozen with fear." Anger suddenly erupted in Hezekiah. He slammed his fist on the table causing Isaac to jump. Hezekiah's voice became hardened as Isaac watched his friend in disbelief. "Damn it! My mother lies up there in the cemetery because of me and the killer is alive because of me."

Hezekiah's voice suddenly became quiet, almost apologetic. "I never told anyone, Isaac. It eats at my insides. When I shot that first man...I froze." His voice choked as he was barely able to speak. "If I hadn't, my mother would still be alive." Hezekiah dropped his head. "I live with that every day...and now every night."

"You can't be blaming yourself for everything that's happened," Isaac said helplessly. "You did your best."

Hezekiah continued, not hearing the consoling words of Isaac. "You remember Eagle Feather talking about some people being consumed with bad spirits. I think I'm one of those. It seems that terrible things happen to every one I love or loves me."

"You can't believe that, Hez. You're a good person. You don't make these bad things happen."

"But what if I am filled with evil spirits, whether it's my fault or not. What if something happens to Kathryn? Besides, I'm beginning to believe I'm going crazy. What kind of torture would I place on her?"

"You're not going crazy. You've been through hell, that's all. Anybody would take time getting over it. Besides, you love Kathryn, and I know she loves you. Let her help you. Don't shut her out."

"I can't."

"Why, damn it? She would want to help."

Hezekiah glanced momentarily at Isaac and then looked away. "Maybe you won't be so quick to think so when you hear everything."

Isaac's eyes stared intently at Hezekiah as though frightened out of his wits. "Damn, Hez. What else is there?"

Hezekiah cleared his throat. "You know," he mumbled and cleared his throat again. "You know that woman in my nightmare I was telling you about...its Christina."

"Christina! What are you saying?" Isaac thrust his hands on the table. Trying to remain calm, he began talking through his gritted teeth. "I understand about the nightmares and I sort of understand you not wanting to burden Kathryn with them...but I don't understand what you're saying about Christina. I thought you were over her. I thought Kathryn was the one you loved."

Hezekiah's teeth were now clenched. "I don't know if I'm saying anything. I was just telling you, which I'm now beginning to regret."

Isaac threw himself against the back of his chair and took a deep breath. "May my soul burn in hell, but I'll never understand." He lurched forward, throwing his hands back on the table. "Christina's the past. I know you love Kathryn. Are you telling me you're still in love with Christina?"

"I didn't say that."

"No, but your implying it. Why else would you be so concerned that it was Christina in your nightmare?"

"I'm afraid she may be in danger."

"It's only a nightmare. It doesn't mean anything is going to happen. It's all in your head."

"Maybe. Maybe it just means I'm losing my mind. I know I don't want to hurt Kathryn."

"I'm afraid it's too late to start worrying about that."

"I know, damn it. If I could only see Christina. If I knew she was all right. Find out what my feelings really are. Until I get things straightened out in my head, I'm afraid I'll never be able to have a good honest life with Kathryn."

Isaac slumped in his chair. The anger that had shown on his face disappeared and sadness replaced it. He looked like a defeated man. His voice became low. "You're the best friend I've ever had. In fact, I've always considered you a brother...almost as though the same blood ran through our veins. I only wanted to help...to help you forget your past. Then when you and Kathryn seemed so happy together, I was sure I had done the right thing."

"What are you talking about?" Hezekiah asked, confused by his friend's sudden change.

Isaac stared towards the saloon entrance. He began to nervously fumble with his empty mug. "I didn't mean to hurt you." His voice had become so soft; Hezekiah had to lean forward to hear. "I know where Christina went when she left Virginia City."

"What! And you didn't tell me? Why?"

"I'm sorry. I thought your past was better left alone."

"Where'd she go...or aren't you going to tell me now?"

"Helena. It's north of here."

"I know where it is." Hezekiah pushed his chair back, stood up, paused, and then sat back down. "Didn't you think I had a right to know? Wasn't it my decision to make?"

"I don't know what I thought. At the time, I felt it was the right thing."

"For who?...You were always jealous of me and Christina." Isaac remained silent. "Weren't you?" Hezekiah said, demanding an answer.

"Maybe a little when we were younger, but that's not the reason..."

"Isn't it?"

"I have Charlotte. Why would I be jealous now?"

"How did you find out she went to Helena?

"One day, about two weeks after you left for St. Louis, I was walking past the freight house as she was coming out. We talked about you for a while, and then she told me she was leaving for Helena the next day to start a new life. She said if it hadn't been for you, she probably would never have found the courage. She decided if she was going to start anew, she should start in a new place. She said if I ever saw you, I was to tell you that you were the dearest friend she ever had."

"And you chose not to tell me all this," Hezekiah said very deliberately.

"I wanted too. So many times, but it never seemed right, and the longer I waited, the more difficult it became and the less important it seemed...until now."

"I need to be alone," Hezekiah said in a tone that made Isaac shiver. Hezekiah pushed his half empty mug away, rose and left without saying another word.

****

Hezekiah had not particularly determined his route when he rode out of town, but he was not surprised when he entered the canyon of Eagle Feather's.

He climbed the knoll towards his old friend. A lone wild flower caught his eye and he bent to pick it. He stopped abruptly as he touched its softness. The seedling had patiently waited through the winter storms so that it might spring to life with its freedom, and the flower had survived the grueling heat of summer to share its beauty with the rest of the world. He would only pick it to watch it wilt and die...like the killer that had taken his mother's life. She had survived all the pain that had surrounded her, and just when she was about to be given another chance, it was taken from her.

"Live and share your beauty for an eternity," he whispered and proceeded on up the hill.

He paused for a short time by the burial platform before sitting at the base of a nearby pine tree. He removed his hat and leaned against it. He let the light breeze brush his face as he tried to feel the earth and all its being around him.

"I love it here, Eagle Feather. I wish my family were here. I'm sure you wouldn't mind. They were good people." Hezekiah rose and walked to the edge of the bluff. "I'm confused, old friend. I wish you were here to give me some answers. I always seem to let everybody down. You must be ashamed of me. I said some terrible things to Isaac. We've never argued like this. I love Kathryn but I've hurt her too. And now I fear Christina may be in danger, and I'm afraid I may be letting her down if I don't do something. I just don't know what to do. I..."

A shivering sound came from overhead. Hezekiah, shading his eyes, looked into the sky. A hawk was circling overhead. Suddenly, with no warning, it dove towards him, giving a shrilling screech. Hezekiah watched in horror as it came within twenty feet of him before returning skyward. It circled and again, with a terrifying sound, it dove towards him. Hezekiah watched helplessly as it came so close he could feel the wind from its wings. The hawk climbed back into the sky, and as Hezekiah stared in shock, it disappeared over the horizon.

"I don't understand, Eagle Feather!" Hezekiah screamed. "Are you angry with me? Are you telling me Christina is in danger? What do you want me to do?"

Hezekiah waited for an answer. None came. He waited an hour before deciding to leave. "I'm sorry if I've disturbed you, friend. I shouldn't have come to you with my troubles." Hezekiah started back towards his horse.

Hezekiah left the burial grounds more confused than when he had arrived. At first, he had been sure the hawk had been some kind of sign from Eagle Feather. But as time passed, he began to wonder if he was only fooling himself.

Hezekiah had become clear about one thing though. He could not let the differences between he and Isaac continue. Right now, he needed Isaac's friendship more than ever.

****

Hezekiah immediately went to Isaac's house when he arrived back in town.

Charlotte answered the door. Hezekiah had hoped it would be Isaac. The way he felt about himself, he did not want to see any more people than necessary.

Charlotte's eyes were red and swollen. "Good evening, Hezekiah," she said, greeting him with a forced smile.

"Hi, Charlotte. Is Isaac in?"

"Yes. He just finished supper. Come in and have some cake with him. Her eyes were searching Hezekiah's face for answers.

"No, thank you. If I may, I would like to speak to Isaac alone."

She nodded and went inside. Hezekiah strolled a short distance from the house, trying to collect his thoughts as to what he would say. His body ached from being so tense, but the intolerable ache was in his heart.

Shortly, he heard footsteps, and turned to face Isaac. Isaac was walking quickly towards him, and then slowed his pace as he approached.

Hezekiah immediately spoke, not wanting to prolong the awkwardness he felt. "We've been good friends a long time, Isaac. We've argued, but never like this." Isaac was nodding in agreement, his eyes saddened. Hezekiah continued, "The pain I feel from our damaged friendship is more than I can bare. I want to apologize for the terrible things I said out of anger. I know whatever you did was what you thought was best for me, and in reality, you probably did the best thing."

Isaac's face relaxed. "I could never go on without making amends either. I'm sorry for not being honest with you. It was your decision to make, not mine. The most important thing is for you to find some happiness, and I want to do whatever I can to make that happen."

They strolled further from the house. "I went to see Eagle Feather today," Hezekiah said. "I was hoping he would have some answers for me."

"Did he?"

"I honestly don't know." Hezekiah stopped and looked at Isaac. "The hawk returned."

Isaac raised his eyebrows in surprise. "Whew. And what happened?"

"To be honest, the hawk scared the hell of out me. I'm afraid that Eagle Feather may be angry with me...I don't know. Maybe my concern for Christina may be true. I'm just not sure what it all meant."

"You know, maybe Eagle Feather had nothing to do with that hawk. He is wise, far wiser than me. He wouldn't make the same mistake I made."

"What do you mean?"

Isaac grinned. "I made the big mistake of trying to make a decision that was yours to make. Now you go to Eagle Feather and ask him to give you answers that you need to decide. Remember that first day we met Eagle Feather, and he told us that he did not want to just tell us the answers, that we needed to think for ourselves, because someday there would be no one there to make the decisions and have the answers for us."

"I remember," Hezekiah answered. "I guess sometimes I heard, but I didn't listen. But still...that hawk...it was frightening the way it came right for me...and the sound. I don't think I've ever heard anything so terrifying. Maybe Eagle Feather was showing his anger with me about our damaged friendship."

"You could be right. So what are you going to do...about Kathryn and Christina?"

Hezekiah stared skyward. "Its probably wrong. It seems my decisions usually are, but I've decided I have to try and find Christina. I need to know if she's all right...and perhaps what my feelings towards her really are. I'm just so afraid what it will do to Kathryn. But I can't continue lying to her. I'm afraid eventually I would hurt her even more."

Isaac's voice was calm. "When are you going?"

"Tomorrow. To delay it, would only make it harder to tell Kathryn."

"What are you going to tell her?"

"The truth...but I still don't know how."

****

Isaac watched his friend walk away. "Hez." Hezekiah looked back. "Have a good trip...and be careful."

Hezekiah waved and smiled. Isaac wanted to tell Hezekiah the warning that Eagle Feather had given him, but his friend was already burdened with so much. Besides, Isaac was beginning to think the danger in Hezekiah's past was Hezekiah's problem dealing with his past-like the nightmares.

If he only knew what lay ahead for Hezekiah so that he could help his friend. Hezekiah said that he never seemed to make the right decision. Isaac was beginning to worry he was also making all the wrong decisions concerning Hezekiah.

****

The last of the twilight had disappeared when Hezekiah arrived at the Richmonds. Kathryn was sitting with Mrs. Richmond on the porch swing. Mrs. Richmond cordially acknowledged Hezekiah, but quickly excused herself as she glanced with apprehension at the young couple.

Kathryn smiled, but Hezekiah could see the tenseness on her face. "Good evening, Hezekiah," she said, rising to kiss him.

He kissed her. "I'm sorry it's so late." How could he ever tell her? She would never be able to understand.

"I don't mind. I wasn't sure if you would come tonight."

"Would you like to go for a walk?"

"I would love too."

Hezekiah could see the concern on her face.

They walked quietly arm in arm for a short distance, as Hezekiah struggled to find the right words.

"Is anything wrong?" she said, glancing towards him. "I want to know," she continued, her voice becoming erratic.

Hezekiah stopped, turned towards her, and gently held her hands. His lip quivered as he looked into her pleading eyes.

"Kathryn, I love you, but what I'm about to tell you, I know you won't understand. I know it will hurt you, and it pains me deeply to tell you." Tears were already forming in her eyes. He struggled to continue. "There is something in my past that requires me to leave for a few days so I can try and make things right in my head."

"Your mother's killer," she said, her voice sounding frightened. "You're not going after him?"

"No. I wish it were that simple. It would be easier to understand...for both of us." Her hands were squeezing his tightly. "When I lived here before, I became good friends with a woman. At the time, I was sure I loved her." He felt her hands loosening, but he

323

clung tightly to hers. "Since I met you, I was sure that any feelings I did have were gone. But lately, she's been on my mind. I'm concerned about her well-being."

The tears began to flood from her eyes, streaming down her cheeks. Her lip quivered uncontrollably. "You think you still love her?"

"I honestly don't know what I think anymore. She is a dear friend to me, and I've had these thoughts that she's in danger. I need to be sure...for us."

Kathryn pulled away, turning her back to him. He could see her brushing the tears from her cheek. "Please, Kathryn. I didn't want to hurt you." He reached for her shoulder, but she stepped away.

"Please go," she whispered.

"Will you wait for me?"

She turned towards him. Her body was shivering. "I know this is where I'm suppose to fight to keep the man I love. But I'm not strong enough. Right now, I don't know what I'm going to do. I've never loved anyone before."

Hezekiah began to speak, but Kathryn raised her hand. "Please, just go," she begged and walked back towards the house.

Hezekiah watched her until she entered inside. He hated himself. He had taken her heart and crushed it. Was she a delicate flower he had picked only to watch her wilt and die? He was absolutely convinced that the bad spirits had consumed him.

****

Kathryn was unable to sleep. She feared she had driven her only love away...perhaps forever. She was sickened by the thought. She was sure she could never love another. How could she have been so foolish? He had said he loved her. He had only wanted to be sure that his past was behind him. He had been honest with her. Could she have been so brave if she had been in a similar circumstance? Now maybe she had pushed him back into his past and he might never return, believing he had nothing to come back too.

She had to tell him she did understand. She did love him. And she would fight to keep him. Otherwise, she would always regret it.

Kathryn rose early the next morning and hurried to Hezekiah's house. She wanted him to know that she did love him. When she arrived, she felt as though her heavy heart would burst from her chest. He was gone.

CHAPTER 37

Hezekiah finished his breakfast of ham and flapjacks, and slowly pushed his plate away. The waitress refilled his cup with steaming coffee and retrieved his plate. "Was your breakfast okay?" she said. A smile came to her pleasant, but plain face.

"Very good," Hezekiah answered, returning the smile.

"You have a good day, now." She smiled again and hurried off.

Hezekiah clutched the metal cup with both hands and slowly sipped the stout brew. He would have to make a decision soon. He had already spent two days in Helena looking for Christina. His search was growing hopeless. An elderly gentleman remembered a woman fitting Christina's description working at a boarding house, but he could not remember the name. The man said he had left for a few months and when he returned, the boarding house had burned to the ground and he never saw the woman again. No one else seemed to recall seeing a woman fitting Christina's description.

Since Hezekiah left Virginia City, all he could think about was Kathryn. He could not forget her tear filled eyes and desperate words. He wanted to return to her and ask for her forgiveness...tell her he loved her and how the nightmare had driven him to this foolish journey. But that was the problem-the nightmares had continued. If he returned now, all his questions would remain unanswered, and his life...his future...would remain in doubt.

326

If the nightmares meant Christina was in danger, then he owed it to her to keep looking for her. Maybe, he thought, as long as the nightmares continued, she was still unharmed. When they stopped-his body tensed-it might mean he was too late.

With a sense of urgency, he pushed the cup away and hurried into the street. Now what? He felt foolish for being in such a hurry to leave the cafe. Where could he go that he hadn't already been at least once? He stood motionless, helplessly gazing up and down the busy street. The street reminded him of the earlier days in Virginia City.

Slowly, he started walking down the street, looking in each shop window, the same windows he had already looked in several times during the past two days. A woman he did not recognize from his prior inquires was working behind the counter in the general store. He would try her.

Hezekiah entered the store and the woman greeted him politely. He began his standard description and information about Christina-the same one he had used so many times during the last two days. But as he hurriedly gave her Christina's description, he watched the clerk shake her head slowly, signifying she did not recognize Christina.

"I'm sorry," she said when he had finished. "I've been here a year now. I've seen a lot of people come and go. There's not many young women, and I'm sure I would remember her."

"Thanks anyway for your time," Hezekiah said, feeling dejected. He began to leave, his faint hope of finding Christina fleeting.

"Excuse me," a gruff woman's voice called out as he opened the door.

A woman dressed in men's clothes approached him. Her face was leather beaten, but her eyes were gentle. "I overheard you talking to Bernice." She smiled. "I've been known to butt in when I shouldn't. I'm Martha Boyd." She extended her hand.

"I'm Hezekiah Templeton." Hezekiah could feel the roughness of her hand that he had felt on only a few men. "Do you know

327

anything that may help me?" he asked, reluctant to have any renewed hope.

"Maybe. My husband and I have a small spread about three miles southeast of here. Our neighbors are the Pearsons. Henry, Mr. Pearson, took ill about a year ago and Susan, such a frail soul, needed help taking care of her husband. Anyway, she hired a pretty, young lady, like the one you described, to help her. Now I'm terrible with names, but I'd bet the sweat off a hog's back that her name was Christina. I remember it because it's such a pretty name."

Hezekiah could hardly believe what he was hearing. He had been so close to giving up his search, and suddenly renewed hope. "And she's still there?" he asked, feeling the excitement building inside him.

"I stopped by just over a week ago to see if there was anything I could do for them. I try to be neighborly, you know. Anyway, she was still there then."

"You say it's southeast."

"Yep. Follow the road east of here. About a mile out, there's a fork. Go right for a couple miles. Their name is on a post at the road. Pearson."

****

Christina helped Mrs. Pearson make Mr. Pearson's bed and assisted him back into bed.

"Thank you, Christina," Mrs. Pearson said, patting Christina's hand. "I'm going to sit with Henry a spell and read him some scripture."

Christina nodded and started to leave, but paused at the bedroom door momentarily and watched the elderly couple. They were in their late sixties, but Christina had seen them age far beyond their years during the last year. But even with their troubles, they had always been so kind and generous towards her.

328

Christina recalled the day she met Mrs. Pearson. One of Christina's rare occasions that she had left the boarding house where she worked. She had stopped at the fabric shop. She knew she could not afford any material to make herself a dress, but it helped to ease her agonizing loneliness. Although she and Sadie had little in common, Christina had felt a friendship did exist between them and she did miss her. But most of all, she had missed her friendship with Hezekiah. It had been a rare friendship and could never be replaced.

Christina, while in the shop, had overhead Mrs. Pearson telling the shop owner her desire to find someone to assist her with her ailing husband. Christina followed Mrs. Pearson outside. When Christina told Mrs. Pearson her interest in the position, brightness came to the elderly woman's eyes that only moments before had been filled with sadness.

"That would be wonderful, honey," she said enthusiastically. "Your vibrant youth would bring a much needed cheer to our home."

Since that day over a year ago, a wonderful relationship had existed between Christina and the Pearsons. The Pearsons treated her more as a daughter than an employee. Christina's heart ached at the thought of leaving them. But it had been Mrs. Pearson, who had encouraged Christina to write to her family. "Time heals many wounds," Mrs. Pearson had told her. "A soul can never rest when there are difficulties with family." Christina knew that all to well. Her heart wept all these years missing her family and unable to return home.

Christina did send a letter to her family anticipating no reply. But the reply did come, assuring her of their love and hope of her return. A weight had been lifted that Christina had carried for so many years.

She began making plans for her return to Philadelphia, deciding she could save enough money in a year. But Mrs. Pearson would not hear of it. "We will loan you the money and you can pay it back whenever you can," she had said. "Mind you, one hundred years would be soon enough."

This time tomorrow Christina would be on her way to Philadelphia. Christina wiped her eyes and left the room that radiated a love between two people that most people would never know.

As Christina reached the bottom of the stairs, the clapper sounded at the door. "I'll answer it," she called to Mrs. Pearson. "It's probably Mrs. Boyd." Mrs. Boyd was about the only visitor that every stopped by the Pearsons.

When Christina opened the door, she stood in shock staring at the familiar face. She had never expected to ever see it again. "Hezekiah!" she screamed, thrusting her arms around him. "Oh, tell me I'm not dreaming. Tell me it's you." Tears rolled from her eyes and streamed down her cheeks as she stepped back to look at him. She joyously looked at his familiar sheepish grin.

"It's me. It's really me."

"How did you ever find me?"

"I had almost given up. Then I ran into Mrs. Boyd in town."

"Bless her soul," Christina said, still wiping her eyes. "Come in. I must know everything that's happened to you since you left Virginia City. I've thought of you so often, wondering how you were."

"How have you been?" Hezekiah asked, still standing in the doorway.

"I'm fine," Christina said, grabbing him by the arm. "Let's go out back and sit under the tree and talk like old times. First let me run upstairs and tell Mrs. Pearson."

Christina raced upstairs and began to hurriedly explain about Hezekiah. Realizing she was making no sense, she giggled. "Oh, Mrs. Pearson, I'll explain later."

A confused Mrs. Pearson smiled. "Perhaps that would be best, honey. You shouldn't keep your guest waiting."

Christina scampered back downstairs. "Come with me, my long, lost friend," she said excitedly. "I can hardly wait to hear all about you."

As they reached the back porch, she stopped. "I must get us some chilled tea from the cooling house. Just like old times."

"That's not necessary, Christina."

"Yes it is. Our tea social, remember? Don't tell me you have forgotten."

Hezekiah laughed. "I remember...all the time. Tea it shall be."

Christina hurried off. Hezekiah sat on the porch step waiting for her return. A minute later she was back with two glasses of tea.

They were soon sitting on a bench under a large oak tree. They sat quietly for a short moment, looking at one another, each remembering, each reliving a wonderful friendship. Christina wished she had dressed more appropriately for her guest. He will think I'm terrible, she thought, remembering how she used to dress specifically for him, even before she had even met him.

"Now, my dear friend, not a moment's delay," Christina said, grasping his hand. "Begin the day you left Virginia City and don't you dare deprive me of one thing."

"What about you? I want to know what you've been doing."

She patted his hand. "In time. But I insist you go first. I can't wait any longer to hear what you've been doing."

"Okay. Really my life hasn't been very exciting."

"Balderdash. I know better. You always try to say your life isn't exciting. Now stop your delaying."

Christina listened to Hezekiah tell his story of his return to St. Louis, about the family, his party, and school. How he had worked and saved money for his return trip to Virginia City, his trip back, about Isaac getting married and the death of Eagle Feather.

"I would have come sooner to find you," he said apologetically, "except Isaac never mentioned where you were until recently. I guess he thought it was best if I forgot my past. Honestly, I was mad at him for not telling me, but I guess he thought he was doing what was best."

"You mustn't be angry with him," Christina said, her eyebrows cocked, "you're lucky to have such a good friend."

331

"I know. He's been a real good friend since I've been back. Anyway, I guess that's about all that's happened to me."

Christina sat quietly staring at Hezekiah. She had listened to him tell his story, but she had heard nothing. Everything he said was about others around him. Something was wrong.

"I'm very disappointed, Hezekiah. I thought we were the best of friends, never keeping things from one another."

"What do you mean?" Hezekiah suddenly seemed nervous.

"You spent all this time telling me about the last year, yet you're not telling me anything. Of course I find your family interesting and that Isaac got married. I feel terrible about Eagle Feather, but I want to know more about you. I know there's more and I feel hurt you're not wanting to tell me."

Hezekiah sat with his head down as he listened to Christina. When he looked back up at her, his eyes were sad. Christina took his hand. "I know something's wrong, Hezekiah. I don't know if I can help, but let me listen. At least sharing your trouble with me will help...Please."

Hezekiah looked away, and then back to Christina. "Okay," he said, his voice raspy. "I'm not sure what to say. Everything seems confusing. You remember after Mother was killed and I had a nightmare remembering what had happened?...The nightmares continued after I returned to St. Louis. At first, they occurred almost every night, but over time they were only coming once in awhile. They had almost stopped completely when I decided to return to Virginia City. Then after I got back, they had completely stopped. I thought they were gone forever. Life seemed to start anew. Then about three weeks ago, the nightmares started again...only occasionally at first, but now the nightmare is there every night, and even worse it haunts me by day. What really makes it so terrible, the nightmare has changed. I no longer see the killer attacking my mother, but it's...it's you, Christina. I was so frightened you were in danger. I had to find you."

Christina listened to the anguish of her friend. The tears filled her eyes. She wondered when his suffering would stop. "Hezekiah,

I...I'm not sure what to say. My heart cries for you. At least you know I'm all right."

"That's what's really important," he said. "I was so afraid for you. I thought I would go crazy."

"You must stop being so concerned for others and start thinking of yourself. If you are happy, then those around you will be happy."

"I know you're right. My stupidity has already caused me to hurt someone."

Christina smiled, her eyebrow cocked. "You have a lady friend?"

Hezekiah hesitated, before a grin appeared, "Yeah," Hezekiah said, his face reddened with embarrassment. "Or at least I did. I hurt her and I wouldn't blame her if she refused to see me again."

"Because you were coming here?"

"Yeah. I don't blame her for not understanding."

"If you go back and tell her everything, she'll understand. A woman in love can be very forgiving. But you must be honest with her...sharing your feelings..., which includes the bad. A woman in love can also be scornful if you lie to her."

Hezekiah stood up and walked a few step away. He turned and faced Christina. His face was somber. He looked at Christina as though hesitant to speak.

"What is it?" Christina asked.

"I'm not sure whether I should. I'm not sure..." he said, hesitating. "I'm not sure that I'm still in love with you."

Christina had mixed emotions...the exhilaration of him loving her, but also the sureness of the direction of the conversation that she would need to follow. For the first time she regretted the day that she had taken Hezekiah into her arms. She had only added to his confusion and pain. She had to set it right. "Hezekiah, I love you. Maybe at one time it was more than a friend. I'm not really sure how I felt. But both of us have a good and beautiful future ahead of us, and although I may feel sad about it, our futures do not include each other. Destiny has chosen our future paths. There is something I haven't told you yet about my future plan. I wrote to my family. They answered and want me to come home. I'm leaving tomorrow for Philadelphia. I've waited so long for this. You'll always be my dearest friend, and I know I shall never forget you, but we must take what is given and move on. Your lady in Virginia City must become the most important thing to you. It is with her where your happiness lies."

"We had so many wonderful times and memories, it's hard to forget them."

"You don't have to forget them. I surely never will. It is a part of us...a part of our past. I would never want to forget them."

"As much as I love Kathryn, it's so hard to say goodbye to you."

"I know. As much as I want to see my family, I dread our goodbyes too. But you must promise me, you'll take my advice and go back to Kathryn and make things right with her. I would feel so much better leaving, knowing that my dearest friend will be happy in the years to come...Will you promise?"

Hezekiah stared at her. It seemed an eternity to Christina and for a moment she wanted to reach out to him and take him in her arms, but she resisted. She could not make that mistake. It would only confuse the situation and make their good-byes that much more difficult.

Slowly he nodded his head. "I will. I promise. I know you're right...And I know Kathryn can make me happy. I just hope I can make her as happy."

Christina was flooded with emotions as he gave his answer. She attempted to keep her voice calm as she replied. "You will. You're too wonderful a person not to be able to make her happy."

"I'll wait 'till your stage leaves tomorrow before I leave for Virginia City."

Christina looked softly at Hezekiah. "I would rather say goodbye here. Anyway my stage doesn't leave until one. I hope you understand."

Hezekiah nodded.

The remainder of the day was spent, talking and laughing, but inside Christina felt the building sadness, knowing all too soon, they would be saying good-bye for the last time.

The dreaded time arrived. "I guess I should be going," Hezekiah said, shifting nervously in his chair. "No sense delaying what has to come."

Christina did not speak again until she stood with Hezekiah at the front door. She did not want to risk loosing control by saying any more than she had too.

"I'm so glad I found you before you left. I'd have been upset with Isaac for a long time if I had missed you."

Christina smiled. "I'm glad too." She knew her voice was betraying her attempt to be strong. She put her arms around him and hugged him tight for a long time, hesitant to let go. She stepped back. "Take care of yourself, Hezekiah. I do love you. You've given me considerable happiness since I've known you."

Hezekiah did not speak, but only waved. Christina knew why. She was having the same problem. He climbed atop his horse. How handsome he looked to her. At that moment she wondered if fate had played a cruel prank on her. But now it was the best letting him go. She had to think of what was best for him. Besides, she did miss her family.

He rode down the road and disappeared from Christina's view. She stood there for some time letting the tears stream down her cheeks. She felt Mrs. Pearson's hand on her shoulder. "I'm sorry, dear," she said. "He was the young man you so often spoke of, wasn't he?"

Christina nodded without turning around. "Kathryn is a lucky woman," Christina said, the words barely able to leave her mouth.

"You love him, don't you, dear?" Mrs. Pearson said, a consoling tenderness in her voice.

"Yes. But most important, I hope he at last finds happiness."

Mrs. Pearson turned Christina around and hugged her. "Cry if you wish, dear," Mrs. Pearson said, gently patting Christina's back. Christina did.

CHAPTER 38

Hezekiah left Helena early the next morning after his day with Christina. He was hesitant leaving Christina before she climbed aboard the stagecoach, but it had been her wish to say good-bye at the house. It was probably better for him too; besides, he did welcome the early start for Virginia City.

The day seemed unusually bright and refreshing to Hezekiah. It had been some time since he felt this good and this confident about his future. Seeing Christina well and happy had eased his mind considerably, and the night had passed without a nightmare...weeks since that had happened. And now only four days and he would be home. His only concern now was Kathryn. Would she be waiting for him and take him back. He feared he had hurt her too much. If she turned him away, he could understand, but he was determined to show her that he loved her and win her heart back.

It was still early morning when he began his ascent up the steep pass south of Helena. Today the mountains looked beautiful and grand...their steep walls rose gallantly around him, and all except for the higher peaks were covered with tall green pines. The white clouds overhead drifted gently by, so close that he felt he could almost touch them. On his trip to Helena, the pass had only seemed like another obstacle.

By late afternoon he had crossed the pass and was moving along a high plateau covered with sagebrush and buffalo grass. He knew it would be late the next day before he would drop down into the valley.

He rode until the darkness began to settle around him. He put up camp along a small creek. The fall night air was chilly. The autumn leaves of red and gold on the trees around him were beginning to make their silent descent to their winter graveyard. But the cold evening air did little to subdue the warm, wonderful feeling inside him. In three days he would be back with Kathryn. And by now, Christina would be safely on her way back to Pennsylvania. How excited she must be, he thought. She had waited so long for this moment. He recalled her standing at the door as he rode away from the Pearson house. The realization that he would never see her again began to set in. Life sometimes was sad, even when the future looked so good. Christina had said fate had determined each of their paths in life. What would it have been like if fate had brought their paths together? They would have been happy. But then there would be no Kathryn in his future. Fate had chosen the best future for him. He was sure of that now. He had to put Christina and all that had happened behind him. He had too much to look forward to with Kathryn.

The next morning, Hezekiah was on the trail early with the beckoning visions of Kathryn. Again he had beautiful fall weather to travel. Perhaps good fortune would follow him now. Life had turned the corner and only good things were ahead of him.

An hour into his journey, a small band of Indians of about twenty-five men, women and children passed a few hundred yards in front of him. They looked weary from traveling. He wondered if they, like Eagle Feather's village, were moving to new lands to find peace. Maybe the white man had uprooted them. Hezekiah had a sudden feeling of guilt. He had never before considered himself one of the white men moving into their land...but he was. Even with that, Eagle Feather had always been kind to Isaac and him.

He began to recall all the wonderful times with Eagle Feather. He had learned so much from his old friend, but he knew there could have been so much more he could have learned. He remembered when after his mother had been killed, Eagle Feather had told him, like all brave warriors, he would have to learn to live with the terrible realization of death. He had said it would not be easy. It had seemed so confusing to Hezekiah then, but now it seemed so simple. He would not be able to change the past, and if he were ever going to find happiness, he would have to learn to accept what had happened and move on with his life. Aunt Jane and Christina had told him the same thing. Hezekiah only hoped that now he had reached that point of understanding and it was not too late.

By the end of the second day, he had reached the valley and began to follow the Jefferson River. He had seen the river swell over its banks when the warm spring Chinooks melted the snow-laden mountains, but now the waters rippled methodically over its rocky bottom like soothing fingers caressing a tired soul.

The third day became colder. Hezekiah began to fear a storm was on its way. It not only could make his journey miserable, but also delay his arrival back to Virginia City. The last thing he wanted was to be delayed from seeing Kathryn. By the end of the day, he was near the headwaters of the Jefferson River. He would be in Virginia City, and hopefully, Kathryn's arms by sunset the next day. He prepared for bed. Three nights had passed with no nightmares. He chuckled to himself. He had almost forgotten about it. He crawled beneath his blanket and studied the darkening sky. There were no stars. He only hoped the storm would wait one more day.

****

The first hew of early light crested the horizon. Hezekiah shivered in the cold early morning dawn. Fear griped his tense body. The nightmare had returned. This time, it was more terrible than ever...He had seen the face of the desperate woman. It was not Christina in his nightmare...it was Kathryn!

"My God!" he shouted. "What have I done?" He had left Kathryn alone and in danger.

338

He quickly rolled his blanket, stuffed his saddlebag, bridled and saddled his horse. "Lady, I beg you, give me everything you have today."

As he mounted, a strange sickening feeling came over him. It was as though he was being watched. He quickly glanced around him. In a nearby tree a hawk was watching him. Its eyes seemed to penetrate right through Hezekiah. Hezekiah sat frozen, looking back at the frightening eyes. "What is it?" he shouted. "Why can't you tell me?"

Hezekiah helplessly watched the hawk lift off from the branch and disappear into the southern sky towards Virginia City...towards Kathryn! He had to get to Virginia City and Kathryn as soon as possible.

Hezekiah urged his mare forward. If Kathryn was in danger, he had to be there.

The valley seemed to stretch out endlessly before him. By late-morning he had arrived at the northern settlements of Alder Gulch. Today, he gave little notice to any of the activity around him. He had only one thought on his mind...get to Kathryn as quickly as Lady would take him. But Lady was becoming weary and beginning to slow her pace. She had been traveling for four days and Hezekiah had not even stopped to give her a rest all day. He dismounted and walked along side of her. "Sorry Lady, I'm not being fair to you. My mind is not working." He found water, and waited for her to drink her fill before traveling on.

The sun laid a golden blanket over the western horizon as Hezekiah rode into Virginia City. He urged Lady forward along Wallace Street, never taking the time to look around him. He rode straight for the Richmond home. He would like to have cleaned up first, but getting to Kathryn was all that mattered right now. He arrived at the house and hurried up the stairs. He knocked. Time seemed endless as he waited for someone to answer. Mrs. Richmond answered the door.

"Good evening, Mrs. Richmond. Is Kathryn here?" Hezekiah asked assertively.

"Hezekiah. I'm so glad to see you're back. We were all so worried."

"Thank you for your concern, Mrs. Richmond."

"Did you stop by your house?"

"No."

"I would imagine she's there. She's spent a good deal of her time there since you've been gone."

"Thanks. I'll check," he said, hurrying to his horse.

"Is everything all right," Mrs. Richmond called out.

"Yes. If Kathryn's all right, then everything is fine," Hezekiah shouted as he nudged Lady into a gallop.

Hezekiah sighed with relief. Kathryn was all right. And she was waiting for him at his house. Once again, he had allowed his ridiculous nightmare to warp his thoughts. It had meant nothing. He had to stop letting it bother him. He could not let it ruin his life. He vowed it would not happen again.

He came to a stop in front of his house. The door opened...his heart leaped...Kathryn appeared in the doorway. She had waited for his return.

"Hezekiah," she said, sobbing as she raced towards him.

He leaped from his horse and grabbed her into his arms. He began kissing her, again and again. "Kathryn, I love you," he kept repeating. "Please forgive me."

"Can you forgive me? I should have listened to you. Isaac explained everything."

"I'm just glad you're still here. I was so worried you might leave." Hezekiah began kissing her again. Kathryn giggled.

"Silly. Not on my life. Now, I think we should go inside before all the neighbors begin to waggle their tongues."

"I don't care. I just love you and that's all that matters to me."

****

Zeke stepped through the saloon door and lit a cigarette. He puffed at it angrily as he gazed out into the street. Since his return to Montana, things had not gone as planned. He had gone to Bannack in search of the gold, but his search of the sheriff's office there had proved futile. Now upon his return to Virginia City, he had found the house where he had killed the woman and child torn down, hindering his recollection of that exciting day. He had also found out that the saloon maid, Christina, was gone. Tonight, he would break in and search the sheriff's office in Virginia City for the gold. If he found nothing there, then his return would be a complete loss.

He glanced at a passing rider that was in a hurry. At first, he paid little attention, but as he watched the rider he began to realize the rider looked familiar. "What the hell," he mumbled. The rider...it was the damn kid he thought he had killed along with his mother. Anger rose inside him. All this time, he had thought that he had been safe...no witnesses to his killings. All this time...now this damn kid appears...he had changed...but there was no doubt, the passing rider was him.

Zeke watched the rider hurry past the saloon and move quickly down the street. Zeke had gone unnoticed. Zeke threw down his cigarette and quickly mounted his horse. He would make sure there would be no witnesses this time. He followed the unsuspecting rider up the hill to an elaborate home. The rider soon remounted and left. Zeke followed, his anger growing.

The rider soon stopped at another house. "Well, I'll be damned," Zeke mumbled, a wry grin appearing on his face. "This may not be so damn bad after all." He licked his lips as he watched a beautiful young woman rush from the house and into the rider's arms. The fire inside him began to grow as he watched the couple. His eyes remained riveted on them until they went inside. "I'll be back," he said, "just as soon as I take care of business." Although Zeke could hardly contain his desires, he was determined to finish his search for the gold and besides it would be too dangerous now. He knew he was going to enjoy this one. He could kill the lone witness and have his beautiful lover too. He turned his horse around and left. Maybe his trip north would be well worth the effort after all.

****

Kathryn and Hezekiah sat and talked late into the evening. Hezekiah told her about his nightmares, carefully excluding his recent one. It would only frighten her unnecessarily, and besides, he was convinced that he was letting his imagination control him. No more, he

341

thought. The nightmare would not ruin his life, no matter how real it seemed.

"I was wondering if you might like to ride up to Eagle Feather's burial site tomorrow," Hezekiah said as he walked Kathryn back to the Richmond home.

"I would love, too," Kathryn said excitedly. "It would mean so much to me, because I know how much Eagle Feather means to you."

"Good," he said as he kissed her goodnight at the steps. "To be honest with you, I can hardly wait until I see you again."

"I'll be anxious too," she said as she waved to him.

"About ten then."

"I'll be waiting," she said, starting to close the door. "Wait," she said, stepping back outside. "Would you mind if I fixed supper for the Kyles tomorrow night at your place. It would be so much fun."

"I think it sounds great. Besides I enjoy eating your cooking."

"You may change your mind."

"I doubt that."

"You're too kind," she said, closing the door.

Hezekiah felt so good. He looked around him, and once he was sure that he was alone, began to skip and whistle down the road. It would seem forever until ten.

****

Hezekiah was at the Richmond home at ten sharp the next morning. He had trouble containing himself until his appointed arrival time.

Kathryn was waiting. She wore her hair down and a laced hat set atop it. When she stepped into the sunlight, her hair glistened with a touch of auburn. Hezekiah was concerned her lace brown dress was too fancy to go horseback riding, but he was glad she was wearing it. She seemed to look more beautiful each time he saw her.

As they rode towards Eagle Feather's burial site, most of their discussion was directed towards the evening meal. Hezekiah found delight that Kathryn was so excited, even though she was nervous having the Kyles for supper.

When they arrived at their destination, Hezekiah helped Kathryn from her horse. Her sweet perfume clouded his thoughts. Everything about her was so perfect. He had made a decision. Tonight, after the Kyles left, he was going to ask Kathryn to marry him. There was no sense waiting. She was all he wanted out of life. With her by his side, any problem would seem small.

They walked up the hill. Hezekiah noticed that the flower he had admired from his earlier trip was gone. For a moment, he felt saddened. But, it will return next spring, he thought.

When they reached the plateau, Kathryn stood silently looking at the burial platform. She turned to Hezekiah. "It seems so peaceful here. From what you've said about Eagle Feather, perhaps he makes it this way."

"Perhaps you're right. I hadn't thought of it that way. You seem as wise as Eagle Feather. He would like you, I'm sure."

Hezekiah suddenly felt a chill. It caught him off guard. He had been expecting the warmth he usually felt and had been wondering if Kathryn would feel it too. His body began to shiver.

"Are you all right, Hezekiah? You're shivering."

"I'm fine. Just felt a chill."

"Really. I didn't feel it. Maybe you're catching a cold."

Slowly the chill began to subside. A shadow passed nearby. Hezekiah looked up. The hawk was circling overhead.

"I think we had better leave," Kathryn said, her face expressing concern. "I'll fix you a hot cup of tea. I don't want you catching a death of cold."

"Okay, but I'm all right...really."

They started back to town. Hezekiah rode quietly. He couldn't understand why he felt a chill and not the warm sensation. He was sure Eagle Feather would approve of Kathryn. That could not be the reason he felt like he did. Here he was again, letting his imagination take control of him. Why could he not accept that maybe he was catching a cold. Kathryn was not making anything unusual about it. But he did feel disappointed that Kathryn had not felt the presence of Eagle Feather.

CHAPTER 39

Kathryn and Hezekiah arrived back to the house by early afternoon from their visit to Eagle Feather's resting place. Once Kathryn was convinced that Hezekiah felt better, she sent him in search of a chicken while she began to prepare the supper.

Hezekiah soon returned with the chicken. He boiled water and began removing the feathers.

After the chicken was cleaned, Hezekiah fumbled around the kitchen trying to find ways to help Kathryn, but soon decided it was best to sit nearby and watch. Kathryn nervously scurried about the kitchen. "It's been so long since I've done this," she said, wiping her brow, "I hardly know where to start."

"You'll do just fine. I'm anxious to feast upon your cooking. You did so well last time."

"Maybe now you can say that, but I think you'd better wait to make any judgment. Cooking for you was difficult enough, but for guests, I don't know. Maybe I shouldn't have made the offering until I did a little more practicing."

Hezekiah could resist no longer and moved in behind his unsuspecting prey, placing his arms around her, and kissed her on the back of the neck. "I love everything about you," he whispered.

"Thank you and I love you too," she said, continuing to peel the potato.

Hezekiah walked to the window. "I think a storm's coming in. I'm sure glad I'm home and not out there somewhere. I thought for a day or so coming home I was going to get caught in a storm and delay me coming home to you."

"Well I'm glad it didn't. Another day wondering if you were going to come back would have driven me crazy."

Hezekiah walked back to Kathryn and held her in his arms. "I'm sorry, Kathryn. I should never have left you like I did. I could never have stayed away. I knew that all along." He kissed her passionately.

Kathryn looked longingly into his eyes. "Hezekiah, I love you and I enjoy your kisses more than anything. But do me a favor. Get out of my kitchen or there won't be any supper. Go chop wood or something."

Hezekiah immediately retreated to the door. He stopped and looked back. "A warning. I shall return."

"Not until supper is ready."

****

By evening, Kathryn had become frantic. Hezekiah kept insuring her everything would be fine, but he was never able to convince her.

A knock at the door informed them the Kyles had arrived. Kathryn, having been besieged with nerves all afternoon, suddenly exemplified calmness as she stood along side Hezekiah. She greeted their guests as though she was a princess at a ball.

Once supper was served, everyone was quick to inform Kathryn that everything tasted delicious. Hezekiah was quick to point out to Kathryn that she had worried for nothing, after which he quickly received a glance in return that he was not to inform the guests that she was nervous.

The men were quickly scurried from the kitchen so the women could clean up. "I know when I'm not wanted," Hezekiah said, not resisting the women's request. "I saw the wrath of a woman earlier today when I invaded her kitchen."

"I've never resisted the opportunity to sit and watch someone else work," Isaac quickly volunteered. "It always does my heart good, and my stomach on occasions like tonight."

Hezekiah handed Isaac a cigar. "Bought them just for this occasion," he said, lighting a match and holding it to Isaac's cigar. Isaac took a long puff and watched the lazy smoke curl upward.

"This one's certainly to my liking," Isaac said, taking another puff.

They sat and stared at the women busily chatting. "I think they wanted us out of there so they could chit chat freely and not worry about what they were saying, "Hezekiah said.

Isaac nodded in agreement, but quickly turned the conversation to one of more interest to him. "So how was your trip?"

"Good. Saw Christina. She was going back to Philadelphia the next day to be with her family. She was pretty excited and happy. I'm happy for her. She does deserve some happiness."

"I guess it took a load off your mind," Isaac said, leaning forward with raised eyebrows.

"It did."

"The nightmare's gone?"

"No. Not all the time, anyway. But after talking to Christina and realizing how foolish I'd been about it, I think I can live with it until it goes away."

"Good," Isaac quickly answered, slapping Hezekiah on the leg.

Hezekiah started to tell Isaac that his nightmare now had Kathryn in it instead of Christina, but decided now was not the right time. He also decided to wait about telling of his chill and the hawk out at Eagle Feather's burial site. Tonight was a night for fun. He wanted to be sure that everything was perfect when he asked Kathryn to marry him.

"So anything new happen while I've been gone," Hezekiah asked to assure the conversation did not falter.

"No. Not that I can think of. Oh, by the way, you might be interested to know Wilbur Sanders is back in town."

"Great," Hezekiah said jubilantly. "I'll probably stop by and see him tomorrow. I've been anxious to hear what he has to say."

"I thought you would be interested. Sounds like he might have something interesting for you. Kind of envy you."

"I think I'm ready to try something different. I hope it works out."

"It will," Isaac said as he tapped the ashes from his cigar. He leaned forward with a grin. "You might be needing a good job here pretty soon," he said, rolling his eyes toward Kathryn.

"Maybe. You never know."

"Not wanting to give your friend any advance tip, huh."

"No tip to give yet."

Isaac sat back and puffed hardily on his cigar. "All right. I guess I can wait like everybody else."

Hezekiah only smiled. He had to be careful with his friend. Isaac was always clever at getting information from him.

"You know," Isaac said, a frown appearing on his face, "there was something strange that happened last night. I heard this morning that somebody broke into the sheriff's office and tore the place apart. Even pulled up some floor and tore out some wall. What makes it even stranger, the same thing happened at the sheriff's office in Bannack a few nights ago."

"Sounds like somebody's looking for something," Hezekiah said, squinting his eyes in thought.

"Yeah. There's speculation that somebody might still be looking for all that gold that never was found after Plummer and his boys were hanged."

"Damn, I wonder if they found it."

"Maybe. Whoever does find it, is going to be mighty rich. I know I could sure use some of it."

"I wonder who it is," Hezekiah said, his mind in deep thought. "I wonder if it's one of the bandits that's returned."

"I doubt it. There weren't too many of them left, and I think any of them that were, are probably too scared to show their faces around these parts."

347

"Yeah...but it's damn strange that after all this time, somebody would be looking for it now." The thought of one of the road agents returning to Virginia City made Hezekiah feel uncomfortable, but it bothered him even more that he was allowing the thought to bother him. Isaac seemed undisturbed by the incident. Hezekiah was convinced he was once again allowing his mind to control him.

The women had finished with the dishes and came over to join them. Kathryn sat across from Hezekiah while Charlotte pulled a chair next to Isaac.

Charlotte eyed Hezekiah and Kathryn curiously. "You two are acting like an old married couple. I hope you're not keeping any secrets from us."

Kathryn blushed and Hezekiah was sure his ears were red. Isaac smiled. "If they are, Hezekiah sure isn't talking," he said, pulling Charlotte's chair even closer.

Kathryn tried to speak, but became lost for words. Hezekiah was determined not to let them get the best of Kathryn and him. "Speaking of secrets," he said, looking directly at the guests, "I would think you might have something to say to us...like another Kyle is on the way."

Charlotte blushed for the first time that Hezekiah could remember.

"It's not because we're not trying," Isaac said deliberately.

"Isaac!" Charlotte screamed, hiding her face.

"We win," Hezekiah said, bursting into laughter.

"I swear, Isaac," Charlotte said, her face becoming more blushed, "when I get you home."

Her remark only added to her embarrassing moment as Isaac twitched his eyebrows in response.

****

Later that evening, Hezekiah and Kathryn watched their guests leave. Hezekiah closed the door. He could feel his stomach churning from nerves. The time had arrived. All the careful preparation of his speech, all the correct words he would use to ask Kathryn to marry him seemed to disappear. It was like the first time he danced with her, only worse. His mouth felt dry as he took her by the hand and led her to one of the chairs. She sat down and looked up at him, her face beaming with innocence. The longer he looked at her, the more nervous he became.

He was ready to kneel in front of her when a knock sounded at the door. "What'd they forget?" Hezekiah said feeling irritated that Isaac and Charlotte were interrupting such an unforgettable moment. "I'll get it," he said, walking to the door. He opened the door to the smiling faces of Isaac and Charlotte.

Isaac had an embarrassed expression. "Sorry for intruding," he said," but Charlotte insisted it couldn't wait until tomorrow."

"We would like the two of you to be our guests for supper tomorrow night," Charlotte said without hesitation as she peered inside at Kathryn.

Hezekiah looked at Kathryn. She was smiling and nodding. "If Hezekiah wants too," she said.

"Okay. Tomorrow at your house," Hezekiah answered hurriedly, with hopes of a quick departure of the Kyles.

Once again, he watched them leave and closed the door. He had to begin building his nerve all over again.

****

Kathryn had noticed Hezekiah's nervousness all evening. At first, she had only assumed he was nervous as she was with being the host for the first time, but as the evening wore on, Hezekiah seemed to become more nervous. Although she had tried not to think about it and be disappointed, she began to believe that Hezekiah was going to ask for her hand in marriage.

After Charlotte and Isaac had left, and Hezekiah had hesitantly set her in a chair and seemed to be looking for the right words to say, she became more convinced of her belief. She feared that the return of their friends would allow time for him to change his mind.

Kathryn sat patiently as Hezekiah for the second time waved good-bye to the Kyles. She could feel the nervousness throughout her trembling body and knew how Hezekiah must feel.

Hezekiah walked slowly towards her. He licked his lips and nervously wrung his hands together.

Without hesitation, he bent to one knee in front of her. "Kathryn, my dear, you must know how much I love you."

"I think so. I hope it's as much as I love you."

He smiled as though receiving confidence from her remark. "Maybe, I'm rushing. If I am, I understand..."

Another knock came at the door. Hezekiah leaped to his feet. His voice sounded agitated. "I don't believe those two. "Don't they have a home?"

"I'll get it," Kathryn said, fearing Hezekiah might be rude this time.

"No. I'll get it. I'll put on my best behavior."

Although Kathryn was not pleased with the interruption, she had to smile at the predicament. It was not how she had envisioned Hezekiah asking her for her hand in marriage, and she was certain it was not how he had envisioned it either.

As Hezekiah was opening the door, she rose and started for the door, not wanting to seem rude. She was certain they would be even more embarrassed this time, although it had appeared to her that Charlotte was not that embarrassed the first time.

As Kathryn approached the door, she was startled to see a horrified look on Hezekiah's face, and the sound of a strange man's voice. "Aren't you going to be neighborly and invite me in," the gruff, unfamiliar voice said.

"Who is it?" Kathryn called out, frightened by the cold sound of the voice. Hezekiah did not answer. He slowly backed away from the door. It was then that Kathryn saw the barrel of a revolver. A man, so terrifying and evil looking, stepped through the door. "Who is it?" Kathryn screamed as her body froze with fear.

"You remember don't you," the intruder said, looking at Hezekiah, a clenched smile on his face. "Aren't you going to

350

introduce me to your little beauty?" He looked towards Kathryn. "As you might have guessed, your man and I've met before." He looked back at Hezekiah. "I could have sworn you were dead that day. All this time, I thought there was no one to point a finger at me, and you were walking around waiting to get me hanged. I'll damn well make sure I'm more careful this time." Hezekiah just stared at the man as he continued talking. "You got yourself quite a fine looking little honey here," he said, nodding at Kathryn. "Hell, I reckon she's finer looking than your mother, and I damn well might say I thought she was quite a looker."

Hezekiah's face showed no fear, only hate and anger. Kathryn feared that Hezekiah might act foolishly and the intruder would kill him where he stood.

"Come here, little one," the intruder said. "Your man seems a little rude. You can call me Zeke. You got a name?" Kathryn did not answer him. "What's your name?" he shouted, his voice filling with anger.

"Kathryn," she said, her voice only a whisper.

"I like Kathryn. It's very fittin' for you. Come here, I want to take a better look at you." Kathryn stood frozen. "Come here if you want your lover over there to live," he said forcefully, motioning his head towards Hezekiah.

Kathryn stepped forward, but was still out of his reach. "Have it your way. I have no problem plugging him where he stands." Kathryn moved closer. He reached out and grabbed her hair and yanked her to him. Hezekiah started towards Zeke, but stopped when Zeke aimed the revolver at his head. "Hold it there or I might get nervous and kill your sweet one." Zeke pressed his unshaven face against her cheek. "You smell awfully pretty, Kathryn. And you're a real looker too I might add. I bet you drive men wild. She drive you wild?" he said, looking at Hezekiah. "I bet she does. She's driving me plumb out of my mind."

Kathryn glanced at Hezekiah. He was rolling his eyes. At first, Kathryn could not understand what he was trying to tell her. Then she noticed his gun belt hanging on the wall, some eight to ten feet away from him. Somehow she had to keep Zeke's attention so Hezekiah could get to his revolver without being noticed.

"What do you want from me?" Kathryn said, hardly able to speak. "I'll do whatever you ask, just don't hurt us...please."

"That's better, honey. I like women who know who's in charge. I'd sure like to see what you've got under all those hideous garments. How about you?" Zeke said, smiling at Hezekiah. "I'll bet you're a pretty one with all those garments off," he said, kissing her cheek.

"I'll take them off...whatever you say."

Slowly Zeke began to ease his grip on Kathryn's hair. She moved slowly away.

"Well, get started," he said impatiently.

Kathryn fumbled at the buttons on her dress. Her hand was shaking so violently, she could hardly undo them. She pulled the dress down from her shoulders and let it fall to the floor. She stepped from the dress, moving in a direction that would put Zeke in a less direct line to watch Hezekiah if Zeke wanted to watch her. Zeke was licking his lips. With each movement, more and more of his attention was being directed towards her and away from Hezekiah. She was afraid to look at Hezekiah to see if he had moved any closer to the revolver. Her stomach was churning so badly, she was sure she would vomit. She had to somehow control the fear inside her. As she began to remove more of her clothing, she could hear the heavier breathing of Zeke. Please hurry, Hezekiah, she kept repeating to herself. She closed her eyes as she began to slip her undergarments from her breast. How much longer could she go on? As the clothing fell from her breast, Zeke began to reach towards her. Kathryn screamed and jumped back.

"You bitch!" he shouted. "I'm going to have you just as soon as I take care of something." He turned to face Hezekiah and pointed his revolver towards him. A terrifying look appeared on Zeke's face. The room exploded with gunfire.

Kathryn watched with horror as she saw a hole appear in Zeke where his left eye had been only moments before. He stumbled backwards and then fell to the floor. He never moved.

Kathryn began to sob hysterically. She looked to Hezekiah. "Hezekiah!" she screamed. Her body froze with terror. Hezekiah's crumpled body lay motionless on the floor.

CHAPTER 40

Frank Stratton arrived home and the Stratton children were immediately called to supper. Jane placed the hot dishes of roast beef, fried potatoes, preserved green beans, and biscuits on the table. Their pleasant aromas filled the room. Roast beef with fried potatoes were always one of her family's favorites, and she proudly watched her family as they anxiously sat anticipating their supper. Frank said a prayer, asking for good health for family and friends. Soon the tinkling of silver against the china became the only sound in the dining room.

Before Jane began eating, she carefully surveyed her children's' plates. "Hannah, I want you to have more of the beans. You know I want you to have plenty of vegetables. They're good for you."

"Says who. I don't like beans, Mother."

"Take some more like your mother said, young lady, or I'll give you more, and I'll make sure you have plenty," her father said sternly. "And I don't ever want to hear you talking back to your Mother. Understood?"

"Yes, Father." Hannah scowled as she added more beans to her plate.

"How was work today, dear," Jane said after testing each of the foods.

"Busy. There seems to be an endless number of people going west. I'll never understand them. Why in the world would anyone give up a comfortable life here for some unknown life with absolutely no luxuries?"

"I'd go," Hannah chimed in without hesitation. "I think it'd be fun."

"No doubt," Frank said, glancing up at Jane. "I'd sure like to know how you ever got that Templeton blood in you."

Jane, catching Frank's devious glance, became embarrassed. "Frank! You're terrible."

Susannah and Christopher looked at each other and smiled. "What's so funny?" Hannah asked, staring at her father as he grinned and continued eating.

"Nothing," Jane said, still eyeing her pleased husband. "Just worry about your beans. Frank, I could slap you."

A knock sounded at the front door. Jane set her fork down. "Whom would that be coming around at supper time," she said, raising her eyebrows inquisitively.

"I'll go," Hannah said already out of her chair and heading towards the door before anyone could stop her.

"Don't people know this is supper time?" Jane said, waiting for Hannah's return.

Hannah quickly returned, excitedly holding a letter. "Mr. Foreman brought us a letter from the post office. It's from Hezekiah. It has a Montana post mark on it."

"Bless his heart for writing," Jane said excitedly. "Bring me the letter, dear. Frank, do you mind if I read it now?" she said, taking the letter from Hannah.

"Of course not," Frank answered, showing his pleasure with the arrival of the letter.

Jane looked at the letter and frowned.

"What is it, Mother?" Susannah asked.

"This isn't Hezekiah's handwriting. It's a woman's writing. My Lord, what's wrong?"

Everyone was watching Jane as her shaking hand tore open the envelope. "Do you want me to read it?" Frank asked, his forehead wrinkled with a frown.

"No," Jane answered, her voice already cracking.

She began to silently read the letter. "It's from a Miss Kathryn Darcy." She read on in silence. "Oh, Lord!" she cried out, "Hezekiah was shot."

"Mother!" Hannah screamed.

Jane's eyes began to move rapidly down the letter.

"What does it say?" Hannah screamed hysterically, jumping up and down.

"Oh thank the Lord. He's going to be all right," Jane said, looking momentarily at her family through tear filled eyes. "He was shot in the shoulder. That's why Miss Darcy is writing this letter." She continued on. "Mercy, he was shot by Sarah's killer. My Lord, Hezekiah shot and killed him."

Hannah was sobbing. Frank rose from his chair and put his arm around her. "He's going to be all right, dear."

Jane continued reading in silence. "Mother," Susannah said with disgust, "Tell us what else it says."

Jane looked up from the letter, tears still in her eyes, but a smile was now on her lips. "Everyone. I have an announcement to make. In the spring, we're all going to Montana. Hezekiah and Miss Darcy are being wed."

Hannah began screaming and dancing around the table. Jane grabbed her daughter and began dancing with her. Supper was eaten cold that night, but no one at the Stratton household seemed to mind, not even Christopher.